Trace:

The Divine Sequence

by

Randy Valentine

Trace:
The Divine Sequence

Copyright 2007   Randall Lee Valentine

Trace: **The Divine Sequence** would not have been completed without the efforts of all those who have made so many contributions to this novel:
Cathy MacGregor, the late Rev. Robert M.A.L. Miller, Dr. James Adovasio, Dr. Ron Helminski, Charles Marr, Tatiana Bogotiva, Robert Heibel, Cheryl Shattuck, Dierdre Kearns, Lynne Bush and Gerri Pelkowski.

A special thanks goes to my wife Amy for her editing and innovative ideas, and my children: Alyssa, John, Drew and Lauren for their support and especially for John's inspiration to start this project as a screenplay in 2003.

Trace: **The Divine Sequence** is dedicated to my brother, John, who inspired a little brother to be better, work harder and aspire higher in keeping with the love and dedication of our parents, John and Edna

Prologue

June 24, 2002   Tralee, County Kerry, Ireland

With a face torn with terror and a body twisted in agony, the bitter bile burned his throat as he tried belching out the searing, penetrating revulsion from looking at this horrible murder scene. With his body craving relief from the all-consuming nausea, County Kerry Homicide Inspector Padraig O'Brien was devastatingly distraught by what was done to one so beloved by everyone in Tralee. "How could someone do such a thing ta another human being, let alone a man a the cloth?" he asked his investigating officers. "What da ya think the people will do if they think this could happen ta them, or their children?" A severely shaken O'Brien was partially paralyzed by these fears resonating through his mind and echoing against the walls of a cranium emotionally evacuated by the sheer horror of this mutilation lying right in front of him.

The parishioners of St. Mary's of Tralee had never loved a priest as much as they did Father Seamus O'Flannery—so wonderful was he, especially with their children. Raised as a child in Listowel, just a short ride on the N69 from Tralee, he entered the service of the Lord with his first assignment at St. Mary's. Diligently served his parishioners did he, and so well-liked that even though he wasn't at Harty's bar when the 'Rose of Tralee' beauty contest was created in 1959, Father O'Flannery grew its popularity so much that many people thought he must have founded it. Many a fair-haired lass, chosen the 'Rose', cherished forever a small kiss on the cheek from the handsome Father. And with his boyish good looks and his trim 6-foot stature crowned with a head of black hair slightly flecked with gray, there were more women than just the 'Rose' who fantasized about such a kiss.

1

At 51 years of age, Father O'Flannery was firmly ensconced in his seat of power as the senior priest at St. Mary's. Yet, O'Flannery always showed his commitment to his flock, especially the less fortunate by taking the late confessional times to serve all who could never come at a more convenient hour.

As was his routine evening habit, the Father took a solitary long walk after finishing his confessional duties. He loved getting out among the people where he could actually see their faces. More than once, he looked at those faces of humanity walking towards him with a sense of amusement regarding who might have been the most interesting sinner of the day or week. His walk took him to the people, through them and finally past them as he went towards the Famine Cemetery. Even 150 years after the Great Famine, he could not walk by without needing to repress a shudder generated by the horrible sadness and pain endured by those subterranean bodily remnants interred in a soil that did forsake them. Yet for Father O'Flannery, God's presence was always there, and he knew his God's love had comforted those residual elements of the flock whose dreams and aspirations were shattered by the unspeakable horrors of the Famine.

This evening, as the good Father took his walk by the Famine Cemetery, where tombstones' shadows encroached upon the sidewalk like dark claws reaching out to grab at his ankles, he heard a sound from deep within. "Help me! Help me, please," came from a body lying on the ground. As he rushed over and knelt down to help the prostrate man, he was shocked by the quickness of the blow delivered to the back of his exposed neck, fracturing the cervical vertebrae and creating within his diminishing consciousness an awareness that he could move nothing; no breath nor any movement of his arms. His last conscious perception, as his head lay terribly twisted against the ground, was the view in the direction from which the paralyzing blow had come. He saw a face, a cold yet apparently satisfied face, staring at him— the last thing that would ever register within his levels of cerebral consciousness. Death came as a quick messenger, dispatching the devoted Father to a confrontation with his Maker.

As the word of the murder spread through the town, the death of Father O'Flannery shocked the people of Tralee beyond human capacity. "Inconceivable!" "A man with no enemies—beloved, nay almost worshipped!" And yet, as the townspeople would soon come to grasp, their Father was now the second priest to be murdered in County Kerry in less than a month. The other priest, Father Ronan O'Leary, cut of the same cloth as O'Flannery, was deeply loved by his flock; a trusted mentor to the children of his parish, especially the sons, and totally devoted to the work of God. Both killed differently and with not a trace of evidence to be found here in Tralee and hardly anything down in Waterville where Father O'Leary was murdered. Surely, after-the-fact, the presence of a foreign-speaking man faking interest in golf aroused suspicions among the Waterville authorities. Especially since he vanished the day of the murder—popped in at a bed-and-breakfast from out of nowhere without any reservations and disappeared just as quickly. The B & B owner's description of some strange markings noticed on this foreigner's skin was the only shred of evidence to be had, and it came far too late.

How could anyone perpetrate such acts of brutality upon men of such love, beauty and charity? No human, only a monster, could commit such foul acts. And the townsfolk of both Tralee and Waterville had no doubts these were murders since the constabulary had clearly and unhesitatingly pronounced them as such—murder it was!

The people of Tralee and Waterville would never come to know the irrefutable evidence supporting the charges of the murders of their beloved priests since it would never be provided to the community at-large. Due to the actions of Inspector O'Brien, fraught with his own fears about the gruesome murders, the sickeningly sordid facts about the identically-horrible mutilations of both Fathers Seamus O'Flannery and Ronan O'Leary would never see the light of day.

Chapter 1

February 14, 2003 Jerusalem, Israel

The hard, cold wooden seats of the conference room's waiting area didn't lend themselves to any warm, fuzzy feelings that Sonja Martin might have towards this Board of Governors of the Jerusalem New Testament Biblical Institute. Her friend Elana Dutros was inside pitching their project to a dubious Board with a disinterested leader and Sonja knew it was best to let Elana lay out their project. Then she could strike—just go in and dazzle them with her genetics concepts sandwiched between layers of biblical education and Christian commitment.

Smugly looking at his Board, the Reverend Simon Lewis disdainfully shook his head. "What do you think is so worthy of not only my time, but that of this whole Board? You girls need to understand we are busy and don't have time to waste on foolish projects!" As irritating as it always was to have so many women intruding into his world of biblical studies, Lewis thought he hid his feelings well when such negative thoughts coursed through his mind. *Why are these girls pushing their way into Biblical studies? This is a man's field! The Catholics have it right—keep the women where they belong!*

Observing Reverend Lewis' clumsy body language with negativism oozing out of every puffy pore, Elana couldn't suppress her thoughts: *Won't even look at me when he's speaking! Pompous little old man with clothes that don't fit and a rear end so big no light from the window escapes onto the floor. A short man with an even shorter man's syndrome! Look up 'arrogance' in the dictionary and there's his picture!* "I...I understand. No disrespect of your time or the rest of the Board's is intended. I hope and believe you will find my proposal an interesting and worthy project for the wonderful Institute you've created here."

Dutiful employee that she was at the Biblical Institute, Elana found it difficult to suppress her disappointment in these biased attitudes of her superiors. Raised in Athens, Greece, she understood the primitive Byzantine perceptions men had about women, especially in the workplace. But these men were Americans and she expected them to be more enlightened, not stuck in that same old mindset of diminished expectations and condescending attitudes so prevalent in the Old World. Elana hadn't spent much time with Reverend Lewis and hardly any with the other members of the Board, but she sensed enough to be anxious about the impact Sonja's unaffected beauty, imposing height and smashing intellect might have on them—especially this little, rumpled, frumpled Reverend Lewis.

Squirming in her seat, yet confident of her ability to face the Board with no hands wringing and no toes tapping, Sonja still couldn't dispel the impact of Elana's last-minute warning: "Just don't intimidate them!" What could she do? She couldn't change her 5'9" height or brilliant hazel eyes framed by long, flowing brown hair, and that's what she thought Elana meant when she spoke about her 'ravishing beauty'. Beauty wasn't something Sonja associated with herself because she never grew up seeking her image in a mirror. Beauty is what she only saw in other people. But her intellect was different, something she frequently needed to hide so as not to intimidate the males in her life. Sonja's deductive reasoning was analytically quick and comprehensively superior. No few males had their testosterone-inflated egos crushed by her problem solving capabilities.

But Elana's earlier words had burrowed deeply into the strata of her subconscious: "Be careful with this Reverend Lewis! His grossly-oversized ego has only a flirting relationship with reality. Those long, athletically-beautiful legs of yours could be threatening to a dumpy little old man who would see them as being longer than he was tall."

After surveying the rest of the Board, Elana now brought her focus back to Lewis. "Once you meet Sonja Martin I think you'll understand my enthusiasm for her and our project. She's uniquely inspiring, as is her concept of biblical genetics." Watching him standing there brought shivers of anxiety through her mind as she doubted men's ability to deal with women in the study of religion. But now, regaining her composure after a momentary pause, she was again keenly focused and her confidence was soaring like the positivism of her thoughts: *We hold all the aces with superior knowledge, insight and judgment. We'll be fine if we can only avoid the YCSS—that Y-Chromosome Suffocation Syndrome where weak men strangle the work of strong women whose minds are too advanced for their fragile male egos.*

Without Lewis acknowledging anything, Elana continued, "Hiring a biblical researcher with a background in genetic research makes no sense under normal circumstances, but these aren't normal times and Sonja Martin isn't a normal molecular geneticist. I think recent events justify adding Sonja to our payroll to develop a unique project; the genetic evaluation of a limestone burial box, the Ossuary of James, son of Joseph and brother of Jesus. A practicing Christian geneticist is unique and exactly what's needed. That's what we get in Sonja Martin!"

Sonja wished she knew what was going on behind that big door, but she trusted Elana to get the job done. They first met three years ago at Strayton University when Elana arrived to do some post-graduate work in the New Testament. Each had spent some time at the home of the other; Manchester, Vermont for Sonja and Athens, Greece for Elana. And now here she sat, eagerly and nervously awaiting the results of Elana's pleas and proposal to the Board.

On the other side of the door, Elana and the four Board members were trying to reach some consensus as the Reverend Lewis had the floor. With his back to Elana while gazing out the boardroom window, he tried to bring this discussion to an honorable conclusion. He was sure these girls were wasting his time, because what could they do for him that he couldn't do? He understood the world had changed, and he also accepted he was more comfortable with men since religion had always been about men's wisdom. "Let's face it," he often said to his manly colleagues, "God is a man. If He wanted women around, He would have created a wife to sit somewhere behind Him." The very pious reverend may have understood this changing world, but that didn't mean he had to like it, nor understand how distant he was from it.

"Miss Dutros," Reverend Lewis caustically questioned while still looking out the window, "how can you begin to think a molecular geneticist can have any potential benefit to this Institute? Even if she spends some of her time doing our biblical research, how do we justify any time dabbling in this unheard-of field of biblical genetics. There is no rationale for it! I understand Miss Martin is committed to our cause, but where does genetics come into play in a world of New Testament manuscripts? My dear girl, maybe it's about business, something you really don't understand."

Ignoring Lewis' stupid slight, Elana resisted the temptation to rise from her chair. She knew her thick brown hair and dark brown eyes, in combination with her height of 5 feet 7 inches, would be far too intimidating a presence for such a small, egotistical man. But she was also concerned her anxiety might show and make her look small and weak. An uncontrollable twitching of her nose erupted when she was nervous, and she hoped now wouldn't be one of those times. She feared this Reverend Lewis would try anything to disparage her proposal. "It comes into play," replied an un-intimidated and un-offended Elana, as she leaned forward on the table and folded her hands in front of her, "on pieces of bone. I know this concept is stretching one's imagination, but Miss Martin's research, based on what is known as the Jewish Priest Study, has created a place for genetic studies in our shared area of interest—biblical research."

7

Turning from the window, and with his hand stroking his ample chin, Lewis admitted to himself he didn't really understand what she was talking about. With a slow and arrogant tilting of his head he looked at Elana, then followed with an imperious raising of all three of his chins. "Tell me more about this study and why you think it has merit for my Institute."

Finally, there's hope I can get these guys to think outside the box. She chuckled at what she just thought, then made every effort to repress an emerging smile. *What a thing to think! I want them thinking inside the box, inside Moshe Levin's limestone box.* She nodded approvingly towards Lewis, acknowledging his superior sense of wisdom and timing, while her own confidence was growing and her nose wasn't twitching.

"Thank you for allowing me to clarify Sonja's work and its potential importance for us at the Institute."

Boredom dominated Lewis and he made no pretense of hiding it as he peered out the window.

An eager Elana started firing on all cylinders. "As you know, the surname Cohen was the name historically given to men who were Jewish priests. I don't think it's presumptuous to assume that we all understand how Jewish priests come only from fathers who were also Jewish priests. It's patrilineal. And since Aaron, the brother of Moses, was the first priest, isn't it reasonable to assume the lineage of priests descends from Aaron to present day Jewish priests? And would they not be genetically related due to this patrilineage? Is it, Reverend Lewis, being out of line to make these assumptions?"

Lewis' body language changed and Elana sensed a light going on in his small, obtuse brain. Afraid he lost some edge by delaying any response, he now gave her a stern look then responded in a very formal fashion, "That is true if there had been a pure patrilineage, only and always Jewish priests descending from Jewish priest fathers. But how can we know that the chain of purity was never broken or tainted by an adopted son or someone who was falsely projected as a son? You know it wouldn't have been uncommon for some women to have been cheating on their Jewish priest husbands."

Nodding approvingly, giving the impression she was aware of his keen insight, Elana repressed her desire to defend the reputations and integrity of these slandered Jewish women. "Well, we can't assume with 100% certainty there are no frauds in the lineage, but we can rely on reasonable degrees of certainty if we provide some genetic link among the men who themselves are linked to the Jewish priesthood. That research is what stimulated Sonja Martin's work at a genetics laboratory called MolecuGen."

"You mean she was trying to find a genetic link among Jewish   priests? " queried Lewis with an inquisitive look on a bloated face framed by his unkempt, arched eyebrows meeting together above his nose to form a shaggy 'unibrow'.

Maybe she finally had him hooked! He jumped at the bait and his curiosity had set the hook. She kept nodding. "The Jewish Priest Study was already done by other people who studied the DNA of many randomly chosen men named Cohen, the historical name of Jewish priests. What did they find? A common genetic marker projecting a shared genetic linkage with the historical lineage of Jewish priests. Sonja used these findings as she focused on the genetic sequence of the building blocks of DNA, things called nucleotides. As individuals, we all have our own unique coding or order of these nucleotides, and Sonja was trying to find something special in their arrangement. While the Jewish Priest study did find special sequencing markers in the lineage of Aaron, Sonja speculated there might be something similarly unique in any lineage of Jesus."

Leaning forward, elbows on the table and left hand stroking his chins, Lewis was now intrigued. He didn't understand too much about genetics, but he thought he understood where this was going. "Speculated?" he asked. "Of what value is a theory if no proof can validate it? Speculation then shifts to sheer stupidity!"

"Your doubt is understandable," replied Elana as she gently, but definitively, pounded the palms of her hands on the table, "but let's bring in Miss Martin to tell you about her work?"

Lewis lumbered over to the door and as he opened it, a surprised Sonja jumped up from her seat and found herself facing this short, heavy-set older man whose gaze shocked her. He appeared interested in her, but his formal tone was absent of any warmth. "Miss Martin, I am the Reverend Simon Lewis. Would you please come in and introduce us to your research at MolecuGen? Miss Dutros has made a very compelling case on your behalf, and now we would like you to share some of your experiences with us. Please... please come in," he said as he extended his hand to her as a greeting.

"Thank you," gushed Sonja as she shook his limp hand and realized she was stooping slightly so as not to tower over him. "I'm pleased to meet you and so excited you've found interest in my project."

Quick to put her at ease, Lewis replied, "I do, or should I say we members of the Board certainly find your research of interest, and would like you to share more of your vision with us."

Almost sprinting into the room, she saw Elana at the table with an open chair next to her. As she moved towards the chair, Lewis was struck by her size—size was always important to him even though he didn't have any and couldn't admit it to himself. *Where do these tall women come from? This Martin girl must be over 5 ½ feet tall with the same dark looks as Dutros.* He pointed to the chair. "Please sit down and make yourself comfortable. We are very interested in what you have to say. Miss Dutros explained the issue of the Jewish priest lineage and your genetic research. While it sounds intriguing, what does this have to do with us?"

Hesitating for only a second, she wondered how much, or how well Elana had described her research. Anxious thoughts raced through her mind: *Just answer the questions. Don't get caught-up with confusion or assumptions.* Then she looked Reverend Lewis right in the eye. "Independent of the Jewish Priest Study, my research at MolecuGen verified their findings that a genetic marker could be traced in men named Cohen all the way back to Aaron, the brother of Moses. I believe Elana already discussed that with you. But I was curious

10

about the very special ordering of DNA building blocks. These building blocks, called nucleotides, are what make up all human DNA, and there are only four of them: adenine, guanine, thymine and cytosine. We usually refer to them only by their letter designation of A, G, T and C. While millions of A, C, T and G are uniquely arranged for each human, there are sometimes recurring patterns called microsatellites such as: A-C, C-G, A-C, C-G. If many patterns were found to be atypically common, the inference is these microsatellites could be uniquely shared by genetically-related people and also serve as a mechanism for the identification of other relatives."

A condescending Lewis nodded, "All very interesting, but what does all this mean for my Institute?"

With confidence building, and while edging up in her chair to close the deal, Sonja looked over at Elana and saw that small nervous twitching of her nose. "Prior to January 7, 2003, it didn't have much potential to be anything other than a theory."

Looking a bit perturbed from being fed in small morsels, Lewis wanted it all in one bite. "What happened on January 7, 2003?"

Quick to respond, Sonja kept her focus on Lewis' face. "That's the day an obscure Jerusalem antiquities dealer announced to the world he had a limestone box, an ossuary, on which carbon dating had been done. The results of the dating showed the box, or its contents, could have come from the time of Christ."

"Was the box 2,000 years old, or just the piece of limestone from which it was made? You know other people have discovered 2,000 year old antiques, so what is so special about this one?" harshly queried Lewis trying to test her mettle to see if she was worthy of any investment.

Repressing her desire to get up from her chair and look down on him, Sonja quickly blurted out, "Actually, for the carbon dating to have any legitimacy, you need organic remains in the box since you can't test the limestone itself. No one has found an antique like this ossuary and on its lid is the chiseled inscription: 'James, son of Joseph, brother of Jesus'."

11

"Are there bones in the box? Do you really think this ossuary is that of James?" now probed a very curious Lewis whose haughty look was one of the last tricks in his arsenal of sexist intimidation.

Unwavering, Sonja didn't hesitate. She knew her position, having reviewed it in her mind hundreds of times before. "The box is listed as being sealed, but something inside was analyzed before it was sealed. Apparently it was found outside Israel in a dry cave complex similar to the site of the Dead Sea Scrolls. I can't say what's in it, be it bones, bone residue or just limestone dust. I can't even be sure if the ossuary is a fraud or not. The man who owns it has a jaded history in the antiquities realm, but this time he's contracted for some legitimizing research from several very prestigious research institutions."

Impatient about how his Biblical Institute might fit into this unfolding mystery, Lewis unquestionably wanted to be on the leading edge of a discovery. But he also didn't want to look like a fool putting his support behind these girls and then discovering the ossuary was a fraud. It would be his and the Institute's reputations that needed protected. He curbed a rising look of eager anticipation while assuming an air of detached aloofness. "Even if the ossuary is 2,000 years old and holds something, how do we know what that something is? If there are bones in the box, how do we know whose bones they were? This could be a genetic detective story with a dead end—a very dead end!"

Struggling to stay glued to her seat, Sonja leaned closer to the table, placed both elbows on it and then prayerfully folded her hands as she then wasted not a second in firing back her retort. "Please bear in mind the chiseled inscription said important things. If the inscription was legitimately chiseled at the time of James' death, it links James to Joseph—something that's not really disputed. However, by saying 'brother of Jesus', ancient people of that time only talked about a brother if he actually was a blood brother. Not a step-brother or adopted brother or anything else. This alone would imply that James was not only the brother of Jesus, but also a biological child of Mary!"

12

"Yes," proclaimed a pompous Lewis, "it would confirm what the Bible said about Jesus having brothers and sisters. It could also confirm what we Protestants believe, and create a basis for a resolution of one of the stumbling blocks in the search for greater Christian unity. God only knows how critical it is that all Christians stand as a unified force against the negative forces emerging from the non-Christian world."

"Precisely," said Sonja, almost jumping from her chair, "but let's take this further. Since Mary was of the lineage of Aaron, if we found some of those unique Jewish Priest Study microsatellite patterns in just a trace of DNA from what we think is James bones, this would support our position of James being of the blood of Mary. It's not perfect proof of anything, but sometimes you have to accumulate a lot of scientific data before definitively proving a hypothesis. Needless to say, just by looking at an inscription in that ossuary lid doesn't prove that any genetic material found inside would be of James."

"Exactly what I was worried about," said a smug Lewis as he turned to look away from Sonja to again show her his back while he mused, "If that is the case, why would we get involved with this ossuary? It looks interesting and tantalizing, yet could lead us to something not provable."

Not able to hold back any longer, Sonja stood up, "I agree what we have may not be perfect, but it's a step in the right direction. And while we don't know from where our next genetic information will come, look at where we end up by tracing this genetic pathway. The thought of the Jewish Priest microsatellite sequencing possibly shared by James makes one wonder if that same sequence might be holy, a Holy Sequence shared by Mary and ultimately Jesus."

Bathing in his unsubstantiated arrogance, the malevolent minister persisted, "How will you know if some DNA you're thinking is James' might not be that of a woman?"

"That's not a difficult issue to verify even in severely altered DNA. You can look at the Amelogenin loci or the base-pair sequences in highly fragmented remains. It's no problem, but not what we're after."

"I see," interjected Reverend Lewis as the quizzical look, raised unibrow included, now returned to his countenance. "Then you're assuming the identifiable genetic material of the Cohen research would have come from Aaron and you're wondering if it could have been shared not only by Elizabeth, but also Mary, James and then Jesus."

"Correct," trumpeted Elana, halfway out of her chair before realizing she needed some restraint. "Excuse me, I... I just couldn't contain myself."

You could feel the emergent energy around the table as everyone had absorbed her enthusiasm as the project unfolded.

"Yes," exclaimed a beaming Sonja. "And," she paused, "if there are any bone fragments in that ossuary whose genetic content is similar to what was found in the Jewish Priest Study, it's reasonable to assume the bone material in the box does in fact belong to James."

A beaming Lewis added, "And an old Christian conundrum would be solved if I proved James was of the blood of Mary, not a stepchild from a previous wife of Joseph, nor an illegitimate or even an adopted child."

Twitching gone, an increasingly confident Elana replied, "Yes sir, you're right." And this time she stayed firmly seated. "We wouldn't have perfect proof, but would have built a stronger data base with this holy sequencing that strengthened the Protestant position. And sir, by doing so, you would be seen as the Great Resolver of the Christian Conundrum—the leader of this Righteous Resolution."

Lewis leapt at the opportunity as a quick thought seared its imprint into his imagination: *These girls can be useful. Why not give them a chance to see what greatness they can bring me that I can show to all the world? If they fail, it won't hurt my reputation, only theirs. If they find something useful, naturally I, the risk-taker and entrepreneur in this venture, can rightfully take credit for it. How can I lose? Take the credit for the good or let them assume the responsibility, as they so rightly should, if they fail me or my Biblical Institute. I'll only further enhance my reputation as the Bold Innovator I've always been.* "Miss Dutros, your recommendation is accepted!"

14

Strutting around the table, this plump peacock of a pastor continued, "On behalf of the Board of the Jerusalem New Testament Biblical Institute, we would like to offer to Miss Martin, a position on our staff. Naturally we will provide all the funding requested," as he winked at her, "but I must tell you a secret. I never had a trace of doubt in you or your project from the very beginning. We on the Board simply wanted to determine if you had the same level of confidence in yourself that we already had in you. Come now! Please stand up and meet your new employers."

Sonja stood up tall, then instantly stooped slightly as a response shot from her lips, "Thank you. I accept your offer and look forward to working with you and Miss Dutros."

Arms spread wide as if to bring the flock closer to him, a joyous Lewis couldn't contain his enthusiasm, nor his smile. "Now where do we go from here with my project?"

Smugly satisfied, Elana replied, "Our first step is to go to the exhibit at King Solomon Hall. Let's see what this Moshe Levin really has."

Chapter 2

3/15/2003, Tarbert, County Kerry, Ireland

Like a brilliant comet streaking across the sky, the super-confident Rigel was always the brightest star, but this time some doubts festered about getting his men focused on this new agenda. *Maybe too much money too soon was the problem*, he thought while wondering whether they could take on his new project—a pilgrimage of sorts. Would these bones of Jesus' brother rattle their cages enough to grab their interest?

Getting up from the kitchen table, Liam's thick, resonating Irish brogue got everyone's attention. Despite his short height and disheveled brown hair half-covering his blood-shot brown eyes, the grimace on his unshaven face projected the doubt in his mind. "It's a bloody mess concerning ourselves with things in Israel. We made our fortunes elsewhere; here in Europe, North America, Russia and from the Saudis. Why now Jerusalem? Is that where we want ta be?"

Liam's words brought to the surface an exploding pustule of underlying uncertainty seeping through him, as well as Conor and Viktor. Conor, like Liam, a devoted ally of Rigel, rose from his chair only to stare out the window at the River Shannon coursing its way out of Ireland to greet the Atlantic Ocean. Same short height as Liam, but more intimidating with the shoulders and neck of a bull, and a ferocious gaze that intimidated no small number of his victims. But now, as he turned towards Liam, the look in his dark brown eyes was only that of a long-standing friendship. Running his fingers through his long, oily brown hair, his Irishness dripped like honey on every ripe word rolling from his lips. "He's never led us astray before, but I'll be damned if I can figure out what he's up ta this time."

A deep Russian voice, coming from the large hulk of an unsmiling man, filled the room with a thick atmosphere of doubt. Viktor Koronovski felt like an outsider since all his partners were Irish, but he never felt so uncomfortable that he wouldn't give his opinion, usually smothered in his slow, halting Russian style. Looking first at Liam, then Conor, he spewed out, "You two are Irish, like him and maybe you grow up trusting each other, but I trust no one but Rigel. Rigel always makes good decisions, but I can't understand Jerusalem. Nothing but religion and hatred there!"

"Right ya are," responded Liam, "and Rigel hasn't told us what's so good there. Why lose our momentum now when the spoils from our Belarus trip generates the power ta make our biggest score?"

The door burst open and there stood Rigel, as tall as Viktor, but with a trim, well-toned body and an undeniable projection of self-assurance. Donovan O'Rafferty, the 32 year old Irishman with the piercing blue eyes coming from under his mop of unruly red hair, was certainly the man-of-the-hour for these men. Forsaking his birth name years ago and now known only as Rigel, he was always the brightest light leading the way. With his ability to lead Orion, the name he gave his pack of larcenous hunters, they were seeking fortune wherever his nose and his brain took them. *A good group of hunters they are,* he thought, *and if I'm their brightest light, I can't keep them in the dark forever.* "Lads, what's in those craniums a yours?" he asked while surveying this collage of confused faces.

A spontaneous Viktor blurted out before anyone else had a chance, "When you not here, we talk. And when we talk, we wonder what Rigel thinks about Jerusalem? Why we go there?"

Rigel's Orion group, together for nine years, had great team chemistry but this was the first time they challenged him.

17

Emboldened by Viktor's bluntness, Liam got off his chair. "Rigel, my boy, ya know we're always prepared ta go with ya, but there's a fog over this mission. We've been making money hand-over-fist, especially after the Vatican, so why change course? Makes no sense ta go ta Israel—it's not part a the plan."

Unfazed by this collective doubt, Rigel still realized he kept his men in the dark long enough. He walked over to the big window in the room, and after flinging its curtain wide open, looked out longingly toward the sky before turning back to them. "Lads, we're off ta Jerusalem and going ta look at an old antique, a relic from about 2,000 years ago. From the time a Jesus if ya can believe it."

Conor couldn't hold back. "But we're not in the antiques business. Why do such a thing when we can make more money in a day looting with our computers than ya can make in a lifetime selling antiques? It might be OK for your old age," Conor laughed as he bent over and mimicked an older person hobbling with a cane, "but for now, haven't ya gone off the deep end just a wee bit?"

Suppressing his sly smile, Rigel reflected, *I guess I need to whet their appetites,* then focused on Conor. "We're not going ta be antique dealers. Already enough crooks there. I'm looking for something a little more legitimate than what we've been doing—something like the business a religion."

Twisting in his chair, Liam spat out, "Rigel, c'mon! Ya say enough crooks are already in antiques, but have ya forgot about religion? Don't ya think there are enough thieves already in the churches who'll make us look like saints no matter how bad we are?"

Sometimes timid, but this time able to speak his mind, Conor chimed in, "Is the mad cow disease making your brain spongy? We know ya hate the Church because a your brother Michael, but religion? You a all people, a religious man ya aren't."

So true, a religious man I'm not. Rigel mused as his mind wandered to a different time. He wasn't religious now, but as a boy, he'd been very religious

18

until he needed the protection of Orion the Hunter. He looked at Conor, then nodded, "You're right. I don't love the Church, but they've been loving me since I was a little lad. What an ingrate ya must think I am!"

Growing up poor in Ireland, there weren't many pathways to success for a very bright little boy. With his father's Irish Disease, never sober enough to give any guidance, Rigel's chances were bleak. His only hope was his mum and the Church. Despite having her hands full with four children, she was able to instill in them a combination of mental discipline and intellectual drive. Like so many women of that era, poor and without help from a supportive spouse, Margaret O'Rafferty did all she could to get her children a foothold in life. She knew they had only one chance, and that was for them to excel in the church school and then maybe the priests would get behind them and push them to success.

But Rigel was the only one to get ahead. He always said his brother Michael couldn't deal with the Church's abuse, which destroyed him. And his sisters? They took the only way out of their destitute lives by becoming nuns. Rigel thought of them often, and how the carnivorous Church had in one way or another consumed their flesh. *The Church*, he thought, *where would I be without the Church? Why was I the only one to escape it with most of me being intact? I could handle the constant pushing, poking and prodding, but my poor Michael couldn't. The Church destroyed him, and for that I'll make it pay.*

Rigel's superior intelligence, and maybe a little help with his mum cleaning the parish house, accelerated him through the local church schools and ultimately to Trinity College in Dublin. But before he got to Trinity, his loyalty to this great benefactor had long since wistfully waned. He didn't have the blind devotion of his mum, and his love of the Church had long since vanished; a love lost just like that for a father not there to protect and love him back.

While still in his pre-university schooling, Rigel realized the Church was not all it was projected to be. He knew it helped men, women and children, but it

19

also created some of the difficulties the Irish people had. With not enough land to farm since too many children were born to most families, the people were dependent on the Church for charity. And with no birth control, the lives of the devout were doomed to over-populated hand-to-mouth poverty. Knowing there was no chance for success, men drank themselves into lives of desperate denial, duly depriving their families of a better life. The Church's emissaries, its priests, were always there to serve the people, and to have the people serve them back—a system of salvation and functional slavery all wrapped into one neat guilt-ridden package.

As a teenager Rigel went from loving the Church, to fearing it and then finally loathing it. He became unsure about all the secrecy and actions from the confessional to the convent, but his mum always said 'ta trust the priests, nuns and the Church' because they were his only hope. 'They'll take care a ya,' she always said, but his unhappiness increased as he grew older and he understood his Michael's mistreatment. That unhappiness with the Church was finally overcome when he followed its own advice, the words he always heard from the pious pulpit: 'When you're in trouble, look ta God—look ta the heavens for your comfort and peace.' And every night when those profound problems consumed him, out to the fields he went to lie on his back to seek his peace and salvation in the heavens. While he never saw his Father in Heaven, he did find something else; the constellation Orion with its three stars in a diagonal row. Why always Orion the Hunter? Were the stars telling him what his Father in Heaven wasn't? From that time thereafter, he understood that heavenly message from Orion, the Hunter, and no longer wanted to be Donovan O'Rafferty, the hunted. And from the brightest star in the constellation, he took the name Rigel, the perfect name for the brightest of boys—and a single name for the most solitary of boys. As Rigel, he would someday settle the score for all the innocents, for all the little ones, especially his little brother Michael!

Like a miracle, the system worked! With the Church's persistent prodding, he was off to Trinity College in Dublin, only to be known as Rigel. At Trinity he came to understand how his powerful ability to lead men combined with his education in finance and international business created a perfect fit for an unlimited future. While his friends at Trinity were of similar educational backgrounds, and whose stars never shined as brightly as his, they would be clustered around his brilliance and become his Orion. And like Orion the Hunter, they would be hunters—hunters of fortune with highly sophisticated computer hacking skills and the knowledge of how the international business world functioned. Forsaking the ideas of that foolish Englishman Robin Hood, Orion would find ways to take from the 'haves' and keep for themselves.

Walking over to the kitchen table, Rigel sat on the only available chair. "Lads, don't ya worry a bit, I won't lead ya ta Jerusalem for a wrong reason. And Liam, don't be doubting our mission. We'll make more money than a supercomputer can count before we're done."

Rigel had taken care of Liam before by saving him from an unruly Dublin crowd which disapproved of his socialist, public provocations. Liam Flynn from Portaferry, Northern Ireland wasn't of the town's Theodore Flynn family which had sired that Hollywood star, Errol. Ever since their first chance meeting at Trinity, Rigel might poke a little fun at him about Errol, but in Liam's mind, he hoped someday to be a real swashbuckler for the cause of Irish independence. Growing-up in Northern Ireland, and like most Northern Irish Catholics, Liam considered himself only Irish.

When Liam traveled the A20 from Portaferry to Belfast and saw those portraits of IRA freedom fighters painted on the red brick Belfast apartment buildings, the fires of Irish nationalism were stoked and burned strongly within him. As a little lad, he always heard, at the knee of his grandfather, and then at the side of his father, the legendary exploits of the IRA patriots, especially the great Dan Keating, who when he turned 100 years old, refused his Republic of Ireland $3,500 award since the President of Ireland was not, in his mind, the President of a true Ireland. While Liam hadn't been a violent participant in any of Orion's business actions—they had Conor and Viktor for that—his aggressiveness and hostility were pent-up for the day he would need them. A day that would come when he'd have the chance to fight for the cause of Irish Republicanism and a united Ireland!

Conor O'Mahoney and Liam were pals since they first met Rigel at Trinity, yet Conor was of a different style than Liam. Conor wasn't one of the typical lads who left Kinsale, County Cork to go to Trinity. He was very bright and took great pride in being Irish, not Northern Irish. But frequently his behavior was an enigma to those around him. Conor always seemed low-key and introverted in his relationships within Orion, but both Liam and Rigel had seen the behavioral transformation that occurred when something or someone outside upset him. For all his life, or at least since he was 14 or 15, something could arise from deep within those tortuous caverns of his psyche, and a bit of a monstrous mean streak would surface that got him in trouble with the priests and the local authorities.

On the streets of Kinsale, more than one inebriated tourist, walking alone at night after a day golfing at the Old Head, had been accosted by this Conor, nicknamed the 'Bull'. They never knew what hit them until the next day when they found themselves free of their wallets and some of their senses. Though not very tall, when he was in a fight, Conor made up for it with a quick, explosive aggressiveness that made him seem a foot taller. And while his dark side never surfaced in his relationships with Orion, Rigel had seen Conor kill a man wearing the colors of the Protestant Orange at a brawl up in the Portadown section of Belfast. It was only Rigel's quick thinking that evacuated Conor from the situation before he was arrested. Conor knew he was beholden to Rigel, the only one able to tame that unstable aggressiveness. Or maybe it should be said that Rigel simply learned to channel it into the directions which best served his Orion.

Liam and Conor were inseparable, despite Conor's chiding about not being a 'pure' Irishman. 'Just a bit tainted by those Northern Irish Protestants' Conor would say when he wanted to get Liam riled-up. Yet, they were a perfect team. Liam was a computer genius who could solve any problem or fix any computer failure. He was a hacker extraordinaire and could create more viruses than God himself. There was no computer system alive he couldn't hack into, and no virus too difficult for him to create, or if needed, prevent. Despite Conor's physical prowess having bailed out Liam several times, it was Conor's mathematical and accounting genius that provided the real support Liam needed. Liam and Conor had been good for each other and Orion had been good for them.

Rigel had met Liam and Conor at Trinity where they realized their feelings about life, society and the Church were very similar, and maybe not acceptable in a Catholic society. If Communism hadn't gone out of style, with its internal decay and flawed designs, they might have evolved into revolutionaries of some kind, possibly spies like the Cambridge men from the 1940's—Philby, Burgess, Maclean, Blunt and Cairncross. Rigel had guided his men to understand if you couldn't change a society, you should take from it. And take from it they did.

Coming to Orion from a different path, Viktor was born in Belarus, then raised and educated in the old Soviet system before being sent to Trinity for post-graduate training. His time at Trinity was a part of an educational program created to bring Christian exposure to the heathens of the old Soviet bloc. But Viktor never seemed to be a real student. He was four years older than Rigel, Liam and Conor, and didn't seem too interested in school. His main strength appeared to be more brawn than brain. Rigel always thought Viktor was a KGB agent, and with the collapse of the Soviet Union, he sensed Viktor's desperation to find some stability without returning to Russia. Viktor chose to forsake the new Russia and allied himself with Rigel who, with Liam and Conor, hacked into the Ireland Immigration and Naturalization Service to create his citizenship papers.

So loyal was Viktor, he had the constellation Orion's three diagonal stars tattooed on his right hand—imprinted forever with his commitment to Rigel. Frequently, a proud Viktor regaled over how he repaid Rigel's trust by leading Orion back home to Belarus where, at a poorly guarded nuclear arsenal, he single-handedly stole two powerful minibombs. Overpowered the guards, bound them with duct tape and drove Orion and the bombs in a stolen truck out of the country before the Russians knew what hit them.

Always Orion's main target for a special brand of financial restitution, the Church couldn't escape the crosshairs of Rigel's aim. Even after the Vatican's banking scandal in the 1980's with Banco Ambrosiano, the Vatican's accounts were easy to access, especially with someone of the talent of Liam. A church dominated by old, white men that didn't trust itself couldn't trust new technology driven by young people of different colors, nationalities and religions, if they had any religion at all. Too many secrets needed to be hidden and that meant keeping as much as possible stored in the old, failing minds of the Vatican. Far too little protection for such wealthy assets, and Rigel knew how to get at them. He also knew how to use one of Viktor's bombs to extort from the Vatican without anyone in the outside world knowing.

"So, Conor," Rigel queried as he surveyed the men around the table and then fixed his eyes on him, "ya think I've gone soft have ya? Maybe I've always been a closet Christian and now it's time ta come out a the closet."

"Are you gay?" said a perplexed and confused-looking Viktor.

"No," laughed Rigel, sensing his confusion, "and I'm not a Christian in-hiding. But I do think this Christian relic in Jerusalem is worth pursuing."

"But Rigel," Conor interrupted, "do the math. How much can we make in the antique business? It can't compare ta what we can steal every day on the internet."

"I know where you're going Conor," replied Rigel, "but let me show ya a new road map ta fortune. And this time we might even look more legitimate, a little cleaner."

"All from antiques?" asked a stupefied Viktor.

Rigel knew it was time to lay all the cards on the table. "Here it is lads," he said as he sat at the table and poured himself a cup of lukewarm tea. "The antique we're going after is a burial box. A limestone box called an ossuary that held the bones from a man thought ta be James, the brother a Jesus."

"The bones a the brother of Jesus?" asked a shocked Liam. "Didn't know he had a brother."

Looking dismissively, Rigel addressed Liam, "That's because we're Catholics, and Catholics and Orthodox Christians don't believe the Books a Matthew and Mark where it says Jesus had brothers and sisters. Maybe they believe the Bible, but they don't believe these brothers and sisters were a Jesus' blood. Could be adopted or stepchildren a Joseph, but the Protestants think different, mind ya."

"Always different," chimed in Liam. "Ya should try living with them— always some kind a yoke around your neck."

"You're right," chuckled Rigel, "they're different. And for our needs, thank heaven they're very different. They believe the brothers and sisters a Jesus were a His blood. Brothers and sisters who were born ta Mary and Joseph after Jesus was born."

"What does this have ta do with us?" prodded Liam.

Smiling as he made eye contact with each of them, Rigel continued. "This burial box, this ossuary, is being offered for sale as a sealed box whose lid has an engraving that says it contains the bones a James, son a Joseph and brother a Jesus. If there're any bones in that box, we might find a genetic link ta Jesus."

"A genetic link?" asked Conor. "How da we make any money with a genetic link ta Jesus, even if ya did find one?"

Wagging a finger at Conor, Rigel quickly replied, "Ya remember Christ was the lamb. Always, some a the flock needs ta be sheared. But we'll do it one better and fleece the whole God-damned flock!"

Ever quick to sense Rigel's direction, Liam intoned, "But how da we get at the flock? How's it that ya see us fleecing them?"

"Liam, don't ya be a doubting Liam," a coy Rigel replied as he stepped towards him. "We'll create the flock, our own flock, and why not our own Church? We can do it if we can find some genetic material and link it ta millions a people who, like us, have been disconnected from their religious roots. Now that they love technology more than they love the God they'd grown up with, why not create some kind a techno-God?"

"And what da we bring ta them?" asked an expressive Liam with both arms held out and his empty palms pointed upwards. "An antique? A limestone box? Da we put the limestone box on wheels and become the Church a the Rolling Stone? C'mon Rigel, ya've been a great leader, but your hatred a the Church, because a your brother, has always been in your craw. Why da ya want ta get us in this religion business?"

A confident smile swept over his face as he answered Liam. "If I'm right, and there's bones a James in that box, I'll link the genetic material ta my church, my Church a the Internet. The world is full a internet nerds and we'll have both God and salvation on the internet for them. These nerds love their technology and we'll make technology, their internet and our genetics, their new god. It'll be a new kind a Trinity replacing Father, Son and Holy Ghost. We'll fleece them twice over. When ya look at how the televangelists have worked over their flocks, especially in the U.S., we'll fleece them even better. Especially all those Protestants who seem ta go for any scam ya can dream up."

"Twice?" asked a confounded Viktor.

Rigel reached over to grasp Viktor's hand and focused only on him. "First we'll get them tithing ta the church and then charge them separately so they can get a little genetic link with Jesus. We'll genetically engineer a little a Jesus from the shared genes a James—engineered genes to be carried into our parishioners' cells using an inhaled spray mist system. No different from what's been already used with gene-altering treatments for a disease called cystic fibrosis."

"What you saying?" asked an even more deeply confused Viktor.

Rigel continued as he made eye contact with all three of his men. "It's already been shown ya can breathe in a mist containing genes which were altered. These engineered genes are then incorporated into your own cells, and in this way, ya can transmit some a Jesus ta each a our flock. And the Protestants aren't our only market. We'll get the Catholics too!"

"How can we get Catholics ta jump ship?" asked Conor, now shaking his head. "If they don't already believe in James being a the blood a Jesus, what'll make them start now?"

Quick to reply, Rigel retorted in a flash. "Except for Christianity only growing in Africa and South America, the world is full a Catholics and non-Catholics who've fallen by the wayside. Church attendance is down so far in Protestant Britain and Catholic France that people are waiting for something or someone ta believe in. We'll give it ta them, and with our Church a the Internet, they still won't have ta change their pattern a not going ta church. My, or someone else's messages will come ta them over the internet. 'Ya've got mail' will come ta mean 'Ya've got God'. Naturally from our Church a the Internet, and for only a small donation."

Viktor stood, then ambled over to Rigel. "I always trust you and will go where you lead. But how we get into genetics engineering with no experience?"

Pointing his right index finger towards his head, Rigel then smiled. "I've already got that covered. Someone who's part a Orion, but not here a part a Orion, will do the deed."

Liam butted in, "Ya said ya had the genetic issue solved, but what da ya mean? Someone who's part a us, but not part a us? Another religious mystery like Holy Communion?"

Glaring intensely at his men, Rigel quickly broke into a smile, "Haven't any a ya taken a phone message for me in some code? Da ya remember the name?"

"Dali, a guy named Salvador Dali," reflexively answered Conor, not only a great mathematician but also the owner of a great memory trap from which nothing escaped. "Some sort a strange guy like that Spanish painter with the waxed mustache and strange paintings."

"Ya got it," replied a detached Rigel as his mind wandered, *If you only knew*, "His code name for us will be just that, Salvador Dali, and he'll only be called by that name until I tell ya differently."

Viktor edged in, "When do we meet him?"

A now impatient Rigel confronted this consortium of curiosity. "I don't know when or even if you're going ta meet him. I'll tell ya when the time comes, if it comes at all." As he walked over to the bay window to look out at the Shannon on its way out to the Atlantic Ocean, the blank stare on Rigel's face conveyed to his men that his mind had now moved elsewhere. *Salvador Dali,* Rigel thought to himself, *if they only knew. An artist? Yea! A creative genius? Absolutely!*

Rigel had known Dali, Dr. Geoffrey Salvatore, for over 10 years since their time together at Trinity when Rigel met him before any others of his Orion group. Geoffrey graduated before the other Orion friendships had evolved and his relationship with Rigel existed outside of the awareness of anyone else.

When Rigel met Geoffrey at Trinity, he was surprised to find this very Italian name belonged to a red-headed Scotsman. And like most people, Rigel was unaware of Italians migrating to western Scotland in the 1600's to work as artisans and craftsmen. While Geoffrey was a Scotsman, he was also a Catholic, albeit a lapsed one. A biochemistry major, Geoffrey was infatuated with genetics, and loved the concept of genetic manipulation. Being a proud Scot, he hoped for a career back in Scotland, the home of so much scientific research.

In the tradition of Sir James Fleming, the discoverer of penicillin, Scottish health researchers had been at the cutting edge of innovation. 'Salvador Dali' hoped he'd get his chance to cut up his share of the intellectual pie, but confided to Rigel that the 'old boy' network might not look kindly on a Catholic

Scotsman with an Italian name who'd gotten his education in Ireland. Despite the fact that Geoffrey needed to expand his genetic research back in Scotland, where the Catholic Church couldn't constrain genetic research as it did in Ireland, he feared never being accepted as a 'true' Scotsman in the eyes of the Protestant Scottish research elite. Symbiotically, Rigel and Dali had been bonded by a religion that hadn't brought them an ounce of peace and tranquility.

Not able to stop looking out that bay window at the water of the Shannon, Rigel's eyes looked upwards as his mind focused, *What the Scots missed, they'll never know.* And he thought of how his very loyal men of Orion might never know who or what 'Salvador Dali' really represented to their plan. "Lads," Rigel said as he turned away from the window, "when the time comes ta meet 'Salvador Dali', you'll be the first ta know."

Chapter 3

April 18, 2003 Jerusalem, Israel

"You bitch!" he shouted while rolling out of bed and surveying the barren walls of his bedroom. Every day was like this for Moshe Levin; empty and talking out loud to that woeful woman, Riva, whose shadow had long fled his bed. "What a fool I was to keep you so long. You'll regret you left because today is finally my day! Today everyone came to Jerusalem to see me, the greatest antiquities dealer in the world."

He always spoke to himself when he was frustrated over his ex-wife or with those questions too often raised about a man whom museums never trusted. But he knew they would be coming today to see his box, not a man whose appearance mirrored his career. With a head of hair that fled just like his many dreams of greatness, the little fuzz remaining was frazzled like his nerves after so many failures. For a short man, his distended belly led the way when he walked and was a reflection of his sense of self-importance—bloated beyond any constraints of reality. But this time, instead of being distrusted by the experts, he would be the center of the antiquities world when he unveiled his limestone treasure box, this Ossuary of James, brother of Jesus.

Moshe's career as an antiquities dealer wasn't even as good as the worst description his ex-wife ever gave. But he had once been a promising young archeologist with great access throughout the Middle East. Born in Israel and educated in Athens, he worked with some of the great names in the field. For Moshe, the future was limitless until he found some relics that were old, but not old enough. The antiquities market had been fueled by rumors and speculation about another Dead Sea scrolls discovery and Moshe had succumbed to temptation. No matter how hard he tried, he couldn't get Riva's words out of his mind, "How could you be so stupid to take papyrus and clay and try to make silver and gold out of it?" He was discovered trying to pass off something newer for being something older, and couldn't comprehend how he so badly lost his moral compass. Now those doubts swirled in his mind and permeated his thinking. *Was it greed? Stupidity? Too young to know better? Or was Riva right, just a fool with not enough character—the second dumbest person on Earth, with her being the dumbest for marrying him.*

Riva stayed with Moshe for 10 years after his exposure as a fraud, but his blemish of dishonesty became even too much for her to bear. She left him alone with no family and no reputation worth mentioning. Having been alone for many years, Moshe had been consoled by his delusions of greatness veneering his mental imprint of failure and deceit. *Someday they will see that Moshe Levin is the greatest name in the world of antiquities!*

Today, Moshe's 'someday' finally arrived, and from now on, it was going to be different. No more persistent questions and evasive answers about the provenance of his discoveries. Now he turned and spoke to each of the walls with their blank expressions reflecting the reactions of his audiences in the past. "How can I be expected to tell you where every old relic came from? They're old! They were lost and somehow I found them. What does it matter where they came from?" But this time there were no ugly questions since he had the ownership papers proving he bought this limestone burial box outside of Israel and could sell it without any restrictions.

His talking never stopped, and a broad smile, like that of an orphan finally finding a home, now graced his wrinkled face. "I promised to deliver the goods and I don't care what they say, I have it—the Ossuary of James. What a treasure for some lucky dealer or museum." And instead of fighting against the tide of doubt that previously engulfed him, he now had experts proving he had the real thing. Never tiring of speaking boldly to his audience of one, Moshe persisted, "Yes! The Ontario Museum Research Center for Antiquities agreed that my ossuary is 2,000 years old. Let the doubters argue with the experts, not with me. Moshe just wants his prize, his fortune for bringing to Christianity a closer link to its messiah."

Like a Lazarus, rising-up from the dead, Moshe saw today's introduction of his ossuary at the King Solomon Hall as the resurrection of his career." *What a choice of sites*, he thought, *the wisdom of Solomon joins the wisdom of Moshe!*

Moshe chose the King Solomon Hall with its semi-circular stage looking out at a lecture hall with seating for 300 people. He expected all seats to be filled because there was such great interest in his discovery, but regardless how many came, he knew only one buyer was needed. Behind the front of the stage was an exhibit floor that would allow the audience to come up and view his prize. They could see it, touch it, measure it or just run their fingers over the words chiseled into the lid: 'James, son of Joseph, brother of Jesus.' He couldn't hold back his admonition, "You can do whatever you want, except open the lid—only I do that". Moshe knew there was something inside the box which could be heard sliding around when the box was tilted. With the lid off, Moshe had been able to see it looked like bones and some residue or dust, maybe bone dust. Now it was sealed but would be opened at the exhibition.

As he prepared to leave, he gave the bedroom one final look and forcefully spoke his last to those receptive, non-judgmental walls, "I don't care what's in the box. Just someone buy the damned thing and I'll be free at last!"

Chapter 4

King Solomon Hall

"Justice, always fleeing like a thief in the night," Moshe mindlessly muttered to himself. "But now I've got them in the palm of my hand—the heat of their intense interest burning and their Christian curiosity coming to a boiling point. Amidst the rape, pestilence and murder in the world, justice finally prevails for Moshe!"

Standing off to the side of the stage, Moshe surveyed the scene as it unfolded right before Him. He was pleased and could feel the explosive energy of the audience as they were being attracted to what he knew was his natural, powerful magnetism. Standing on the stage and looking out at the filled seats of the amphitheater which surrounded and embraced him, he was elated. Now he could gloat, and naturally deserved to! Sticking out his belly, thumbs in his trouser's pockets and rocking back-and-forth on his heels, he cast his magical aura over this assembled flock. *They've all come to bathe in the luxuriant light of my great vision and integrity.*

While Moshe thought he had the vision of a genius, unfortunately it was channeled through a narrow, selectively-filtered prism, letting in the colors or thoughts of his choosing and screening out the impurities that conflicted with what he wanted to see. But now his keenly-focused visual and psychological prisms were only letting in the purest of light as the symposium leader prepared to announce the introduction of the Ossuary of James.

"Ladies, gentlemen and honored guests," fluently flowed the words from the lips of the deeply-tanned and very patrician Dr. Aaron Rabinowitz, curator at the Antiquities Museum of Galilee. "it is my distinct pleasure to welcome you to share in the discovery and evaluation of a treasured ancient relic—an ossuary from 2000 years ago. And," he paused as he took his right hand out of his jacket pocket and extended his large boney fingers toward the covered ossuary, "you will have the opportunity to not only evaluate this wonderful box, but also meet its owner, Mr. Moshe Levin. As many of you know, Mr. Levin has a long history in the antiquities field, and we think you will be very interested in evaluating his wonderful discovery. Please, allow me to introduce Mr. Moshe Levin."

As Dr. Rabinowitz's hand gracefully gave the signal that now was his time to appear, Moshe, with his bouncing belly leading the way, eagerly sprinted into the spotlight. The exuberant applause rocked the hall as everyone was eager to finally see what this 'rock star' of archeology really had.

Adjusting the microphone, Moshe spread his hands out wide to virtually embrace the curiosity of the audience and compel them to be drawn to him. Exultant, he knew his time did finally come. "Ladies and gentlemen here to see this wonderful link back to the time of Jesus, my enthusiasm for presenting this ossuary can only be exceeded by my confidence that it is a genuine link back to that time." Polite applause was followed by a low level buzz as these researchers were dissecting every word. *These biblical experts would be constantly talking among themselves,* he thought. *They can never keep quiet, no matter how important the speaker.* Peering out into this energized audience, he saw heads bobbing and weaving as each strained to hear what their neighbor was saying. How long could he keep their attention until the perfect time to unveil his ossuary sitting on the stage and covered with a brilliantly-white satin drape?

In the audience, some interplay was evolving as people tried to converse with those next to them. The handsome, blue-eyed man with the Irish brogue and an unruly head of red hair was one of them as he leaned over to the attractive, dark-haired woman to his left. "Might ya be able ta tell me if the research particulars are in our handout packet? I don't seem ta have any."

Somewhat irritated, and without turning to him, Elana whispered, "I don't have anything either. Wait til he's done, then we can talk."

Chastised by her words and body language, the Irishman responded with an equally appropriate whisper. "Sounds lovely."

Feeling the exhilaration of one who had the soul of the audience in his grasp, Moshe decided to boast about the ossuary's validation process. "This burial box, and its contents, being what has been described as the bones of James, brother of Jesus, have been evaluated by the Ontario Museum of Antiquities with carbon dating. I am pleased to confirm what had so often been stated—this box is from the time of Jesus! I now ask Professor Grover Newbold to speak to the validation process as we take a better look at this Ossuary of James." While the lights on the stage dimmed and a spotlight from above shined down, Moshe dramatically pulled off the pristine white satin cover, now making it everyone's focal point.

Leaning over again to whisper to Elana, this Rigel couldn't cease commenting. "Looks nice, but if they've already confirmed the box is 2,000 years old, why da we have ta hear it again?"

Trying to focus on Moshe, she whispered even softer and slower to this obviously obnoxious stranger, "We must listen because he controls the microphone, and we're curious about what's in the box. Look, it's the dues he wants us to pay."

Dr. Newbold rose from his chair and stepped to the front of the stage. For a man in his 60's, he had that disheveled, old professor look, with too little hair, as gray as it was, too many eyes with his heavy spectacles, too many pounds around his waist and too few pressings of his trousers. His height of 6 feet, but diminished by his noticeable stooping, only magnified his scholarly appearance as he proceeded to present his report in a decidedly arrogant style. "We at the Ontario Museum of Antiquities, using the most advanced carbon dating techniques, have committed ourselves to thoroughly research this ossuary's contents – what appear to be bone residue and some organic matter which is embedded in a chiseled animal figure on the underside of the lid. While the box and its lid create the impression of being from the same approximate time in history, that doesn't mean they are from the same time as the organic material within the box—the bones and the reddish coloring in the carving of the animal."

A voice arose from the back of the audience. "What do you mean, 'same approximate time'?"

Turning to the questioner with a glaring look, Newbold rightfully responded, "We can say they are approximately from the same time in history, but naturally, one can't say the lid and the box are from the exact same time since carbon dating couldn't even tell the age of the sea shells which formed the limestone tens or even hundreds of thousands of years ago. We can't even say if the box and lid were inseparable, since no one knows if they were always paired together. Despite the fact the chemical compositions of the lid and the box are exactly the same, and might have been mined from the same site, they may not have been always together," Newbold finished while pointing to Moshe's treasured box.

A hatless, gray-haired woman, quite trim in a blue print dress covered with white and yellow flowers, slowly rose from her seat, "Regarding the chiseled animal on the lid, are you implying it is 2,000 years old?"

Newbold turned away from her as he prepared to address the rest of the audience. He reached over and ran his hand along the ossuary's sealed lid, glanced her way for a second, then chose to look away again. "Our carbon dating says the organic, reddish coloring within the carving is approximately 2,000 years old. Could it have occurred that the carving was chiseled into the lid 3,000 or 5,000 years ago with the reddish coloring only added 2,000 years ago? Yes, but we are only stating the two organic items inside the box, the bones and the reddish coloring, are of the same approximate age which appears to be somewhere around 2,000 years. My dear woman," he replied, still not looking in her direction, "I hope this answer is satisfactory."

"Dr. Newbold," came a very British-sounding voice from the assemblage, "might you comment on the engraving on the outside of the lid—what it says of the inhabitant of the box?"

Newbold paused and looked briefly at Moshe Levin as if to give him a chance to answer, then disdainfully stared at the questioner, "As you should know, the lid is engraved with the message, 'Herein lie the bones of James, son of Joseph, brother of Jesus'. From a biblical perspective, this engraving is truly noteworthy since it not only links James to Joseph and Jesus, but also links James to Mary since the designation 'brother of Jesus' would, in the style of those ancient times, only be for a blood brother. Therefore, it would appear this ossuary may help resolve the issue as to whether, as Protestants believe, James was a child of Mary, or if he was an adopted child or from some other kind of a liaison that Joseph may have had with some woman other than Mary."

Not intimidated, the Brit shot his hand up again, and without giving Newbold a chance to ignore him, asked another question. "Do you really believe an ancient engraving on a lid could be sufficient evidence to resolve an issue of such ecumenical importance between Orthodox, Catholics and Protestants?"

"Absolutely!" Newbold defiantly responded while suddenly standing taller at the podium, head erect and posturing like a cobra rearing its head and ready to strike—ready to spit out his vicious, venom of verbal invective. "Only a fool wouldn't believe this engraving from 2,000 years ago sheds light on this issue of James' maternity."

A persistent pest, the same questioner was not to be deterred. "Was there anything else noteworthy on the ossuary?"

Newbold pointed to the lid of the box, "When we removed the lid, there was an engraving of what appeared to be an animal on the underside. It is barely discernible, and even with enhanced visualization techniques, we can't be certain what type of animal it might have been. One can only speculate that the animal carving may have been the brand or logo for something or somebody, if I may use a modern term like logo for something that could be so ancient. It also had some color, some red residue that was the organic material we carbon dated."

Seated on the other side of Elana, the side away from Rigel, and looking radiantly beautiful in a simple white blouse and brown pleated skirt, Sonja raised her elegant right hand and rose to ask a question in her very confident, yet not presumptuous style. "Dr. Newbold, would you hazard a guess regarding what's inside the box? Could the bones be human or animal? What opinion might you have?"

Briefly looking down his long beak of a nose at her, Newbold then turned away, refusing to make further eye contact as he arrogantly responded, "Based on carbon dating, one can't be certain exactly what is inside. But when the box was opened for us by Mr. Levin, and since an ossuary is something to hold bones, we made the assumption that what we saw was in fact just that—bones and bone residue"

"And the bone remnants," replied Sonja as she put one hand on her chin and the other on her hip as a sign of her defiance of his style, "can you speculate from whom or what that might have come?"

With a smile that trivialized her question as well as her person, Newbold replied, "As you probably don't know, with carbon dating technologies, we can't tell if the bone is human or animal. But if DNA testing shows the bones are human, they could be those of James, since that is what the lid says."

Not to be marginalized by this obnoxious older man, Sonja quickly shot back, "Could there be bones of an animal in there? If it was an animal, could it have been the animal whose image you said is chiseled on the underside of the lid?" Now she was rapid-firing her questions, not giving him a chance to butt in. "Could the bones have been a favorite pet of someone who memorialized it with its image chiseled on its burial lid? And will we get a chance to open the box to see what's inside? "

After that questioning onslaught, Newbold craved to be done with this pest and looked to Moshe for help. Knowing now was the time to step in, Moshe moved to the microphone and added in a condescending tone while at least making eye contact with Sonja, "For now, we really don't know what's inside and won't until some fortunate person or institution purchases this ossuary and then performs their own DNA testing of the residue. But please, now that we have discussed this Ossuary of James, I would like to welcome all of you to come up onto the stage and evaluate it for yourself, including the lid which I will now remove. But please refrain from reaching into the box to sample its contents, they are uniquely precious. After this period of evaluation, we will have another report on the scientific analysis of this wonderful relic from 2,000 years ago. Dr. Newbold," Moshe said as he turned towards him, bowed, then started to applaud, "please allow me to thank you for your wonderful and expert report."

As the audience rose and started to make their way to the stage, Rigel turned to Elana and Sonja. "Forgive my schoolboy pranks a speaking during the lecture, but I couldn't help notice your keen interest in this ossuary. It's simply lovely ta see two women here who bring some brightness ta this audience. I'm called Rigel," he said while extending his hand, "and who might the two a ya be?"

Shaking his hand with her customary firm handshake, Elana replied, "I'm Elana Dutros and this is my research associate, Sonja Martin. We're from the New Testament Biblical Institute here in Jerusalem. And, Mr. Rigel," she continued with an impish smile on her face radiating from some exploding warmth she couldn't control, "what's your first name?"

"It's Rigel. Ya just might say I've really only one name and that's Rigel."

"Well Mr. Rigel," said Sonja as she pushed her hand past a noticeably infatuated Elana, "I'm Sonja, and I'm pleased to meet you. And since you're obviously Irish, what brought you here from Ireland, or do you live just around the corner?"

39

A look of disarming innocence radiating from those twinkling blue eye preceded his reply, "I did in fact come from Ireland, from Bantry. My company, Bantry Ancient Elements has an interest in not just ancient relics, but any materials that survive for long periods a time. Ya must understand, I'm more a materials person than a religious man. But my dear Elana, what brings the two a ya here?"

Struck by his reference to Elana and sensing some evolving chemistry, Sonja withdrew to the side and nudged a timid Elana forward.

Feeling an emerging attraction for this virtual stranger, Elana fought to regain her composure. "Our interest isn't only in the religious history of the ossuary, but also what might be in the box. Sonja is our Biblical Institute's resident geneticist."

Eyebrows raised, head tilted and with a dubious look all over his face, Rigel looked directly at Sonja. "Ya don't say! Resident geneticist are ya? Why aren't ya just ta be studying old bibles?"

Chuckling as Rigel turned her way, Elana sensed a twitching of her nose, "It may seem a little out-of-place to have Sonja with us, but this project is why we hired her. You just might say the two of us are the creators of the specialty of biblical genetics. If there's something in the box that's human, or was human, we'd like to know who it was from, or to whom they were related."

"And how da ya know such a thing?" asked a glib Rigel. "Get on the telephone ta call their ancestors, or look them up on the internet?"

Taking the cue, Sonja thought she would straighten out this intruder with a no-holds-barred assertiveness. "Well Mr. Rigel, there are some comparative genetic tools which allow us to follow a trail all the way back to Moses—and maybe this bone residue is part of that trail."

"Really?" said an obviously interested Rigel who was struck by her positive, yet very confrontational style. "And how will ya do that? Look for Moses' name on some lost DNA, or is his DNA on file somewhere?"

"No," said Elana, being a bit conciliatory as a buffer to Sonja, "but there's a comparative mechanism we have that can give us a read on whether any genetic material inside that box could've been of James, or related to James. If that was the case, you can make the argument, a very legitimate argument, that James was related by blood not only to Mary, but also to Jesus."

"Good heavens my lovely lass, it'd be heresy ta say James was a the blood a Mary. Not very lovely at all if I say so myself." he replied.

"Not lovely only if you're a Catholic or Orthodox Christian. But if you're a Protestant, you already believe James was of the blood of Mary, and the genetic trail just might tell us what we need to know," spoke a smiling Elana as she started moving towards the stage. "Let's go see what this ossuary is all about."

Elana and Sonja led the way to the stage with Rigel close behind. He looked around to gauge the audience's level of interest, but it seemed everyone was already on-stage, running their hands over the lid of the limestone box. Every irregular surface was touched hundreds of times with delicate, probing finger tips, looking or feeling for some explanation or inspiration. At one point, with Moshe Levin supervising, the ossuary lid was removed in order to expose the faintly chiseled image on its underside. An animal? Rigel's thoughts were dubious, *With a naked eye, it's hard to be sure what it is.*

Running their hands over the chiseled figure, Elana and Sonja noticed an old man dressed in a black suit and holding a black hat. He looked up at them and spoke very formally as he saw their fixation on the lid, "An animal? A dog or a wolf? You should know this type of image was no stranger to ancient Christianity, but was not seen before the time of Jesus. Look, you can see some reddish coloring residue within the figure." He paused briefly, then continued, "If I'm not being too intrusive, may I ask if you are familiar with this type of carving?"

"No," replied Elana as she extended her hand and then pointed to Sonja. "I'm Elana Dutros and this is Sonja Martin. I'm not a stranger to ancient Christian relics and antiquities, but I've never seen or heard of such a carving."

"And I am Abraham Weissberg," he said while extending to Elana his pale, boney hand with its blue veins popping out. "You are right," said the old man very precisely and with his sad-faced countenance projecting the look of a

41

serious ancient biblical scholar. "In ancient Christianity, there is no mention of this symbol. But among those of us who have studied the Old and New Testament and other relics from the time of Jesus, the stories and legends of some symbols of an animal, a dog or a wolf, have always been present. It may have been taboo to talk about animals in the ancient Church since it might have caused fears about some form of animal worship."

Fixing her gaze on Abraham, Sonja sensed their two sets of eyes linking with a fusion of immediate trust. To this man, exuding such gentleness, she asked, "Do you think this animal carving gives any legitimacy to the ossuary?"

Before Abraham could say more, Moshe took the briefly-squawking microphone, and barked loud enough to get everyone's attention, "Please, please, everyone to their seats. We are excited to hear a report from our next expert."

As Sonja and Elana were departing the stage to get back to their seats, Abraham meekly suggested, "If you would like, we could talk more about this carving."

Jumping on the opportunity, Sonja replied even before the last decibel of Weissberg's words disappeared, "I'd like that," then continued on to her seat.

Once everyone was seated, Moshe blew into the microphone, and after a few taps on it, announced, "Please allow me to introduce Dr. Theodore Tavlarides of the Hellenic Archeological Institute. Dr. Tavlarides had the opportunity to study this ossuary, especially the letters chiseled on its lid." Beaming with unconstrained pride, Moshe gestured for Tavlarides to proceed to the microphone. "Dr. Tavlarides, the podium is yours."

With polite audience applause, Dr. Tavlarides, barely over five feet tall and dominated physically by the other men, took the podium. After running his hand through his thinning gray hair, he pulled the strands of his goatee to a point as he stepped up onto a box positioning him to be tall enough to reach the microphone. Clearing his voice, he started speaking in Greek-accented English. "Thank you ladies and gentlemen. I am pleased to be able to provide our scientific testing results on behalf of the Hellenic Antiquity Museum. We at the

42

Museum believe this gives us the opportunity to show how science and religion can work together for the good of not only religion, but also mankind."

The audience warmly applauded its approval and Dr. Tavlarides continued. "At our modern research facility, we have done carbon dating on the contents of this ossuary, in addition to the reddish material which gives color to the poorly-defined chiseled form of an animal on the lid. All the work has been done at our own laboratory with the most modern techniques. We are also of the opinion that the lid and the box are of such absolutely similar chemical composition that they were probably from the same stone source. Naturally, carbon dating can't tell us how old this ossuary really is, but the dating done on the organic contents—the bone residue and the colored material are approximately 2,000 years old." Looking over in the direction of Moshe, Dr. Tavlarides could see his nod of approval. "However," Dr. Tavlarides remarked as he turned back to the audience, "we must make a statement of concern regarding the lettering carved into the lid."

Moshe's head jerked so violently his vertebrae cracked—a sinister sound shattering the satisfaction and redemption the symposium had rebuilt. Barely able to avoid shouting, thoughts of despair burrowed deeply into his heretofore impenetrable psyche while a flood of depression cascaded through his mind. A warming heat flushed down the back of his neck and spread to his whole body. *A statement of concern? What do you mean you fool?*

Tavlarides precisely proceeded. "A close examination of the carving of the letters shows the edges of the letters exhibit different wear patterns. The word, or in this case the name 'James', shows different wear patterns, with more wear on the edges of its letters, than do the words 'son of Joseph' and 'brother of Jesus'. Therefore, it is very reasonable to assume the words 'son of Joseph' and 'brother of Jesus' were added at some later time in history because their letters have very angular, sharp edges with virtually no wear on them. These newer letters may not even be one hundred years old."

His piercing brown eyes projected an aura of finality for the project, as Dr. Tavlarides scanned the audience and then Moshe, before noticing more than a

43

few mouths had fallen open in surprise—with Moshe's the most cavernous. His report continued. "Please bear in mind we understand that some ossuaries may have been produced in quantity, an early form of mass producing. It was not unusual for some pre-death, generic chiseling to be done, such as 'herein lie the bones of' with a blank space for the name to be added later. In this fashion, early engravers could have used their downtime to a greater degree of efficiency. Later, after someone died and their bones needed a final resting place, the addition of names and dates was done. In the case of what we are calling the Ossuary of James, we believe that aside from 'Herein lie the bones of James', the rest of the letters were added years, or possibly centuries, later. We must therefore conclude that this limestone box, known as the Ossuary of James, may have been just that, the ossuary of someone named James. With regard to it containing the bones of the 'son of Joseph' or the 'brother of Jesus', we believe that is fraudulent."

A collective gasp went up from the audience. Having had a preliminary positive report from Tavlarides, or what he thought was positive, Moshe was crestfallen. Arms falling to his side and every bone in his spine morphing into jelly, he slithered into a chair. By the time he recovered his resolve, he could sense the mood of the audience had shifted as one thought immediately ran through his mind—*Another fraud!* He jumped to the microphone and snatched it away from Tavlarides. "Professor, there must be some mistake! I... I can't believe that after your very positive preliminary report you now believe this Ossuary of James is a fraud. Could you somehow be mistaken?"

With his jaw defiantly thrust forward, the diminutive Tavlarides responded with a resounding firmness. "No! Mr. Levin, I understand your frustration since our preliminary report, based only on the carbon dating of the organic material inside the ossuary, did project an age of approximately 2,000 years. But an analysis of the physical characteristics of the lettering does lead an impartial group of well-qualified researchers to a different conclusion. We think this is similar to other fraudulent articles of antiquity which have come from Armenia. What is the provenance of this ossuary?"

44

Trying to speak with a cotton-dry mouth, Moshe could barely spit out the answer. "Armenia," half- chokingly escaped the words as he turned away from Tavlarides and smacked his right hand to a forehead already bubbling with pregnant beads of sweat.

A voice rose from the audience. "Dr. Tavlarides," asked Abraham Weissberg, "what about the carving of the animal? What was your opinion about it?"

Taking the microphone and then looking at Abraham, Tavlarides responded. "We can't be sure, but we assume the oldest lettering chiseled on the lid of the box, about James, might be of the approximate age of the animal carving. Mind you, this is speculation, but all of these edges and wear-patterns are similar."

Barely able to walk, and holding both hands to a head now trying to shake itself free of his neck and his bewilderment, Moshe stumbled to the microphone. "Professor Tavlarides, what about the contents inside the box? Have you no interest in what is in there? You, yourself said the contents are approximately 2,000 years old."

Tilting his head and with his pointed chin now elevated and aimed someplace above Moshe's head, Tavlarides' critical look matched his equally abrasive tone. "What is in the box is of no interest to us. From our perspective, this box is of no value in any biblical research. We believe the chiseled attribution to Joseph and Jesus is fraudulent, and therefore we would question the legitimacy of anything in the box as it relates to being from, or a part of James. It might be from some James, but there is no way the bones and residue, which may rightly be human, can be accurately attributed to the James described in the Book of Matthew as being a brother of Jesus."

The agitated and angry crowd started to leave in droves with their heads shaking and tongues wagging as they moved out of their aisles. Moshe could see not only that they were leaving, but their animated tongues were probably saying it again—another fraud from Moshe Levin! Even though he knew better, he wondered if his ex-wife was hidden somewhere out in the audience, triumphantly leading this defamatory exodus.

Sonja and Elana rose to leave as Rigel quickly turned to Elana. The mellow Irish brogue was quick to flow, with a slight sense of the forceful desperation a male can project when a desirable female appears to be leaving and not showing a reciprocal interest. "Not a good day for biblical research, but a lovely day for meeting new friends. Don't ya think? Would ya consider sharing a pint a Guinness with me?"

With her eagerness energetically radiating from those big brown eyes fixated on Rigel, Elana was quick to respond. "I'd love to, but I don't know what Sonja has in mind." She turned to Sonja, "What are your plans?"

Looking in the direction of Abraham Weissberg, Sonja paused for a second and then turned back to respond while only giving a cursory nod to Rigel. "Yes… yes, that sounds fine, but how about tomorrow? I'm going over to speak to Mr. Weissberg now, so make it tomorrow?"

Seeing how intently Sonja wanted to speak with Abraham Weissberg, Elana disappointedly acknowledged the agreement, but still craved to cement some contact with this handsome Irishman. "Yes, why don't we meet tomorrow? Where?"

Sensing the different needs of the women, Rigel honed in on Elana like a predatory raptor. "Why don't the two a ya meet me tomorrow afternoon at 1:00 at the King David Hotel Lobby Bar on the first floor. OK with ya?"

Both Elana, and a clearly distracted Sonja, nodded to Rigel that his suggestion was fine.

Rigel smiled, nodded back in approval and after a hesitation, added, "But before we leave, I need ta impose on ya ta get a quick photo a the two a ya. It'll make my employees back in Ireland very jealous when they see the local Jerusalem scenery."

Giving their approval, Sonja and Elana posed quickly for the photo on a small digital camera that appeared out of nowhere. "There, my lovelies, what a wonderful picture. I'm sure I'll have far better memories a this day than will Mr. Moshe Levin. Forgive me if I'm nosey and ask one more thing, but why da ya both have the same purse? Don't women like ta avoid having the same thing as somebody else? Are ya such good friends there isn't a wee bit a jealousy?"

Impressed he would notice such a thing, Elana was still embarrassed that he did. "We don't get paid that much at the Biblical Institute, so we bought these purses together as a packaged deal. Simply a better price when you make a volume buy, and since they're the only ones we have, we bought good ones."

Nodding his approval, he took his program and opening it to a blank page, he started to draw directions to the King David. "Follow these directions and you'll have no problems finding your way tomorrow."

Busy getting directions to the location of the King David, Elana could see Sonja was still looking longingly for Weissberg. "Why don't you just go over and see Mr. Weissberg before he leaves. I'll take care of our plans with Rigel."

Turning in the direction of Abraham Weissberg, Sonja called out to him, "Mr. Weissberg! Mr. Weissberg, may I talk with you before you leave?"

Seeing her genuine interest, Weissberg waved her over. "How may I help you?"

As this long-legged woman eagerly strode over to him, he could see in her face and body language that her enthusiasm and attentiveness were strong and sincere. She never lost eye contact with him as she spoke, and he loved her confidence—just like he did when she refused to let that Newbold fool intimidate her. "The carving of the animal still intrigues me, and you said references to this type of carving have been around since the time of Christ, didn't you? Do you think Professor Tavlarides' lack of interest in the carving was significant?"

Shrugging his shoulders, Abraham replied, "I don't know what Tavlarides knows. I can accept some people don't grasp this field of relics, but when I keep reading about or seeing this carving or similar carvings, I suspect there is something behind it. This might be from the time of the crucifixion since there have always been rumors of the existence of items from back then. Who knows, maybe this carving, this animal, could be related to these rumors."

47

Persisting, as an inquisitive look defined her face, Sonja's intensity inundated the old man. "Do you really think there still could be relics from 2,000 years ago?"

Weissberg responded in his soothing, paternalistic way. "Miss Martin, was this ossuary not of that time? Was the animal carving not of that time? Is it not possible that other types of materials, other types of items, who knows what, could have survived until this time in history? You must remember we are dealing with a very dry climate. Look at how long objects were maintained in the Egyptian pyramids. The Dead Sea Scrolls, were they not more fragile than some of the items of the crucifixion?"

Tenaciously questioning, Sonja wouldn't let up. "I know some items have been preserved for hundreds, even thousands of years, but is this something only you thought of or are there other people who believe items could still survive from the crucifixion?"

Finally realizing the depth of her conviction through the persistence of her questions, he broke into a smile, an infrequent visitor to such a solemn face. "For years, there have been many rumors among Christians and Jews that something or things still exist. I strongly suspect something is out there, and probably at the old Christian monasteries that hoarded so much material even from the 2nd century. There are others here in Jerusalem who believe the rumors are true, and if you have any further interest in what we old relics dealers think, why don't you come to see me in a few days and we shall speak then. I can introduce you to someone else who may help you on this path."

"Don't take me the wrong way Mr. Weissberg, but why would you be so helpful to me? Why don't you go searching for these mysterious relics yourself?"

Lowering his eyes, he sheepishly looked back at her. "Miss Martin, I did go searching once, but you must understand how difficult it is for an old Jew to gain access to Christian establishments. An old, haggard-looking man whose eyes and smile are of a time past and don't have the sparkle in them that a young person like you has. My time has passed, but I will be happy to help you with whatever I can. It was very clear to me you had a strong interest and unique insight in this ossuary, but I was shocked everyone else but you dismissed the issue of the animal carving. Let me see if I can help you along the way. But remember, there may not be a pot of gold at the end of this journey."

"Thank you Mr. Weissberg. Thank you. I can't wait to meet with you. Is tomorrow too soon?" said Sonja as she reached over to Weissberg's hand to take his business card. "When can I come?"

Realizing this young woman had brought a smile to his face and a long-absent warmth to his heart, Weissberg nodded, "Please come tomorrow, after lunch, at 1:30, and we can speak. Who knows, you might find more than you could ever imagine."

While Elana and Rigel waited in the main aisle for Sonja, a few people still lingered and were passing by. Alone on the stage sat a very distraught Moshe Levin. Sonja went over to him as Elana and Rigel could see he stood up when Sonja was talking. He then wrote something on a piece of paper, appeared to speak, handed her the piece of paper, then followed with a handshake. Sonja reached into her purse and appeared to be writing on something that she handed to Moshe. With a mutual nod of approval, they parted with Moshe going back to his chair to stare off into space while Sonja walked quickly back to Elana and Rigel.

As Sonja approached her partners waiting alone in the aisle, Elana was almost leaning out of her shoes waiting to ask, "What was going on up there?"

Making eye contact only with Elana, Sonja sensed her co-worker's legitimate concern. "You might say I was just keeping my options open. We'll talk about it later."

Sonja, Elana and Rigel proceeded up the aisle, while behind them, up on the stage, unfolded a drama with Moshe Levin bending over his ossuary. His hands were over the box as if in some form of prayer, while his head bowed down to touch them. Moshe was now all alone—alone with this box, his last hope, his resurrection, his redemption. As the stage lights dimmed, so did Moshe's prospects for raising his reputation from the dead. No Lazarus would his reputation be!

Chapter 5

What can they bring me, these handmaidens for the needs of men? In Rigel's mind, women worked so men could thrive—even though that attitude, in impoverished Ireland, was his mother's prison, and one that she, like all poor women, could never escape. Unfortunately, the intense love for his mum hadn't spilled over into his feelings for all women.

The King David Hotel wasn't hard to find. Its dominant presence was not only physical, but also historical due to its role in the creation of a modern Israel. The old King David Hotel was blown up by the Menachem Begin-led Jewish freedom fighters in their quest to throw off the strangling British yoke of oppression. The King David, overlooking the walls of the Old City, was absolutely the place to stay in Jerusalem, and its Lobby Bar was the place to be, and be seen for the young and young-at-heart. For Elana, the thought of her charming newly-found acquaintance made the Lobby Bar a 'must' stop. The King David just might be Elana's place where a different kind of explosive relationship could begin.

Exiting her taxi, and cutting a stylish figure in dark blue slacks and with a crisp white blouse opened at the neck more than she might normally consider, Elana wondered if Rigel might be disappointed since she was the only one coming. *Was it me or she he wanted to see?* raced through her mind. Her intuition told her she was the one, but normal doubts about relationships always creep into a psyche as you meet a confrontation with reality—especially when relationships with men were virtually non-existent. *I'll find out soon enough what this Mr. Rigel is all about—I hope.*

Entering the hotel's opulent glass and marble lobby, she barely had time to look around before Rigel's voice called out as he stood up from the deeply-cushioned sofa immediately to her right. "Elana, Elana," Rigel called as he rose quickly from the sofa, "I'm so delighted ta see ya! It's so lovely we can be together. And did Sonja come with ya?"

Like a shearing tornado, doubt ravaged her confidence leaving it torn in tatters and with confusion littered across her mind. *There he is, asking about Sonja. Maybe she's who he wanted to see.* Keeping her composure, she looked right into those beautiful blue eyes. "It's great to see you, but Sonja couldn't come. She's meeting that antiquities dealer from yesterday and forgot we discussed meeting here. Having actually bought that ossuary from Moshe Levin, that's what they were doing up on the stage, she can't think of anything else. And now she's fixated on that animal carving and can't wait to see what Mr. Weissberg has to say. She sends her apologies and hopes I can make your stay worthwhile."

With beaming eyes focused back on hers, and a wisp of that reddish hair falling over his forehead, his words melted her heart. "I'm glad it'll be just you and me. Ta be able ta spend only a few minutes would be enough time ta make any man happy. It would be OK if Sonja were here, but I'm happier you and I have this time together."

How did he know to say just what she was thinking? Ever since Sonja joined the Institute, they were like co-joined twins, joined together at the Bible, and she realized some of her own identity was lost to Sonja's. "Frankly, I've had some of the same feelings, especially since Sonja seems to have gone off on a tangent over that carving. That Mr. Weissberg told her he and some other antiquities dealers still believe some relics of the crucifixion might exist. Her hunch is that carving could be related to the relics."

Deftly treading along a path of questioning without seeming too interested, Rigel continued, "So, ya said that chiseled animal caught her interest? But why if the ossuary was a fraud?"

"Now she's an animal lover, or at least that carved animal since Weissberg's ideas about crucifixion relics consumes her. And the fact it's 2,000 years old sealed the deal."

Seductive was his charm as the words flirtatiously flowed from his lips. "Whatever her interest in the box might be, I'm more interested in what ya think. I'm sure more interesting than some animal carved in stone."

As they walked arm-in-arm through the lobby and up the escalator to reach the Lobby Bar, Elana couldn't help thinking of how interesting this place was going to be. A very charming Irishman and a welcome break from the stagnation and boredom of everyday biblical research.

Overlooking the hotel lobby, the Lobby Bar had a very special table where Rigel continued his Irish charm. Pulling her chair away from the table, he put his hand on her arm and in a most polite way asked, "Elana, my dear, may I seat ya so ya can see all who come into this wonderful hotel? And quite frankly, when they see ya, they'll wish they could trade places with me."

Gazing into one of the mirrors lining the walls, she knew she was blushing and needed to say something to get his focus off her face—that bothersome nose twitching seemed ready to erupt. "Why should I take the best seat when you're stuck looking at the wall or out a window into the sky?"

Leaning forward to grasp her hands in his soft and perfectly manicured hands, he didn't let a flattering opportunity pass him by. "It's I who'll have the best seat. While ya can look at the lobby, I'm able ta look at you—and a far more enjoyable sight it is."

"Enough of this," she said pulling her hands away and taking a drink of water to cool that internal furnace of emotions erupting inside of her. "Not about me anymore! Tell me about you and what really brought you to Jerusalem. Why was this ossuary trip worthwhile?"

Tilting back in his chair, and with his handsome face framed by the green fern-like branches of the plantings behind him, Rigel gave a bigger smile before answering. "My business brings me into contact with issues like this ossuary, and while the box was bogus, the database regarding the expert evaluation a materials was important ta me and my company, Bantry Ancient Elements."

A quizzical look accompanied her response. "How so?"

"Our work centers more on the materials a the manuscripts a the Middle Ages. It's a period when the Irish saved so much a the written works in Europe that some say the Irish saved civilization. The Irish were geographically so far from the barbarians ransacking Europe that Irish priests did actually save much a European history."

Unknowingly drawn towards him, she spoke without sensing that emotional gravity. "But why be interested in a period so far from the Middle Ages?"

Looking at the veins on the back of his hands, he paused, then looked up and caught her gaze. "I was more interested in what they would do ta validate the ossuary. Our needs for verifying manuscripts relies on chemical applications, and the chemistry a the ossuary validation was worth the symposium trip. But since the ossuary was a fraud, what'll ya do next?"

Elana caught herself subtly shaking her head negatively and stopped it. "I thought we'd be in a different direction by now, but if Sonja can't pull a rabbit out of the hat, I don't see how we can keep her at the Institute."

Projecting a most understanding look, Rigel wanted her to expand on their pursuit of the ossuary without appearing too interested. "I admit ta being very intrigued when ya told me about your genetic interest in that ossuary, but how da ya go from a leap a faith in the Bible ta a genuine curiosity about genetics?"

Now she was nodding in approval. "It might seem odd that in an issue of science, I'm asking for faith which is usually in conflict with it. But we felt a genetic marker discovered in a genetic study could be used to biologically link Jesus' brother James to Mary. We were looking to see if genetic material in that ossuary was similar to what we had from a Jewish priest DNA sequencing marker."

Trying to soften his tone, he wanted to disguise the intense interest of his inquiry. "You're asking me ta believe if that box contained residue a James' bones ya might've shown a genetic link ta Mary?"

"Believe me my dear Mr. Rigel, if genetic material in that box was similar to the genetic material of the Jewish Priest Study, we would've projected James was the blood son of Mary. All because they would've shared genetic material from the lineage of Aaron—the genetic beginning of the lineage of the Jewish priests and also a part of the lineage of Mary."

"How did ya get the genetic material from Jewish priests?"

"From men named Cohen because Cohen had always been the historical name of Jewish priests."

Now a dubious look arose, matched by his curiosity. "Let me get this straight. You're saying if ya take a large sample a Jewish men named Cohen and look at their DNA there'd be a significant percentage who shared some a it?"

Virtually bounding out of her chair, Elana was elated he grasped her direction. "Yes! And since Cohen was the ancestral name for men who were Jewish priests, and you could only pass on the title if your father was one, you could be tracing that DNA linkage up the fathers' ancestral tree all the way to Aaron who was the first Jewish priest. Now can you see why we had such interest in that box?"

A consoling look now replaced his inquisitive intensity. "I do, but where da ya go now since that box had nothing a James, not even his car keys or his credit card."

A laughing Elana quickly retorted, "For us, James is history, but who knows what Sonja will find this time? But frankly, she better find something good or her career with the Biblical Institute may be toast—that's an American saying that means her career will be finished with us."

With his curiosity smoldering, Rigel needed to appear disinterested. "Obviously there's more ta what ya were seeking than meets the eye. But enough science, tell me what da ya do for fun in this old city?"

Sitting upright and stiff, even a little threatened by his inquiry into her personal life, Elana was afraid of exposing her lack of social sophistication. "I'm focused more on satisfaction than fun, and my work at the Biblical Institute is that, very satisfying. Fun and elation are temporary states of mind with too few peaks and valleys that can become far too deep. But satisfaction based on faith brings me a consistent plateau of peace."

"And ya say, for a beautiful and charming woman like ya are, there's no room for fun or exhilaration?" He winked at her as he smiled. "You'd have a hard time convincing an Irishman a that."

Now leaning forward again, she clasped her shaking hands over her face as her nose was twitching to the beat of her heart. "There's always room for fun. That's why I was looking forward to spending this time with such a charming Irishman."

Realizing he wanted to put his hands on her arm, he thought the better of it. "You're wonderful for my ego, but I still want ta know more about ya. Where'd ya come from? What da your parents do?"

Unaccustomed to such questions, she reflected on how she had so little exposure to sophisticated men. Life at the Institute was always dominated by dealings with old biblical scholars or clergy. "My dad was a history professor and my mother a museum curator. Both interested in things old and worth finding. As the only child in the family, it seemed only natural that both of their careers influenced me."

Rigel burst out smiling, with those blue eyes radiating intense warmth and sincerity. "But where were ya from? Where were ya educated by those two intelligent parents?"

"Born and raised in Athens, and went to the university and studied the Greek language. Then off to graduate work in the United States, at Strayton University, focusing on the history of the early Christian Church. That's where I first met Sonja."

"What brought ya ta the Biblical Institute? Seems odd for a beautiful young woman ta be stuck in such a dull field."

A flattered smile broadened as her sensuous lips parted exposing two rows of perfect sparkling white teeth bordered by those luscious waves of crimson. "It is pretty boring at times looking at old manuscripts and providing information to scholars throughout the world. But now it's my turn to turn the table. Tell me about yourself. How did you emerge from being a small Irish lad to what you are now?"

Sitting upright, he wagged a finger at her. "Ay, a fair question. What I should expect from someone with such a background." He sat back in his chair, distancing himself from her as he continued, "I was one a two boys and two girls, living together as a family until the Irish Disease got the best a my 'da'."

Noticing a chill that suddenly crept between them, Elana leaned forward to close the chasm opened by his reflexive movement away from her. "Your 'da'? Is that your dad? And what's the Irish Disease? Some kind of plague?"

Elana noticed, but wasn't sure if Rigel was aware of how he was subtly shaking his head up-and-down. "Yes, da—my dad. And the Irish Disease? It's the plague a Irish alcoholism that soaks through so much a the fabric a Irish life. I think it's a bit about our DNA, then a little about the environment."

"Why?" she asked with her eyes fixated on his.

"Excuse me please," said the waiter who reluctantly chose to interrupt this intensely occupied couple. "Would you like something to drink?"

Looking back at Elana with a gleam in his eye, it seemed he welcomed the break in the conversation. "What would ya like my dear?"

A quick smile was followed by a dismissive reply. "I would like tonic water with a wedge of lime—fresh Israeli limes to perk-up the tonic water!"

"Ahhh, no alcohol? No Irish Disease for ya my lovely lass?" Rigel asked with an inquisitive look pasted all over his face covering the smile he was trying to suppress.

"Pardon me," said the waiter. "I don't know this Irish Disease drink, but if our bartender doesn't know it, he'll find it on the internet."

Both tried to hide their amusement as Rigel cleared the air. "No sir, we'll limit our drinking ta tonic and lime for her and a Guinness for me."

As the waiter turned and walked away, while stifling their laughter, Elana edged to the front of her chair, eager to continue with their discussion. "Getting back to what I was asking, how is it you believe your dad's Irish Disease was part genetic and part environmental?"

An abyss opened between them and he was talking not to her, but through her about the Irish Disease. "Take some genetics and history, then mix them with a little restrictive geography and see what ya get. Scientists know there's a gene predisposing ta alcoholism and it's in all people ta varying degrees. When ya take island people, and Ireland is an island, if people don't get off the island, they tend ta in-breed. Not getting enough genetic mixing with the other tribes a Europe and only concentrating their own genetic flaws. The alcoholism gene would then become more genetically concentrated in the island people such as the Irish. No different than those American Indians—forced onto reservations and genetically concentrating their alcoholism. Hell, probably none a us has any greater genetic predisposition ta the Irish Disease than those pompous Protestant pricks living in London." He paused, as his hand came up to his mouth and he realized his hatred of the English had escaped. "Sorry for my gutter language, but an Irishman can't hide the contempt he has for the emasculating English."

"That's OK, but tell me more about this history and geography issue."

"The history a the Irish is they were stuck on that island and, since they were Catholics, never heard a word about birth control. And with an island's limited land mass ya can't create any more farmland. If ya kept having too many kids, pretty soon there wasn't enough land ta support all their families. If ya wanted ta raise wheat, ya needed about 30 acres a land ta keep a family, but if ya relied on potatoes, ya only needed 5 acres. So everybody with smaller farms grew potatoes. Then along came a potato famine and without enough food, it further destroyed the strength a families. This led ta the environmental problems, not in the air or water, but in the psychological pollution a men. When ya can't farm ta make a living, and there's no industries bringing good-paying jobs ta men, what da ya think happened? They despaired and damn it, they drank! Evolution made men think they had ta be providers and if they can't provide, they got depressed and fell in love with the booze. Did I offend your very proper Christian beliefs by talking about evolution?"

"Not at all," an apologetic Elana responded, realizing she wanted to soften the conversation since she might have opened some deep, psychological wounds. "Evolution and Christianity were compatible in the religious debates in my family."

"Ya were lucky indeed ta have a family like that—a family that stayed together and talked together. In Ireland, when the plague a the Irish Disease stuck its infected head into so many families, the 'da' left, some by body and some only by spirit. My 'da' left ta work in England like so many others, but we never heard from him again until we got his body sent back in a cheap wooden box. The English postal authorities mocked him by calling it 'Paddy-in-the-box'."

Reaching across the table to touch Rigel's folded hands, Elana sensed a stream of sadness structuring a barrier between them. "I'm sorry I asked. That's such a sad story."

Rigel couldn't hide the mist clouding his eyes. "As a little lad, the life I had was the only one I knew. But my mum? She knew a better life, a life a love before the Disease made it so difficult. With four little mouths ta feed, what choices did she have ta keep us alive. My mum was a saint; a saint that doesn't get the proper respect in the Church. And not the only one! She shared that mantle a greatness with so many women in the world, all doing whatever it took ta keep their offspring alive and moving ahead. When I think a the Lord's Prayer, I can't get myself ta say 'Our Father who art in Heaven'. It's always 'My Mother who art in Heaven'."

Reaching her hand over to cover his, she couldn't repress her thoughts, "What a tragic life for your mother and you kids. With all that instability, how'd your mother ever get you where you are in life?"

Up he perked, both physically and emotionally. "It was the Church. I'm what I am because a it, even though I still won't say the Our Father."

"But how'd the Church do so much for you?" she asked aware of the sense of empathy creeping into her voice as well as her consciousness.

"In Ireland, if ya are a poor boy, ya can still have a chance if you're smart and if ya let the Church dominate your life. If you're smart enough and obedient enough, ya just might be able ta rise above your poverty. My mum cleaned for the parish priests and that's what probably got them ta pay attention ta me and my brother Michael. My sisters Shannon and Molly didn't get the attention Michael and I got, probably because they were only girls in the eyes a the priests. I was smart in school, smarter in many ways than Michael. I guess we were all pretty smart because a our mum. She may have been seen by some as only a cleaning lady, but ta us she was a genius Smarter than anyone in the Church, and at least for her sake, she knew it, and of our love for her."

With eyes fixated on his as the depth of his story was so profoundly impacting her, Elana still craved more, "Did the Church send you to school?"

Discarding the raw emotional edge invading his mind, Rigel looked away briefly, then locked his gaze on hers. "I went ta the Church school until I was old enough ta go ta university. The Church paid my way ta Trinity in Dublin and they were behind me every step a the way. Prodding, pushing, making sure that I did what they wanted. Always making me feel guilty for being their special boy."

With nary a blink to break her concentration, her eyes never wandered off his. "And your brother, Michael, and your sisters, did the Church do as much for them?"

"The Church? It owns my sisters—they're nuns," he said keeping his focus on Elana's face. But he turned away again, glancing momentarily out somewhere into space before turning back to her. "But my Michael, he's not a this earth. He's passed, and with him went the dreams a my devastated mum. And now it's just me, stuck with this bitter residue from a lost brother and the need ta rectify the situation."

Sensing a chill that displaced the warmth in Rigel's face, and even though it might be risky to go further, she craved to know what he meant. "Rectify the situation, what's that about?"

"Got an obligation—an obligation ta my Michael! I was his older brother and didn't protect him from the Church and its unnatural intrusion into the lives a little boys. Couldn't keep the perverted priests from getting their filthy hands on him! Failed him in life, but won't fail him in death."

Captivated by the look on his face, she couldn't stop now. "You mean he was abused by the priests?"

Nodding his head, Rigel then turned away, avoiding her eyes.

"I feel so horrible for you, but this shouldn't be your burden. And what do you mean you don't expect to fail him now that he's dead?"

The pain that had invaded his face now fled, but an intimidating tone emerged in his voice. "Oh, I'll make them pay someday, somehow and someway. But for now, please, let's not talk about it. A part a this needs ta stay away for some other time."

Toying with the lime in her drink, and not wanting to face him, her courage now sprouted as she looked up. "OK, I understand, but once you graduated from Trinity, did you work in chemistry or engineering? How did you get into this Bantry Ancient Elements business?"

"Once I got through Trinity, I could figure out how ta get ta the London School a Economics on my own. Business and international finance were my interests, and I moved into the chemical field as a business venture. Consulted for a distressed chemical company and saw a way ta buy it. Now I'm in the chemical business, or so ya might say when ya consider how I deal with chemicals and antiquities."

With eyebrows raised and her head tilted to one side, Elana was aware her nose wasn't twitching as her focus was on him, not on her own emotions. "So you found yourself getting educated and then finding a good deal? Is that the Irish way?"

The change of expression on her face was missed by Rigel as his answer was directed over her shoulder, to somewhere far more distant than merely across the table. "Ya might say my life is one a being a hunter—a hunter for good deals."

61

Now was clearly a good time to change directions, and she took advantage of it. "Is genetics a special interest of yours? When we first met at that ossuary, you seemed to have a keen interest in it."

Out of nowhere appeared a big toothy smile, but with framing teeth tainted by the mistreatment of poverty. "Ya got me there—I must admit ta being a closet geneticist."

A quizzical, yet dumbfounded look couldn't be suppressed as she asked, "Why in a closet?"

His smile was snatched by the seriousness that found a home in his psyche. "I've always had this idea that's probably not acceptable in the world a genetics. Afraid I'd be laughed at if I raised a question about my controversial concepts."

Intrigued, she leaned in towards him. "What's so odd about your ideas? You can share them with me, and maybe, you might be surprised what I think. Come on! What's locked away in that cranium of yours?"

Like a canary sitting on a perch, Rigel was ready to sing. "It's all about genetic memory. I've always studied the histories a people, like that actress Shirley MacLaine, who think they've lived in another time as one or maybe more than one person. Ta me, I believe their ability ta recall incidents from another life comes from their ability ta transfer memory data onward from past generations through the only mechanism available—their DNA. I don't think they recall their previous lives, but those lives a their genetic ancestors."

Sitting back in her chair, right hand on her chin, her westernized sophistication overtook her. "Certainly a leap in imagination! Projecting the brain can process events in a person's life and then cause some sort of mutation in the genes that transmit this information onward to succeeding generations. A little hard to accept since usually mutations are random or caused by chemicals or radiation energy."

"And that, my dear Elana, just might be the answer. The chemist in me, or the chemist in me since I bought the company, thinks certain chemicals might induce mutations at the exact time significant historical events occur—events that are then imprinted within the DNA a the person being exposed ta the chemicals. Ya have chemical transmitters, like serotonin, involved in the transmission a nerve impulses. Ya also have forms a energy called brain waves. Here we have chemicals and energy, and both can cause mutations. Didn't ya say so yourself?"

"As I said before, quite a big leap in imagination, but you need a good imagination to be successful."

"Ya can understand why I don't talk too much about my theory with the scientific community, but I believe it's true. Ask the Buddhists who believe a person's spirit is inherited from another life. Inherited how? Through DNA? Am I any different than Columbus or Alexander Graham Bell who challenged conventional wisdom?"

Whimsy overtook her and her raised right eyebrow broadcast it. "Probably not much different at all! Either ahead of your time or, on the other hand, maybe just a hopeless Irish dreamer."

"A hopeless dreamer, but not much different than two young women I met looking at a stone box, hoping ta get DNA from a stone or a bone. How many years ago would people have thought ya ta be daffy in the head or just hopelessly incurable dreamers?"

"Message well taken! Let's just hope we both live long enough to see what happens with your genetic memory theory."

Rigel laughed. "Or at least long enough ta share many more wonderful evenings while being able ta search for the challenges a our dreams. Speaking a dreamers, tell me about the other one, your partner Sonja who's off with some old antique dealer looking for God knows what. How did the two a ya come together ta work at your Biblical Institute? "

Elana's eyes lit-up as she picked up on the warmth of his tone. "Sonja originally came to the Biblical Institute as a consultant for the evaluation of the bone residue of James in that ossuary. Had a great religious background from a Christian university in the United States, Strayton University, yet her religious beliefs didn't conflict with her advanced degree in molecular genetics. She got an education in genetics in Boston, but I met her after I'd gone to Strayton for some graduate work. When we were looking for someone with some genetic credentials and a strong religious background, Sonja was the right candidate."

Rigel's eyes stayed fixed on hers as he tried to stifle the projection of his own curiosity. "How long have ya been working together as a team?"

Sensing his powerful, penetrating focus on her, she quite ably returned his steady gaze with one of her own. "About three months."

Looking away briefly at some ever present, ever distant point off in space where he was communicating with someone or something, Rigel finally turned back to make eye contact. "If ya haven't any genetic research for her ta do, especially if the antique dealer finds nothing, will ya keep her at the Institute?"

Surprisingly, Elana was able to maintain her eye contact with Rigel without blinking—something notable for her since she didn't often have this type of contact with male friends. "I'm not sure. I'll try to, but who knows how the Institute values her? I suspect she knows there's pressure on her with nothing coming from that ossuary. Maybe this is why she's so interested in this dealer, Abraham Weissberg. He might hold the key to the salvation of her career."

He blinked momentarily, then looked down at his hands as he inquired, "Does she have any family?"

Keeping control of the conversation, Elana kept her focus on him even as she sensed his far-off look whenever he discussed the issue of 'family'. "Yes, both her mother and father are alive, and she has one brother. They're a very close family."

While waiting for the waiter to take their order, Rigel schemed to connect with Elana via the internet. As he wrote his e-mail address on a napkin, he leaned over to her and handed it to her. "Enough a this about Sonja. Since ya said ya communicate with everybody by internet, might I be considered ta be in your 'everybody' group? Here's my e-mail address. Please e-mail me tomorrow and let me know if ya still think my genetic memory theory is foolish dreaming. Just a simple answer like Dreamer if ya still don't have faith in my concept, or Visionary if ya think my idea has merit. I'll respond ta whatever comes my way."

Pleased he shelved his serious side, she shot an amused look back at him. "And what if I haven't decided whether you're a Dreamer or a Visionary? What should I say then?"

Returning an equally-amused look, Rigel replied, "Think about it for a wee bit. Take your time and I'll look forward ta your e-mail decision."

The young couple took a diversion away from their genetics discussion as they looked around the room and commented on the art, architecture and the diverse people either working or drinking at the Lobby Bar. Rigel finished his Guinness and Elana was only toying with the lime in her mostly-empty glass. Rigel got up to leave and as he took the back of her chair to help her away from the table, he replied with a big grin on his face, "Say anything that ya want, but just say something. I'll be expecting your e-mail tomorrow with some message. Even 'I don't know' is OK as long as I get something from ya."

Striding away from the table, Elana's spirits soared while Rigel, with his arm intertwined with hers, was equally confident he would get his much-needed internet communication from her.

The next day, Rigel was not surprised to see Elana's e-mail. While he thought 'Visionary/Dreamer' cute and politically safe, he was more pleased when Liam was able to figure out which webmail service she used. After some digging he was able to derive the appropriate IP address to the webmail service's servers where he would be able to data mine and retrieve all the emails she sent. Whether he was on the internet here in Jerusalem or back home in Ireland, Rigel and his Orion would now know what she knew. And Liam knew he'd have no trouble getting at anyone else's servers who communicated with Elana.

Chapter 6

Sonja Martin's hometown of Manchester, Vermont was where she got a transfusion of antique shopping in her blood and perfected the ritual of looking in old homes and barns hoping to find some overlooked gem. Her mother and father, Rachel and Henry, were devoted to antique browsing, as well as the restoration and resale of whatever they found and didn't keep. Sonja had wood stain and varnish on her fingernails long before she ever thought of using brightly colored polish. But this search was different because now she was chasing something that maybe hadn't existed for over a thousand years.

The small alley off Agrippas Street, where Mr. Weissberg had his shop, was just that – small. It was virtually an alley, narrow enough in its own right, but since so many people were showing their wares, there was barely enough room for two people to walk side-by-side without bumping into someone's stand. Even though dressed modestly, she could still feel the men leering and the women glaring. *Get out of here as soon as you can!* rambled through her mind. Fortunately, Mr. Weissberg's shop was just up ahead as she accelerated her pace to cease being the center of attention in this circus of gawking heads and huckstering mouths.

Approaching the weathered, wooden door, she saw no doorbell and felt the sweat of anxiety as she sensed all those eyes behind her still watching every move. Knowing this wasn't the time to be timid, she rapped on the door, then boldly turned the knob and pushed as the door gave. There she found herself in what must have been a display room. Looking around at the shelves, she saw vases, jugs and identifiable pottery shards that appeared to be from very distant times. Some metal items such as candelabra, of different metals and finishes, were positioned on tables around the room, while the metal candleholders on the walls were of such a rough finish you could only wonder if they were from an ancient time, or simply new and finished to look old? In the antiquities trade, no one was to be totally trusted, even though Abraham Weissberg seemed to be uniquely different.

Saturated with the anxiety of possible rejection from a stranger who might have lost his interest in her, she was relieved when he passed through a curtained doorway from another room. "I hope I've come at a good time."

The warm smile on his face embellished the words coming from his lips. "You are fine, Miss Martin. I was expecting you and very much looking forward to your visit."

Sonja couldn't contain the enthusiasm that rolled off her lips, "I couldn't wait to see you— couldn't sleep all night. That animal carving has me fixated and befuddled at the same time. I can't get if off my mind, but still wonder if it might be a clue to something that will allow me to continue at the Biblical Institute."

Like a cloud blotting out the sun, his concern snuffed out his smile. "Are you thinking of leaving?"

The emotion of possibly losing a job caught up and her voice cracked as she awkwardly looked down at her folded hands. "I may not have a choice since my reason for being at the Institute was to research whatever was inside that ossuary. My friend Elana, you met her at the symposium, and I based my job on finding something there. But with the box being a fraud, my job might also be false."

Wanting to support this young woman was easy, her effort seemed noble, and she even nobler. "But you did find something, the carving on the box. And did you not also buy the box for the Institute?"

"I did buy it, but for me with my own money. When I opened it last night, I couldn't take my eye off that carving, and now I need your help to see if there's something else to be discovered."

Weissberg's eagerness for Sonja's visit wasn't because she was a beautiful young woman, which she certainly was. It was her unbridled enthusiasm, vision and ability to see past the disappointment of that ossuary to focus on the animal carving. No one else in the lecture hall understood it may have been the most important thing there. She saw past the residue of disappointment to envision the fertile foundation of the next discovery. Now was the time to help her accomplish things no longer available to him.

Some special bond was fusing him with this Sonja and he didn't understand it since he never mentored anyone before. His marriage to Elsa had been barren of offspring, and only lately had he come to understand the impact of that famine of fertility. After Elsa died five years ago when they were both 67, he had nothing left inserting any enthusiasm into his life. They had been the rising sunshine at the beginning of each other's day, and when the real sun departed, they grew closer together to let their personal warmth interact. The energy they had for each other was what kept them satisfied and the lack of children wasn't ever discussed as a shortcoming in their lives. But once Elsa died, he realized her sun had fled his universe, abandoned his countenance and with her critical mass of humanity gone, so was the reason for so much of his existence. Now for the first time in five years, Abraham was enthused about something else— Sonja's project. It would be his reason to share some part of his life as she brought a renewed energy source to his.

She reached her right hand over to touch his left arm. "Do you really think there can be something left from 2,000 years ago? Other than the ossuary I bought?"

Placing a hand on top of hers, he gazed at her like an old grandfather looks at his grandchild— warmly and supportive. "Do I really think there could be something here? Yes, I do, but I am not sure if what we can find will be what you need in this search-and-rescue mission for your job."

Squeezing his thin, boney hand, and then turning away, the confrontation with reality hit her like a smack upside her head. Stunned with his analysis, she looked back at his curious face. "You're right. This is a search-and-rescue mission for a career that never seemed to get much of a start."

His eyes never left the simple honesty of youth emanating from her face. "Tell me about yourself because I am not sure what you can achieve with me. Don't forget, I am a very old man."

Sonja realized that in his gaze there was some level of trust allowing her to speak freely, without any concern of whether she might look foolish, or simply too young. "I was hired at the Biblical Institute as a result of an old contact I made with my friend Elana. She convinced the Institute's Board my background in genetics and biblical studies was a unique package. But after that ossuary scam, I'm having trouble justifying my job."

With his right hand stroking the unshaven stubborn stubble on his chin, Weissberg found himself nodding. "I can understand where you have been, but how will that help us as we go on from here?"

She walked over and plopped down into one of his stuffed chairs, slammed her hands onto the tops of her knees, then bolted upright on the edge of her seat. "Maybe my genetics background won't be any help searching for relics, but my religious background, coupled with a healthy dose of curiosity, and topped off with the determination of a pit bull might provide our best chance to find something."

Eyebrows arched and a frown found his face. "What do you mean, 'a pit bull'?"

Embarrassed, she put her hand to her forehead, "I'm sorry, it's an American saying about a very determined dog whose jaws are so strong once it grabs a hold of something, it won't let go."

Turning his back to her, he then abruptly turned around as he spoke. "So you really think you have what it takes and you won't let go of this search? What will you do if you lose your job? Stick with the search?"

A steely resolve came over her as she got up from her chair, stood ramrod straight, pursed her lips and thrust out her square, but delicately chiseled chin.

"Whether I work at the Biblical Institute or not isn't the issue. The carved animal is. I'm here for the total search, whether it's with or without you!"

Weissberg couldn't contain his smile. "Very well, you might be a worthy partner in this search nourished by the memories of not just this old man, but others as well."

The narrowness of her squinting eyes projected the breadth of her questioning mind. "Others like you? Still around here?"

Slowly moving to a chair, he spoke without looking. "There are other men here who also heard the stories of crucifixion relics. And I know the carved animal has been around for a long time, based on actual descriptions of what was found or seen in times past. I saw an example of the carving years ago."

With eyes lit-up like firecrackers, her enthusiasm exploded. "What did you think it was all about when you first saw it?"

Sitting back in his chair and rubbing his nose, he replied. "I wasn't sure whether it was a family symbol or from the builder of the limestone box—what we now call a logo. Does that seem to make sense to you?"

"Yes, but what else could it be?" Sonja questioned as her excitement exceeded her curiosity.

"It could be a symbol for some group of men responsible for creating or protecting what was in the box. From our 21st century perspective, we would have expected Christians to put a cross on something they wanted to identify as theirs. Could it have been that people who didn't know they were even Christians, or what we now call Christians, simply had chosen a symbol such as an animal that made sense to them? Could this animal have been an alternative sign for Christians who realized their secret identity could be compromised if they also used a fish symbol? What if they thought the Romans, or whoever they feared, would figure out what the fish meant. Why not go their own way and create their own secret identity? Whatever meaning exists for this chiseled animal, it is old because the elements of aging, which didn't alter the newly carved letters in the ossuary of James lid, did affect this chiseled animal. Its edges were worn by the years of its existence even though it was on the underside of the lid."

Up again, out of the chair she sprung with uncontainable enthusiasm in her eyes. "Do you think the chiseled animal might be an original carving for the box's first use?"

"We need to assume that the animal has some meaning which may have even preceded that box. And my gut feeling is the animal, with its reddish coloring, was more than just a simple decoration."

Now her methodical intuitiveness emerged. "Based on what I've said and you've thought, where do we go from here?"

His old gray eyes locked on hers. His perception of work was always serious, and he expected the same from Sonja if he was to be involved. "Where and to whom? To consider where we look, you must understand there are very few connections that far back in history. Only the old monasteries go that far back, and my recollection is that the other carved animal may have come from one of the ancient monasteries."

With her left hand on her hip, she was consumed with her inquisition. "But how ancient could they be? Monasteries didn't come into existence until hundreds of years after the time of Christ."

Moving over towards her, he then leaned upon a desk that was between their chairs. "The monasteries didn't need to be around at the time of Christ, but only later when they could have been havens for safe keeping of the sacred texts and relics from the time of the crucifixion. Their abilities to hide valuables could have persisted for many centuries afterward, especially at the time of the Crusades."

She sat back in the chair and looked up at him with a sense of frustrating finality dominating her inquiry. "And you think there are monasteries worth researching? Have you ever been to any of them, or known anyone who had? "

"I haven't been to them and don't know anyone who has, but, I think there are two that fit our needs. Khor Virap in Armenia and St. Catherine's on Mount Sinai."

Following his words closely, she watched every muscle movement of his face as the name Khor Virap flew right by her. "Why those?"

"For the best of reasons, especially their long history. They have been around a long time with great proximity to issues of the Christian faith."

"Such as?" Sonja asked so quick she feared she was rude.

He laughed at her obvious enthusiasm. "I can see you are now getting very eager, but be patient. Khor Virap, in Armenia, looks at Mt. Ararat, directly across the border with Turkey. The monastery's position allows it to look directly at the mountain which many believe was the final resting place of Noah's Ark once the great flood receded. And, tracing the trade routes of ancient times, you will find that Khor Virap was on the route to ancient Israel. Following the pathways of ancient traders will tell you how something got from one place to another."

"And St. Catherine's? I know a little about St. Catherine's on Mt. Sinai, but do you think it's relevant because Moses got the Ten Commandments on Mt. Sinai?"

"For our purposes, St. Catherine's value is that it was always such a physically impregnable fortress. If you had something to protect, it would be as good a place as any, especially in ancient times. Some people tried to get into St. Catherine's and found it impossible, while others got in but couldn't find what they went for. There is a conundrum at St. Catherine's that may not be resolvable --- you may get in but may not get anything for your efforts. "

Struggling to suppress this cross-examination of Weissberg, Sonja softened her inquisition. "OK, we discussed the 'where', but who is the 'who' you mentioned?"

Weissberg reached over to a paper pad and scribbled something. "There are two other men here in Jerusalem I want you to meet. I have talked to them about your interest and they agreed to meet you. One is a Greek, Theodore Protopolis, and the other, Shlomo Levi, is Jewish like me. Here, take their addresses," he said as he handed her the paper, "and tomorrow you are to see Levi in the morning at about 10:00 and then Protopolis after 2:00 in the

72

afternoon. I will do more research and will meet with you in two weeks. After that we can determine what we know and where we go."

"Thank you," said Sonja while giving a hug that reminded him of that wellspring of human affection that fled his life five years ago. "I can't thank you enough for what you're doing for me. How I can repay you?"

As he still held onto her and gave her a smile that conveyed his understanding of her thoughts and mission, his barrier of formality softened. "You can repay me by finding out what all these things mean. Understand that while you first saw the animal on the box lid and were curious, that was my second time and now I am even more curious. Go find the answers, and don't delay, because at my age I can't wait forever. Be gone now with good health, even greater energy, and hopefully an abundance of luck."

When she said her goodbye and turned to leave, she couldn't help but sense a sprouting confidence that she was on a trail to not only keep her job, but hopefully lead to something even greater—hopefully something to strengthen the relevance of Christianity in the modern world.

Leaving the area where Weissberg's shop was located, Sonja knew the shops of these other two men were nearby on similar alley-like streets she had passed along the way. But she couldn't wait to share her discoveries with Elana, since while she was at Mr. Weissberg's, Elana was negotiating Sonja's future with the powers-to-be at the Biblical Institute. Sonja thought she might have a future finding some relics, but didn't know if she had one at the Institute.

Looking out the window at the Institute, Elana saw a jubilant Sonja approaching the building, she couldn't wait to see what put such a bounce in her step. When Sonja finally entered the office complex and turned the corner into Elana's cubicle, Elana jumped up to give her a welcoming embrace as words just spewed from her mouth. "What've you found?"

Negating the question with a shaking of her head, Sonja countered, "No, more importantly, what've you found?"

With both hands on her hips, Elana jokingly digressed into a very juvenile style, "No, you tell me. I asked you first."

"Well," she paused, "I think there's something there. Mr. Weissberg has heard for years about something existing from the time of the crucifixion. He also thinks the chiseled animal on the underside of the lid may be an important link to early Christianity. Now, it's you turn. Am I a jobless, impoverished waif about to be cast out onto the hostile streets of the world?"

Stepping back, Elana's chemistry changed as the sobering sense of Institute business definitely needed addressed. "You still have a job, but I can't say for how long. The Board thinks we should keep you on since maybe you can help with our basic New Testament research, but there's no interest or funding for any relics search. And, they're requiring routine e-mail updates on anything you're doing."

Sitting down next to the computer, Sonja motioned Elana to come over. "Let's send them an e-mail right now and tell them I'm on a hot trail to find some items from the time of Jesus. And to legitimize it, I'll give them the names of the antique dealers who'll help us navigate these uncharted waters of discovery."

Typing the e-mail, Elana couldn't keep up with Sonja. "Slow down, you're getting ahead of yourself and me. I can send this right away, but you still need to figure out how to fund this venture, because nothing at all will come from the Institute."

Sonja gave her a mischievous look. "Tell them what I said, and also that I'm in the process of securing funding from my alma mater, good old Strayton University."

Stunned, Elana stopped typing. "When did this occur?"

Up from her chair, Sonja turned away from Elana for just seconds, then quickly turned back. "Today! Once your e-mail gets sent, I'll e-mail the President of Strayton University, Dr. Harlan Smathers, and see if I can get his attention."

"Do you know him, or do you think he just might remember those long, beautiful legs of yours?" Elana added with a devilish grin.

"Don't be so shallow. No, I really don't know him personally, but I did meet him since I was fairly unique among their collective student body."

"Unique in his mind, or only yours?"

Sonja plucked at an imaginary pin on her blouse. "They didn't have too many people who won the Smathers' Gold Medal as an Honor's Scholar in the Bible and then did graduate studies in molecular genetics. In fact, I'm the only one ever to do that. Just a Strayton poster child, of sorts, for how religion and science can work in harmony. The President may have forgotten me, but I think I can jolt his memory."

Laughing in jest, Elana pretended to reach up and grab things from the air. "And you expect him to just snatch money out of the air and give it to someone he may not even remember? For a person who may be out of a job at any minute, why do you think you're going to get some financial 'manna' from heaven?"

"My dear Elana, let me explain. Dr. Smathers was, and still is, a very important and powerful man, and he personally made that university what it is with his legendary fundraising skills. Since he raised all the money, and reports to no one, he spends it in whatever way he wants. Fortunately for Strayton, he spent it on honorable things—even built such a strong New Testament department they have a professorial exchange program with the Vatican. Now let's see if our relic search can redirect his imagination our way."

Turning back to her keyboard, a trace of sarcasm found a home in Elana's comment. "OK, I'll send my e-mail then you can fabricate yours to this Dr. Smathers."

Sonja reached over to touch Elana's shoulder. "No, I'll use my woman's prerogative and change my mind. Send your e-mail to the Board and I'll wait until after I see these other two antique dealers before I send my message to President Smathers."

Watching Elana send the e-mail, Sonja found her confidence grew that this would buy her some time if the Board would be interested in what she had to say. Little did she know, at the same time, a computer in Tarbert, County Kerry, Ireland, next to the River Shannon, lit up with great satisfaction for the hacker who was monitoring Elana's computer. Unaware of what was being transmitted north to the Emerald Isle, Sonja left Elana to get some rest for what would be an interesting tomorrow with Protopolis and Levi.

Morning came quickly to Sonja after a restless night filled with images of old, secretive relics' hiding places. At the designated time, she walked down the narrow street to Levi's shop, and could've convinced herself she was walking down Mr. Weissberg's little alley. And the people still looked the same, staring bug-eyed as she wove her way between items on display and small grills cooking angry little pieces of meat. The masses of people seemed to see every move she made even though she wanted so badly to just melt into the crowd. As she finally got through this morass of humanity, she was at the shop looking at the sign: Shlomo Levi Antiques.

Emboldened by her experience at Weissberg's, Sonja opened the door, walked right in and saw a man sitting behind a small table with only a single piece of pottery on his shelves. He didn't look very successful, but maybe what he had was so valuable he hid it. Walking over towards him, she extended her hand to shake his. "Mr. Levi, I'm Sonja Martin, and I believe Mr. Abraham Weissberg spoke to you about my interest in some relics from the time of Jesus' crucifixion."

Levi nodded his head in approval as nothing else moved except his right hand as he shook Sonja's. There he sat, motionless in his black clothing with only a hint of skin color and with only the gray of his beard breaking the monotony of the boring, bleak blackness. "Yes, Abraham spoke to me about you. You are the one from that bone meeting, that Ossuary of James. You wanted a box of bones from 2,000 years ago?" he asked somewhat derisively. "I have better bones, at least 200 years older than that, and I won't charge you any more for my dry-aged bones than what you would pay for those fresher 2,000 year old bones."

Immediately disillusioned with this Levi character, Sonja still pleaded, "I'm not here looking for bones, just for something from the time of Jesus' crucifixion. Might you have something?"

Pitifully shaking his head, Levi then stopped to look at her. "Miss Sonja Martin, I am very sorry, but Abraham misunderstood something. I hear of people hoping something like that exists, but I know of nothing from Jesus' time."

Sonja's reflection in a mirror on the wall showed the agonizing distortion of a face as her frustration was uncontainable. "What about the chiseled animal, a dog, a wolf, that Mr. Weissberg and I found, have you ever seen anything like that?"

He got up from his chair and walked over to Sonja. "I don't know how he got this so confused. I told him I remembered something about a chiseled animal somewhere, but now I don't know if it was a dog, a wolf, or even a snake. I'm sorry you wasted your time, but you must understand that Abraham is very old and gets confused. I am much younger in mind and know more than he knows, but don't tell him I told you so. And I know he arranged for you to see that Greek Protopolis, but he can't be trusted—don't turn your back on him."

Sonja turned to leave and bade farewell to Levi, "Thank you for your time, and I'll take your recommendations about Mr. Protopolis under advisement."

As she left Levi's shop, she had to face those crowded streets, teeming with a greater density of snooping and sneering humanity than existed just those few minutes earlier when she went into his shop. Sonja increased the pace of her walking but despite this increase in human congestion, with hundreds of eyes out there, she knew every eye was on her. As she tried to quicken her pace, she wondered if anything ever occurred on a street like this that no one ever saw.

The trip to Protopolis' shop was a similar experience, and she wondered how anyone could escape this dense accumulation of humanity jamming every nook and cranny of these streets. Everyone must know everybody else's business, and maybe that was part of the pricing/haggling you could constantly hear as you passed by the different merchants. Sonja realized she needed to get out of this area as soon as she could once she knew if Mr. Protopolis was a better source of information than Levi.

Approaching the green wooden door to Protopolis' shop, Sonja saw a man's face appear through a small window and then the door quickly opened. "Miss Sonja Martin?" inquired the man.

Extending her hand towards his, she responded. "Yes, I'm Sonja Martin, and I presume you are Mr. Theodore Protopolis? Am I correct?"

"Yes and it is my pleasure to greet you because our mutual friend, Abraham Weissberg told me you would be coming."

Scarred by her experience with Levi, Sonja realized she was being somewhat abrupt. "Is it presumptuous to ask if you agree with Mr. Weissberg that some relic or relics still exist from the time of Jesus' crucifixion."

Completely bald and somewhat stooped over, Protopolis chuckled and struggled to contain his response. "You are to-the-point with your questioning, but no, it is not presumptuous at all to ask that. For many years I heard of suspicions about relics from that time, and possibly even from the crucifixion itself, but I have never been sure what to believe."

She looked him in the eye with an unwavering stare and a firmly set chin. "And Mr. Protopolis, what do your sources tell you about these relics?"

Leading her over to some chairs, his pleasant manner radiated in the midst of the drabness surrounding them. "I believe if anything can exist, it must be in one of the old monasteries. If not there, maybe in some dry cave like the Dead Sea Scrolls, but if in some caves, who knows which ones and where? I know Abraham is doing some additional research for you, and please allow me to do the same. I think if I see you in two weeks, the same day you see Abraham, I may have more information for you."

Even as she was sitting in the chair, she knew she was desperate to continue her questioning. After the Levi experience, she saw no reason to waste time, or worse yet, lose a good opportunity to learn what she needed. "Mr. Protopolis, what do you think about the chiseled figure of an animal on the ossuary lid? Have you seen anything like that before?"

Pausing for a few seconds, he then responded while nodding. "Yes, I think I have in a monastery many years ago, but this is another of those issues I need to study before I can be sure. Please come back and see me in two weeks and I will tell all that I know and maybe even more, if I discover anything else."

Blocking the Levi experience from her mind, Sonja knew this Protopolis was a gentleman, direct, informative and eager to help. Her prospects were looking up as she told him good-bye "Mr. Protopolis, thank you for your help, and I'll look forward to seeing you in two weeks."

Upon leaving Protopolis, she was able to quickly navigate her way out of the congestion and confusion dominating the street. Bad enough to be a woman having men staring at her in normal circumstances, but here, everyone was doing it and then they'd probably forget her in a heartbeat.

After a quick taxi ride back to her office, Sonja sat down at the computer she shared with Elana. Now was the time to e-mail President Smathers that she was on to something, and needed to project this level of confidence to him thousands of miles away. She had the president's e-mail address from previous alumni correspondence and knew what she needed to say. Though unsure how her e-mail would be received at Strayton University, she was absolutely unaware how the message would be received in Ireland.

Chapter 7

Power personified President Harland Smathers, and both publically and privately he always projected absolute power. As president of Strayton University, he didn't get to where he was only to be bound by the constraints of mealy-mouthed men spooked by their own shadows of doubt and desperation. Looking out his office window as Eric Stanfels walked briskly towards his building, Smathers wondered if Eric would be up for this task in the same way he would have been if he were Eric's age. He had no confusion about Eric's history of being embroiled in an intelligence fiasco in the Middle East— some blast furnace of an inferno. Maybe now wasn't the best time to ask him to return there, but in reality, it was the only time. And Smathers knew Strayton needed Eric as much as Eric had previously needed Strayton. Harland Smathers was not about to allow a Strayton alumnus to forget about his obligation to the University.

Nestled in the Appalachian foothills of North Carolina, Strayton University was founded as Strayton College in 1870 by textile manufacturer Elijah Strayton. A biblical college from its inception, its mission was 'Do Good Deeds in the Name of the Lord'. It wasn't until 1975, when Dr. Harlan Smathers ascended to the presidency, that the school established itself as an international force in the world of New Testament research.

Harlan Smathers had come to Strayton College as a student in 1958 from a very simple background in rural, southern Virginia. After receiving his Bachelors of Divinity degree at Strayton, he enrolled in the Yale Divinity School for advanced studies in biblical history. While his intellectual growth

80

was stimulated by the different perspectives of the New England schools of religious thought, it was at New Haven, Connecticut that the young Reverend Harlan Smathers became introduced to the concept of building great endowments for a university. He thought it odd that he was learning the 'tricks of money raising' from some of the most pious of religious educators, but gradually he came to understand the symbiotic nature between the wealthy and their religious institutions.

While the south didn't have the concentration of wealth that Wall Street and Boston provided for the Yales and Harvards of New England, when the Reverend Dr. Smathers left Yale to return to Strayton, he understood how to be a 'relationship builder' with some of the great families of the geographically-diffuse South. He had unprecedented prowess in raising not only money, but also emotional commitments to Strayton from individuals who had no previous affiliation with the school. Smathers was a man who knew his place and power as the President of Strayton University, and as such also controlled the finances with an iron fist. He had no delusions about who created the wealth at the institution, and he had no reservations about when and where to spend it. He raised the money and he treated it like it was his God-given right to dispense as he wished – just like it was his own! And tucked away in some deep recession in his mind, he thought of his alumni as people that he, or least Strayton, also owned.

Entering Smathers' sumptuous office, Eric Stanfels was in awe of the exquisite elegance of the room with its beautiful burled chestnut walls, heavily-beamed ceiling and massive Chippendale-style conference table with its twelve matching chairs supported by ball-and-claw feet. And there waiting for him was President Smathers, with his extended right hand, and as usual, dressed in what probably was a remnant of his Ivy League exposure—a navy blue, chalk-striped 3-piece suit. At age 67, with his full mane of silver-gray hair framing a handsome well-tanned face, Smathers still kept his athletic body in good shape, and the buttons weren't popping off his vest. Being 6 feet tall, he enjoyed looking down on most people who came into his office, except Eric who had him by an inch.

"Great to see you Eric! Always enjoy it when the two of us can have the time to get together."

"Thank you President Smathers. It's a pleasure being in your company."

"Thanks, but skip the formality. You know you've always had a special place in our collective hearts here at Strayton, and especially here, you're family." Smathers then pointed in the direction of a chair. "Have a seat. I need your advice about something." Smathers sat at his desk as he continued, "Are you familiar with what happened in Jerusalem regarding a limestone burial box supposed to be that of Jesus' brother James?"

Sitting opposite the President's desk, Eric crossed his legs as he leaned forwards. "I've seen the reports that the box supposedly held the bones of James, but was exposed as a fraud."

"Good, then I don't need to review that. But as a result of some research done by a Strayton alumna at a biblical institute in Jerusalem, there's unbridled optimism about relics from Jesus' crucifixion. Here," he said as he handed Eric a copy of the e-mail, "take a look at this e-mail, then read it to me. I want to see how it impacts you."

Taking the copy of the e-mail, Eric scanned it for a moment before reading aloud, "Dear President Harlan Smathers. As a recent graduate of Strayton University, please allow me to impose upon your good graces regarding a consideration of my proposal. I am presently located in Jerusalem and have done extensive research on the 'Ossuary of James' which we now know was a fraud. My associate and I at the New Testament Biblical Institute in Jerusalem have discovered the possibility of one or more relics from the crucifixion of Jesus. As our financial resources are depleted, I am making a request to you for financial support for this mission—for the sake of Christianity in these very compelling and turbulent times. Sincerely, Sonja Martin, Class of '98."

Looking up at Smathers and before the words could roll off his tongue, the eager President beat him to the punch. Smathers had already thought a lot about

82

this Sonja Martin, and remembered her well—to him her beauty was unforgettable. "How does this strike you?"

Uncrossing his legs, Eric twisted sideways in his chair as he spoke. "Mr. President, I read it in several ways. The request may be worthy of your interest and secondly, the requester, Sonja Martin, may be worthy of your support. I certainly do remember her as a student of mine."

Smathers smiled as his mind wandered, *How could you forget her?* then came around from behind his desk. "I knew she was a student of yours. Researched her religion courses and you were one of her professors, and your investigative background made you a more interesting choice to talk to about her request. I get requests all the time, but what's your gut feeling on this one?"

Gazing out the window, as a smile crept over his face, Eric turned to Smathers. "As I said, I remember her since she was so unquestionably unique," and now his head was unconsciously nodding, "quite unique... and quite beautiful."

"I understand where you're going. Great religion scholar who gets a degree in molecular biology. Aren't many of those in the world, let alone here at Strayton. She even won my Gold Medal for biblical research as an undergraduate, and quite frankly, I still remember when I fastened the commemorative pin on her blouse—what a stunning young woman."

Choosing to sublimate the beauty issue, Eric paused to find the right words. "The fact she's an alumna doesn't legitimize her request, but her uniqueness does make me give it some serious thought."

Smathers' smiling face now had a sudden, serious transformation. "Was she truly unique or was it her beauty clouding some of the total picture?"

Vigorously shaking of his head, Eric gave a laughing response. "Unique to say the least. Also very beautiful, very bright and not a person you could easily forget. Each class has someone beautiful, maybe even more beautiful than she, but with Sonja Martin, beauty was even greater in her persona, her intellect and her faith. I taught her during my first year back at Strayton, the first year back here after my 'Problem' when I was trying to re-admit myself into the sanctity of Strayton and God. If I'd met her at a different time in my life, and naturally,"

83

he chuckled, "when a professor-student relationship wasn't forbidden, I would've tried to know her better."

Sarcastically, Smathers spoke back to this denying young buck. "I know what you mean. She was quite a fireball of a student in my University."

But Smathers' words caused Eric to drift off to somewhere else. 'A fireball'! The *Problem* had insidiously invaded his mind as he focused on that time warp wafting somewhere out in space. It was always there. He put some of it behind him here at Strayton, but knew he couldn't lose it or its devastatingly destructive impact. Frequent flashbacks brought a haunting level of re-emergent conscious and subconscious awareness of a time in his life when all had gone so wrong— all up in fire!

"Eric? Eric? Did I lose you?" Smathers almost shouted. "I asked what you thought of Miss Martin's request?"

He brought his focus back to Smathers, making and sustaining direct eye contact with him. "The request is intriguing. As I recall, Miss Martin had exceptionally good judgment, so I'd be inclined to not dismiss this too lightly. Naturally, her request must be tempered with what costs you invest in this venture, or should I say adventure?"

"Oh Hades, man," replied Smathers smitten partly with the proposal and partly with the proposer, "I've raised more money than I can spend on reasonable or unreasonable ventures, but my inclination is to support her. She's worked on that ossuary and been exposed to fraud and deceit but still thinks this new search has merit. Funding this isn't an issue, because the real issue here is whether or not you want to be Strayton's point man on this mission?"

With a calmness covering his underlying concerns, Eric laid open and exposed the palm side of both of his hands. "Why me? I haven't done any type of archeological research. I'd be a neophyte, a fish out of water."

Making a quick, dismissive wave of his right hand, Smathers knew he had to address the real problem with this trip. "I know this really isn't your field, but it might be, and it will be unless your past experience creates a conflict. I'm asking you to go back to the Middle East where I know you had some problems before. Am I being unfair to ask that of you?"

Focusing intently into Smathers' strong, stable eyes, Eric was the first one to blink. "I hadn't thought of going back, but that doesn't mean I won't."

Turning his back on Eric as he walked over to look out his large picture window, Smathers dug deeper. "I've never asked you what happened over there, but I know you came to us right after what I suspect was some sort of disaster. Is this the time to talk about it?"

Speechless for a moment, aware he hadn't confided in anyone about his Problem, Eric knew his past was something he wanted to just stay there—in the past. But he also suspected he couldn't completely compartmentalize that part of his memory or psyche and deny its existence. With Smathers now walking towards him, Eric responded. "You might be right. Maybe it's time to talk. If I'm going back to the Middle East, I need to put the past as much behind me as I can, or at least try to deal with it better."

Smathers sat in the chair next to Eric. "Only tell me as much as you want. There's no need for me to know more than that."

Leaping back to a different place in time, Eric's mind went not to the time of his venture into the Middle East, but back three generations, two generations, then to only one. He came from a line of ministers who graduated from Strayton. His great-grandfather, Adam Stanfels, was the first in the line to serve the Lord, then followed by his grandfather, Aaron and finally his father, Jacob. With Eric's outstanding academic record and his family heritage, it was naturally assumed he would also travel that same principled path into the ministry. But something changed and his Stanfels shadow never graced those doors to the Strayton Seminary. Instead, Eric walked into a CIA embrace that would ultimately become an emotional and moral abyss—his Problem.

There was no question Eric Stanfels loved his God, but he did question how the love of God could penetrate the violence and hatred saturating the world. Eric's vision was to perpetuate God's love by making the world safer and more open to change so people could focus on their spiritual lives instead of just trying to stay alive. For him, by detouring from the ministry and joining the CIA, he'd be able to open the doors of the world to Christianity by creating peace and democracy. This would be his mission—spreading Christianity by establishing peace. When he left Strayton, Eric couldn't foresee how terrorists and terrorism would become the perverted pieces that didn't fit in his jigsaw puzzle of humanity.

How could Eric's parents see it the same way? Jacob and Anna Mae Stanfels were simply devastated by Eric's CIA choice since they couldn't see how forsaking his Christian duty for a labor bordering on hatred could in any way serve their God. With his gaze still fixed on President Smathers, Eric worried Smathers might misunderstand his actions back then and how that impacted his life now here at Strayton. He knew it was time to open the floodgates to that period of his existence when life became so badly blistered and his morality mired in the waves of human hatred. Now Eric's mind came back from that distant place to Smathers' office, and his look was that of someone who wanted to unburden himself. "I'll tell you all that you'll ever need to know, and then you'll understand what you gave me here at Strayton resurrected at least part of my soul."

It all came back too quickly as he discarded the present and regressed into an emotionless monotone accompanied by eyes staring off into some other place in time.

As the two men sought shelter under the grove of olive trees, the cold night wind cutting through him made no concession to the chill from those penetrating doubts Mordecai Rubin always seemed to have about these Americans. No, not the one flying high in the sky above him who was probably belched off some aircraft carrier out in the Mediterranean, but with this one, this operative who had been entrusted to him for such a mission. Mordecai's thoughts stuck to him with some neural glue that prevented him from getting rid of the frustration and anxiety such a high stress mission brought when you couldn't totally trust your partner. *Why do those damned Americans always send boys to do a man's killing? Babes sent for a mission they glamorize but then can't pull the trigger when it counts.* He felt this way too often on these joint ventures with the CIA. Mordecai looked over at the peach fuzz framing the American's cheek, shuddered and turned away in disgust.

Eric Stanfels didn't join the CIA to do reconnaissance like this, spending a cold night in the hills overlooking this small village in Gaza. In the month he and his partner were on assignment, Eric had little to do but watch this guy chewing on a toothpick—twirling it between his lips like some acrobatic gyration. Checking and rechecking data, reports, sightings and histories while this Mordecai character was chewing on enough toothpicks to deforest half of Brazil. And fighting a war against terrorists was more difficult than it must have been in the old days when cell phones weren't part of the equipment of a thoroughly trained terrorist. And Hassan al-Azziz was no ordinary terrorist. He was schooled by the legendary Carlos, the Jackal, before Carlos became fat and careless. Al-Azziz wasn't careless and was thought to be a leading organizer and, more importantly, the primary bomb maker for all the terrorism taking place in Gaza. "Mordecai," Eric whispered to his Mossad partner, "where's this dog? How many nights do we wait before getting a shot at him?"

Mordecai Rubin had eleven more years than Eric in the anti-terrorism business. Being 35 years old compared to Eric's 24 was not just an issue of age, but of devotion to a cause. When Mordecai first joined the Mossad 15 years ago, he had no delusions about what was in store for him. Israel had always been a target of terror, and if you worked for the Mossad, you were going to see your share of random terrorism, innocent death and devastating destruction. Fulfilling his sworn duty to protect the State of Israel, Mordecai knew two things always to be true. You always spent a lot more time watching than doing, and what you thought you might be doing was usually not what you ended up doing. It was a nasty, boring, psychologically-destructive career, but it had to be done by someone if the people of Israel were to be kept safe.

"Our sources are reliable," replied Mordecai. "They've been monitoring this house for several weeks, and Al-Azziz comes and goes sometimes with family, sometimes with terrorist friends. Our information is usually accurate and I've got a feeling tonight, when he comes home, just might be our night."

This should be the night? Ha! Eric thought as he caught himself shaking his head as a reflection of his doubts. There'd been too many nights like this since he'd forsaken his duty to follow in the family line of ministers. As Eric sat on this hill in Gaza, he asked himself his father's questions which were thrust upon him when he announced he'd joined the CIA. *How could you do the CIA's dirty business? Why not be God's emissary, not the CIA's? When you've had enough, please come back to Strayton, come back to God!* He knew they'd never understand how he could smite God's foe and do His work—bringing peace and love to the world. But now, on this desolate, windswept hilltop, the doubts arose as he wondered if he could fulfill that destiny. Looking over at Mordecai, staring hard for a moment, he spoke, "Don't you get tired of this? Spending your whole life sitting, watching and chasing shadows? Don't you ever wonder if you really accomplish anything?"

Mordecai looked at Eric and couldn't suppress the thoughts, *Why do they all look the same? Scrubbed faces, rosy cheeks, perfect teeth. Disgusting! Right out of the movies.* Mordecai knew his years had taken their toll, and maybe he was just jealous because the demands of his job were showing. Slightly less than Eric's height, but carrying too many pounds draping over his belt. Most of his brown hair gone, like too many of the terrorists he tracked. The sandpaper of stress and the corrosion of alcohol had left pits and fissures on a face that defied plastic surgery. Without speaking, he looked at Eric for what seemed a minute, twirled that toothpick, then spoke, "Always boring when you stake-out a site, and I've spent more time watching and listening than ever doing anything. Watch and listen better and you have fewer screw-ups."

Impatient, Eric interrupted. "But how often have you made a difference? When does the shadow chasing give you something substantial, like something that justifies what we're here for?"

Mordecai shot back with his own impatience vaulting into his voice, "Intelligence work doesn't usually give you anything you Americans say 'you can put your hat on'—it only takes away from you. It takes away your life, your innocence, your optimism, your ability to love and your faith in mankind. And sometimes it even takes away your belief in God. Is that a lot to lose, to give-up? I don't think so. As Israelis, we serve our state, our heritage and our God as sons and daughters of Abraham and Moses. But being a Jew means always being the focus of someone else's hatred. Always in the sight of someone else's gun who planned to enslave or annihilate our people, our lives never had a full dose of innocence, optimism or faith in mankind. Whether we died at Masada or fueled the flames at Auschwitz, Jews never got their fair share of manna from heaven. I'm not complaining about what I've got to do tonight or any night. I just do it because I know it needs to be done for my people and my God. But you, what about you? Can you guide that laser bomb into al-Azziz's house?"

Looking away for a moment, then without turning back, Eric talked only to the night. "For me, the task is different. I'm here to kill al-Azziz and create a more peaceful Middle East. Will it bring justice and peace? I'm not sure. Will the world be safer for all God's children? I think so."

An indignant Mordecai interrupted. "Killing makes the world safer? You haven't killed before, have you? And what do you think killing does to a man's faith? Time will tell what it'll do for you, but for now, my only concern is if you can guide a bomb into that house?"

Bristling at the insinuation he might not be a reliable partner, with his nostrils flaring, a defiant Eric answered while pointing in the direction of the small, one story mud-and-brick house. "No, I haven't killed before, but I'll guide that bomb home tonight."

Turning to look at two men jumping out of a just-arrived green Range Rover, Mordecai pointed and spoke in hushed tones, "I told you tonight is our night— al-Azziz and his aide. Once he's inside, radio your pilot to bring the bomb. But if you can't guide that damned thing home, gimme the guidance system and I'll do it for you."

A glaring Eric focused on Mordecai's murderous eyes, "Your men are sure the house was empty before those two went in?"

Mordecai returned an even more intense glare. "Trust my men, the place is empty."

"Yea, well trust what I'm telling you! There's no room for screw-ups. Justifiable assassination is one thing that's understood no matter which side you're on. But collateral damage is unacceptable—an intolerable Rorschach imprint of horror in the psyche of civilized people. Am I clear?"

"Clearer than the purest waters of the Red Sea! No murky residue in the superficial analysis, but red with the blood of intent as you probe deeper. Look Eric, my men don't make mistakes. We're a civilized society in a fight to the death with barbarians, but we don't have to act like them."

After activating the guidance system to start the operation, Eric and the pilot were in a morbid countdown mode preparing to direct a bomb directly into that hovel of hatred. After only a few seconds, the bomb was released and as it dove to earth, Eric's guidance brought it directly on a path to annihilate the house and its contents. Seconds before the bomb hit, with its final plunge directed by Eric into the despairingly darkest depths of destruction, a door opened and a woman and two children stepped out. Within seconds, the exploding bomb hurtled their bodies through the air. In that instant of explosive color, colors that would revisit Eric from this point on, three dark body forms seemed like bats fleeing an intrusive, glaring light. But this time, nothing moving was alive. The crushing percussive force of the explosion, which killed the terrorists inside the building, also mercifully tore the life out of the woman and her children before any level of consciousness could comprehend what happened. But the level of consciousness within the mind of Eric Stanfels had also been altered—a permanent destructive permutation occurring within a split second that eons of time wouldn't be able to heal.

Despite his right leg being lacerated by a piece of flying metal, Eric screamed over the echoes of the explosion, "Mordecai? For God's sake, what in the hell did we do? You told me no one was in there before al-Azziz came. What were you thinking? How could you not have known there were other people in there? Or didn't you give a damn?"

Faltering for a few seconds, Mordecai tried to aggressively assert, "We were told the place was empty with no one in that house before al-Azziz arrived. I didn't know they were in there. The Mossad avoids killing innocents—I don't know what went wrong. Maybe our informants were wrong or maybe they set us up. If I'd known someone was in that house, I'd have told you! But don't forget, in counter-terrorism sometimes it's not enough to kill the leader and leave the worker bees alive. Their honey, as sour as it is, only nourishes the hatred that later kills you and all that you stand for."

To a boiling point came Eric's frustration as he realized his sense of innocence, or what little of it remained, was fried in a flash. "You rotten son-of-a-bitch!" Eric yelled over the resonating explosion still echoing through his head. "You should have died there, not that woman and her children."

Letting the hostility of Eric's remarks bounce off , Mordecai stared resolutely into his empty eyes while slowly shaking his head from side-to-side, " I'm not a rotten whatever you call me, just what your government and mine needs me to be. And that's not much different than you!"

"Bullshit! What the hell did we do here?" Eric asked partly to Mordecai and partly to the depressive darkness now shattered with this beacon of death.

Mordecai paused before answering—he had seen it all before. Men too young; too virtuous; too naïve and too American. They didn't understand at the gut level what they were doing here, and when the shit hit the fan, they couldn't comprehend the destruction they brought into peoples' lives—including their own. Now Mordecai tried a conciliatory tone. "The destruction of innocent lives is horrible, but it happens, and you better realize, this life is not for you. You're not tough enough, so get out now while you still have some semblance of a soul. This swamp of destruction will only suck you further into the muck and soil you forever."

Eric's hostility for Mordecai erupted like a Vesuvius, "Jesus Christ, Mordecai! God-damn you and… " But he caught himself before he went further as the

91

shame and horror of taking his God's name in vain had clarified his complete spiritual collapse. Now he was shaking his head despondently as thoughts bolted through his shattered mind: *How could goodness grow in a spiritual desert, with soiled psyches gone wrong, judgments warped by the distortion of hatred, and innocent death splattered on the canvass of humanity?* He turned away from Mordecai and then spun back to look at him. Eric knew that with this failed mission he had been devastated by chance, but his God, he destroyed by choice. That he couldn't live with! Nor could he forgive his partner for leading him into this moral quagmire. "Mordecai, may our God in heaven damn you and all the killing you stand for!"

Listening intently, until it seemed Eric was lost in another world completely disassociated from the room, Smathers asked, "Eric... Eric, can I help you?"

With sweat dripping from his chin and tears flowing from his bloodshot eyes, Eric looked up to an utterly anxious, yet understanding face of President Smathers, "Now you can see my Problem. I gave away a big part of my soul for something I thought I believed in. My road to Hell was paved with good intentions, but instead of doing good I wove a web of hatred that ensnared, strangled and then discarded my soul. Enough?"

Smathers looked at him impassively. "Only when you think so. If you need to tell me more, go ahead."

Averting Smathers' gaze, Eric continued. "I'll only add that despite the severe leg wound I got, being able to physically and mentally come back home to Strayton was critical. Here I've had a chance to regain some access into that realm of spiritual purity I once coveted, but foolishly threw away. Hopefully, the healing of my psyche and soul have progressed enough I can go back to the Middle East. Maybe it's time to go back and face it!"

Smathers looked Eric right in the eye. "But having gone through what you did, is there still be some residue? Are there nightmares? Any awakening in the middle of the night with the sweats or any kind of emotional distress? Wouldn't be unusual."

Shaking his head, Eric negated not the past trauma, but Smathers' new concern. "I think I've been able to compartmentalize things pretty well, but there are occasional flashbacks to that night when I see even the smallest fire. Overall, I think I'll be OK."

The smiling President now sat serenely in his chair. "Good, not just that you can go back to serve Strayton, but that you feel you're ready to go back. And since you're presently on sabbatical, there are no logistical or class scheduling problems if we make immediate plans to send you to Jerusalem to help this Sonja Martin."

Eric reached over to give President Smathers a handshake, and as he did, gave him a look Smathers knew would be of steely resolve. Eric smiled and spoke, "I can go immediately. Passport's in my safe deposit box and I know how to dress for this time of the year. Just e-mail Miss Martin that I'm coming to support her mission."

Smathers gave Eric's hand one last, but firm shake. "Good, then it's all set. I'll have my secretary send an e-mail to her right now."

After his secretary, Mrs. Youngk came into the room, President Smathers spoke. "Please send this to Miss Sonja Martin at her e-mail address on the message she sent to me. Dear Miss Martin. Strayton University is pleased to share an interest in your quest for relics of the crucifixion of Jesus, and I am sending Professor Eric Stanfels to assist you. He will have Strayton's full financial and legal authority to assist and support you to whatever level the two of you agree. Please make immediate plans for his housing for at least one month. He will be flying to Tel Aviv in two days. I will wire you money to cover any immediate expenses you may incur before he arrives. Please know you have our complete confidence in this project. Lastly, thank you for keeping in touch with us at Strayton University. Sincerely, President Harlan Smathers."

Turning away from Mrs. Youngk, Smathers focused on Eric. "This e-mail opens the door to your next adventure. While Miss Martin may be unforgettably beautiful, I expect it'll be her intelligence, judgment and perseverance, all traits that we helped mold here at Strayton, that'll lead you to success with her search.

Go now with good luck and Godspeed, and tell Miss Martin I'll be thinking of her."

Caught up in the moment, he shook Smathers' hand again, a vigorous, pumping shake. "Thank you President Smathers, for all the help you've given me in the past, and for this expression of confidence in my future."

As Eric left the room, he stopped at the doorway and turned to take one more panoramic view of the room. He understood he was expected to come back with something of real value to Strayton University, and he was determined it would be something of value also to him—a renewed Eric Stanfels.

Chapter 8

"Professor Stanfels will be coming to help and finance this search for the relics of the crucifixion. Isn't that marvelous! He'll be able to help us find what we're looking for."

> --- Sonja, commenting to Elana after reading her e-mail from President Smathers.

"Professor Stanfels will be coming ta help and finance this search for the relics a the crucifixion. Isn't that marvelous! He'll be able ta help us find what we're looking for."

> --- Rigel, speaking to his men after reading the intercepted e-mail to Sonja.

No need existed for an internet service in Sonja's small apartment since she spent so much time at work using the Institute's. After sending her e-mail to President Smathers, she spent the morning at work filled with anticipation of a return message. It was only one working day since e-mailing Strayton University, but she sensed today just might be the day. Sonja's enthusiasm, laced with small doses of doubt, was evident every time an e-mail arrived. Looking over at Elana at the computer, she asked for the fifth time, "Anything for me?"

As if not even hearing her, Elana maintained an emotionless facade, then broke into a big smile. "Your long, tortured wait has ended." Elana said mockingly. "Your beloved Strayton University didn't forget you. You got an e-mail from PresSmathers@ Strayton.edu. Come look at it." She couldn't help but add, "Let's see if you still have a job."

Her relationship with Elana had always been strong and she was the only person Sonja knew she could always depend on. "I'm expecting President Smathers will address me as 'my dear friend Sonja'."

Watching Sonja devour the message, Elana saw the enthusiasm casting a glow all over her face. "Are you going to share this tidbit of good news with me or just sit there basking in your newly-found radiance?"

With a huge smile on her face and the light of a thousand stars glowing in her eyes, Sonja reached over to grasp both of Elana's hands. "It's good, no, great news. Better than I could've imagined! I was asking for a single but instead hit a home run."

"And my dear Sonja," a confused Elana asked, "what may I ask does that mean? You forget, I don't speak Americanese."

Raising up her hands as if she was surrendering, she conceded, "OK, OK, I understand. I'll try to speak understandable English. It's this way: I was asking for something small, but they're giving me much more than I ever thought to ask for."

Still not enough for a confused Elana. "What does this mean? What do you think they're giving you that's so great?"

Sonja assumed a deep, super-sophisticated voice, "My dearest Elana, you know I requested some financing, and naturally some small commitment from Strayton for this project. Now President Smathers has committed to me," she paused as she quickly acknowledged the slight, "I mean to us, the financial resources we'll need."

"Then you should be excited. You got what you wanted. I'm excited for both of us—a team not to be torn apart."

With both hands, Sonja grabbed Elana's shoulders and brought her face-to-face with her.

"No, I got more than that. President Smathers is also sending additional help—one of his associate professors to assist us. And not just any associate professor, but one of the most handsome and wonderful men I'd ever met. I can't believe he's sending Professor Eric Stanfels to finance and assist our search for the relics. Isn't that marvelous?"

Keeping a smile on her face, Elana hoped the doubts in her mind weren't leaking out for Sonja to read. They had been such a good team working together on all the assignments the Institute had given them. Even on this wild goose chase for the Ossuary of James, they paired-up well and let intellectual integrity override any tendency for their enthusiasm to distort their judgment. Now there would be three of them. Obviously this third element interjected into their equation would change the dynamics, for good or bad. Seeing the impact of this message on Sonja, Elana wondered if there was more to this than just an old professor coming to help them. "Now tell me, my dear Sonja, my dear glowing-like-a-million-kilowatt-bulb-Sonja, is there more to this Professor Stanfels than meets my eye?"

Raised eyebrows gave away hints of more emotion than might be found in her words. "Yes and maybe, no. Professor Stanfels was one of my religion professors at Strayton. At that time he had to be in his mid-twenties. Handsome, yet quiet. Elegant, not stuffy. Attentive, but not in a patronizing way. Stylish, but not in a pretentious way. And full of mystery. Professor Stanfels was the kind of man a woman would just die for. Is that American phrase too hard for you to understand? The type of a man you would give up your family for. The type of a man you would leave everything for if he asked you. Am I making my simple, American-self clear?"

Wrapping her arms across her chest, with a simulated hug and with a swaying of her shoulders, Elana couldn't resist giving some romantic impact to the scene. "Yes, very clear. Yes, a wonderful man. Yes, a charming man. But what about the mystery? What do you know about him, this Adonis of yours?"

"Cloaked in mystery and probably still is. And I admit not knowing enough about Eric Stanfels, and I'd like to, but naturally only in purely a platonic way."

With a look that said, 'Don't try to fool me', Elana slowly pronounced, "Ahhhhh. Now I see it moving into the more personal Eric. Pretty soon it becomes 'my dear Eric' doesn't it?"

"Oh Elana, no! It was never anything like that. But Eric Stanfels, Professor Stanfels to you my dear, had a very mysterious side no one at Strayton was able to decipher."

Now a more serious, inquisitive tone emerged. "Mysterious in attitude? Mysterious in intent? Mysterious in action? Mysterious in history? What was it Sonja? What was it that struck you so mysteriously?"

Picking up on the change in attitude, Sonja responded in-kind. "Probably mostly mysterious in history, if I can say that. The mystery was about his history, or what he'd done prior to coming back to teach at Strayton. He'd done his undergraduate schooling there, and it was well known he came from a family of ministers. Also well known, or at least thought to be true, that he didn't follow into the ministry because he went to work for the United States government in some capacity. That's where the mystery begins."

Trying to temper her questioning so as not look too divisively cynical, Elana feared her tone may have been too harsh. "Is that all there is? You think this guy is mysterious since he left Strayton and worked for the government, possibly even cleaning floors at the White House? And now he comes back to Strayton. Maybe he just couldn't get a job elsewhere. Maybe he couldn't stop spilling the wash bucket when he was mopping the floors. I'll ask you again my dear, is that all there is?"

Sonja ignored Elana's tone as she now reflected on her own history back at Strayton. "No, there's more. Some may be rumor, such as that he probably worked on some secret intelligence operation."

Taking off her restraints, Elana's cynicism ruled. "Do you mean like some double O-Bible? Like James Bond, 007, but O-O-Bible instead?"

Shaking her head and rolling her eyes, she wasn't going to let Elana get away with this. "Very cute, Elana, but not so cute. I do know he was involved in something, and from the looks of it, probably something important and pretty bad."

"Important and bad? How?"

Sonja sat in her chair and motioned for Elana to do the same. "Sit down. At the time I was a student in his class I did a lot of jogging. One day I was jogging through the campus and saw him standing by an old concrete bench. Wow! What a man. Tall, dark and handsome --- you know, the complete picture. Over six feet tall, brown hair and blue eyes – and in very good shape. In wet, clinging jogging clothes and with sweat rolling down his face and legs, that's when I noticed his leg. A large disfiguring scar on his right leg went from his knee to up under his shorts."

With raised eyebrows and an impish smile, Elana couldn't resist giggling, "Did you see how far up it went?"

Again, shaking her head in dismay, Sonja tried to regain the gravity of the moment. "Not very funny and obviously you didn't take enough, or any, religion courses. Anyway, still a young woman trying not to look like I was gawking at him, I stammered the obvious, 'Hi, I'm Sonja Martin—in your Religion 104 class. Looks like a great way to rehab your body back here at Strayton. Jogging I mean', I clumsily blurted out. He probably felt more compassion for my stumbling and bumbling than for his own injury."

"And?" Elana asked.

"That's when he answered and noticed me looking at his scar. 'Yes, Miss Martin, I remember you from my class, and you're right, jogging is a good way to rehab your body. But I'm not here to rehab my body, only my soul. That's why you come to Strayton, a great place for your soul, and a great place to enrich your faith. Look, I'll see you in class, but for now I better keep running while I'm still warmed-up.' Elana, that's when he jogged away, with a slight limp."

"Are you telling me he jogged away into the sunset just like the Lone Ranger?"

"C'mon, let's be serious! And you can't fool me, you did pick up some Americanese with that corny Lone Ranger stuff."

99

A serious pall covered Elana as she sat on the edge of her seat. "Tell me, my sometimes naïve Sonja, why did you feel so compelled to think this was a man of great mystery?"

Looking away from Elana as she struggled to describe what she saw and felt, Sonja paused, then turned back. "The scar, that scar was hideous, and not like a burn since the surrounding flesh looked normal. Like a huge gash. More importantly, when he spoke about rehabbing his soul, a mysterious, distant look came over him. Not a look of pride or accomplishment, but a look of being lost in some far-away place. There's deep mystery there, but I don't know where it leads to."

Finished with the wise remarks, Elana knew it was time to be serious. "How will you figure it out now if you couldn't figure it out then? Will this mission be about finding relics of the crucifixion or the lost relics of the psyche of the good and handsome professor? Do you think he'll be a good 'fit' with our team? I know we need the money, but what do we give-up to this handsome ex-professor of yours to get it? Are we going to lose our ideas and discoveries by having this Strayton guy taking them away from us?"

Putting her hand to her chin, Sonja rested her elbow on the desk top. "I'm not worried about him taking something from us. More importantly, President Smathers believes he'll bring us something. President Smathers' e-mail mentioned Professor Stanfels would be sent as a source of investigative strength. I'm assuming he knows more than we do about the strengths of Eric Stanfels. Come on Elana, don't get down on what you're not up on."

Nodding in agreement, Elana stopped the foolishness. "OK, let's do what we need to and see what fate brings us. What's Strayton expecting us to do for our guest?"

Leaning back in her chair, Sonja felt relaxed as she realized how much of her time she'd been spending simply trying to justify her perceptions of Eric. "We'll only need to get him a room with arrangements for at least a month. Other than that, he can do what he wants when he gets here. I've a car and don't know if he'll need one. Let's wait and see how it goes once we pick him up at the airport."

Realizing she created some unnecessary tension, no matter how good-natured it was, Elana sat back in her chair and added a conciliatory tone. "When does he come?"

Sonja brought her chair back on all four legs and got up. "He'll be here tomorrow, so we'll need to move quickly. The e-mail said he'll be flying to Tel Aviv tomorrow, and we need to find him an apartment."

A 'good soldier', Elana stood up and mimicked a salute. "At your service for whatever you need?"

Exasperated with her friend's antics, Sonja shook her head as a smile drifted over her face. "I know you're at my service. We're sisters in this search, but why don't you e-mail the Institute's Board that he's coming and bringing financial and investigative capabilities to our project. That'll get their interest while we plan on picking him up at the airport."

In Ireland, President Smathers' e-mail was equally well-received. Looking out his big picture window, Rigel was pleased the hacked e-mail came through just as Liam said it would. This spot in Ireland, where land and sea joined, was a perfect place for Rigel to have his lair. It was here he and Orion could share in the news of his new friend, this Elana Dutros.

Speaking as he looked over at the computer, Rigel had Liam's attention. "Hear we've got mail. What da ya have for us, my boy? What's falling into our greedy little hands?"

Without turning away from his screen, Liam answered, "Rigel, didn't I tell ya we could get what we wanted with that little bit a hacking. First we know who all these antique dealers are that help them, and now we find these women are going ta get help from somebody else. It's wonderful this friend a yours, this Elana, continues ta be so kind ta inform us a this."

Always quick with an answer or a question, Rigel fired back. "Liam, what's she telling ya boy? What's she dropping in our laps?"

Taking his time to read what was sent from this Strayton University to Ms. Sonja Martin, Liam's pride was evident in the tone of his voice. "Seems these girls hit the jackpot! This Sonja had the testicles ta ask her university for help and they're either dumb or smart enough ta agree. They're also sending over one a their professors, a Professor Stanfels, ta help the women. This Strayton University must have tons a money and they should be duly thanked for it. Maybe in the future, we should help them lose some a it."

Rigel smiled at his Liam. "Don't get carried away in another direction, just tell me what they're saying."

With his nose still stuck to the screen, Liam gave Rigel a synopsis. "From what I see here, this university sent this Professor Stanfels and he'll not only bring financial support, but he'll also bring his investigative talents. Da ya think that's good or bad for us?"

Thinking for a moment, while taking his time to look at all three of his men sitting around the room, Rigel's response was nothing short of enthusiastic. "This is great. These women have done the basic investigative groundwork and this university will now be able ta send their man into this project. Professor Stanfels will be coming ta help and finance this search for the relics a the crucifixion. Isn't that marvelous? He'll be able ta help us find what we're looking for. We'll see if he'll lead us ta where we want ta go, or if he'll just get in the way."

The irony of this situation struck Rigel. Wasn't it like all the things he saw with the Church. Here again, the women doing all of the work, and the men swoop in like vultures and steal the credit, glory and riches. Not much different than it was for his mum and all of those other millions of culturally-, religiously- and economically-enslaved women. Kept under the relentlessly pressuring thumb of the Church, these women would maintain their loyalties to it, and most importantly, to their children. Where would he be without his mum? Where should his brother Michael have been with such a wonderful mum, if it hadn't been for the Church? The thoughts of his mum were always on the surface of every supercharged neuron in his brain— she was his salvation!

Not totally sure where this was going, Conor turned away from looking out the bay window. "Rigel, even if we find these relics a the crucifixion, what'll we do with them. And what if the women and their new hero find them first? What'll we do then, or should we even be doing anything at all? Mind ya, we've more money than we need. With our haul from the Vatican, why go back ta the Church. Leave it alone damn it, screw it! My God Rigel, what's your affliction with the Church? Isn't it time ta move onta something else?"

Conor's remarks struck home with Rigel, because money they didn't need. They used one of those super minibombs so cleverly to blackmail the Vatican at Castle Gondolfo that no intelligence or police agency knew what was done until after Orion had looted their most secret bank accounts. Placing an un-activated super-mini bomb outside the Castle, right under the noses of their security people, was enough of a message of what would happen at St. Peters with an activated bomb. Vatican and Italian security were so threatened by the bomb they had no choice but to capitulate to Rigel's demands. Liam's internet accounts were so scrambled with his virus talents that nothing could be traced. For a simple $15 million, the papacy was safe and Orion was rich. And with an embarrassment so great for the Vatican and their security forces that everything was hushed up with not a word to be leaked about the theft and extortion.

Looking towards Conor, Rigel winked, then nodded his approval. "You're right, we don't need money. Ya've been wonderful in our quest ta redistribute the wealth from the richest ta the needy—good old needy us, but ya mustn't forget our church. Even though that Ossuary a James was a hoax, there's still a chance there's a pot a gold ta be found with this relics chase. Maybe something ta build my church on."

Sitting in an armchair large enough to comfortably hold a man of his size, Viktor looked on somewhat bemused. He was never totally sure of their discussions because these Irishmen had a different way of communicating. He spoke in his slow, halting style. "Rigel, you think you build church if we find this relic or something?"

Turning his attention away from the computer screen, Liam chimed in, "Rigel thinks he's another St. Peter. Not ta build his church on a rock like St. Peter, he's going ta build it on some relic. Good God, Rigel, what are ya really all about? Have ya been a closet Christian all along and now you're finally coming out a the closet?"

In a very serious tone, matching the look on his face, Viktor quickly added, "No! Rigel's not gay. Isn't coming out the closet! I think he loves this woman Elana."

Not to be distracted, Liam persisted, "Viktor, I wasn't talking about Rigel being gay. I only meant he might be a hidden Christian. Someone who always professed ta hate the Church, but who, deep within his heart and soul, does truly love it."

Now Rigel's concerns focused on how this foolish thought could divert his mission. Orion needed to stay on course and doing so probably required he open up with his men and let them know a little more. "No, I'm not a closet Christian, but the Church screwed my family and I'll screw it back. Now let's get back ta business."

Conor knew he could always say what he wanted. "Are we now going back ta our business and leaving this damned Church issue, your Church a the Internet, behind us?"

Not about to let them stray, Rigel returned to his plan. "Not really. There's good money ta be made in this church scheme, and cleaner money it'll be. There'll be respectability in this business if we find what I'm looking for."

Viktor was, and looked confused. "And we're going to get all that from some old relic?"

Although focusing on Viktor, Rigel's message was for all three men. "Yes. If we can find these relics, and they're from the crucifixion, my previous scheme for the Ossuary a James will still be viable."

"Rigel, still thinking about some genetic issue ya can manipulate from these relics?" asked a dubious Liam who's screwed-up, twisted look on his face

104

reinforced his lack of confidence in the concept. "What da ya expect ta find? What's the genetic contribution ta your cause."

"If there are any relics left a the crucifixion," Rigel started to say as he scanned this assemblage of his men, "there aren't many options what it, or they could be. Liam, after the crucifixion, what happened ta Jesus' clothes?"

Liam threw up his hands. "I've no idea what happened ta the clothes."

"Does anyone else want ta make a guess where the clothes went?" Rigel asked as this question was then met with dumbfounded silence. After a moment's pause, he answered his own question. "They were spread among the people at Golgotha. And as cloth, it's extremely unlikely they could've lasted 2,000 years. Not impossible, but unlikely."

"What could still be around? What would've lasted?" asked a very attentive Conor.

Now Rigel knew he caught their curiosity. "I see four different things that might have a chance ta last after the crucifixion, and they would've been made a materials that had some durability. First, the cross itself could have lasted."

"Being a wood, could the cross last this long?" asked Conor, not taking his wary eye off Rigel.

Sensing a problem with Conor's doubts, Rigel found himself focusing on him. He knew Conor's trust was crucial to the mission. "No, I don't think so, but, I could be wrong. If the Dead Sea Scrolls lasted, and they were a parchment, the wood a the cross could've lasted if it was stored at some dry place. But I'm still going ta guess this is not what we'd expect ta find."

"Then you would be thinking about something metal?" asked Viktor.

Rigel nodded approvingly. "Metal is what I believe is the only material that could have any long-term life. And if metal it is, then it must be one a several things. Liam, what da ya think these could be?"

"If I'm right," Liam responded, "they could be the Holy Grail, the cup that Jesus used at the Last Supper, or the spear that the Roman soldier used to pierce Jesus' side."

"Yes, my Liam," Rigel responded, "but I don't think either the spear or the cup are ta be found."

In jest, Conor chided Rigel, "Ya've still got ta be a closet Christian. Ya still know too much a that Biblical history."

Holding his hands out like Jesus on a Crucifix, Rigel shot back, "So crucify me! I had ta do something ta get ahead in that church system. But you're right, I retain a lot a what my dear old mum taught me. Me, her dutiful son, always at her knee listening ta her."

In his slow, Slavish, halting way, Viktor asked, "Why don't you think these are items?"

Rigel now let his focus stay on Viktor. "Both a these items have been searched for over the centuries, and we aren't going ta find what millions a people and dollars have already sought."

"And the spear that stuck him in the side?" asked Liam.

Rigel turned away from his men as some psychological gravity pulled him over to the bay window to look off into the distant heavens. Then he turned back when he was ready to talk. "Same reason! That spear was the focus a attention for thousands a years. From kings ta explorers, the efforts were made, dollars spent, and I'm sure, lives lost over the search for that spear. Legend has it that it was found and even Constantine owned it. Then the Hapsburgs a the Holy Roman Empire had it. Some king even took what he thought was the spear and used it in his coat-of-arms. I really don't think the spear is going ta exist for us. And even if it or the cup did exist, they would be a no value ta me, or more importantly, ta my genetic ambitions."

"Why?" the ever-inquisitive Liam persisted.

Rubbing his chin and patiently pausing before focusing his attention on Liam, Rigel continued. "Lads, I'm looking for blood or blood residue. What would ya do if ya had a nice cup or spear? Would ya polish it over the years? Would someone hundreds a years later, trying ta show their wonderful devotion ta this item of the crucifixion, would they not polish the cup or spear? I suspect they would. Who would've wanted ta show off a filthy bowl or spear?"

106

"If not the cup or spear, what da ya have left?" added Liam.

Rigel went over to the wall of this large living room. There adjacent to the large picture window with the view of the Shannon Estuary was a framed landscape painting hanging on the wall. He lifted the painting off the wall to expose the nail on which it had been suspended. Tugging the nail out of the wood, he turned to his men and saw the smiles on all of their faces as they now understood. "This, my lads, the nail! I can only hope if anything survived not only the elements, but also the thousands a years a searches, it would have ta be one or more a the three spikes that nailed Jesus ta the cross."

"But what you expect to find on spike?" asked Viktor.

A smiling Rigel couldn't wait to answer. "If the spikes a the crucifixion were stored someplace safe, there's a good chance there's some blood residue on them."

"Rigel, didn't ya say ya would have expected someone ta polish the cup and spear? Why not the spikes?" asked Liam.

Without leaking a hint of doubt, Rigel quickly responded. "Metal cups and spears were precious. They were smooth, made ta be shiny. Spikes were not. They were rough, unfinished metal. Lots a little spaces and nicks where blood could go. And while they may have been wiped off at some time, it wouldn't have been the custom ta polish them. Too rough and irregular with pits and grooves! If we find the spikes, and if some fool hasn't sand-blasted them, there's a good chance we'll find some blood residue."

Conor added his two cents. "What if ya find the spikes and there's blood residue still on them? Is it something a scientific value? Can it be recovered?"

Rigel's confidence now peaked, and he was on a roll. "If there's blood residue, it can be recovered. Scientists have taken blood off stone knives that butchered wooly mammoths 20,000 years ago and been able ta isolate DNA from that blood. There's no reason ta think we can't do the same thing here."

"Even if we find the spikes and there's blood present, what da we do with it?" asked Conor. "None a us has training in genetics."

Rigel's confident smile only got bigger. "That, my good friend Conor, is where your mysterious Salvador Dali comes into the picture. He's really Dr. Geoffrey Salvatore. And Conor, not a physician is he, but a Ph.D., a research doctor. Dr. Salvatore's a research scientist in molecular biology, what ya might call a genetic researcher or genetic engineer."

"But Rigel," Conor asked, "isn't that what we also heard from ya about this Sonja woman? Isn't she in some genetics field?"

"Yes, I probably did tell ya that from my meeting with Elana Dutros. Sonja Martin was keenly interested in that Ossuary a James so she could examine any bone residue. But, from the little I know and what we see on the internet, I'm not sure she's focusing on these relics as a source a genetic material. I might be wrong, but that's my hunch. Elana led me ta believe Sonja's work at her Biblical Institute was tied into that ossuary being the real thing. I suspect since she's probably desperate ta get some success that'll please her employers, she's going after any trail that looks hot ta her."

"Da ya think she'll eventually see this relics issue the same way ya see it as a genetic research issue?" asked Liam.

"It's hard ta say what she'll think, but if there're spikes ta be found, and since she saw that ossuary as a genetic opportunity, she's too smart ta not figure out the same potential that I see."

Always feeling a little on the outside of these conversations, Viktor wanted to be included in this questioning ritual. "You mean she's going to start church and compete with you?"

"Not really." Rigel now found himself having to stifle a laugh. "I don't think she'll start a church and be my competitor for the disenchanted Christian flock, but I do think she, and her two pals, will be some competition for these relics if they exist. We need ta make a quick move ta find out what those antique dealers know before the women go back ta them. This guy Stanfels can certainly help them if he leads them ta the relics, but we need ta get the information first."

A new confidence descended on Liam, and he looked the part. "What da ya have in mind for us ta do? Do I need ta change my computer surveillance?"

"No Liam, we need ta go ta Jerusalem and have a consultation with these dealers. We need ta see them before the women go back ten days from now."

Wanting to impress Rigel that he was on-board with the project, Conor added his insight. "Shall we split our group so we can see these three dealers a little quicker?"

"Not really," replied Rigel while giving a negative shake of his head. "First of all, I think we only need ta see the two who have information for her. We only need ta see this Weissberg and Protopolis. And we don't want ta split up because we might need the strength of our black Russian brother Viktor ta get some information from them."

An indignant Viktor stared at Rigel for a moment. "I am not black Russian, but to be called your brother pleases me. I am White Russian from Byelorussia, what now is called Belarus. Belarus always White Russia. I am White Russian!"

Sure that Viktor understood his intent, Rigel teased him, "You're my black Russian, ya do the black deeds for me. How da ya say in Russian, 'my black Russian brother'?"

A huge smile of acknowledgement and acceptance erupted on Viktor's face. "Moy chornee Ruski brat. My black Russian brother. But Rigel, I am still White Russian!"

Rigel reached over to grasp and then shake Viktor's hand while he patted him on the back, "You're my black Russian and my White Russian, moy chornee Ruski brat. C'mon, tomorrow we fly out a Shannon Airport ta London and then ta Tel Aviv. So let's make it a quick and sober night my boys because tomorrow will be a long day.

Chapter 9

Long and tiring and not too different from his first trip to Israel, this one was under far more favorable circumstances. But when the plane's engine shot out a far-reaching flame, nothing could suppress Eric's flashback to al-Azziz's home; to the explosive carnage and the Problem. He didn't lie to President Smathers because those flashbacks did still come like some dreaded form of demonic devastation driven deeply into his psyche.

The rough landing jolted Eric into reality since he didn't know this young woman he was to be meeting. He doubted he could recognize her, but he did recall her dark brown hair, her finely defined facial features, and her tall statuesque beauty like that of a runway model. Thinking about her brought him nothing but confusion. *What does she look like now*? And he wondered if she would know who he was, or would there be two lost souls roaming through the Ben Gurion Airport not knowing who they were looking for? After all this identification anxiety, he still had to figure out if he could help this dream team of young women and bring some value to them in terms of work, not just in money. Same held true for Strayton, as he wondered if he was worth their investment.

During the flight, Eric had time to analyze the task ahead, but now that he landed, he realized he hadn't come to any conclusions. Sure, if something was to be found, it had to be strong and somewhat indestructible, but what it was, he didn't know. He had great confidence in this Martin woman's intellect and judgment, but time would tell if he was wrong. Still, he preferred to believe Sonja Martin was all he and the President had hoped she would be.

110

Traveling to the Ben Gurion Airport at Tel Aviv, Sonja was a mass of internal conflict: excitement, anxiety and downright fear. Thank heaven Elana was driving since Sonja's concentration was elsewhere. Just the thought of Eric Stanfels shot an electric impulse through her body, and maybe now she could admit to herself that no other man in her life had stimulated her imagination, both professionally and personally. She lamented how the personal side of their relationship might only exist in her mind, and not in his.

But some of the anxiety Sonja experienced was more professional than personal. She knew the strain of performing for the Biblical Institute Board to justify her existence, but now, as this Stanfels meeting was imminent, she was acutely aware of the professional risk involved. She had doubled the number of institutions placing a bet on her judgment, and now the deepening doubts were starting to sap the strength in her mind. Disappointment was something she didn't deal with often in life as she was usually prescient in her thinking and pre-emptive in her actions. She had doubled, even tripled, the ante, and could have set herself up to fail not only the Institute and Strayton, but also her belief in controlling her own destiny. Sonja didn't suffer fools, and didn't want to be seen as one of them, at least not this time with Eric Stanfels. The magnitude of failure would explode exponentially if she failed him personally as well as professionally. Now she sensed her stress was rising like her temperature as the sweat under her blouse trickled down her torso, and left her worried it would leave a dark stain. What a great first impression!

The chameleon-like change in Sonja was quite evident to Elana on this drive to Ben Gurion Airport. Silence had been a seldom-seen stranger for Sonja, and now its presence nurtured Elana's suspicions about there being more to Sonja's memories of this Stanfels than she cared to admit. The incessant movement of Sonja's hands surprised Elana who always thought Sonja was in complete control of her emotions. And the changes in Sonja reinforced Elana's previous misgivings about adding Professor Stanfels to their mission. Any third person, not necessarily only Stanfels, would interfere with the internal chemistry of their team. She could only speculate how Stanfels' presence with the antique dealers would impact their commitment since it was Sonja's personal credibility that opened the doors with both Weissberg and Protopolis. Elana hoped this professor would be an equal partner in this venture instead of an alpha male who thought his wisdom and superior guidance were desperately needed. As she drove her car to Gate 03 at the Greeter's Hall of Ben Gurion Airport, she knew she would soon start to find some of the answers to her nagging concerns.

Carrying his luggage out the exit from the baggage area, Eric was stunned at his reception and a smile came on a face finally freed of its anxieties. Two women were standing there, with one holding a sign, 'Strayton Alum'. He was going to guess she was Sonja anyway, but the sign took away the doubt. He knew Elana's name from a follow-up e-mail, but now he had a face to go with it. He strode directly to Sonja, with an outstretched hand and greeted her first, "Miss Martin, I presume."

"James Bond, I presume," responded an amused Sonja as she tried to cut through some of the tension in the air. She extended her hand to shake his. "Forgive me Professor Stanfels, but that seemed like the appropriate response. And allow me to introduce you to my friend and associate at the Biblical Institute, Miss Elana Dutros."

Turning to Elana, Eric extended his hand while his dazzling blue eyes focused on hers. "Miss Dutros, I'm pleased to meet you since I know about your collaborative work with Miss Martin," he paused while looking at both of them, "and I look forward to being of assistance to you in any way I can. This is your venture, and Strayton University and I are here only to assist you."

Elana was impressed and felt the tide changing about her impressions of this Eric Stanfels. *Maybe Sonja was right. Maybe he's for real.* "Professor Stanfels, it's my pleasure, on behalf of the Biblical Institute to welcome you to Israel. Have you been here before?"

Caught off-guard by the question, Eric didn't forget his training to deny any CIA aspects of his past. "I've been here before, but never in the midst of such good company."

"Here before on business or pleasure?" Elana asked as Sonja could feel the tension rising as Elana's questioning took on a surprisingly sharp edge.

"Business before, but this trip, hopefully will be just pleasure. Have I imposed upon you too much to obtain lodging for me?"

Realizing he sidestepped her questioning, and then hesitating too long, Elana allowed an anxious Sonja to interrupt, "It was no problem at all, and we found a place not far from our Biblical Institute. Let's get into Elana's van and take you to your apartment."

After leaving the terminal, Eric sat in the back of the van as Sonja sat in the front passenger seat, next to Elana. Leaning forward in his seat with his arms resting on the headrest of each front seat, Eric stuck his head between them. "What brought you together for that ossuary project?"

Elana seized the initiative before Sonja had a chance to open her mouth. "I hired Sonja at the Biblical Institute because I knew her and of her unique ability to bring a genetics perspective to our religious endeavors."

Eager to be included, Sonja quickly turned in her seat to face Eric. "Since the ossuary was originally advertised as having been sealed before the owner opened it for testing, we, or probably more accurately, I, questioned if there might have been some residue of James' bones still in it. I had access to some previous genetic research that created a DNA data base all the way back to Aaron and Moses. And I thought it could biologically link James with Mary if we could find some DNA in that ossuary. This would've been a pivotal moment for Protestant theologians."

A mask of skepticism covered Eric's face after that remark. "Sure, and it would also upset the applecart for the rest of Christianity. But since the ossuary opportunity is gone, what's your interest in this new search for some relics? Purely biblical or is there some genetic issue?"

Still flexing her seniority over Sonja, Elana replied, "I think I also speak for Sonja that we see this purely as a biblical venture with no real genetic implications."

The discussion on the drive back to Jerusalem gave Eric an opportunity to determine what had been done, and for what reason. E-mail messages don't carry a lot about meaning or intent, and since emotion is lost in them, he needed to get a read on the depth of the commitment these two really had for this search.

He spotted Elana looking at him in the rearview mirror and spoke to her image. "What do you think you'll find? Something from the crucifixion itself or something from the time of the crucifixion? I'm thinking of something like one of Jesus' tools because he was a carpenter. Technically, Jesus' hammer from that time would fulfill the requirement of being from the time of the crucifixion, but not of it."

Eyes back on the road, Elana spoke with occasional glances to the mirror. "I haven't given this as much thought as Sonja has, so ask her what she thinks."

Sonja couldn't wait to chime in. "Yea, my thought process is a little further along than hers, and I can't rule out anything, even something as flimsy as parchment."

Pausing for a second, he looked at both of them, then added, "Who knows what we'll find, but what if it's something from the actual crucifixion? Elana, what do you think it would be?"

"I'd suspect either wood or metal. Cloth and parchment are probably too fragile to last 2,000 years, so that leaves us only with wood or metal."

Now leaning back in his seat, Eric wasn't done. "Cloth would definitely be too fragile, and who knows about parchment, so let me ask both of you Biblical Institute warriors, wood or metal? What'll it be?"

Too occupied driving to answer, Elana pointed her index finger at Sonja who got the message and responded as she turned back to face Eric. "Metal or wood? Don't rule out parchment. It could last 2,000 years under ideal

114

conditions, but the wood of the cross would have a far better chance to last than parchment." She then rapped her knuckles on the vehicle's metal dashboard frame. "Metal? If it were metal, it would probably be the spikes that nailed Jesus to the cross. Even though metal can rust, just like any of the other materials we've discussed, whatever it is, it had to be stored properly. And professor, you can't overlook cloth since intact 2,000-year-old cloth was discovered in 1950 in the Cave of Letters which is close to where the Dead Sea Scrolls were found."

Leaning forward, gazing in the mirror, Eric saw Elana's eyes follow his movement towards Sonja. "Do you think that's the origin of these new relics?"

"That's hard to say, but my feeling isn't that where they might be now is where they've been stored since the crucifixion. If the antique dealers are correct, we're going to be looking for help at one of the old monasteries. Some of the oldest are high in the mountains, but not necessarily where you have the same dryness as at the Dead Sea. None of the monasteries were in existence back at the time of the crucifixion, but the oldest ones had some chance of collecting valuable items from early Christianity. You just can't assume anything about where relics might've been for the last 2,000 years."

Eric's focus was fixated on Sonja and her unadulterated beauty. "I don't know what Elana thought of your answer, but I'm curious why you said that if it's metal, you'd be thinking of the spikes and not maybe the spear that pierced Jesus' side or the Holy Grail. Why not those?"

Sonja twisted in her seat to make eye contact when she spoke. "Wherever the spear and the Grail are to be found, I don't think they're going to be where we're looking. Those two items have been searched for, found and then searched for again. If we're going to be lucky and find a relic of the actual crucifixion, it's probably going to be wood from the cross or one or more of the spikes. Milan's Duomo Cathedral thinks they have one of the spikes and the Trier Cathedral in Germany claims they have another. Then some people claim there were four spikes instead of three. May not be a trace of truth to any of these claims. Who knows what we're looking for?"

115

Eric's eyes were riveted on Sonja. "Have a guess?"

Confident, yet absent of arrogance, Sonja answered. "I'd guess the spikes. Regardless how many there are, if they're rough, we just might find some blood residue on them."

Intrigued by Sonja and not realizing how intensely he was focusing on her to the exclusion of Elana, he continued. "And if we do, what's next?"

Turning her head away from him, her answer was immersed in a laugh. "Thinking about genetics again, you're throwing my mind into a tizzy. Finding residual blood on an old spike that was never reused and carefully preserved is not unrealistic. If we find some residual blood on the spikes, we could use that Mary-to-Elizabeth-to-Aaron trail which could lead us to the Jewish priest DNA study. But I don't know if you're aware of that study."

Unbuckling his seatbelt and leaning further forward in the backseat, Eric tried to get even closer to them. "I'm aware of that study because of your contact with Strayton. I found it odd that a molecular geneticist found something interesting in the Ossuary of James, but when I knew I was coming here, an internet search led me to the Jewish Priest Study. I was toying with you about what you were expecting to find, because if we find anything, my hunch is we find the spikes."

Elana added, "So you thought all along it would be the spikes. Why?"

Seeing Elana looking back at him in the rear-view mirror, Eric hesitated, stared at her eyes then answered, "Pretty much for the same reasons as Sonja. There's been a tremendous focus on the Holy Grail, and it's not going to be discovered on the simple word of an antique dealer or two. Same for the soldier's spear, wherever it is, we aren't likely to be bumping into it any time soon."

As Elana drove to Eric's apartment, the atmosphere in the car changed to one of quiet relaxation. He was tired and had fallen asleep until Elana raised her voice to bring him back into the real world. "Sorry to wake you, but we're at your apartment."

An overly-eager Sonja added, as she looked back at a travel-weary Eric, "Let's get together tomorrow morning and plan our work with the antique dealers."

"Make it around noon," Eric said somewhat groggily. "I need some time to get acquainted with the city."

"Sorry," Sonja said, "we forgot how many time zones you've flown through."

Eric shook his head. "That's not really the issue. I'll adapt quickly, but I need some time to look at the city, and to get a feel for it. Let's not plan anything before 11:00 AM."

"Well for now, let's get you out of here," Sonja added as she opened her door to get out and help him. "Let me help you with your bags."

"No, I'm fine. See you tomorrow at your office," Eric said as stepped out of the van and proceeded to trudge up the steps.

As Elana drove away, she looked at Sonja and saw nothing but sheer rapture reflected from her glowing face.

Turning in her seat to face her, the words couldn't come quick enough out of Sonja's mouth. "What do you think of him?"

Elana's eyes rolled as she was forced to acknowledge, "He appears to be just as you described, but I really haven't had enough time to get to know him. I hope I wasn't too aggressive in my questioning, but there's no doubt he's mysterious."

With eyebrows raised, Sonja added, "I was more concerned with your questions than he appeared to be, but at least he didn't seem shaken with you being the Grand Inquisitor."

Elana laughed. "Maybe I was being too nosey. My mother always told me you can get your nose cut off when you act like that."

"Well I think it's OK, but you can't be looking forward to tomorrow's meeting more than I. Probably my old Strayton loyalty showing through."

"Enough's enough!" Elana said jokingly. "I can't stand it anymore. It's not those old loyalties showing, it's a woman with a deep and serious case of infatuation."

As both women were now going their separate ways, their departure was a positive reflection on a day that had gone well. One probably couldn't find three more happy people in Jerusalem, with the exception being the four men landing at the airport from a trip that started at the Shannon Airport in Ireland. While their El Al airliner would arrive two hours later than Eric's, they didn't drive to Jerusalem. They had money to spare and luxuriated in a limousine from the King David Hotel. With this Stanfels now helping the women, their focus was on pre-empting the women's access to the antique dealers.

Chapter 10

The most elegant hotel in Jerusalem was the King David, and Rigel saw no realistic reason his men shouldn't stay in one of its most luxurious suites with individual bedrooms and a large conference room. They earned their money and Rigel had no qualms about spending it 'ta spoil me Orion'. With no one in Jerusalem knowing who they were, and with Europeans out-and-about, Rigel knew they could move about the city with impunity

From his panoramic view off the King David's balcony, the Old City lay before him and Rigel sensed a special identity with the history of the Jewish people. Their struggle over the centuries was against oppressors of various religions and nationalities while he had only one oppressor, the Church. Reflecting on how the Jewish freedom fighters, the Menachem Begin-led Irgun, bombed the King David in 1946 to punish the British and achieve their goals, Rigel thought of the parallels to his threat of blowing up the Castle Gondolfo in order to achieve his. Thoughts of the dominating Church constantly crept into his consciousness and festered from burrowing so deeply into his wounded subconscious. *This trip might be just what I need to be free of the Church's yoke, just like the Irgun threw off the yoke of the damned British. Why couldn't the Irish do that?*

Taking their seats surrounding his sofa, Rigel was finally able to open up with his men. "Any more e-mails about the women?"

An always-scanning Liam was quick to add, "Nothing we don't already know 'cause they're just waiting ta go back ta the antique dealers in two days."

119

Speaking with a forcefulness that would underlie what he planned for the dealers, Rigel didn't hide the aggressiveness tone in his answer, "Good! No reason ta take any chances because ya never know what'll happen since they've added this professor. Get this man involved and he could screw-up everything before we have our way with the dealers."

With a smirk on his face and a chuckle in his voice, Conor interrupted, "Rigel, can't a man do anything right in this world?"

Flashing back to what the absence of a dad meant to his mother's plans for the future of her family, Rigel somehow kept a sense of humor. "A man can do anything he wants, but too often he screws-up the best-laid plans a women. Ya might say he's the most important link in the chain we call a family, because the most important link is the weakest link. But for now, let's not lose the focus on our plans since they're built on what these women will do."

"What do you mean?" Viktor asked with a deeply resonating voice echoing against the walls of the room.

Up from the sofa and over to the window Rigel sprang to gaze at the hustle and bustle of the Old City. He then turned back to Viktor. "We'll do what the Church always did. Let the women do all the work, and carry the load without a whimper. Then screw them out a the riches, the glory and most importantly, the responsibility and influence. Isn't that just like the Church? Jesus was wrong. Saint Peter wasn't the rock the Church was ta be built on, it was women! Always been, and always will be women who are the rock and foundation the Church was built on. The stupid old white men a the Church can't figure it out, just like all the old men everywhere who screw up the world. It's them, not women who do the damage. We'll let this Sonja and Elana find out what they can, and then steal their work while they only get a little bitter manna from heaven."

Sensing this conversation needed to be turned to the task at hand, Liam interjected, "Rigel, if we need ta move today, since the whole day's ahead a us, what da ya want ta do?"

Flipping an approving hand gesture Liam's way, Rigel continued, "You're right, don't get me started on the Church. We'll need ta move quickly, but Liam, stay here while the rest a us go first ta this Weissberg's shop, then off ta Protopolis. Any questions?"

No one batted even an eyelash.

"Good, then let's go down ta the bar for a Guinness. That's why I chose this place, it's got Guinness at the bar."

"Do I need to drink that sludge?" came the Slavic voice.

"No," chimed in a laughing Rigel. "ya can drink your vodka."

But Conor couldn't resist, "Why da ya drink that Chopin vodka? Chopin was Polish."

"I drink Chopin vodka because most people in Belarus have Polish blood in them, and I like Chopin's Polonaise Symphony. He make good music and good vodka."

Not wishing to let this moment of frivolity pass, Conor's words swiftly shot back at Viktor, "Chopin's dead. How's he making good vodka?"

With a serious look on his face, Viktor answered, "I don't know, but this White Russian likes it better than old Russian potato vodka."

Laughing with a frivolity that masked the intent of their mission, they quickly left for the bar. After spending an hour drinking their libations of choice, Rigel, Conor and Viktor went off in three different taxis to Weissberg's, where each of them would be deposited at different points within one block of his shop. Each was to walk alone as they followed Rigel's lead down the alley. Three European men walking together down the alley might raise suspicions, so Rigel directed them to individually browse among the vendors rather than just going straight to Weissberg's.

The plan was activated; the men deposited by taxi and Rigel led the way down the alley. Upon reaching Weissberg's address, he opened the door to the shop, then looked back and saw Conor sticking his nose into different merchants' displays. Rigel could only assume Viktor, even though he couldn't be seen, was doing the same. But knowing Viktor, he was probably buying something to feed his face. He had an insatiable Slavic appetite for anything he could get his hands on. Probably a result of growing up in the luxury-starved Soviet Union! In Ireland, you knew if you ever found some money, you could buy something good with it, but apparently that wasn't the case for Viktor where deprivation, physical, psychological and economic, caused many White Russians to be blue Russians. Blue Russians, 'blue' with the depression of a depraved land; 'blue' from the constriction of their blood vessels being exposed to the constant cold; and 'blue' from the awesome allocations of alcohol that staved off the constant lack of hope for a better life.

Abraham Weissberg routinely left his shop door unlocked and wasn't too surprised when a man entered with a greeting of 'Good day'. He recognized the voice as that of a European, but couldn't differentiate between an Englishman, Scotsman or an Irishman. Looking up from his desk, he saw a handsome, red haired man of approximately thirty years of age, but he chose to ignore him. Better to haggle over prices when the customer thought you weren't interested or too eager to sell.

"Good day to you. Look around if you like," Weissberg replied as he recorded this visit with a notation about the customer on a piece of paper. He'd been robbed once by a team of thieves and never forgot to make a record of who came in.

Looking around and wanting to give Conor some time to get to the shop, Rigel gave a friendly reply. "Don't mind if I do."

After observing Rigel for several minutes, Abraham inquired, "Is there something special you are seeking?"

Before Rigel could answer, Conor burst into the shop. Avoiding any acknowledgement of Conor, Rigel stayed focused on Weissberg. "Yes, I'm interested in some very old pottery from as far back in Christianity as ya can find."

The newly-arrived Conor avoided any eye contact with Rigel and Weissberg, and neither Irishman saw the old man writing something down on his paper. Weissberg's discomfort was starting to grow since he had been robbed before by a pair of men. *But these men don't seem to know each other*, he thought while pointing at the wares on his shelves, "There are different types of pottery vessels from vases to bowls, and all marked with the approximate time in history when they were made."

Separately browsing, Rigel and Conor looked at the different items on display, but Viktor now came through the door and created such a sinister synergy with the two men that the old man suddenly sensed trouble.

Weissberg looked at this third man and a sharp pang of fear followed the chill that had already run down his spine. He spoke quickly to Viktor while watching the impact of his words on the other two men. "How can I help you?"

Trying to appear unaware of the other two men, Viktor strode over to Weissberg's desk and picked up a cup that was being used as a pencil holder. As he wrapped his fleshy right hand around the cup, Weissberg couldn't help but notice the tattoo on the back of Viktor's hand.

Smelling the old man's fear seeping profusely through his pores, Viktor smugly smiled, "Yes, old man, I would like to see metal antiques you have."

Even at his old age, Weissberg knew this man's English had a Russian influence since there were so many Russian Jews in Jerusalem. "If you want to look for metal objects, look in the lower drawer over on the wall." Pointing to the drawer, he had gotten Viktor to focus there and walk over to it while he had enough time to sketch the tattoo. "Feel free to open the drawer and look for yourself." he told this third man without looking away from his drawing.

On cue, and with perfect timing, all three men turned to Weissberg with Rigel moving quickly to grab him by his shirt. "We're here for something else, and if ya shout or cry-out, my man will shut ya up forever. Da ya understand?"

An intimidated Weissberg squeaked like a little mouse, "Yes."

Shoving his menacing face into Weissberg's, and with a shower of spittle covering him, Rigel heaped his hostility on this old man. "We're aware you've

123

been helping this Sonja Martin. And we know you've told her there might be some relics from the time a the crucifixion a Jesus. Don't be confused because we know everything you've already told her, but we don't know what you're going ta tell her next when she visits ya. If ya don't tell me all you and your friend Protopolis know, I'll have my Russian interrogator get it out a ya with his truth serum. And I'll guarantee ya won't like it!"

"I don't have more to tell," whimpered the shaking, frightened old man.

Knowing that Weissberg's bone-chilling fear would override his sense of honor to Sonja, Rigel patiently persisted. "We know ya told her something could be at some monasteries, but which ones, and why?"

Weissberg answered in that same squeaky, fear-weakened voice. "Yes, I did tell her about the two monasteries, Khor Virap and St. Catherine's."

With a vise-like grip, Rigel tightened his hold on the old man's shirt, and with his face so close their noses touched, he could smell the fear on Weissberg's breath. "And why da ya think something's there?"

Partly out of fear and partly due to a sense of residual loyalty to Sonja, the old man hesitated long enough for Rigel, impatient with his progress, to turn to Viktor. "Give him a bit a your truth serum."

With a lightning move, Viktor grabbed Weissberg by the throat so he couldn't scream and in a threatening, guttural voice spoke slowly, "If you don't tell what we want, I keep squeezing your throat til your spit and blood mix together. Then you tell us all we want to know. Tell me what I want or drown in your blood."

Never before had Abraham Weissberg experienced this kind of fear. Not just the presence of three hostile men, but also this strangling suffocation of his throat. "Please," he barely spoke, "let me talk."

Removing his strangling claw, Viktor shoved him towards Rigel. "Scream and I have your throat in my hands before sound gets out!"

Rigel interceded in a conciliatory, good-cop style, "Please Mr. Weissberg, we're not trying ta be unreasonable, just tell us what you're going ta tell Miss

124

Sonja. Why those two monasteries? What more have ya learned since ya last spoke ta her?"

Partly from fear and partly from gasping for air, Weissberg could barely speak, but he choked out his words. "Those two monasteries are the oldest with some connection to the times of post-crucifixion history. Khor Virap is older than St. Catherine's and always had a reputation as a special hiding for centuries, St. Catherine's was the safest place for hiding hundreds of old Christian items."

"Why?" pointedly asked the irate Irish inquisitor as his voice raised in tone and implied violence.

Abraham continued after taking two deep breaths. "St. Catherine's was the place for Christian articles in the 4th Century. St. Catherine's is not as old as Khor Virap, but impenetrable to any outsiders, and no one could get into it due to its position on Mt. Sinai and it's unique structure. No one ever successfully raided that monastery, and it is thought to have a treasure of ancient items, and probably too many even for them to count."

"Why look at Khor Virap?" asked Rigel.

With tears bathing his old, dark eyes, and with a downturned mouth ready to give out a solicitous whimper, he pleaded, "Let me be. Please, don't hurt me."

But Rigel was relentless. "Tell us why you'd look at Khor Virap?"

Through his tears and fears, Abraham Weissberg was barely able to respond, but he still tried. "Khor Virap was a part of the early Jewish territory and on a trade route to Jerusalem. It had a unique place in Biblical history, across from Mt. Ararat where Noah's Ark landed. I don't know what they have there, but it and St. Catherine's are the only places I would look."

In a conciliatory gesture, Rigel eased his grip. "And what did ya learn from your friend Protopolis?"

Weissberg seemed to gain strength as Rigel loosened his grip. "Nothing that he wanted to share with me! I think he wanted to see the beautiful young woman again."

"Good," said Rigel as he turned to Viktor. "Take him into his backroom and see if he's holding back anything on us."

Before Weissberg could utter a sound, Viktor's big hand closed around his throat stifling his scream. Viktor hauled the old man into the back room from which emerged a series of muffled noises, a thrashing sound and then a silence of finality. After a few minutes, Viktor emerged from the other room and grabbed a curtain to dry his bloody hand. Indifferent to his actions, he turned to Rigel. "Not able to tell more. Truth serum worked, and he wasn't lying."

"He wasn't able ta tell us more?" Rigel said as he turned to Conor. "Now we need ta go and find what the Greek knows. Viktor, leave first and I'll follow shortly afterward. Conor, wait at least five minutes after I leave before ya go, then we can meet as planned over by Protopolis' street."

Leaving in the sequence Rigel pre-ordained, each man walked back the alley and browsed again at the merchandise and foodstuffs that were available. Nothing seemed abnormal about these men as they wove their way out of this small artery at the heart of the city's small business operations. True-to-form, since Protopolis' shop was on a street not far from Weissberg's, Rigel's plan was for each of them to separately walk there.

The small side street to Protopolis' shop served as the chief conduit of commerce for a group of merchants who looked no different from those near Weissberg's. Ready to turn down this congested alley, Rigel commented to Conor and Viktor, "Same as before—same timing and same attempt ta look at all the wonderful things for sale." As they nodded, Rigel added, "Ready mates, let's have at it, and don't be all stopping at the same vendors. Mix it up just a bit."

Dutifully leading the way, Rigel looked, browsed, and even did a little haggling with one vendor. Conor followed at a delay that shouldn't have created any sense of relationship between the two. When Conor could see Rigel entering the antique shop, he turned and saw Viktor winding his way through the shopping stalls. The timing looked good as he proceeded towards Protopolis' door, but he didn't see the disturbance surrounding Viktor. Always hungry, Viktor couldn't pass the small grill which was cooking lamb over a charcoal fire. Reacting, but not thinking, Viktor reached over to the grill and snatched a skewer of lamb and proceeded to walk away without any thought of paying for it. As the shopkeeper protested, Viktor waved him away with the same meaty right hand that had snatched the lamb. As the vendor persisted, Viktor held the lamb in this left hand and used that club of a right hand to push him away. Only when the vendor's wife joined in the fray and kicked Viktor did he relent and pay for the morsel of lamb. After a cacophony of hostile voices calling him every foul name in the Hebrew language, Viktor finally arrived at Protopolis' door.

On the door into Protopolis' shop was a simple brass bell which gave out its beckoning call as Rigel entered. Not wanting to look hostile or sinister, Rigel immediately extended his hand to the reluctant merchant and introduced himself with his best British accent. "Hello my good man. Might you just be the lucky proprietor of this shop?"

"Yes," replied a disinterested Protopolis without looking up. "This is my shop, and as you can see on the door, I am in the business of antiques. What can I do for you?"

Wanting to allow some time to lapse so that Conor could come through the door, Rigel turned to look at what was on the shelves. Turned left, then right and finally towards the old man just as Conor entered the store. "I'm looking for something nice for my wife, something special, like a vase or a bowl for holding fruit. I'll look around at your wares if you would like to take care of this man." Rigel said as he pointed to Conor.

"Thank you, but I'll be just looking for some ideas to be found on your shelves," Conor said in a poor French-accented style as he dismissively waved the shopkeeper away.

Protopolis nodded towards Conor as to imply that he would be with him once he served this other gentleman. To Rigel he asked, "Does your wife know what you are looking for? Most women don't trust men to purchase antiques, or anything."

"Oh, I'm sure she'll like anything I choose," Rigel said with a dismissive hand gesture.

No sooner had these words escaped Rigel's lips than Viktor came barging into the shop. Forgetting to remain silent and appear independent of Rigel and Conor, Viktor spontaneously commented, "Stupid woman kicked me over a piece of lamb." Realizing his mistake of speaking, he reflexively put his hand over his gaping mouth. "I be quiet."

Exposed as a collaborator, Rigel responded by grabbing Protopolis by his shirt and, making no pretense to be British, berated him in his most-Irish of voices, "Don't even think a making any noise or my big man will kill ya in a heartbeat. Stay calm and still and ya won't get hurt. But if ya try ta make any contact with your phone or if ya scream, he'll hurt ya. Da ya understand?"

"Yes, yes ... I understand," whimpered the very frightened Protopolis. "What do you want here?" he asked barely able to spill the words from such trembling lips. "Who sent you?"

Rigel sugar-coated his duplicitous lie with a phony grin. "The woman sent us here ta find out what ya want ta tell her about the monasteries. Is it Khor Virap or St. Catherine's holding the treasure for Sonja Martin?"

Shaking his head in dismay, Protopolis asked, "Why are you here? You don't work with Miss Martin? Leave before I call the police."

Twisting the old man's shirt even tighter, Rigel spewed words and spittle into Protopolis' face. "You'll not be calling the police or anyone else. We're here, just like the Martin woman, looking for the relics from the crucifixion. We know from your meeting with her ya think there's something out there somewhere, and now we need ya ta tell us where. We've already talked ta your friend Weissberg and he told us we needed ta talk ta you before the woman does."

"Rubbish!" Protopolis spat out through clenched teeth. "I have nothing to tell you."

"We know Weissberg thought you knew something, and if you don't tell us, I'll have my man here give ya a Russian interrogation? Then you'll tell us all ya know, but ya won't be able ta share the joy a giving if my Russian gets his hands on ya."

Firm in his resolve, the diminutive Protopolis defiantly straightened his spine and stood his tallest. "No, there is nothing else I know. Abraham was mistaken. I don't know where he would have gotten such an idea that I knew anything else. You should go back to talk to him and insist this time he tell you the truth."

Shifting his gaze from the old man to Viktor, Rigel added, "My dear Protopolis, I can assure ya we've gotten from Mr. Weissberg all he can tell us, and I know you're going ta do the same before we're done."

With a discrete nod of his head, Rigel gave a signal to Viktor who unleashed a mighty right hand quickly thrusting over the short distance to Protopolis' throat. With gurgling sounds generated from a severely stressed face, Rigel and Viktor knew it would only be a short time before they got what they needed.

"Please, please," pleaded a panicked Protopolis as he wet his pants and barely got a sound out, "don't hurt me. I will tell all I know if you take your hand off of my neck."

With a nod from Rigel, Viktor loosened his grip and spoke slowly, "OK, you talk, but if you make a cry or scream, I kill you with my bare hands."

Desperation dominated the dealer's darting eyes, seeking some solace from Viktor, then Rigel and finally, Conor. Like a condemned prisoner facing his eager executioners and knowing there was no way out, Protopolis still mustered up the hope that one of these faces just might hold some small spot of sympathy for him. The cold chill of reality swept over him like an arctic wind blowing over his fragile landscape, leaving no hope in sight. He knew there was no way to resist, and probably no way to escape with his life.

Resigned to his fate, yet still clinging to a small shard of hope, Protopolis relinquished the last tidbit of information he knew. "If there is a relic, it is probably at the Russian monastery. That's all I could get from a very old man who heard all the old stories. He said no one other than the Russians seemed to have control of any relics."

With an increasing impatience past its boiling point, Rigel grabbed Protopolis by the throat and demanded through clenched teeth and an ugly, distorted mouth, "What da ya mean the Russians? Are ya saying there are no relics at either a the two monasteries? Should we not waste our time at this Khor Virap or St. Catherine's and go ta Russia?"

"No," replied the shaking, old man, "The Russian monastery is where I heard there might be relics. For years, the old men said there was something at a Russian monastery. Since Khor Virap is in Armenia, but was a part of Russia, this is where I think they were talking about."

Looking at Viktor, Rigel nodded toward the back room. "Take Mr. Protopolis ta the back a his store and try your truth serum. I'll leave now, and Conor, follow me in five minutes. Viktor, when you're done, then ya can leave. None of us needs ta do any shopping, but don't appear ta be in a hurry. Now, go, Viktor, go!"

Grabbing the hopelessly resigned Protopolis by his arm, Viktor shoved his other hand over the old man's mouth so he couldn't scream even in a reflexive fashion. As Rigel opened the door, he could hear the scuffle in the back room that he assumed was going to be a last dance, a death dance so to speak, for Mr. Protopolis.

As the minutes passed slowly, Rigel and Conor waited for Viktor to finally pass through the vendors in the small street. Where they stood at the end of the street, they could see Viktor making his last steps. However, the compulsive eating urge, wedged deeply within Viktor's primordial brain, compelled him to take another chunk of lamb as he passed the cursing wife of the previously-abused vendor. This time, Viktor threw enough coinage to more than pay for the lamb. But that mighty right hand that stole the lamb and then begrudgingly paid for it was not to be forgotten by an old wife who would remember the particulars of any person who ever abused her loyal, if very meek, husband.

Turning the corner off of the small street, on to Agrippas, Viktor was confronted with Conor's questioning. "Did he tell ya anything else?"

"He said nothing more. Maybe gave him truth serum too soon."

"What da ya mean 'too soon'?" asked Conor.

"His neck snapped before he could say much more."

An annoyed Rigel quickly shot back, "Da ya mean ya killed him before he had a chance ta say anything?"

"He said he'd told us all he knew. He said to ask Weissberg if we needed more information. I told him Weissberg was dead. That's when he tried to shake loose and maybe I squeezed too hard."

Leading the way as they walked over to a taxi, Rigel disgustedly spouted, "Just follow Conor and me, and we can get a taxi back ta the hotel. Then we need ta plan on how ta get ta this Khor Virap. Da ya speak Armenian?"

Shaking his head, Viktor couldn't look at Rigel as he answered. "No, but all Armenians speak Russian. That was requirement of old Soviet Union. They be able to speak to me. Be no problems unless they need some truth serum."

A very frustrated Rigel pointed for Viktor to get in the taxi. "For now, let's see if we can get what we need without killing anyone else. Let's go and see if Liam has heard anything."

Chapter 11

She was sure the dynamic changed, but didn't know why. She certainly suspected it was more than just some confusing cloud surrounding Eric's history and even this present mission. Sonja seemed increasingly infatuated with her Strayton colleague, and Elana knew it was up to her to keep Sonja and this relics project on line. It wasn't like much had really happened between Sonja and Eric in this short time, but Elana could feel the intensifying glow, with its simmering heat, probably representing the escape of some repressed, energized emotion from her previous infatuation at Strayton.

Understanding the changes in Sonja wasn't complex, but Elana still couldn't fathom the depth of the dark mystery masking Eric. She had no trouble acknowledging some tinge of darkness based on Sonja's descriptions of his mysterious past. Maybe something coming from deep within some cavernous abyss related to an Eric that Sonja didn't know could even exist. Elana concluded that reading him, with the limited information she had, was like trying to read hieroglyphics without a Rosetta stone. But she also knew she needed to avoid getting negative since there was no confusion they needed Eric's money and, to some degree, maybe even his experience. That nagging feeling about Eric had burned its brand in her brain, and she didn't know if she could, or even should douse it with the coolant of naïve confidence that Sonja had been serving.

Even though he didn't want to start work too early, it was evident Eric was an early riser, and Elana couldn't accept his late arrivals since she and Sonja were always at work by 8:00 AM. While Eric said it was necessary to just get reacquainted with Jerusalem, Elana's doubts grew whether his return to Israel had something to do with issues other than representing Strayton University. Where did he go for so long in the morning, and what was he looking for that was not a part of their search for the relics? As she noticed a slight twitching of her nose, she couldn't help thinking, *Yes, he is mysterious, but hopefully his mysterious past doesn't mean a mysterious future for me and Sonja!*

Not having seen much of Jerusalem on his previous posting with the CIA, now was Eric's chance to visit the holy places of the Bible. But even his immersion in this pool of Christian spirituality couldn't eradicate the ghosts of his pathetic past posting. Couldn't disassociate himself from those psychic returns to his traumatic past in Gaza, and couldn't repress the moral inferno that erupted so explosively into his consciousness.

Wandering along one of the small streets where vendors were busy preparing their stalls with the goods for the day, Eric didn't anticipate what was about to happen next to him when an old woman lit her lighter fluid-soaked charcoal. An explosive eruption of fire startled him as he physically jumped back a few feet while his memory, even quicker, leapt back what seemed like eons in time to the night of the bombing in Gaza and to the Problem. He sensed, felt, and saw bodies flying everywhere even though the only thing flying was the black shawl the woman vendor was wearing. It took only seconds to regain his composure, but the psychic wounds had been re-opened and immediately started to fester. He hoped being here again might suppress those damaged neurons still dripping with the electric charges that digitized this horrible picture in his mind, but apparently he was wrong since no escape could be crafted. He was forced to admit these deep, searing intrusions from his subconscious were a reminder of that time when everything had all gone wrong. And now that time had come again, and the ravages of the deepest inferno of his psychological Hell had re-surfaced into a mind that desperately begged to find only barren ground for such memories.

Unable to constrain her enthusiasm for her visit to the dealers, Sonja had been nearly out of her wits waiting for the day to arrive. Sitting in her office cubicle, she sent an e-mail to the Board of the Institute stating she was going to finally find out what these dealers knew. She knew the e-mail would make them happy since it implied she was making progress on their behalf even with this helper from Strayton. Whether her e-mail had the intended effect on the Board was unknown, but it certainly made some Irishmen very happy since they could now gauge their position relative to the progress of this Sonja and her pals.

Concentrating on her computer, Sonja was startled as Eric poked his head around the corner of her cubicle. "Miss Sonja, are you ready to be the Grand Inquisitor with the dealers?"

Looking curiously at his funny grin and his head cocked sideways, she answered with an ever-present smile, "Am I ready? You bet! Are they ready for me? Who knows, but I'll try not to intimidate them too much. Do you and Elana want to come along?" she asked as she rose from her chair.

The grin stayed there as he cocked an eyebrow. "Why? Don't you have a charming chemistry with them? Maybe these old guys only want to see you, not two tag-alongs. Or, are you afraid of something?"

Staring back, no smile graced her face. The radiance of her hazel eyes was diminished as they squinted to match the harsh features of her mouth replacing what had been a most pleasant and somewhat sensuous smile. "Not afraid, but I don't like that little alley with all those vendors staring at me. To you it may not seem so threatening, but to a woman, you know there are hundreds of eyes watching your every step, and probably leering at every movement of your anatomy."

Trying to be a supportive buddy, he put a hand on her shoulder. "Don't sweat it. We'll go, but are you concerned about the dealers?" he asked as he took his hand away and leaned back on her desk.

"No, not really other than maybe a little anxiety about them changing their minds and not wanting to help," she said as she turned her attention to what seemed like someone coming to her cubicle.

Popping into the cubicle with a buoyant step, Elana brought an upbeat tempo to what had evolved into a more serious discussion loaded with doubt and indecision. "What are you two conspiring about?" she asked in a lighthearted tone. "Did the two of you go to the dealers this morning and leave me stuck here holding the bag?"

"No," replied Sonja with the tone of her voice rising to the elevated attitude that Elana infused into the cubicle. "We're just talking about going to the dealers as a team. You and Eric with me, but I'll be the only one going into the shops."

"Sounds good to me because Eric and I can shop the old marketplace while you hash things over with the dealers."

Vigorously nodding his approval, Eric added, "Makes sense. Let's grab a taxi and we're on our way." He led the way as the women followed him out through the front door and onto the street to flag down a taxi.

As the taxi started and stopped, bumped and swerved along the narrow pavement toward Agrippas Street, there wasn't much said until Sonja broke the silence. "Weissberg's street is more like an alley than a street. Small and loaded with people selling, browsing or buying is how I see it. Just a narrow alley, too tight for way too many people."

"I saw how small it was, and I agree," said Eric as Elana's head snapped towards him—a startled turn he didn't notice since he was looking away from her.

"Have you been there before?" Elana immediately inquired while trying to suppress her surprise, but still unable to repress a reproachful look that was more serious than it should have been.

Eyes roaming, not making any visual contact with either Elana or Sonja, Eric rapidly responded. "Yea, took a taxi yesterday to see where this street was. Probably an old habit of scouting out the area before we go for the visit."

Oblivious to the evolving tension between Elana and Eric, Sonja asked, "What did you see?"

Ignoring their gazes while looking at the taxi driver, a determinedly detached Eric replied, "Just passed by in the taxi, but slow enough that I could see how small it was."

"Did you see anything or anyone else?" asked Elana.

He continued to look away, gazing out the taxi window. "Not really, but you can understand why Sonja felt uncomfortable walking through that congestion to get to Weissberg's shop. The street to Protopolis' shop is a little larger, but it's still filled with the same mass of humanity doing the daily commerce of Jerusalem."

Not able to hide her surprise or suspicions, Elana was now sharply inquisitive, "You were at Protopolis' shop?"

Still looking away as his eyes surveyed the streets pedestrians, "Same as with Weissberg's, only drove by to make sure where we were going."

The taxi ground to a halt at the junction of Agrippas and Weissberg's alley. Once they finally got out, and still brimming with curiosity about what he'd been doing on those early morning trips, Elana persistently pestered him with her questioning. "Is it easy to get a taxi when we're done, or did you have to wait long when you were here?"

"I think taxis are always around, but I'm no expert. I only passed by and didn't stop for anything or anybody."

Meandering through the mass of mankind clogging the alley to Weissberg's, Sonja led the way. She walked with the confidence of her team being with her, not with the meekness that saturated her previous trip. After what was only about 50 yards of walking, but seemed like a mile, Sonja finally led her team to the door of Weissberg's shop where she was confronted with a band of broad yellow tape wrapped across the door. In Hebrew was printed, 'Stop' and some other words she couldn't understand.

Decidedly dumbfounded, she turned back to Eric and Elana. "Can either of you read this?"

136

Trailing behind Sonja and Elana, Eric was quick to sense the situation and responded by moving to the front of his team. "I think it's a crime scene, and the yellow tape is probably telling us don't tamper with anything."

With a limited, but better grasp of Hebrew than the others, Elana added, "That's what it is, a restricted area due to some crime." Elana then turned away from her partners and looked for the nearest vendor. Needing more information, and quickly, she confronted a shopkeeper who was warily eyeing them and asked in her limited Hebrew, "Do you speak English?"

"I do some English," spoke the man as he lifted his gaze up from this collection of beads and other jewelry laid out on his table, "but what do you want here? Can't you see the police closed that building?"

"Yes, we see that," responded Elana as she waved her hand towards Sonja and Eric as a gesture to show they were together, "but why? We're supposed to meet Mr. Weissberg today."

Moving closer to the merchant, Sonja took over. "I was here over a week ago and was to meet him today."

Missing no part of her anatomy, the merchant eyed every bit of her from head-to-toe and then, fixating for a moment on the beautiful sensuousness of her long, graceful legs, looked up and slowly replied, "I remember seeing you before when you passed my shop and bought nothing."

"I know, I know," blurted out a frustrated Sonja, "but where's Mr. Weissberg? Is he OK?"

With a dismissive gesture, the merchant replied as he looked away from Sonja and gave the same scan of Elana. "Abraham is not OK. He is dead! Can't you understand why the police have put up that yellow tape? Weissberg is dead and the police don't know who killed him."

The shock set in as Sonja immediately realized the affection she had for the old man who'd been so kind in such a short period of time. Her knees started to buckle as she propped herself against the side of his building.

Seeing the devastating impact on Sonja, Eric took over the questioning. "What happened? When was he killed?"

Now fixing his gaze on Eric, the vendor took his time to reply as it appeared he was processing what was being asked of him. "Weissberg was killed two days ago. Some men came to his shop. They then left. When he didn't close the curtains at the end of the day, I got suspicious and went in to see him. He was dead! What more can I tell you?"

Continuing with his line of questioning, Eric moved closer to the merchant. "You saw my friend here come to visit Weissberg. Do you remember the men who killed him?"

The merchant now started to face Eric and as he replied, he then shifted his gaze back to Elana. "Yes, I saw them. They didn't come all at once. There were three of them. They didn't come all at once, and they didn't leave all at once. But when they left, I guess Weissberg was dead."

Eric persisted, even moving slightly to his right to get back in the wandering face of the manipulating merchant. "You remembered what my friend looked like, but do you remember what these men looked like?"

The merchant now looked into Eric's face and his answer shot a powerful shock and then suspicion through Elana's mind. "They looked like you."

"What do you mean, 'They looked like me'?" a flustered Eric asked.

The merchant raised his arms as if to beseech to the heavens. "They looked like you, just like you. They looked like they were Europeans or Americans, just like you. They weren't Jews or Arabs from here."

Trying to insert herself into the conversation, Sonja moved away from the building and forced her way into this small hub of questions-and-answers. "Was there anything else you saw? Were they the same size? Short? Tall? Walk funny?"

"What do you mean 'walk funny'?" asked the man as his eyes started at Sonja's waist then penetratingly met hers.

Not deviating from the task, or his deviant ways, she kept her eyes firmly focused on his. "I mean, did they walk in a different way? A limp or anything special?"

His eyes now left hers to view Elana, who was now also intently searching his. "No, no limp or anything, just like I told the police. Three men, Europeans and one was bigger. Taller and heavier! They all wore denim pants and dark jackets. That's all I know."

"When did you tell the police this information?" Eric probed so direct and now forceful that the merchant quickly turned back to him.

"The day they came the day Abraham was murdered. I told them all I knew, but I didn't say anything about this beautiful young woman visiting him," he said with a hint of a smile.

"Have they been back to talk to you again?" Eric continued as he clearly was taking charge of the questioning.

Becoming irritated and seeing no reason to continue this dialogue, the merchant's belligerence partnered with his diminishing patience. "No, they haven't been back to see me or to Abraham's shop. Now, go to the police if you want to find out more. You are standing in the way of my business and keeping people from my shop. Your lady friend didn't buy anything when she was here before and you aren't buying now. Only asking questions, so leave... go!"

Annoyed and impatient with the man, Eric fired right back, "Fine, fine. We'll go to the police. Do you have the name of the policeman you spoke with?"

"Yes, I will give it to you," he said as he reached under the counter for a piece of white paper that he handed to Eric. "Here, take it, see some policeman at this department, but now, just go!"

"Thanks," said Eric in a sarcastic shout. "We'll be gone and leave you to your thriving business." Now turning to the Sonja and Elana, he spoke without the hostility. "Let's go to the police and see what's happened."

Briskly walking their way through the crowded alley out to its junction with Agrippas, they looked at nothing other than the crowd now separating to let them through. Once freed of the congesting constraints of the crowd, Sonja reached over to Eric's shoulder and grabbed it to turn him towards her.

As Eric turned to Sonja, he grabbed Elana's arm as she might have kept walking. Sonja abruptly asked, "Do we want to go to the police or to Protopolis'? He's only blocks away and may know something about Abraham."

"I agree," added Elana as she was aware of the sudden twitching that was convulsing the tip of her nose. "Let's go see Protopolis first. Since he was a friend of Weissberg, maybe the police contacted him."

"Only if the police knew Protopolis was a friend," replied Eric. "But, OK, let's see if Protopolis knows anything."

Hailing a passing taxi and then after a short ride, the three found themselves on Protopolis' street. The seriousness of their mission energized a briskness in their step as they shoved their way through this second crowded bazaar-like setting. Sonja led the way since she not only knew where to go, but was also so emotionally-driven to see Protopolis as soon as possible and find what could be learned about Weissberg. As she walked through the bartering and bantering mob, she got the same stares as before, but for a different reason. Now she was aggressive, pushing aside anyone in her path, and could care less if she was getting any stares or hearing the cacophony of complaints. Her mission had her focused and her sense of mourning for Abraham Weissberg had her moving like a wounded animal—driven to survive regardless of the presence of her pain.

Approaching Protopolis' shop, Sonja was struck with a crushing blow as the same type of buttery yellow tape was covering the door. She turned to Eric and Elana and with a muted scream pleaded for an answer. "My God, what's happened? Eric, what's going on?"

"I don't know," he replied as he grabbed her arm and brought her closer to him. "Let's see if anyone knows anything". Eric turned to his right, walked to the nearest storefront and could be seen engaging in an animated conversation with the owner before returning.

Pointing at the vendor he had just spoken to, Eric recounted. "This guy knew Protopolis and confirmed the police taped off this area as a crime scene. Protopolis was murdered two days ago by three men who looked like Americans

140

or Europeans. He said many of the shop owners on the street saw the men go into the shop as individuals and then leave the same way. He doesn't know much more except the police talked to a number of people on the day of the murder."

Speaking in a rambling fashion while looking away from her partners, Sonja lamented, "I meet two men and now both of them are murdered. Because of me? Did I cause this?"

Pulling her face-to-face with him, Eric confronted her doubts, trying to dismiss any guilt, "This can't be something that happened by accident or coincidence, but why would it have anything to do with you? Who would know anything about what you were doing with these men?"

"My thoughts exactly," said Elana in a very supportive tone. "Who other than the three of us has any knowledge of what we were trying to do? It's only Sonja, me," and after an uncomfortable pause, "and you who knew about these men and our work."

Not wanting to get caught up in some game of sniping speculation, Eric persisted, "Could someone wanting to rob antique dealers have randomly chosen these two?"

"Not likely, but not impossible," answered Elana while shaking her head 'no'.

"No, not likely. But why? How?" were the words gracing Sonja's lips as she gave Eric a painfully questioning look. "What's this all about?"

Eric's eyes quickly met Sonja's, but just as quickly moved to Elana before roaming to view all that was around them in this market place. "Makes no sense at all, but our only option is to go to the police. Instead of one dead antique dealer, we've got two, and once we talk to the police, we might also be suspects since we knew these men."

Startled at the insinuation, and with her nose twitching again, Elana looked first at Sonja then to Eric before asking in desperation, "We could be suspects?"

"Yes." Eric said since it was obvious to him the police would want to talk to them, or at least Sonja. "You, Sonja and I are about to be seen in a different way than when we left the Institute, but we have no choice other than to find what the police know."

Chapter 12

Three desperate relics voyagers jumped into the back seat of a waiting taxi and were immediately confronted with the repulsive remnant odor of someone's vomitus spew saturating their collective noses. But, bundled between layers of apprehension and guilt, their eagerness to reach the police station overrode this residual offensive cloud. Unspoken thoughts rambled around that back seat cocoon of emerging despair as Sonja, Eric and Elana struggled to come to grips with whether they somehow caused the dealers' deaths, or if they were to be targets of a murder investigation. Eric leaned forward to give the driver the police station address, but the driver, looking back in amusement, slowly spoke, "Don't need it—been there too often."

After driving for what seemed like only a few minutes, the driver suddenly jammed-on his brakes in front of a gray, angular concrete and steel building with a sign reading: Mishteret Yisra'el. Eric leaned forward, somewhat mystified by the sign since he only had an address, then annoyingly asked, "What's this?"

The indignant taxi driver looked over at Eric while berating him. "This is police station. If you can't read our language, listen to what I tell you. Now, pay your fare and get out!"

With the taxi's stagnant atmosphere dripping with tension, none of them was the least bit insulted or embarrassed as Eric paid the money and got out without uttering a word. *An odd taxi driver dumping us out at an odd building,* he thought while viewing the building's asymmetrically angled front surface. Such a modern look it was easy to think the building was something other than a police station. Eric's pause to analyze the building's design was just enough delay for Sonja to push by as she couldn't wait to get this investigation moving.

As she approached the building's doors, out of nowhere appeared a security guard who, in a firm monotone confronted Sonja, "What is your purpose for coming here?"

Choosing to be assertive, and not looking solicitous or guilty, Sonja replied without batting an eyelash. "We're here looking for information about the murder of two people I knew."

"Are you a suspect in these murders or a witness?" asked the guard in a cold and detached fashion.

An impatient Eric interrupted, "Neither, but we might know something about the motive. Who do we see?"

"I will give you this pass for the building," said the guard while handing a card to Eric, "and go to section D on the third floor. You may enter now," she said while opening the door with a hand-held device.

Leading the way, Sonja dropped only a cursory "Thank you" as they rushed by and disappeared into the bowels of the building. An elevator immediately to their right suddenly opened as two uniformed officers came off. The three hopped on as Sonja hit the button for a third floor confrontation with reality.

Off the elevator they spilled into an open seating area serving four offices. To their right was a large D on a sign immediately under some Hebrew lettering. They approached the male clerk at the desk as Eric held out his business card. "I'm Professor Eric Stanfels and I want to speak to someone in charge of the murder investigation of Abraham Weissberg and Theodore Protopolis."

Warily eyeing them with a cold, penetrating stare, the clerk looked down at the card and then returned his sterile stare to Eric. "Pro-fessor Stanfield."

With a temperament imploding with impatience, Eric insistently pointed to his name on the card. "No, it's Stanfels, Professor Stanfels—just like it says on the card. I'm with Strayton University in the United States."

Without blinking, and peering right through Eric, the clerk replied, "Professor Stanfels, what is your business here?"

"We want to talk to you about your information on the murders," replied Eric.

Folding his hands while looking only at Eric, the clerk continued in a very condescending tone. "Mr. Stanfels, we don't share information with just anyone who walks in off the street. Why would we open our files to you, maybe a murderer trying to find out what we know?"

Thinking a woman's touch was imperative, Sonja interjected, "We can help because we think we know why these men were killed."

Absent any hint of interest or enthusiasm, the clerk looked up at Sonja, then at Eric. "I will have a detective contact you if he can find you? This card says someplace in America but we aren't going to send a detective there just to talk with you."

"No!" sharply added Elana, with frustration fermenting in her voice as she fumbled to find something in her purse that she handed over, "We're with the New Testament Biblical Institute here in Jerusalem. I'm Elana Dutros—here's my card, and my partner here is Sonja Martin. We're all headquartered at the Institute. Who'll contact us?"

The clerk avoided looking at Eric as he smiled while speaking now to Sonja. "You will be contacted by the detective-in-charge, Mordecai Rubin."

As if struck by a lightning, Eric was jolted by the shock. He accidently dropped his wallet on the table as the two women were startled at his atypical response—a response inconsistent with what the clerk said. "Mordecai Rubin? Mordecai Rubin is the detective?" asked an incredulous Eric.

"Yes, Detective Mordecai Rubin," answered the noticeably agitated clerk as his head turned to face Eric. "Do you know him?"

Eric's answer was met by surprise not only by the clerk, but also by his two partners. "I know Mordecai Rubin, and couldn't forget him no matter how hard I tried. The Mossad agent, or now the ex-Mossad agent, fallen from grace so far he's now a policeman. A man eating more than he's thinking, and always with a toothpick hanging out of his mouth like a wooden tumor growing on his lip! How could I forget Mordecai Rubin? Worked with him only one time and it was a disaster. He should've retired long before he ever started working."

Trying unsuccessfully to stifle a smile, the clerk was shaking his head, "Yes, I see you know him. Obviously an old friend, I'm sure." Turning away from the three, he reached for his telephone and dialed a number. After a brief, undecipherable conversation, he turned back. "Mr. Rubin wants to talk with you." As he got up from his desk and motioned for them to follow, "Please follow me to Mr. Rubin's office."

Entering through a large metal door, they saw three glass-enclosed cubicles in one of which sat a rumpled-looking man who rose from his desk when he saw them. Just as Eric remembered him, there stood Mordecai Rubin, larger than life. At 5 feet, 11 inches in height, Mordecai wasn't imposing, but his girth was much too great for the overstretched shirt that failed to contain it. As he walked from behind his desk, Eric saw that ever-present swagger, almost humorous with so much weight being carried. And the ever-present toothpick, still dangling from his mouth. Eric remembered everything about Mordecai Rubin no matter how hard he tried to forget.

With his hand extended out to the women he greeted them. "Ladies, I'm so pleased to meet you. What good fortune brings you here, especially with such a wonderful old friend?" After shaking their hands, he turned to Eric, and with his thick, all-encompassing hand aggressively shook Eric's. "And Eric, my boy, how can I be so lucky to see you of all people and with some information about the murders of those unfortunate antique dealers. It truly is wonderful to see you again. I've thought of you often."

Confusion clouded the women's faces and Eric concluded a clarification was in order as he struggled with how much he hated Mordecai's condescending 'my boy'. "I do know Mr. Rubin from my past time in Israel. You might say we worked together on some projects of interest to the United States and Israel. Mr. Rubin was the reason I returned to Strayton University, and while he talks about his good luck, I'm in some time-warp, wondering why such bleak, black, bad luck brought us together again."

146

"Don't be so negative, my boy. Since your friends don't even know me, why sow such seeds of slander?" Turning away from Eric, Mordecai asked of the women, "Which of you is Sonja and which is Elana?"

Not shy, a bold hand extended out to his, "I'm Elana."

"And, I'm Sonja," she replied while reaching over to shake that thick, all-enveloping hand.

After vigorously shaking their hands, Mordecai folded his two meaty hooks together. "It's my pleasure to meet you ladies, and," he hesitated as he turned towards Eric, "it's an even greater pleasure to meet again with such a long-lost friend."

More agitated than joyous, Eric tried to cut through the sugar-coated pleasantries. "Mordecai, what are you doing here? As sloppy as you were, obviously the Mossad didn't want you, the CIA didn't want you, and I certainly don't want you." As soon as the words exited Eric's mouth, he realized he had leaked to Sonja and Elana more about his past than he would have liked.

With a dismissive wave of his hand, Mordecai trivialized Eric's remarks. "Eric, my boy, don't be so negative, because you know emotions like that only distort your analysis. Who knows, maybe I'm looking for a little redemption with you. Like you Christians say, I'm looking to resurrect my soul, or at least the part of it that relates to my dealings with you. Let's allow the past to remain there—in the past. Now tell me, what really brings you here to Jerusalem, to my office?"

With the conversation clearly focused between the two men, streams of static energized the distance between them as Eric confronted Mordecai's gaze. "I'm here on a relics search with Sonja and Elana who work for the New Testament Biblical Institute. I represent Strayton University, in the United States, and we're providing some support to them."

Tilting his head to the side, Mordecai gave Eric a quizzical look as he read his business card. "Providing just money or some other kind of help?"

Oblivious to the subconscious shaking of his head 'no' as he looked at Mordecai, Eric replied, "We're helping them financially and in whatever way they need me. Sonja and Elana discovered information on some relics from the time of Jesus' crucifixion and they needed help. That's why Strayton sent me. Once I arrived in Jerusalem, we found their two information sources, the antique dealers, were dead. I assume murdered since you of all people know it's unlikely their deaths are a coincidence. What do you know about them?"

Mordecai's head was now nodding 'yes'. "You're probably right. You know, from our times together, deaths like these are rarely a coincidence. In fact, in the death of two people living not far from each other, you simply don't find any coincidence at all. You find planning and implementation, and never coincidence." said Mordecai as he twisted the toothpick around with his tongue.

Trying to break this frigid psychological polarity that bound the men and isolated the women, Sonja butted-in, "Mr. Rubin, how much do you know about these murders?"

Mordecai turned his attention to her. "Not much, but the three of you may have the answer since it must've been about the relics you were mentioning. Somebody obviously thought or heard these men knew something, so now the relics create some linkage between the deaths and a motive."

"But how would anyone know anything about the relics?" asked Elana with her eyes riveted on Mordecai, who turned to meet her gaze. "We thought Sonja was the only person dealing with those two men."

Elana was Mordecai's focus as he continued, "I can't begin to guess how that happened, but other than the three of you, who else knew anything about Weissberg or Protopolis? At your Institute, who knows anything?"

Sonja spoke directly to Mordecai, "I told my superiors what we found, but I've a hard time thinking these old, wimpy men would be involved in these murders."

The cross-examining professional that he was, Mordecai persisted. "You're sure that none of those men could have given or sold the information to someone else?"

148

Elana intervened, "Anything could happen, but I know these men on the Board and they're just as Sonja described – old, passive, decrepit and somewhat useless when it comes to any bold activity, especially a crime."

Mordecai slowly surveyed the sullen faces of all three of these youthful and naïve fonts of curiosity. "Regardless of age, vitality and so-called honor, greed can get the best of all men, even old men. Who else knows anything about your venture?"

Elana couldn't suppress what a compelling urge forced her to say. "Only Eric, but he's been outside this project up until the last few days. While he knew of it when he was in America, he's only been here for a short time, and that's during the time when the men were killed. Other than that, I can't think of anyone else. Can you, Sonja?"

Sonja's head jerked around to focus on Elana. "Technically you're correct since Eric has been here only a short time, but certainly you're not accusing him of complicity in these murders—or are you?"

It was obvious some intervention and clarification were desperately needed by Eric. "Both Elana and Sonja are correct since I knew of the project and, to some degree, what possibly could be had from these men. But I didn't have anything to do with their deaths. You know, from our past relationship, death follows me like an ugly, sinister shadow. Since that time, I've preferred to spend my days in life's brilliant sunshine. What do you know from your investigation? "

Mordecai shook his head. "Nothing. The people on the streets, even next to the shops, knew very little. We know there were probably three men, all Europeans or Americans, and one was much larger than the others. Probably the enforcer for the group! Don't know if anything was stolen, but we're going back to the crime scene today since I was short-handed that first day."

"Can we go with you?" asked Eric. "Can we go now, just the four of us?"

Studying Eric, and then the women, Mordecai finally nodded. "OK with me as long as you don't disturb the crime scene."

Eric rudely added, "Have you disturbed the scene? Is there evidence you've taken that we should see here before we go?"

An impatient incisiveness crept into Mordecai's tone. "No, Eric, the scenes haven't had any evidence taken from them and we haven't really questioned the witnesses as thoroughly as possible. I told you I was short-handed."

Eric got up, ready to move. "Then let's go. With you there, we'll probably get more from the vendors than we could get by ourselves."

As he got up to lead them out of his office, Mordecai's biting sarcasm flowed. "Why would they tell you anything if you look like the killers? Why would they even talk to you?"

The ride to Weissberg's shop was quick and the walk down that narrow alley was unimpeded as an opening, like the parting of the Red Sea, was created for Mordecai's swagger. His authority clearly visible on his sleeve, there was no confusion this strutting peacock was someone to be reckoned with.

Arriving at the shop, with the yellow tape still across the door, Mordecai ripped off the tape, opened the door and all four walked in. As they looked around at such a small and unimpressive shop, Sonja was the first to comment. "What was here that someone would kill for?"

Sensing Sonja's pain of perceived responsibility, Elana added, "This is horrible, it's just a small business. What was worth killing for?"

Mordecai interjected. "May not be an issue of what was here, but what did he know about somewhere else. Any relics probably weren't here, but let's look around. You can move things with a pencil, but don't pick up anything—no need for any new fingerprints. Eric and I'll look in the back room where his body was found."

As the women watched the two men wander into the back room, Elana moved over towards that side of the room. "Let's get started. His desk is as good a place as any."

Weissberg's desk was cluttered with papers scattered all around. The impression to even the untrained eyes of Sonja and Elana was that Weissberg must have had some papers in his hands and threw then around, possibly when he was hit or grabbed by the intruders. Partially covered by the papers was a tablet on which were dates, names and a drawing. As both women were looking at the tablet, the men came out of the back room.

Mordecai spoke first. "Other than a little blood, I can't see anything back there that might be evidence." He glanced over at Sonja. "Anything out here?"

With a pencil, she pointed at the tablet left undisturbed on the desk, "We found nothing but this tablet with dates and names, and even a drawing of some figures."

Moving over to the desk with Eric close behind, Mordecai picked-up the tablet. "Look at the dates, the last was the day of his murder, and the entries in most cases aren't names. He listed names sometimes, and mostly what appear to be descriptions of people at other times."

"What do you make of it?" Eric asked.

Mordecai didn't make eye contact with anyone as he scanned the contents scattered on the desk while twirling away with his toothpick. "Who knows, but I guess he was writing descriptions of who visited this place."

Sonja quickly added, "But why names sometime and then descriptions the next? Could he have been describing the customer that he named?"

"I don't think so," said Mordecai. "He has several different descriptions of people under one name. Like here, 'Eisenstein, woman and husband,' and below it on the same date, 'short, fat man, skinny wife with dirty clothes'. He must have been describing people who entered his shop. If someone had an appointment, or if he knew them, my guess is that he listed their name. If he didn't know who walked through his door, he may have tried to describe their appearance."

"Why would he do that?" asked Eric.

Mordecai was still occupied with the desk, opening drawers and leafing through the contents. "When we got the report of his death, the computer check for his name showed he had been robbed within the last year. Maybe just trying to make a record of who came in his door. I don't know what those figures are with their points and triangles, maybe stars, but they're not Stars of David. Put the tablet in the evidence bag," Mordecai said as he handed the bag to Sonja, "we can use it for reference later. But let's get out of here, I've seen enough."

The ride to Protopolis' shop was short with Mordecai's flashing red light opening the way through the traffic. As they made their way through the alley, Mordecai's bull-rush style parted the crowds just like the Red Sea did for Moses. At Protopolis' shop, off came the yellow tape and Mordecai led the barging foursome into a place stinking of musty old rugs, spices and death.

"Same thing," Mordecai said as he looked at Eric. "Let's go to the back room where the corpse was found," as he turned to the women, "and you two look around and see what you can find. Forget the fingerprint stuff."

After an hour of looking, Sonja and Elana were partly exasperated and completely bored with finding nothing. When Eric and Mordecai came out from the backroom area, as they were greeted with the look of defeat on the faces of the women, Mordecai mockingly said, "Now you know it's not easy finding clues, they're not always jumping out at you. And we didn't do any better. Nothing back there! Let's go back to headquarters."

"Any interest in talking to the vendors outside?" Elana asked Mordecai.

He dismissed her question out-of-hand. "No, I'm tired and know my men did that already."

A suddenly hostile Eric turned as he looked Mordecai in the eye, "Yea, that's what I heard from you back in Gaza. 'My men did a thorough job'. And where the hell did it get us? Literally in hell! How many innocent lives will be lost now because we trusted your men to do the job? WE need to talk to the vendors, and WE need to do the job, not YOUR men!"

The women were shocked at Eric's eruptive hostility, but Mordecai wasn't fazed as he stared resolutely and spoke sarcastically, "Yes, yes, yes my dear Eric. I forgot how your previous brush with the underside of humanity left you physically and emotionally scarred. Forgive me. Let's talk to the vendors as we leave."

As the foursome left, they fanned out to the different vendors' stalls inquiring about any possible witnesses. Mordecai did have some information from the stalls immediately adjacent to the dealer's shop, but it was just about three European or American men. Nothing else was being turned up despite their efforts, but just as they decided to stop this fruitless investigation, Mordecai was confronted by a little old woman, dressed in black and smelling of the charcoal that grilled her husband's lamb. She jabbed him in his puffy, protruding paunch and asked, "Why don't you talk to me instead of only the men?"

Caught off-guard, he answered her disdainfully, "What can you tell me that no one else can?"

Excitedly continuing, the old woman spoke about the big man, the biggest of the three who greedily took some lamb and only reluctantly paid for it.

Mordecai's fuse was getting short. "What do you want me to do? Arrest this man for taking a piece of your husband's precious lamb when I have more important things to do?"

The irate woman berated Mordecai, "Don't be a pigheaded fool! I'm not here to talk about some lamb. Why don't you ask me about the big man I saw and his big, fat, greedy hand?"

Mordecai appeased her aggressiveness, "Enough already, what else did you see?"

"I saw that hand when he took the lamb on his way to poor Protopolis' shop, and I saw that big, ugly hand when he took the lamb and then overpaid for it. But what I really saw was three stars on that hand. Three tattooed stars, not in a straight line, but on a slant like this." she said as she took his pen and drew, on the back of her hand, three stars on a diagonal line.

Mordecai's three partners were getting bored and frustrated with this conversation, but when the old woman drew the three stars, Elana's interest was ignited. "What's she doing? Those look like Weissberg's drawings on his tablet. Were you telling her about the tablet?"

He turned away from the woman to include the others in this conversation. "No, I haven't told her anything, but she's telling me one of the killers had three tattooed stars on his right hand. She saw them when he took some food and paid for it."

"Just like the drawing at Weissberg's," said Sonja, "That's what those points and triangles were—stars, and three stars in a diagonal row."

"I think you're right," said Elana. "Let's get back to the car and look at that tablet."

Looking sarcastically at Mordecai, Eric repeated what Elana had said, "Yea, let's go back to the car. We wasted our time here because Mordecai's men did such a thorough job, so thorough this woman had to find us since his men wouldn't find her. Come on, let's go back to the evidence envelope and see what's there."

Settling into his car, Mordecai opened the envelope and removed the tablet for the other three to see. While nodding his head in approval, he acknowledged, "You're right, they look like stars on a diagonal line, especially after what we just saw. Are we satisfied it's solid evidence?" he asked as they all nodded in agreement. "C'mon, it's late, so let's get out of here. I'll take you to your apartments and then we can meet tomorrow afternoon."

"Hold on," Eric replied with one hand raised to stop the action, "take me back to our office. I need to send an e-mail to Strayton."

Caught off-guard by Eric's request to go back to the office, and a little suspicious of his intent, Elana added, "Take me back so I can check my e-mails. But don't worry Eric," she said with a just a hint of acid in her tone, "I'll let you use the computer first."

The weaving police car cut through the light traffic as all four occupants had different things on their minds. Sonja couldn't eliminate the thought of poor Mr. Weissberg and Mr. Petropolis being killed in the back rooms of those empty, lonely shops. Elana couldn't shake the persistent doubts she still had about Eric. Obviously something bad happened between him and Mordecai, but this only added to his dark, mysterious persona. Eric's thoughts centered on the concept of a 'hit team' sent to Jerusalem to kill two antique dealers. The 'why' of these murders wasn't yet comprehensible, but he accepted as fact they existed and that one of them had these star tattoos on his hand. Mordecai? Mordecai was hungry. His only thoughts were about food. He couldn't get out of his mind the thought of lamb sizzling on a grill.

When they arrived back at the Institute office and Mordecai then went on his way, Elana checked her e-mail first as a smile graced her lips while reading a message about an invitation to dinner. It had been an ugly day, chilled by the deaths in those little shops, but now she felt an explosion of warmth in her heart just from reading Rigel's e-mail.

Ever impatient to use the internet, Eric sensed something good from the smile spreading across her face and the sparkle radiating from her eyes. "Good news?"

"I'm having dinner tomorrow evening with my friend Rigel."

"Is this the Irishman Sonja told me about?" Eric asked with a smile creasing his face and a look of mischievous curiosity framed by his arched eyebrows.

"Yes," responded an enthusiastic Elana. "Quite a nice Irish gentleman, if I say so myself. Wouldn't you agree Sonja?"

"Absolutely," Sonja added with a smile, the first of the day. "I agree, quite an Irish gentleman."

Eric's impatience now got the best of him. "Fine, but get off the internet as soon as you can. I need to send an e-mail to Strayton University about what's happened and our thoughts on this Armenian monastery."

"What'll you tell him?" inquired Sonja.

"When they were alive, our sources focused us in the direction of the Russian monastery."

"Well, you go right ahead and use the internet because I'm done," a pious Elana said as she deferred to Eric and got out of her chair. "But what's next?"

Sonja's attention turned to Eric. "That's what I was thinking, what's next?"

Tired and mindlessly running his fingers through his tousled hair, Eric added, "Tomorrow I'll meet you both at 8:30 and we'll plan our trip to Armenia."

With a lightheartedness that reflected the mood Rigel's e-mail created, Elana jabbed at him, "Is that AM or PM?"

"AM my ladies, AM. Now I've got to send this e-mail, so I'll see you in the morning."

Mordecai did go on his way, straight to his office and sent an e-mail to all detectives within the Jerusalem and Tel Aviv jurisdictions to look for a large, European man with three diagonal stars tattooed on his right hand. What Mordecai didn't know was the e-mail would not go to the border passport-control authorities. Even though Rigel and his men would be leaving Israel, no one at the borders would be looking for tattoos on someone's hand. Simple dumb luck had worked on behalf of those who deserved it the least.

Chapter 13

Early morning meetings were scheduled for two groups in Jerusalem who were not more than two miles from each other, yet light-years apart with regard to intent and prospective actions. Blood was the underlying theme for each— the search for the blood of Jesus for one group and the willingness of the other to shed as much blood as needed.

Sweeping into the suite conference room at 7:30 AM, a confident Rigel surveyed the scene. A tired Liam was peering out the window, while Conor, not quite awake, was still trying to look attentive. And Viktor? As usual, stuffing his face with the breakfast sweet rolls he was dunking in his sugar-laden coffee. Despite the less than enthusiastic appearances gracing his meeting, Rigel knew these men would be willing and able to rise to the occasion as the demands arose, since they always had.

Turning away from the window, Liam asked, "Rigel, what're we going ta do. Ya always have everything thought out and we follow ya, but where are we going now?"

As Rigel walked towards the table to grab a cup of coffee, he smiled at Liam. "Ya flatter me, but I admit it pleases me ya trust my judgment. It'll be off ta Armenia for us, but first two issues need ta be dealt with. First I'll meet my beautiful friend, Miss Elana, for dinner tonight. Sent her an e-mail and she responded late last night." He chuckled and looked at the others. "Liam already knows that since his e-mail snooping told him before I saw it. Right Liam?"

Moving his chair closer to the table, Liam nodded. "Right, and I hoped ta find some juicy, romantic message instead a only a simple 'yes'."

157

Looking more asleep than awake, Conor queried, "Other than for the affairs a your cold, cold heart, why is it ya want ta meet this woman?"

Unresponsive, Rigel sat focused on the coffee circling in his cup as he stirred the black liquid It looked clear in contrast to the dark thoughts traversing the multiple compartments of his brain—thoughts that never found a home in his conscience. "I need ta meet her because I'm not sure we can get all the information we need from the e-mails. There's more going on than we think with this story about the Russians and the monastery. It's more like the Russians and their monasteries."

"The antique dealer told us the place ta look was a Russian monastery. So what's difficult about that?" asked Conor. "Doesn't this Khor Virap monastery in Armenia seem ta be it?"

Shaking his head from side to side, Rigel looked up and then over to Conor. "Yes and no. Its Russian, sort a, and that stands out ta us. But the other one had some Russian influence in its early years, so be cautious lads, we can't rule out anything."

Looking up from his sweet roll, and lost in this discussion, Viktor needed some clarification. "How do you know this about other monastery?"

Rigel turned his attention to Viktor, who could barely wait until his last word was out of his mouth before he stuffed it with sweetness. "This Professor Stanfels sent an e-mail last night ta his university telling them what he thought about chasing down these relics at the Armenian monastery. Obviously the dealers provided that information ta the woman when she first talked ta them. But his university told him the Russian Orthodox Church controlled St. Catherine's monastery for many years. I'm not sure if the dealer was saying ta us 'Russian monastery' or 'monasteries'. For sure, this Professor is thinking about both monasteries."

Still looking very confused, and with his mouth still stuffed, Viktor looked at Liam and Conor and then asked Rigel with barely discernible words, "What has this to do with meeting woman for dinner?"

"Moy chornee Ruski brat, I need ta meet with her and plant a listening device somewhere on her so we'll be able ta know what she's thinking different from what she's e-mailing."

"What da ya have in mind?" asked Conor.

Taking something out of his pocket, Rigel held it up for all to see. "I can plant this listening bug on her, probably in her purse, and hear what she's been saying whenever we want."

"Won't we need ta be close ta her ta hear it?" asked Liam.

Rigel nodded. "Right, but with a burst-transmitter bug like this, we can access it when we're within a half mile a her. Would be nice ta hear everything just when she says it, but we can't do that unless we're always close ta her. With this device, once we get around her, or at least within a half mile, we can access the bug and hear what's being said as well as what's been said."

"But Rigel," Conor questioned with a facial expression projecting nothing was clearer than the heaviest fog coming off the Irish Sea, "what're we going ta do about going ta this Khor Virap monastery?"

"OK, let's get this back in focus. I'll take care a the woman and then off we go ta Armenia."

Liam stood and looked back out the window. He pointed outside, somewhere out there in space. "How'll we be 'off ta Armenia'? How're we going ta get there? Where da we leave from?"

Getting up and walking over to Liam at the window, Rigel put his arm around his shoulder. "Don't worry, I've figured this out early this morning before the three a ya were even awake and reservations are already made. Khor Virap is in the Ararat province a Armenia, and we're going ta fly out a Tel Aviv on the Austrian Airlines ta the city a Yerevan—a city a 1.4 million people where we won't stand out in a crowd. We'll rent a van and drive ta this Khor Virap."

"How far da we drive?" Conor asked Rigel.

Rigel responded as he turned an invisible steering wheel. "About 90 kilometers on a reasonably good road. We can do our business at Khor Virap, then fade away in the urban sprawl a Yerevan like shadows scorched by the sunlight."

"What da ya know about this monastery?" added Liam.

Responding without hesitation, which was usually his style, Rigel was in complete control of their operations, "The monastery isn't too sophisticated and there're usually only a handful a monks there at this time a the year. Thank heaven we're not going around Easter time."

"Why not?" asked Viktor. "Easter is always wonderful time of year."

Rigel addressed Viktor, "Not for our needs. At Easter, the Armenians believe they need ta go ta the monastery and re-vitalize their religious fervor. If we had all a these people ta deal with, we'd have total chaos. Liam, you'll stay here ta monitor the internet action and what ya pick up from the bug. Hopefully, it'll work for us."

Never completely comprehending Rigel's plans, Viktor asked, "When we leave and what to wear?"

"I'm having dinner this evening with this Elana, then we fly from Ben Gurion Airport at 8:38 AM tomorrow morning. Wear comfortable outdoor clothes, but when we get close ta the monastery, I found some clothes we'll put on. We need ta be out a here by 6:00 AM, so make sure we all get enough sleep."

This day's morning meeting at the Institute also included Mordecai who, awakened by Eric's early telephone call, showed all the signs of having arrived too early and with too little sleep. Being a senior detective, Mordecai was accustomed to arriving at the office anytime he pleased, as long as it wasn't after 10:00 AM. The black coffee helped, but wasn't able to jump-start his tired, haggard appearance. "What's on your mind?" Mordecai asked between yawns.

Surveying the faces of his three partners, Eric stopped at Mordecai. "You'll need to make the plans to go to Khor Virap monastery in Armenia. I have no idea how to get there with Syria and Iran between us and Turkey cradling Armenia from the West. Can we even get to Armenia directly from Israel?"

160

The last question seemed to shake Mordecai from his slumber. "Not to worry! We can get to Armenia from here."

"I suspected that," Eric caustically replied, "but can we get there without having to go through a dozen other countries hostile to Israel? There are a lot of people who'd love to shoot down an Israeli plane any time they could and I don't want to be on it."

Mordecai took a sip of coffee, hesitated a few seconds, then indifferently replied, "Eric, my boy, don't fret for a moment. We can fly directly from Tel Aviv to Yerevan, Armenia. From there, I don't know what it'll take to get to this monastery, but I've a contact in Yerevan I can rely on."

"Someone from your Mossad killing days?" Eric asked sarcastically as he gave a glaring look that would have frozen a lesser man's mind and tongue.

Leaning forward on the table, Mordecai folded his hands together and then pointed them at Eric with an equally assertive stare that communicated, 'enough is enough'. "Now we need to have an understanding. What happened with you and me in the past needs to stay there—in the past. If you want my help and connections, we need to move forward from here. And yes, this Armenian is someone I knew from my past life, but now it's important what he knows and how he can help us. I'll contact him about how we get to the monastery and for whatever else we need. But, I think with all this public bickering about what we can't change, Sonja and Elana deserve some explanation about your one-sided bitching. It's just exploding excrement from out of your haunted past."

Eric nodded in agreement. "OK, I'll tell them."

"No, I'll tell them because you're too damned biased. You'll distort the truth to support your own weak-kneed, guilty-conscienced perception of our past," fired back Mordecai as he turned towards Sonja and Elana and took the toothpick out of his mouth. "Eric and I were collaborators on a joint mission between the CIA and the Mossad. We were a bad mix of oil and water; youth and experience; idealism and pragmatism. Most importantly, a mixture of conflicting objectives. Eric came as an idealist working to further the interests of his nation and his God, while I brought my battle-hardened perception that it wasn't any good to do anything other than annihilate the enemies of the State of Israel. My team was sloppy, either consciously or subconsciously and Eric paid the price. Lost his integrity and his soul all because he worked with me, a man too jaded about the motives of the Arabs and their terrorist friends who I spent a lifetime chasing and killing."

"Is that the total dark side of your past?" Elana asked Eric as she turned towards to him.

Looking directly into her eyes, he nodded, "Yes, it's an eternal fire searing my soul since, because of me, innocents died when I thought I was saving the world. Now I'm stuck in a flaming hell hole and no amount of praying, wishing, or begging for forgiveness can smother even the smallest embers of that fire."

"That's why you came back to Strayton?" asked Sonja with a sympathetic look led by eyes covered with a film of moisture, a smile lost to the tightness of pursed lips and a hand that reached out to touch his arm. "Is that why you told me at Strayton you came back to heal your soul?"

Taken by surprise, Eric replaced that surprised look with a hint of a smile that moved across his lips. But the warmth of that emergent smile couldn't change the lost, empty look that now owned his eyes as he sought Sonja's. "I remember that day when we met on some jogging trail, but what you couldn't know is that you were the only person I ever spoke to with even the faintest hint about why I was there. And I can't believe I opened up to you.   But speaking of Strayton," he said as he pulled away from her, "I've already heard back from them after yesterday's e-mail."

Elana looked right at him, but fixated on Sonja, Eric was oblivious to her until she spoke, "You've already heard from them?"

Now she got his attention, or at least a part of it, as he turned away from Sonja to meet her questioning eyes. "That's the benefit of e-mailing a country many time zones away."

Anxious about losing their funding and Elana's hostile attitude, Sonja nervously asked the question for which she may not have wanted the answer. "Are they still interested in us?"

With a palpable fear written all over her face, Eric lightened the mood with a laugh and an upbeat answer. "Don't worry, they still like the project, but, the concept of the 'Russian' monastery has opened up a new issue. President Smathers knew St. Catherine's had been under the control of the Russian Orthodox Church up to about 150 years ago, but now he thinks any reference to a Russian monastery could mean Khor Virap or St. Catherine's."

Busily fingering the new piece of timber he took off his lips, a serious Mordecai asked, "What does that mean for our planning?"

"Our? What you mean 'our' planning?" asked an incredulous Eric. "Since when did you become a part of our team?"

"For God's sake Eric, let it die," said Elana, now disgusted with his small-mindedness. "It makes perfect sense having Mordecai on our team. Sure, it'll take him out of his jurisdiction here in Israel, but look at his contacts elsewhere. Look at what he's done already with this trip to Armenia. What makes you think you can do better?"

Stumped to say something, Eric knew he couldn't and looked away from Elana's probing eyes.

Surprised with his attitude, Sonja was decidedly disappointed with Eric's belligerence. "I agree with Elana—he's a great addition. Get over it Eric!"

Shame replaced his holier-than-thou hostility as he averted eye contact with anyone. "You're right. It was just some old baggage coming out of those deep pits of my past. If it's OK with all of you, let's move on. We do need to plan on going to both monasteries, unless we find something special at the first one. I already sent an e-mail from Elana's computer to President Smathers letting him know we'd probably also go to St. Catherine's."

"Do you have enough funding to expand this project?" inquired a dubious Mordecai. "Who knows where it will take us?"

Knowing he was important to some aspect of this venture, a small sense of confidence and self-worth sprouted in Eric. "Funding won't be a problem. President Smathers told me this project is very important to him, and he'll fund it at whatever level I recommend."

"Unlimited support?" responded Sonja as she got up from the table to pour herself a glass of water.

Beaming with pride as his sense of value was almost completely restored, Eric looked first at Sonja and then at Elana and Mordecai. "He told me I had up to a million dollars to spend if a relic of the crucifixion was findable. And, if we had to spend more to buy the object or objects, I could do that if what we found could be worthwhile to him."

"Worthwhile to him? What can be worth so much to him?" came back a confused Mordecai. "Why is he so interested?"

Raising his middle and index fingers, Eric addressed Mordecai's question. "There were two issues Smathers identified. He liked the concept of James' ossuary since he was hoping it would shed some light on a very personal issue for him—the conflict in Christianity between whether or not James was the blood brother of Jesus. Actually, Strayton has two New Testament scholars living presently at the Vatican doing research on this subject. They've always had a close relationship with the Vatican, although the Vatican has never known that resolving this issue, naturally on the side of James being the blood brother of Jesus, has been what was partially behind our involvement with them."

Looking puzzled at this pronouncement, Elana asked, "Is that what's interested him to fund us? He must have tons of money and no reporting responsibility. To his Board, this might look like, as you Americans say, a crap-shoot with a lot of money wagered on what Sonja and I think we stumbled on."

"I agree," said Mordecai as a sinister smirk crossed his face.

Eric was pleased his team now had some grasp of what forces were really behind their mission. "Wait, there's a little more to it than that. He also thinks there's more to be found at this St. Catherine's than meets the eye. St. Catherine's has a storied history regarding not only its treasure of ancient holdings, but also about its confusion regarding what it really has hidden in its old stone vaults."

"What do you mean by that?" asked Mordecai, letting curiosity overcome his sinister side, "If they're confused, how can they help us?"

Now knowing he regained control, Eric was confident of his contributions. "Hold on Mordecai, there's even more than that. President Smathers sent me an attachment with that e-mail today. The attachment relates to not only their confusion, but also a potential problem St. Catherine's may have with us that could hinder getting help from them. They don't care for Protestant biblical researchers, since they got burned in the past by a German Lutheran researcher and now prefer dealing with Catholics or Orthodox. That's why President Smathers wants me to go to the Vatican to meet with his contact there and see if he'll intercede with St. Catherine's on our behalf."

With narrowed eyes squinting with suspicion, Elana keyed them in on Eric's baby blues, "You're always spending some of your time away from us. Now what's this all about, this story about a Lutheran researcher? St. Catherine's being confused? Why are we getting so far away from Khor Virap?"

Trying to close the growing gap developing between them, Eric reached over to touch Elana's arm. "Let me explain as simple as possible what we're facing with a Protestant problem at St. Catherine's. In the 1840's, a Lutheran minister, Tischendorf, worked his way, and I mean 'worked his way' because traveling conditions were horrible, to St. Catherine's on Mt. Sinai, where Moses got the Ten Commandments. He was looking to find one of the oldest pieces of the New Testament that was rumored to still exist. He ended up staying for days and found nothing. On his final day there, while preparing to leave that fortress-like monastery, he noticed a monk burning some trash. Tischendorf went over to see what he was doing and found the monk actually burning the priceless document he'd traveled to St. Catherine's to find. Unbelievable!"

"Yes," said Mordecai with a sleepy nod. "Too much of a coincidence—coincidences just don't happen."

Raising his hands with his palms facing outward to stop this runaway diesel of doubt that was Mordecai, Eric continued. "Hold on. Wait a minute, hear me out. It only gets worse. There were 43 pages to what Tischendorf took, but there were 86 other pages that the monks wouldn't let him take, even though he said he wanted to take them for the Czar. And don't forget, those were Russian

Orthodox controlling the monastery at that time. So he went back to Europe and these 43 pages became the Codex Sinaiticus and were lodged in London, where they still reside. He went back to St. Catherine's in 1860 with special permission to get the other 86 pages but nobody could find them. They were lost. This time again, when he was getting ready to leave, a monk invited him to dine in his cell. And lo and behold, what did they find in an Old Testament Bible? The 86 pages! He took them back to London and that's where the trouble began. St. Catherine's thought they loaned the material to him and he thought it was given to him. He wouldn't return anything and St. Catherine's has been distrusting of Protestants ever since."

Mordecai's increasing impatience was stretched to the limit, "Look Eric, where are we going with this?"

Mordecai's protestations weren't strong enough to stop Eric's runaway train of information. "Don't lose sight of what I'm telling all three of you, and what Smathers is telling you and me. The main issues here are there must be a lot of stuff at St. Catherine's, and they don't really know what they have. They could have what we're looking for and who knows what else?"

Something still wasn't kosher, and Mordecai needed to speak his piece. "What are you three really looking for? I know you're talking about relics of the crucifixion, and that's what you thought the dealers would help with, but is there more? Do you have any real idea what these relics might be?"

This Mordecai-Eric dialogue had become too exclusionary and Sonja decided to butt-in. "If there's something to be found from the crucifixion of Jesus, we're inclined to think it'll be metal, although it could be wood. If it's metal, we would expect it to be the spike or spikes which nailed Jesus to the cross. Other metal objects from the crucifixion have their own histories and provenance which we believe are outside of this place and time in history."

Focused on Sonja but with a questioning look still dominating his face, Mordecai continued, "And what if the three of you find some spikes? What good will a spike be? How will you be different from these swindlers we always find in Jerusalem trying to pass off old nails as being from the time of the Romans?"

Replying with a calmingly confident tone, Sonja laid her hands on the table directly across from Mordecai's. "If we find relics, and if they're spikes, carbon-dating will establish the age of any organic residue on them, and our hope is there'll be some residual blood on the spikes."

Now she had his attention. "And what happens if you find some?"

Sonja's resolve never wavered. "If we find some, we'll do a DNA extraction."

"What'll that show you?" asked a confused Mordecai as he got up from the table with loads of doubt saturating his scientifically-starved brain cells.

A woman on a clear-cut mission, Sonja continued, "A DNA analysis of Jesus' blood could show he only has the DNA contributions of a woman who would be Mary. And that speck of DNA will allow science to prove that Jesus was divine since we would then be proving there was no evidence of a male's genetic contribution.

Mordecai had his back turned away from Sonja and kept talking to her as he looked out a glass window. "So what?"

With dwindling patience, she responded, "Look Mordecai, if we can prove Jesus' DNA only had a contribution from one human, Mary, then Elana, Eric and I would be showing God exists since He had to create Mary's pregnancy, not her husband Joseph. And since God would have no human DNA, rather than repudiating religion, for the first time, science would actually be proving its legitimacy."

"Then what'll you do with it?" asked Mordecai

Eric jumped into the dialogue. "If we get what we think is Jesus' blood, President Smathers will have no trouble figuring out what to do. It'll be a bombshell destroying the negativism of non-believers, and even converting more than a few."

Getting more than a little frustrated with this three-way dialogue, Elana tried to move the conversation along. "OK, what's next? Off to St. Catherine's now or after Khor Virap, as we had planned?"

Eric took the lead. "In his e-mail to me, President Smathers recommended two things. First go to Khor Virap since it's older than St. Catherine's, being built in the 4th Century while St. Catherine's was built in the 6th. Secondly, he recommended I go to the Vatican—what I told you earlier. Mordecai, I'm going to suggest you make plans for us to go to Armenia four days from now. I'll leave tomorrow to go to the Vatican to meet this Monsignor Bertani who is President Smathers' contact. Then I'll return with more than enough time to go to Armenia."

Mordecai nodded his approval. "OK, I agree with what you have in mind and how we're going to do it, but let's change the tone of the day and have dinner tonight. At my home, and no business discussed."

Elana chimed in, "I already have plans for dinner, but why don't the three of you go ahead since we'll have more than enough time together in the future." A stream of guilt swept over her face as she added, "Sorry, but I do need to bow out tonight."

Smiling approvingly at Elana, Mordecai took the toothpick out of his mouth. "Don't worry, I'll do my best to entertain these two, and maybe even this President Smathers," Mordecai said with a chuckle, "if he sends us anymore e-mails today."

Chapter 14

The allure the magnificent King David held for Elana was nothing compared to the magnetic attraction drawing her to Rigel. Just the thought of seeing him elicited an electrifying sensation streaming through every vessel and bone in her body. She couldn't wait to see him and hoped this highly charged feeling was the same for him. There was no denying a certain amount of foolish, young love had crept into her life, and with her existence in Jerusalem void of any hint of romance, what a welcome addition it was.

Aside from the pangs for romance, Elana hungered for a really good meal, and it was no secret the King David had the best cuisine in all of Jerusalem. Her appetite for food and romance were both in for what she hoped would be a long and productive evening.

Meeting Elana at the King David Hotel was simply perfect for Rigel. He and his men were living *incognito* on the 7th floor in their spacious suite; he loved the food at the La Regence Grill Room; and most importantly, they served his beloved Guinness draft. But this evening wasn't a social occasion—he was only there to involuntarily recruit Elana for his informational network. He needed a way to eavesdrop on what this Stanfels was contributing to the women's search since he knew this Smathers had focused them on not just Khor Virap, but also St. Catherine's.

Alighting from her taxi at the King David, she was greeted by a polite doorman who held her hand as she exited the vehicle. But within seconds, a simply suave Rigel snatched it away. "Elana my dear, it's wonderful ta see ya. Let me help ya into this lovely hotel."

Stunned from looking at the radiance of his blue eyes and that perfectly charming smile, she couldn't hold back, "It's so wonderful to see you, and quite a treat to dine with such a world traveler."

Walking arm-in-arm through the lobby, he felt her snuggle even closer to him. He gave her a small kiss on her cheek, then flattered in his very Irish style, "But my dear Elana, the treat's all mine. It's certainly been worth the trip from Ireland just ta see ya, and ta be able ta dine in such a fine restaurant as the La Regence. I don't think there's a better place ta be—other than maybe Ireland."

With eyes sparkling with the light of love, and a smile warm enough to melt the glaciers of Greenland, Elana's emotions were just plastered all over her face. "Your flattery serves you well Mr. Rigel, but tell me, what's brought you back to Jerusalem so soon?"

As they rode the escalator up to the La Regence restaurant, he thought of how he needed to disguise his interest in her business. "Let's get seated and then talk about what's going on in your world." Turning to face the maitre d', he spoke with a confident air, but no sense of arrogance or self-importance. "Sir, might my lovely date and I impose upon ya for your best seat in the house? One with a wonderful view a the Old City."

"Most assuredly! Please follow me," replied the tuxedo-clad man with his French accent. "I know just the right table for two young people like you." With enough said, the maitre d' led Elana and Rigel to a properly positioned table providing them the exact view Rigel had requested.

"Perfect!" said Rigel as he slipped a gratuity to the man after he finished seating Elana. "Could ya please have someone bring a bottle a sparkling water for my lovely companion, and with some fresh lime. For me, ya can bring a pint a your Guinness, please."

Once the maitre d' gave the menus to Rigel and Elana, he disappeared and sent the waiter with their drinks.

Trying to bridge the gap between them, Elana leaned forward to get closer to Rigel. With a mischievous smile gracing her luscious red lips, she playfully confronted him, "Now, I'm going to give you a chance to answer what I asked you a few minutes ago."

He matched her body movement by also leaning forward. "Oh yes, my dear, how could I have let that man distract me? I really came back ta Tel Aviv ta follow up on some work we'd been doing with Tel Aviv University."

"What were you doing with the Tel Aviv University—something you'd been doing when we first met?" she asked as a curious look now defined her face.

With a quick flip of his hand he pushed his floppy red hair back in place and answered in an equally quick manner. "Yes, more-or-less a continuance a what I'd been doing when I first met ya. It wasn't the only thing we were working on, but it's what brought me back ta Israel. And since it's only 70 kilometers from Tel Aviv ta here, it's a small distance between good friends?"

Elana reached her hands over to cover his. "I'm simply flattered you could find the time to drive here to see me and make my day, or maybe my month. What are you doing at the university? Some form of chemical analysis?"

"Not really, it's chemical preservation, not analysis. With my company's chemical background, our expertise in preserving ancient books and manuscripts is what interested Tel Aviv University. They've a Department a Biblical Archaeology where numerous ancient texts need some re-vitalization. That's where my company specializes—the preservation and restoration a ancient writings."

"Enough to keep you busy?" asked Elana.

"Yea," he said with a carefree flip of his hand, "We've more work than we can handle. Every university or museum that has something a value written on some material wants ta maintain it. We're simply overwhelmed with work, but what about you? What are ya doing now, and is that Sonja still doing it with ya?"

Placing a napkin on her lap, she momentarily took her eyes off Rigel, before beaming back to meet the abundant sensitivity of his. "We're doing fine. She's still working with me, pursuing a project she developed at the symposium."

"Da ya think what ya have can convince your Board it'll be worth their support?"

Nodding tentatively, Elana then surpassed it with a confidence-exuding smile. "I think so, and we think we could be onto something big, and possibly related to the crucifixion of Jesus."

The waiter came to take their order, and when both ordered a rack of lamb, Elana was fascinated by the similarity of their tastes. "What a coincidence we both like rack of lamb. Is that what you grew up on in Ireland?"

Rigel's Irish brogue found a serious note. "Back in Ireland, ya never saw a rack of lamb, or at least not on your table. The good cuts went off ta the English. If there was any lamb ta be had, it was the scraps turned into a stew—a potato stew with only a fleeting visit from a lamb's shadow. There was less meat in those stews than ya would find on a starved hummingbird."

Laughing politely, Elana sensed what he said might be cute, but also represented a very serious and probably deprived phase of his life. "Tell me about your life back home in Ireland. Was it bad for everyone or just your family?"

Looking over Elana's shoulder into a fog of family faces, Rigel spoke with a soft voice that lost its vitality. "Everyone, or at least everyone who was a Catholic. As a child, we never had enough ta eat, and there was never enough balance in our food. Always potatoes done 10 different ways! Ya didn't eat anything else since food was too expensive, and ya didn't have things like a salad. That's why tonight I ordered their special 'seasonal' salad. I'd never had a salad until I left home. Back home, if there was a salad, I'd have thought I was eating some kind a potato dyed green. But now, about you! What did ya mean when ya said there were some problems ya had ta work through?"

As if being ashamed to discuss the issue, she spoke while looking away from him. "It's kind of embarrassing since we needed financial help to pursue what Sonja discovered. Her university sent someone, but now we have to put up with him since he controls the purse strings."

That got his attention as he leaned in towards the table. "What da ya mean 'put up with him'?"

"He's taken over some aspects of the work we developed, and he's got this mysterious background from working for the CIA. He and this Mordecai, the detective who was once with the Mossad, worked together and accidentally killed some people during an anti-terrorism mission. You can see the tension between the two—so thick you couldn't cut it with even the sharpest knife."

Leaning back in his chair, Rigel didn't want to appear too interested. "So this Eric is becoming a problem for the two a ya? Is he some kind a alpha male taking over the whole project?"

She missed it. The name 'Eric' coming from Rigel's lips simply passed by with no recognition that she hadn't spoken Eric's name to him. "Not really taking over the project, but frankly I'm suspicious of what he's doing. I mean, he comes to Jerusalem but won't meet us at the office before noon. He says he's roaming the streets, getting a feel for the city, but during the time he's been in Jerusalem, the two antique dealers we counted on have been killed."

Now was his perfect time for a little sympathy, and the seeding of a lot of doubt. "I can understand your frustration, but da ya think this Eric is involved with the murders a these dealers?"

"No, probably not, but I'm really not sure of what he's up to. It's too much of a coincidence that he arrives and our antique dealers get murdered. His murky past, even with this old Mossad agent, still needs some purifying for me to totally trust him."

Twisting in his chair in such a way that he could cross his legs, Rigel looked almost detached from this drama which consumed his interest. "Now I understand why ya don't trust him, but what about the old Mossad agent? Can ya trust him? If ya've really stumbled upon something, maybe they're working as a team ta steal from ya. How much money does a policeman make? So much he can't be tempted?"

"Maybe I'm being too negative. I think both men are probably trustworthy, and seem to be resolving their hostility, but our search would move along better without this CIA-Mossad sideshow of repentance."

His head tilted and was followed by an intensely inquisitive look, "Who is we? You, Sonja and this Eric?"

She held up one finger. "Plus one—we added this Mordecai to the mix. Now he's officially part of our team."

Uncrossing his legs, Rigel leaned towards the table. "I thought ya said he was a Mossad agent?"

Spellbound by those seductive blue eyes, she couldn't take her mind off them as her words came more from her heart than her head. "He was, but now he's a police detective here in Jerusalem. The deaths of the two dealers fell under his jurisdiction, and he thinks the dealers' deaths have something to do with us."

"Ús ya say? Da ya mean you, Sonja and Eric, or just you and Sonja?" he asked with his arched eyebrows broadcasting the extent of his doubts about Eric. "If this Mordecai and Eric weren't hitting it off so great in the beginning, what's binding them together now? Maybe the detective suspects Eric."

The blue-eyed spell popped, with bewilderment and confusion running rampant in her mind and on her frowning face. Turning away to look out the restaurant window as she regained her composure, she quickly redirected her focus back to Rigel. "You're raising too many doubts. Maybe I've not thought things out as clearly as you're making them, but your suspicions have hacked a hole in my reservoir of trust for Eric."

An uncomfortably long lull of speechlessness was ended as dinner was served and Rigel decided to change the subject. "Enough a this conspiracy talk. If ya have more on your mind, e-mail me if ya need ta, but for now, let's just enjoy this wonderful dinner."

Her beautiful smile and sparkling eyes buoyantly rebounded. "You're right. Forgive me for unloading all my problems on you, because the rack of lamb looks simply wonderful and I don't want anything detracting from this lovely feast."

Long, elegant fingers gently caressed his knife as Rigel started to carve the rack. But then he turned and pointed the knife at Elana. "If ya watch closely, you'll see I can cut my lamb and talk at the same time—something not all Irishmen can do." A self-imposed laugh cleared the air after his self-generated attempt at humor. "But in all seriousness, this lamb is the reason I stay here at the King David. They cover the rack with a coating a Dijon mustard, crushed garlic, merlot wine and bread crumbs, then it's sprinkled with rosemary. Bake it in the oven at 425 degrees Fahrenheit for 17 minutes, then finish it under the broiler ta crisp the outside. Like that," he snapped his finger, "it's done and ready ta be served with a merlot sauce."

Laughing at his theatrics, Elana paused for a second and gave a seductive smile, with her red lips oozing sensuality, then coquettishly questioned, "And how do you know so much about making this lamb?"

Pointing his knife now towards the kitchen, he teased, "I went back ta the kitchen the first time I had it. Was alone then, not with such lovely company as today! Who was ta complain if I rudely left the table ta go see the chef, and made him show me how ta make his merlot sauce."

Uncontrollably laughing, she acted like a little schoolgirl; something that hadn't happened for quite a long time. She paused to catch her breath and to stifle any more laughing. "I'm surprised you didn't ask him to show you how he prepares the lamb. Can you butcher it?"

Scraping his knife and fork together, as if he was sharpening the knife, he wasn't about to let the moment pass. "Well, if ya must ask, I'm very adept at butchering this rack. Ya take a very sharp knife and meticulously cut through the plastic shrink-wrap in which the rack a lamb is delivered ta your store. Once you've thrown away the plastic, put your knife away. Don't be foolish enough ta think ya can improve on what some butcher in Australia or New Zealand already did."

Now the laughs returned, but she was able to contain them. "OK, OK, I'm done, I won't ask anymore." she said raising her fork to eagerly consume a wonderfully delicate morsel of this overly-described lamb.

After watching her humorous meltdown, Rigel sensed he could get back to business, or at least his business. "How's your job at the Institute? Stable? I see you're still carrying the same purse, the one you and Sonja bought together ta get a better price. Aren't they paying ya enough ta get a second purse?"

Even though she was looking away from him, her eyebrows raised up like the flush of heat from her embarrassment. "OK, I admit the pay isn't as much as the satisfaction I get, but even though this is still my only purse, it's because of my choosing, not out of financial necessity."

"But didn't ya and Sonja get some financial help for your relic search?"

Her eyes now met his very focused orbs, but their blueness was faded by a force field of projected seriousness that dulled the light in his eyes, but sharpened her awareness of his probing. "There's no way the Biblical Institute has the deep pockets that Strayton University has. Strayton's generosity is the difference, and without them, it would be good-bye relics and good-bye Sonja. The President of Strayton, has given Eric authority to spend up to a million dollars if he's convinced something from the crucifixion is still around."

Rigel heard enough about Elana's team and didn't want to appear too interested in this Eric. Now was the time for some meaningless chatter about the food and the Guinness, as his superficial sincerity displaced intelligence gathering.

Looking at her plate, Elana summoned the courage to ask what was haunting her since their last time together. "I was struck with the depth of your devotion to the memory of your brother Michael. Do you really think you can make the Church act responsibly to get some sense of closure for your pain?"

Tilting back on his chair and pausing for a moment, he smiled as he found her eyes off her food and searching for something in his. "I don't worry about that. I'll fulfill my duty ta my brother in a way the Church will understand how many lives it's ruined. But don't ya worry a bit about this, I'll take care a it just like I'll take care a this bill." Rigel then waved to the waiter for his bill.

The waiter apprehensively approached the table, not wanting to disturb the two as they dreamily looked out the window at the Old City while the sun's beams were piercing through the prism of glass separating them from the outside world. When Rigel noticed him, he said with his hand reaching out, "Please give me the check and I'll pay with my credit card."

The waiter handed the bill to Rigel who clumsily dropped it and watched it flutter under the table. Fumbling and bumbling, he dropped all his credit cards on the floor and exclaimed, "I'll be damned, how clumsy a me! Under the table, but I'll get them." he said as he pushed aside the crouching waiter. Down on his knees under the table, he had access to Elana's purse. Taking the small burst transmitter out of his pocket, he secured it in the lining of a middle compartment, and zipped it closed. Such a small item couldn't be noticed by even the most curious of people, let alone a woman running her hand through a purse for some large object like a wallet, keys or sunglasses. But a transmitter like this could pick up anything that was said, and now the placement of this 'bug' was successful. Mission for the evening was accomplished.

Emerging from under the table, Rigel gave the check and the credit card to the waiter with a perfunctory "Thank ya. Once I escort my friend ta her taxi, I'll return ta sign the check." Turning to Elana, he walked behind her and helped slide her chair out from under the table. He spoke with rivulets of emotion, dripping over a cloak of intrigue, while looking into her beautiful brown eyes, "The thought a leaving ya simply shatters my heart, but I must go. Even though it's certainly been a wonderful evening, unfortunately it must come ta an end, but I'll escort ya ta your taxi."

Getting up from the table, she couldn't take her eyes off him. "It's been that, a wonderful evening, but when will I see you again?" she asked with a finely honed focus on his eyes delivering the increasing intensity of her emotions. But now she abruptly walked away from the table before he could answer, and peered back with a coquettish grin that conveyed she expected an answer.

With only a few quick steps, he caught up with her while grabbing her arm in semi-desperation. "I'm not sure, but I do expect ta be back ta Tel Aviv within the next week. Maybe we can get together then."

Her right hand reached over and squeezed his arm. "I'd love that. E-mail me when you know when that'll be. I only have one commitment over the next week that might interfere."

Walking along, Rigel couldn't help inquiring, "Will ya be away for long?"

"For several days. Sonja, Eric, this Mordecai and I will be going up to Armenia in about three days to look at a monastery for our relics search. I'm not sure when we'll leave, but if you e-mail me, I'll be in touch with you about when we can get together."

His head spun over this confrontation with his confusion. *How did I miss that?* He thought to himself. *A little gem of information that almost slipped by me very ears.* "Once you're back from Armenia, e-mail me and let me know what ya found, or if this Eric and Mordecai tried ta steal ya blind," he said while laughing. "Be careful with them, 'cause those men always want something from ya, and ya never know exactly what or when. Believe me, I grew up seeing how the men in power take all the hard work a the women."

Walking from the restaurant towards the revolving exit door, Elana tightly grabbed Rigel's arm, and he responded with a more intimate clutch that heightened her anticipation of some warm, fuzzy end to the evening. Finally outside, the doorman opened the taxi's door while Rigel put his arms around Elana and gave her the kiss he assumed she was expecting. Not as long as she might have liked, and not with the intensity of affection that she had hoped for. No simmering heat, no stars bursting and no emotional intensity. A little too lifeless, even too chilling—or was it too cold and empty? But it was a kiss, the first kiss and she wasn't going to let this chance drift away. She grabbed around the back of his neck and gave him a hug and bigger kiss than she was receiving. She felt it was her time and she wasn't going to leave without putting her mark on the evening. As she got into the car she looked back into his beautiful face and added, "Good night Rigel. It was wonderful to be with you again."

"Marvelous ta be with ya, my dear. But hopefully the next time we can spend more time together." With that, Rigel slowly closed the door and as the car pulled out, he waved back to the waving hand of the lovely and lovelorn Elana Dutros. He knew it was time to go to bed since he had a long day ahead of him tomorrow, and tragically for Elana, he hadn't a thought or even a memory of her kiss. Rigel wasn't going to let a little thing like romance derail his agenda.

Chapter 15

Austrian Airlines flight 641 circled the Armenian countryside as it approached the isolated Zvartnots International Airport from the east. Rigel's and Conor's panoramic view of the landscape surrounding the city of Yerevan was just as the tourist pamphlet described: a city ringed by magnificent mountains. To the south, Mt. Ararat dominated the skyline with its snowcapped peak, and on its east side was the small Lesser Ararat. And to the northwest were the four peaks of Mt. Aragats, just like a crown ringing this lovely jewel of a city. *1.4 million people,* Rigel mused to himself thinking how he never expected there could be this many people in all of Armenia. When you came from a small country like Ireland, you needed to fight the sense of geographic parochialism that existed within most people. He shook his head in amazement as the thought stayed in his mind, *There's a much larger world out there than you realize.*

After the plane's rough landing, compounded by some wind shear turbulence, Rigel was glad they weren't flying on a Russian Aeroflot plane where there was no assurance, even in good weather, you would land in one piece, or even in the right country. Glancing over at Conor, Rigel saw the relieved look on his face since flying was not one of his strong points. Viktor slept through the complete landing and needed to be awakened once it was time to exit the plane down a steep staircase and out into the Armenian air. The air seemed just as they advertised in the tourist pamphlet—clean, fresh and even sweet.

The Zvartnots Airport, still a remnant of the time Armenia was The Armenian Soviet Socialist Republic, was painfully short on creature comforts and minimalist in architecture and passenger hospitality services. Just a bare-bones airport reflecting on the time when the people of the old Soviet Union didn't have the opportunity or money to travel.

Once inside, Rigel scanned the terminal and saw the Armenia Lada rental car company had a booth. He had pre-registered for a Mercedes van and booked it with the same false passport used for the airplane flight. Upon providing his papers to the man behind the counter, this rental agent was immediately trying to sell him some options to his basic rental agreement. *Why do these people always try to make more money on you? Just rent me a car, and no, I don't want any insurance. And yes, I'll bring the car back with a full tank of petrol,* he thought as he lamented this unfortunate part of renting a vehicle anywhere in the world.

"Please Mr. Morgan, sir," the car rental clerk beseeched Rigel with his new identity, "please take wonderful vehicle, sir, and enjoy Armenian countryside. When will you be return it?"

"Tonight... back ta ya tonight," replied Rigel, knowing he would be going out tonight on the airplane, but not under the same name. And the van might never see the light of the next day.

"Your van, sir, over in lot across street," said the agent while pointing to the lot. "Please, have good drive, my sir."

The route south from the airport was relatively simple to find with Viktor behind the wheel since he was able to read the road signs. Driving southward, they couldn't ignore that the towering presence of Mt. Ararat, not even in Armenia, but within Turkey, was a clear directional beacon on this main north-south road out of Yerevan.

Speaking loudly to make sure he wasn't falling asleep at the wheel, Rigel startled Viktor. "Da ya know where we're going? Can ya really read these road signs?"

Trivializing Rigel's concerns, Viktor gave a simple wave of his right hand lamb-claw. "No problem, I read well Armenian signs. Spend one year here with KGB. They know how important to understand what religions thinking, especially with Muslims everywhere."

Conor added his 'two cents', "Da ya mean even at the peak of its power, the old Soviet Union still didn't trust its own people?"

Giving a quick glance over his shoulder, Viktor replied, "Soviet Union never trusted anyone. Was country spying on its spies who were spying on own parents, children and friends. Never a union of people, but bunch of people never trusting, always fearing each other. Not you Irish, you bound by Church and people's poverty."

Conor couldn't hold back, "Don't ya get started with that bullshit about the damned Church. Now we'll have ta listen ta Rigel tell how it ruined the life a the people." He turned to Rigel. "Right?"

"That ya are," replied Rigel while looking out the window at the countryside. "But don't ya get started with that discussion, we've got more important things ta do here."

Angling toward Viktor, Rigel continued, "We're taking this road basically all the way ta Khor Virap. It takes us into Ararat Province and then wind along the banks a the Araks River. Once we get close ta the monastery, we'll need ta find directions."

Driving for 90 minutes, following the Araks River as it moved southward and then into the area where Khor Virap was to be found, they were now confused about where to go next. "Rigel," Viktor boomed loud enough to shake all the dandruff out of Conor's hair, "not sure where to go, but are in right area since Mr. Ararat is on right. Across from us, not south anymore. Somewhere up on left will be monastery.

Viewing the bend in the river, one could see it was paralleled by the bend in the road, and coming around that bend, Viktor saw a road going off to his left and turned onto it. This stone-paved road steeply ascended away from the river to what appeared to be some distant village life.

With his arm reaching over to Viktor's hand on the wheel, Rigel said, "This is a good place ta stop before we go too far. We need ta put on some priests' clothes ta make us look more legitimate."

Quickly into the van after slipping on the robes and collars of priests, Conor spoke mockingly to Rigel. "Ya look so priestly, maybe ya should've been a priest or even a Pope."

Rigel laughed. "In my Church a the Internet, I'll be the Pope and you, my worthy lads, as a reward for your devotion and obedience, will be my cardinals. But don't ya worry," he mocked them, "there'll be no vows a celibacy in my church—just looking like a priest is bad enough."

Leaning forward in his seat, Conor asked. "Is there much of a monastery here?"

Not able to take his eye off Mt. Ararat, Rigel answered. "It's mostly a ceremonial place for their patron saint."

"A resting place for their saint?" asked Viktor. "Sounds good, no?"

"Maybe," replied Rigel, "but who knows? There's just a hole in the floor where their patron saint, St. Gregory, was held prisoner. Supposedly it contains his bones."

Driving along, they looked up the hill and saw an older man riding on an oxcart. As they got close, Viktor stopped the Mercedes and waved for the man to stop. Viktor turned back to Rigel. "Give me map. I get directions."

Rigel and Conor watched Viktor go over to the old man, thrusting himself along the way as a massive hulk of intimidation. Viktor's right index finger became an instantaneous, jabbing probe into the man's chest. Barking something in Russian, Viktor then held his map in his left hand while that same offensive right index finger pointed to it. Viktor finally left the hapless farmer and returned to the Mercedes.

"What did he tell ya?" asked Conor.

Proud bully that he was, and seeking his master's approval, Viktor focused on Rigel. "He said stay on road. At fork in road, go right 6 kilometers and see monks' home. Has white cross on front of it."

Conor's words came out first. "It's good ta have this Russian with us. We'd be lost without him."

Sitting up straight in his seat and staring at Conor, Viktor's words were laced with indignation, "Not Russian! Am White Russian!"

Rigel reached over to pat Viktor on the head, "Don't ya forget, you're my black Russian, not White Russian."

Always seeking some Irish approval, Viktor looked first to Rigel and then to Conor, before smiling. "Fine! Am very black White Russian!"

The van and its deceitful contents drove onward; bumped and jostled by the badly-rutted, muddy road with its brown pools of muck grabbing at the vehicle's wheels. But just as the old man had directed, up ahead was the monastery with its rectory behind. Parking their van, they walked over to the monastery but saw it was closed. Redirecting over towards the rectory, Rigel added, "We'll do the rectory first, then check out the monastery."

When they got close to the rectory door, Rigel turned to Viktor, "Come up front. I need ya ta tell these monks we're traveling Irish priests and want ta see what relics they have from the crucifixion."

"I to tell them, me sounding like Russian who they don't like, I to tell them I am Irish priest? Good God Rigel, I not Irishman. They will think me a Russian."

At the rectory front door, Viktor knocked several times before it was answered. A little, pot-bellied, red-faced monk, looking like he just dunked his face into a bowl of borscht, answered while eyeing them curiously.

Viktor spoke in Russian. "These Irish priests are searching for some relics of Jesus' crucifixion. Do you understand their English?"

"I understand English," said the monk, now looking somewhat warily at this odd threesome and knowing this big Russian wasn't of the cloth.

Rigel impatiently stepped in front of Viktor. "Da ya have any idea where they keep the relics a the crucifixion?"

In his broken English, the monk replied while warily eyeing these three very peculiar strangers. "I am here 15 years and never heard of relics."

184

Persisting for a different answer from this brown butterball of a man, Rigel shot back, "Anyone else here who knows about the relics from, say, 2,000 years ago? We've come all the way from Ireland ta look at your relics a Jesus' crucifixion."

The monk's spine stiffened and his face projected a firm resolve. "I am senior monk here and can tell you with absolute authority, we have nothing of crucifixion. The oldest things are bones of our St. Gregory, the Illuminator."

The impatient Viktor gave a mighty push and forced the door open as the monk flew back into the hallway. Towering over the monk, he smacked him, grabbed him by the throat, then threatened him, "Listen old ball of fat, we want relics of crucifixion. Where to look, here or in monastery? Lie to me and I kill you!"

In a trembling voice, with blood dripping from a torn lip, the old monk whimpered weakly, "We have no relics of crucifixion. We are poor monastery in very poor country."

Grabbing Conor by the arm, Rigel turned to walk back outside towards the monastery. Before exiting the doorway, he turned to Viktor, "Do whatever ya need ta get the truth from him."

Outside the rectory, Rigel and Conor could hear a violent commotion in Russian. The sound of broken glass and an old man's screams left no doubt regarding what avenue of interrogation Viktor had introduced. As the rectory door swung open, out came Viktor dragging the old man.

Holding the monk upright, like a prized stag, Viktor triumphantly spoke. "Can you believe he volunteered to help? Said there is something important in the monastery."

Viewing this pitiful old man, Conor turned back to Viktor, "Da ya believe him? Da ya believe ya ever get the truth when ya torture?"

An exaggerated positive shake of his head characterized Viktor's reply. "I gave him dose of his own truth serum. A taste of your blood works every time. He told all he knows. Let's go to monastery. This monk, Brother Barda, responsible for monastery for next six hours and is only one here."

185

Pointing Conor toward the van, Rigel directed. "Get the metal detector from the backpack."

Turning to Viktor, he added, "Take us ta the monastery and let's see where ta go."

Pushing and dragging the monk along the large pebble path to the monastery, Viktor led as Rigel followed closely. Conor ran back from the van to catch up with them.

At the monastery, the monk unlocked the large wooden door whose ancient huge metal hinges creaked as it was pushed open by Viktor. Brother Barda then led them past a simple exhibit area where the faithful could see some drawings and text about St. Gregory.

On a tripod stand was some text about the beloved saint. After looking at it, Conor turned to the old man, "What did this St. Gregory do for Armenia that ya thought so much a him?"

In a voice weakened by the beating and the rough transport out to the monastery, the monk, cowed by his handling, tried to avoid eye contact with anyone. "He converted the ancient King Khosrov to Christianity and then converted the whole country."

An increasingly annoyed Viktor raised his right hand and the monk saw the stars on it right before it crashed down on his weakened shoulder. "Move faster old man! Don't have all day. Where are relics you talked about? "

The old man went to a large limestone slab and pointed down at it. "Under this is the only relic at Khor Virap, the bones of St. Gregory."

Viktor bent down, readily slid the large oblong-shaped stone over the adjacent stones, then picked it up to expose an underground compartment. "Too dark to see!"

Pointing to a light that Rigel was getting out of the backpack, the monk answered, "Take the light and look, but don't break our ossuary. Inside are the most prized possessions of Armenia—St. Gregory's bones."

Quickly down into the hole, Viktor's light was on the stone box which he picked up and pushed it out onto the floor. A proud Viktor spoke to Rigel,

"Knew he couldn't wait to help us." Looking back towards the monk, he asked, "This all you have?"

Tears of shame flowed as Brother Barda couldn't escape how he had forsaken his vows to keep safe these precious bones of St. Gregory. He badly mumbled, "For 1700 years we have kept his bones in the dungeon where he was held prisoner."

"Whose bones are ya blubbering about?" asked Conor. "Jesus' bones?"

Incredulous, Rigel asked, "How could they be Jesus' bones? If ya believe the Bible, he was resurrected and His bones and body were gone ta Heaven. There are no bones a Jesus ta be had."

Handing Viktor the light again, Rigel told him, "Take the light and sweep that whole area so nothing gets overlooked."

With the three men standing above the hole, Conor held the monk upright by his collar to prevent him from collapsing into the hole. Viktor finally stuck his head outside the hole and pronounced, "Nothing here."

With pressure building, just like two tectonic plates preparing to let loose their pressurized devastation, a frustrated Rigel turned and grabbed the monk by his robe, "Is this the only hole?"

"Yes," said the shaken monk in a trembling voice, "the only one. The holy one."

Turning to the ossuary, Rigel tugged at the lid until it fell on the stone floor and cracked. He could still see the exterior surface of the lid and thought of how it had no lettering on it. Looking at the inside of the ossuary, Rigel finally turned away in disgust, "Nothing but some old bones and dust in the bottom a the box." As his frustration peaked, Rigel grabbed the monk by the arm and jerked him violently. "Did your monastery ever have any other relics?"

The monk half whispered, "I am 'Keeper of Oral History' at Khor Virap. My job is to know the history that wasn't written down. In ancient times, we had something from time of Jesus, but we sent that to drier climate about 1100 years ago."

An agitated Viktor stuck his finger in the monk's chest, "How do you know that? Why you say 'drier'?"

Gasping for breath, the old monk was barely able to speak. "Said so in our ancient written records. Old records are gone and head of the monastery is required to memorize history and pass along to two monks to keep the monastery's secrets."

"Why send it ta a drier climate? What was it? Where was it?" asked Rigel.

Pausing to take several deep breaths, the monk replied. "The records didn't say what it was but it was sent to another monastery in a drier, desert climate. They needed dry place that would protect whatever it was."

"Where da ya think they sent it?" asked Rigel again with his disdain for this development getting greater with each unanswered question.

For a few seconds, the monk regained his composure. "Not sure, but probably was St. Catherine's. It is in a remote desert and with Russian Orthodox connections. Monastery always had some relationship with St. Catherine's."

With the bitter taste of failure filling his mouth, Rigel turned to Viktor, "We've wasted our time here. Conor and I are leaving, but do what ya must."

Having just passed by the tripod display of St. Gregory, Conor and Rigel heard the pleading of the old man and then a quick scuffle and a heavy grunt as Viktor dispatched him to the ground with a death-dealing blow to the back of his neck. Not caring how he left the scene, Viktor turned and followed Rigel and Conor to the van.

Sitting in the van, tapping his fingers on the dashboard, Rigel couldn't hide his disappointment. "Wasted a lot a time here lads. Should've gone ta the other place."

Playing the role of a diplomat, Conor intoned, "Aren't we still days ahead a the women? When they get here, they won't even have this monk ta give them the information we got."

Turning away from Conor, Rigel was captivated by the view of Mt. Ararat dominating the skyline over to the west of them. "You're probably right. We're still way ahead a them, but for now, take these robes and throw them in the rectory furnace. Let's get back ta Yerevan and leave our van in an old run-down part a town where it'll disappear. The van and the three a us all disappearing from Armenia with no trace left behind."

Descending down the stone road toward the river, they again passed the old farmer. Recognizing the vehicle, he noticed those men, but now without their robes. And no one in the Mercedes noticed this insignificant man as they drove by with their steely gazes focused on something other than the local farmer who wouldn't forget them.

Chapter 16

Ben Gurion Airport was always a busy hub for business and tourist activity, and this day was no different. Proceeding through security to the El Al departure gate, little did Eric know, nor could he have understood how much he had in common with the three men who he unwittingly passed at the Austrian Airlines boarding area for flight 614 to Yerevan, Armenia. While ugly fate didn't yet have their paths intersecting, the Ben Gurion Airport represented the first focal point of their physical and conceptual proximity, and soon they would be enveloped into conflicts of ideas, values and physicality.

Eric's flight out of Israel evoked thoughts about fleeing his Problem as well as the continuing Middle East quagmire with too many hostilities and too few genuine opportunities for peace. The antique dealers' deaths, while personal with their impact on Sonja and Elana, couldn't compare to the systematic dispensation of death and horrors scattered throughout the eastern end of the Mediterranean basin. Eric's Strayton adventure had taken a psychological U-turn—deviating from an experience of intellectual curiosity towards a caustic cauldron of death and horrific hatred of humanity that too often found residence in the region's shifting sands. Try as he might, Eric Stanfels couldn't shed his own snakeskin of Middle East psycho-trauma by simply doing good for Strayton or his partners in their search. Now finding himself back in this pit of vipers, the deaths of these two old men was the venomous neurotoxin that told him on some subconscious level he may never be able to flee this heritage. Hopefully, this trip out of this land of holiness and hatred and off to the Vatican might serve as a cathartic experience, fleeing this remorseful psycho-complexity of Jerusalem for a sense of spiritual tranquility. El Al flight 314 just might be his 'angel flight" taking him to a land of better promise.

Hailing a taxi at Rome's DaVinci-Fiumicino Airport was no problem since the lines were long and the homogeneity of the drivers, all enthusiastic about their city and country, made for a welcome greeting for any traveler. As he jumped into the back seat of a taxi, Eric was overcome with a tourist's rush of euphoria that accompanied a first trip to Rome, certainly an emotion that was absent his first time in Jerusalem. As the taxi sped toward the Vatican, his inner sense of satisfaction buoyed his confidence for his soon-to-be encounter with the Operational Director of the Division of New Testament Studies at the Vatican, Monsignor Carlo Bertani. For the past 14 years, two Strayton professors per year were at the Vatican researching the New Testament due to the dynamic vision of Dr. Smathers' and his longtime friend, Monsignor Bertani. President Smathers' e-mail for Eric, sent to Sonja Martin's computer at the Biblical Institute, had expressed his undaunted confidence that Monsignor Bertani could and would be the person to facilitate Eric's access to St. Catherine's.

Deposited at the appropriate Vatican address, Eric looked up in awe at the imposing buildings caressing, surrounding and snuggling in a sense of spirituality he had never seen. Despite growing up in a family of ministers, there had never been any interest in seeing the Vatican since his family was more in step with a narrow Protestant mindset that had very little use for any aspect of Catholicism. Yet, as he stood in the midst of this universal epicenter of the Catholic Church, a spiritual power enraptured his emotion-charred soul and brought a sense of shame that Christians could create artificial barriers between themselves which only served anti-Christian agendas. Feeling like a sponge soaking-up this serum of spirituality that imparted an enhanced energy to his own committed Christianity, Eric couldn't take his eyes off the surrounding structures. So lost was he in this realm of rapture that he never heard the security doorman who asked, first in Italian and then English, if he could be of service.

Confused, he replied with his struggling staccato sentences. "Oh...no! Yes... I'm sorry. Yes... please, I'm here to see Monsignor Carlo Bertani. My name is Professor Eric Stanfels from Strayton University in the United States. The Monsignor is expecting me." He now dropped his passport, and then after retrieving it, handed it to the doorman. "Here... you'll find all my papers are in order."

After carefully analyzing Eric's passport, the doorman gave a stern look for a few seconds, then quickly followed with a broad smile broadcasting a warm greeting, "Welcome Professor Stanfels. Monsignor Bertani is awaiting your arrival. Please," he said as he opened the door, "please enter and go straight ahead and then to your right at the last corridor. You will see the Monsignor's office directly in front of you. Have a pleasant and holy stay here at the Vatican."

Thanking the man who shook his hand, but didn't want to let go quickly enough, Eric hastily entered the building and proceeded along the corridor. He thought it noteworthy that the walls, which could serve as space for numerous religious paintings or portraits, were devoid of any trappings of opulence. Certainly not what Eric had expected based on his anti-Catholic upbringing. The sturdy doors to the various offices were of beautifully-finished wood, but the lack of any decorative frills conveyed a sense that the people in these offices were workers, not dignitaries. Finally facing the large, double doors to the Monsignor's office, Eric was overwhelmed by the intimidating projection of absolute power, not unlike what he felt around President Smathers. Sensing anxiety seeping into his brain from some hidden reservoir of doubt, Eric dried his sweaty palms and opened the door. With his boldest of strides, he walked directly towards a priest properly positioned behind a reception desk.

"I'm Professor Eric Stanfels," he said as he handed his business card to the priest, "Monsignor Bertani is expecting me."

Staring at him for seconds, the priest then replied, "You are correct Professor, Monsignor Bertani is awaiting your arrival. Please follow me," he said as he rose and led Eric to a door opening into the massive office of the Monsignor.

Ensconced behind a large mahogany desk was a man whose gray hair contrasted with his stark black robe. Out from behind the desk he came with his hand extended towards Eric as he spoke with a sense of propriety and formality that was consistent with his office. "Professor Stanfels, it is my pleasure to meet you," he spoke as he shook Eric's hand. "I can't tell you how excited I am to have this occasion to serve you and your president, my dear friend, Dr. Smathers. What a man of courage and Christian conviction!"

"Thank you Monsignor," Eric rightfully responded as he continued shaking the Monsignor's hand while intently focusing on his dark brown eyes with their great sensitivity and a penetratingly powerful projection of integrity. "I'm very pleased to meet you and certainly honored to be here on behalf of President Smathers and Strayton University."

"Please, the pleasure is all mine! Your Strayton's biblical researchers are a invaluable addition to our thought processes here at the Vatican. I am embarrassed to admit it is much too easy to fall into a very parochial mindset when you are in place so isolated from the diversity of Christian thought."

Eric couldn't hide that huge 'Strayton-Pride' smile smeared all over his face. "I'm sure our scholars feel the same way about being here. We all need some person or experience to help shed the myopic blinders that limit our vision and our perceptions."

"Well said," replied the Monsignor as he pensively placed an index finger on his heavily-dimpled chin, only then to use it to point at a three-legged Oriental Chippendale coffee table, "but, please don't stand there, come and have a seat at the coffee table. There's coffee or tea, and some sweets that are simply marvelous. Come... please help yourself."

As the two men ambled over to the coffee table, the reception priest exited the room, leaving only Eric and the Monsignor to enjoy their treats and discuss their intended area of mutual collaboration. The Monsignor's social face took on a firmer business facade with his eyes now seeming to darken and his chin dimple getting decidedly deeper. "Professor Stanfels, if I am correct, you are here because you have an interest in gaining access to the St. Catherine's monastery. Is that so?"

Compelled by his eagerness to reply, Eric edged forward in his chair but his mind was leaping further and faster than his body. "Yes! My colleagues, Sonja Martin and Elana Dutros, and I would like to travel to St. Catherine's to gain their assistance in our search for some ancient relics."

The seriousness was shed and the warmth returned to Bertani's face as his eyes lit up to a sparkle. "President Smathers told me that and how your enthusiasm for this search could be infectious. What is it you are seeking? Something you know definitely exists at St. Catherine's," Bertani said while tilting his head and projecting a look of doubt by his unevenly arched eyebrows, "or is it possible that, as you Americans say, you are on a wild goose chase?"

Sensing a dose of doubt in the Monsignor's question, an almost apologetic Eric tentatively answered in a conciliatory tone. "I admit we might be on a wild goose chase, but one with enough basis to justify our efforts—so strong a basis that two men assisting this project were murdered."

"Oh my," replied Bertani as a frown quickly covered his face and the wrinkles on his forehead pulled those bushy eyebrows into contact with them. "Are you sure their murders were related to your work?"

"Very sure! The two murdered men were actually two of three relics dealers who met with my associate, Sonja Martin. Of the three dealers, the two who were murdered were the only ones who gave her any information. The third had no information, wasn't harmed and didn't have any suspicious visitors at the time the other two men were killed. Apparently the killers knew who provided information to Sonja and only went after them."

Standing up and moving behind his chair, and with his left index finger back on that dimpled chin, the Monsignor turned towards Eric. "Have you considered that maybe they did know what was said, and by whom?"

Eric nodded. "We're guessing that, but we're not sure who, how or why."

Looking down on Eric, still seated in his chair, Bertani towered over him both physically and intellectually. "These relics must be important to the three of you if people have been killed over them. What can be so valuable?"

Looking away to regain his composure, an energized Eric turned and responded by looking directly into those brown eyes that now seemed to be tinted windows of inquisitiveness, or even skepticism. "My colleagues and I think there might be relics still existing from the crucifixion of Jesus."

Swiveling back into his seat, Bertani leaned towards Eric. "Professor, I can understand your commitment, and also that of President Smathers, but may I ask what you are expecting to find?" A look of amusement now crept over his face as a mischievous twinkle came back into his eyes. "The Holy Grail or some such thing?"

"Frankly Monsignor, the three of us aren't sure, but we aren't expecting to find the Holy Grail or anything as fragile as cloth or parchment."

The smile stayed, but a serious, probing tone emerged in Bertani's voice. "Might it be wood or metal that you are expecting to find? Like the spear which pierced the side of our beloved Savior?"

His confidence was growing and the Monsignor could read it in his reply. "Metal is what we think might exist. But the spear? No. That spear has been the object of searches for hundreds of years and was thought to be in the treasure of some king or on the crest-of-arms of some ancient ruler, probably a Hapsburg. No, the spear isn't it."

"Then what is it you seek?" asked Monsignor with a look of impatience now visiting his face.

Eyeing the Monsignor with a surprising sense of empowerment, probably too confident considering how little information he actually had, Eric continued. "If we're lucky, we'll find something like the spikes that nailed Jesus to the cross."

Shocked and surprised, and with his eyebrows separated from his scalp only by the deep furrows of doubt across his forehead, the Monsignor continued. "The spikes? Very intriguing, but the Middle East has been rife with unscrupulous relics dealers who have been peddling spikes or nails from the time of the crucifixion. Some people think there were four spikes, not three, while others claim they found several of the spikes. How do you think you can find anything that won't be a fraud? Even if St. Catherine's has something, who can prove if it was from the crucifixion?"

Eric's confidence thermometer was rising. "If we find the spikes, we can do sophisticated testing to prove their legitimacy."

"Professor, I am aware of carbon dating and how it might be used to show the spikes to be from the time of the crucifixion, but what good would that be for you?"

In somewhat of a pleading gesture, Eric extended both of his hands toward the Monsignor. "You're right that with the use of carbon dating there are still other problems, but we think the discovery phase can be taken further once we show what we find is 2,000 years old. Actually, you can't carbon date metal spikes, so for our purposes, we need to find some organic residue on the spikes—the organic residue is what gets carbon dated."

Leaning forward, the Monsignor reached over to clasp Eric's hands in his. "And my dear Professor, what kind of organic residue might you expect to find?"

Taking his hands away and sitting back in his chair, Eric fixed his eyes on the intently staring brown globes of Monsignor Bertani. "To be honest with you, the only organic material I would expect to find on those spikes, if there is something to be found at all, would be blood.
But we can't get anywhere if we can't get past the monks at St. Catherine's. We know they don't like Protestants because of some problems from the 19th century. This is where we need your help if I can be so bold as to impose upon your graciousness."

Sitting motionless for a few seconds and then, whether consciously or subconsciously, Bertani started nodding his head, "I know the history of the pilfering Protestants at St. Catherine's. Old memories fade away slowly, especially when you are dealing with old men in religious orders with too much time on their hands. Fortunately for you, I have a good relationship with Archbishop Bournias, the power who controls everything at St. Catherine's."

"How do you know him so well?" asked Eric.

"It's all about the New Testament. While we have research programs with Strayton, we also have numerous relationships of a similar kind with other religious groups and institutions. St. Catherine's has a treasure trove of New Testament materials which is why the Vatican has been all too happy to collaborate with them in order to gain access to their New Testament reservoirs of information."

"And this is how you know the Archbishop?" asked Eric.

"Yes. He is the only person who can give authority for anything to be studied, and with absolute certainty, I can tell you anything at St. Catherine's to be studied must be done at their monastery. Nothing leaves the monastery without that rare permission from the Archbishop. The wounds inflicted by that preposterous Protestant Tischendorf still sear within the collective psyches of all those monks at St. Catherine's. The mere mention that Tischendorf's Codex Sinaiticus, or more rightfully so, St. Catherine's Codex Sinaiticus, resides in London brings back hostile memories that are deeply imbedded within the collective DNA of the monastery."

Leaning further forward, and with his hands clasped together like a pleading beggar, Eric did just that—begged. "Is it presumptuous of me to impose upon you, on behalf of Strayton and the New Testament Biblical Institute, in order to arrange a meeting for me with Archbishop Bournias?"

Bertani reached over to approvingly pat Eric's hands. "I can assure you I will do all in my power for all of you, especially my good friend President Smathers. But I will need to begin work immediately since the Archbishop actually will be coming to Rome in a few days." As he looked, a smile broke across Eric's face. "Did I surprise you with that?"

Eric's newly-found smile expanded so the corners of his mouth almost touched his ears. "You certainly did!"

"Then please forgive me for now ending this meeting since I do have work to do regarding what will hopefully be our meeting with Archbishop Bournias."

"I'm sure I speak on behalf of President Smathers in thanking you for what you are willing to do, but may I ask you for one additional favor? Do you have the internet here that I can use to e-mail to my co-workers at the Biblical Institute? They're dying to hear about our meeting."

"Surely! Use my computer over there." said the Monsignor pointing to the computer desk off by a window behind where they had been sitting. As the Monsignor got up from his chair and walked over to activate the computer he added, "Send whatever you need, but now I must leave. When you are done, just go out the door you originally entered."

"Thanks so very much for your time and consideration." said Eric in such a manner he worried it might be too solicitous.

"Please Professor Stanfels," the Monsignor said while tilting his head towards Eric, "the pleasure is all mine. And do give my best wishes to your President Smathers. I hope you will share with him what you are e-mailing your co-workers."

An exuberant Eric contemplated how he would break such wonderful news to his partners. "Yes, I will to all of them. Thank you again."

Striding elegantly out of the room, with his perfect posture and the edge of his robe brushing over the Oriental rugs, Monsignor Bertani looked back at Eric to wave good-bye, but saw only the back of a man already immersed in his e-mailing.

Eric's first e-mail was to President Smathers. Simply emphatic that Strayton and the Biblical Institute should be honored to have a friend like Monsignor Bertani—a wonderful man eager to help their cause. Eric closed Smathers' e-mail with an optimistic message about the potential for more good news in the future.

To the Biblical Institute, using Elana's e-mail address, his message was different. Eric's message was full of hope and optimism. He told of his confidence about some level of support from Monsignor Bertani. He caught himself smiling while speaking out loud with his last e-mail lines, "Will get back late tonight on El Al flight 416. Tomorrow, all four, including Mordecai, must have lunch around 12:30 at the Golden Ram restaurant. Saw it one day, and they have a large outside dining area where they cook a lamb in an open pit. Look forward to seeing you there tomorrow."

Elated and empowered, Eric arose from the computer, satisfied his message conveyed a sense of enthusiasm that he could open the doors to St.Catherine's. He knew the message would be well received, as it was by President Smathers, Elana and by Liam.

Chapter 17

Delayed due to mechanical problems, the return flight to Tel Aviv and then drive deposited Orion in Jerusalem at 1:30 AM. When the weary Rigel, Conor and Viktor finally came crashing into their beds at the King David, they missed the note Liam left on the table.

Morning came quickly with the sunlight streaming through windows whose blinds barely blocked these unwanted rays of intrusion. But Liam knew he had to awaken these bone-weary travelers, and did so with a cup of black coffee—the Middle Eastern stuff so thick you could peel it out of your cup and chew it. "Welcome lads," he barked as he raised the feeble blinds and placed the tray of cups on the table, "it's a beautiful morning and ya don't want ta miss it. Stayed up late ta greet ya, but ya took so long, I went off ta bed. Did ya read my note?"

"God damn ya, Liam!" belched out a belligerent Rigel. "What in God's name are ya doing? We need ta sleep, not hear ya singing about a beautiful morning."

Persisting in bringing these vagabond voyagers back to reality, Liam kept pushing. "I know ya've had just a small sleep but ya need ta face a bigger day, and do it right now. We've work ta do, or at least plan on doing."

Being the only one stirring, Rigel looked at the bright light then turned to Liam with a mouth so cotton-dry he almost couldn't speak. "For Christ's sake, what is it ya know that we don't? How da ya know we have work ta do when ya don't even know what work we did?"

With the sense of utmost urgency refusing to yield, Liam raised his voice almost to a shouting level, "I don't give a damn what ya did yesterday, we've work ta do here and it needs ta be done soon. Obviously ya didn't read my note last night."

Knowing he couldn't stay in bed any longer, Rigel conceded to stop Liam's persistent pestering. "No, we didn't even see a note, so tell us what it said."

Now that all the men were awake, before continuing, Liam passed each a cup of coffee, remembering to add heavy sugar for Viktor. "I read their e-mail and found this wonder boy, Stanfels, had a good day at the Vatican with some Monsignor Bertani. Now he's eager ta tell his mates the good news today. Flew in from Rome yesterday and probably got back ta Jerusalem as late as you. And he's planned a lunch today at 12:30 in a restaurant called the Golden Ram. Said it'll be 'all four a them'. Who da ya think this fourth is?"

"What is time?" asked a groggy Viktor stumbling slowly into the conversation.

An edge of impatience sharpened Liam's voice as he turned away from Viktor to Rigel. "It's eight o'clock now and that's why I woke ya so early."

Briefly hesitating after taking a long sip of his steaming coffee, Rigel was now awake and ready to assume control. "What about the bug? Did ya go over ta her office ta hear anything?"

Liam's head shaking said it all, "Went over, but heard nothing important."

After turning away from Liam to look out the window to the heavens, that routine embedded into his brain when in he was in deep thought, Rigel was ready to turn back to face the men. "Ya were right ta wake us, but give me a second ta think." He paused for a second. "Four a them ya say?"

His slow moving and even slower thinking comrades were fanning the fires of Liam's increasing impatience. "Yea... ya heard me correct. The professor is talking about having lunch together—today. Don't ya think we need ta do something?"

Weary and aching from too long on a plane, and not long enough in a bed, Rigel got up off his chair. "OK, we need ta see who this fourth is."

"The professor's e-mail from Rome referred ta a Mordecai, so it must be him," a cocksure Liam proudly proclaimed as proof he could analyze, not just copy messages.

"Mordecky?' asked a very confused Viktor.

"No, Viktor, it's Mordecai. Mor-de-cai!" spouted an impertinent Liam barely able to keep his frustration from leaking further into his speech.

Sensing the rising tension, Rigel took control. "Whatever his name is, we don't know what he looks like, or even what the professor looks like. Liam, do yourself a good deed and find the address a this Golden Ram."

The words barely escaped Rigel's lips before Liam proudly spoke, "It's at 532 St. George Street, over by the American Colony Hotel."

"Good job, my Liam," added Rigel with a nod of his head in Liam's direction. "Good job, my Betelgeuse. Now we need ta deal with the issue at hand—these four lunching at the Golden Ram. We need someone ta go there and take photos a these two men." Turning to Viktor, he asked, "Can ya use that cell phone ta take the photos."

Nodding a head still weary and weaving from tiredness, Viktor responded. "I do that, and can't wait to take photos of the women."

Unable to suppress a laugh, Rigel raised his hands to 'give-up'. "Sorry mate, take as many as ya want as long as no one sees ya doing it!" As he spoke, Rigel reached over to his briefcase on the table and extracted the photo he had taken at the Ossuary of James symposium. "But here's what the women look like, so any men with them are who I want ya ta shoot."

Caught in a conflict of psychological blurs created by his deadly KGB training, Viktor was puzzled. "I thought you wanted photos. Now you want me to shoot them?"

Realizing the confusion, Rigel added, "Sorry lad, but ta shoot them means ta take their photo, and that's what I want ya ta do; take their photos, don't kill them. Go early, scout the Golden Ram and sit where ya can see all the tables and where no one can see ya."

The hyper-informative Liam added, "The professor said it had an open courtyard in the middle with a place for a lamb ta be cooked. They'll probably sit where they can see the cooking pit."

Moving over to gaze out the window, Rigel then turned to Viktor. "Get there early, by 12:00. Scout the place and expect them ta be where they can see the lamb. Take a good look at this photo, and when ya see them at their table, call me."

Viktor rose to get his sugar laced with coffee. "What you want me to say? Use code?"

"Yea, use code," said Liam as he pointed his right index finger to his brain showing Viktor what a good idea it was. "Ya didn't forget your training. Use that Russian phrase, 'my black Russian brother'. What's that again?"

A rare smile, an infrequent visitor to Viktor's face, now found a home. "Moy chornee Ruski brat?"

Rigel's confidence in Viktor was clear. "Ya got it; so when ya call me, just say Moy chornee Ruski brat, nothing else."

Beaming with pride, Viktor jumped up and saluted. "I only say 'Moy chornee Ruski brat', then shoot photos, not people."

Wrapping up the discussion, Rigel added, "I'll e-mail my dear Elana ta have lunch with me. Then we'll see if their professor discovered something we're not hearing about."

Chapter 18

Exhilarated with his Vatican experience, Eric's euphoria was exploding as he looked forward to his lunch with Elana and Sonja. But he sensed an unwelcome intruder had entered their lives as a distant attitude embraced Elana with a corrupting chill thrust into their relationship. Maybe it was his rejuvenated attitude, but now he was able to see what he might have missed before—this underlying emotional current rippling between them and drowning the trust that should have been binding them.

Parking the Institute van behind the Golden Ram, Elana, Eric and Sonja casually walked around towards the front of the building, where Elana, still harboring some suspicions, decided to engage Eric with some light, provocative conversation. "How'd you stumble onto this place?"

Eric's flippant response was innocent enough. "I was out and about on one of the mornings."

Not realizing the shocked look she cast, Elana still knew the tone of her voice raised an octave. "How'd you choose this part of Jerusalem? I've never been over here. Hope I didn't look too lost driving to some place you obviously knew better."

"Of course you didn't," interjected an anxious Sonja sensing how Elana's inquisitiveness had taken on a harder edge.

Eric stared at Elana as her serious vein of doubt had surfaced. "If you're that curious about my morning gallivanting, just say so. Considering what Mordecai said about us, you obviously know I worked before in this region."

Elana's distrustful look was dominated by piercing eyes and a caustic tone. "For the CIA?"

"Yes Elana, as Mordecai correctly told you, for the CIA. And back then, my first night in Jerusalem was spent at the American Colony Hotel. I came over here twice since I've been working on this relic project just to re-visit a time in my life when I was much younger and more idealistic."

Stopping at the restaurant door, Elana turned towards Eric. "And what did you find? A rebirth of your youth, or just your innocence?"

"Neither," he smiled. "Just a chance to see if the city had changed or if it was only me."

"What was the agent of change?" Elana fired back much too quickly. "You, the city or the CIA?"

"All of the above," Eric said as he reached to open the door and close the subject, "but now let's concentrate on what I hope will be a great dining experience. On one of my morning walks, I peeked through the windows and saw an open-air courtyard with a lamb cooking on a spit. It must be a good restaurant. Using my old friend Jasper Myers' criteria, only go to a place that has a lot of cars in the parking lot. This fits, so let's give it a try."

Feeling the tension tingling in the highly-charged air between Eric and Elana, Sonja tried to keep the conversation rolling in the right direction. "Looks like a great place to me," she said while anxiously looking for some sign of agreement from Elana. "What do you think?"

"I agree," Elana said while looking around. "Peering into that courtyard, it seems a lot of people are having a good time."

Upon entering the Golden Ram, its short, chubby host, in his white shirt, black flour-dusted pants and a white apron, rushed to greet them in his perfect, if halting English. "Can I help you?"

Bubbling with enthusiasm, Sonja couldn't wait to answer. "Yes. We'd like a table where we can see the lamb being roasted."

"Follow me," he said to Sonja with a bow that allowed him to view the total vertical dimension of this beautiful woman—from her ankles upward. "We are about to light the fire to finish the lamb. We partially cook it in the morning, then finish it when our customers are here. This way its skin is nice and crisp and the lamb, as its final act, provides a little entertainment as well as nourishment."

Following the meandering host, Eric could see most of the tables were in the open-air part of the restaurant, but some tables were tucked back in the shade and coolness of the perimeter roofing. But on this day, the temperature was mild and the open-air courtyard was the choice for the people who already were seated. Despite the cooler temperature in the shade, some of those tables had a scattering of men sitting by themselves, drinking coffee and reading newspapers.

The host wove a path from shade, to sunshine and then back through the shade again. Finally, as they were back in the brilliant sunshine and approaching the open charcoal pit, an employee lit the accelerant-soaked charcoal. The flick of a match was followed by a sudden explosion with its bright orange and yellow fingers reaching out to snatch at Eric. He froze not out of rational fear, but from a psychological regurgitation of that Gaza explosion whose intrusive flames still reached deeply into his psyche still saturated with bat-like body forms flying and innocent lives dying. His Problem was always there!

Walking slightly behind and to the side of Eric, Sonja saw what happened and was stunned to see Eric's face frozen in-time and with his eyes darting wildly, left and right. Instinctively, she grabbed his hand but there was no response. She grabbed his other hand and spun him towards her to make some facial contact with him, as well as to get him away from the flames. "Eric! Eric! What's wrong? Eric, look at me! What's wrong? Look at me I said—just look at me!" she pleaded. She allowed his unresponsive hands to slip from her grip and placed her two hands on both sides of his face. She wanted to draw him near to her, to get his focus on her. But in a millisecond she realized how close she came to just reaching up to kiss him, to see if this catatonic frog would turn back into her prince.

After a few seconds, with a face now flushed with life, Eric was still partially immobilized by the psychological crisis that precipitated the breakdown. For

Sonja, those few seconds seemed like an eternity. Now his hands finally reached up to hers and grasped them with a soft, yet powerful grip as he took them from his face, brought them to his lips and kissed them. "Sorry. Sometimes I go off to another place in time on a journey I can't control. The flames...the flames just threw me back to my Problem. Sorry," he stammered, "sorry."

Sonja grabbed his arms to pull him closer to her. "Don't be sorry, and don't worry, but what do you mean by the 'Problem'?"

Looking away from her only momentarily, he then turned back and his gaze locked onto her eyes. "I guess that's how I refer to my time with Mordecai; that time when it all went bad. That's my Problem, and I can't shake it. The explosion caught me off-guard and threw me back into a time-warp I've tried to escape for a long time."

"Don't kid yourself! You weren't the only one who was shocked. It caught us all by surprise. We're lucky Sonja was here," added Elana realizing the seriousness of the incident required a personal tone warmer and lighter than she exhibited outside. "If Sonja hadn't been here, everyone might have thought you fell in love with that lamb on the spit—it really had your attention."

While her tension was evident only a few minutes ago, her tenderness now had its intended effect. "Thanks, dear," Eric replied with a warmth in his voice that confirmed she was a friend not an antagonist. "Let's follow this guy and find our table."

That sashaying, expansive backside of their host led the way to the table, with Eric, like a bobble-headed doll, looking around to evaluate the crowd. As his intelligence background had trained him, he surveyed the scene while making eye contact with no one. But Eric was unaware that he wasn't the only one observing the restaurant and its customers—someone else had intently watched the drama unfold at the charcoal pit.

From deep within the shadows of the perimeter of the restaurant, at an angle where he could clearly see Eric and the two women, Viktor was pleased with his choice of locations. Even though the second man, this Mordecai, hadn't yet arrived, and Viktor liked what he saw with his straight shot of Eric, he knew Rigel would expect him to be patient and wait until Mordecai came. But in this boredom, Viktor's mind wandered. *But what if he doesn't come? What do I do then? How long should I wait if he is late? If he doesn't come, will these three get up and leave?* Viktor reminded himself this Mordecai was to join them for lunch at 12:30, and if he wasn't there by 12:45, he would call Rigel, give him the password and then take a picture of this professor and the women.

Realizing he would be late, Mordecai called Eric. "It'll take me five minutes, so don't think I stood you up for a better offer."

"Don't worry about it," Eric jokingly replied in a way that brought smiles to the women's faces, "I can see the lamb from here, and it won't get eaten before you arrive. When you get here, look for our table just past the cooking pit."

Distracted for a second by the traffic he was stuck in, Mordecai then blurted out, "OK, see you in a few minutes."

Seeing the frivolity after the telephone call, Viktor guessed it might have been from Mordecai. He would be patient until this Mordecai came to meet the other three, then he would get what Rigel wanted.

Now aware he might even be later than he projected, Mordecai was on the phone again. "I'm going to be even later than I thought, so go ahead and eat. I'll eat when I get there."

"That's fine," Eric laughingly replied, "but when you get here, you'll see us out in the middle of the open-air courtyard, soaking up the sun."

Even over the phone, Eric could perceive the change in Mordecai's voice. "In an open courtyard? Are there people around you? Are you visible to everyone?"

"Yes, out in the courtyard—a lovely spot that even an old gasbag like you will like."

Mordecai's voice catapulted his concern to an alarming level. "What are you thinking? Have you forgotten your training to never sit anywhere in an open-air courtyard? Never, never out in the open like some sitting duck waiting for something bad to happen!"

Trying to bring some levity to a conversation that already slid too far downhill, Eric countered, "C'mon Mordecai, sometimes you need to forget that every corner, every rooftop or every shadow might be a repository of horrible devastation. You need to lighten-up."

"Not me!" Mordecai replied with his voice still at the alarm level. "You do the lightening-up for me. When I come into the restaurant, I'll sit elsewhere. Don't even look for me, because I don't want to be seen by you or anyone else."

Entering the Golden Ram a few minutes after the caustic cell phone conversation, Mordecai was greeted by the same host. Surveying the outdoor area, and not about to be told where to sit, he pointed and brusquely told the host, "Sit me there, in the shade under that overhanging roof."

The intimidated host meekly replied without peeking at Mordecai, "My pleasure, follow me."

As he sat at his table, Mordecai briefly looked at the menu and then peeked over it to view the eating area and his partners. He came in so inconspicuously he was sure they were unaware of him. As the waiter brought water, Mordecai only ordered coffee, the very strong kind, then sat back to monitor his surroundings.

Growing impatient over the absence of the fourth man, Viktor thought waiting until 12:45 was long enough. Now he realized the code made sense because some people were seated so close to him. He dialed Rigel's cell phone, and upon hearing his voice, Viktor spoke the magic words, "Moy chornee Ruski brat." Then terminating the call, he proceeded to use the camera option to take the pictures of this professor and the two women. He took several photos, but was so engrossed in leering at the women that he didn't realize the lone man seated at the table to his right was intensely focused on him—studied thoroughly might have been a better description of how Viktor was being scrutinized by Mordecai.

No confusion existed since Mordecai knew exactly what was said! His parents fled the Soviet Union for Israel in 1951 when the repression of Jews was again showing its nasty face. Raised as an Israeli, an English-, Russian- and Hebrew- speaking Israeli, he was proud of his impeccable language skills. And Mordecai was no small amount suspicious when he heard the man at the adjacent table speaking in Russian, 'my black Russian brother' with no verbs or implied action. A slave to intelligence long enough to trust his finely-honed suspicions, he couldn't take his eyes off this thick man looking like a Russian and speaking in Russian what was probably a coded message. And from the angle this man was shooting his photos, Mordecai could only assume the camera was focused on Eric, Sonja and Elana.

Desperate for a good look at the Russian, Mordecai took his cell phone out of his pocket, and faking a call, prepared it for a photo. Assuming a guy speaking in code had some intelligence background, Mordecai realized a distraction technique was needed if he was to have any chance of getting just one shot. As he rose from his seat with his coffee in one hand and his camera deceitfully cradled in the other, he turned towards Viktor. Faking a stumble, he intentionally spilled his coffee on Viktor's shirt and pants.

With the horrific howl of a wounded Russian bear, Viktor jumped up in such fury he never realized Mordecai had snapped the photo. "You dumb Jew!" shouted Viktor in Russian-tainted English. "How could you be clumsy? You make mess!"

"Sorry... I'm sorry!" exclaimed Mordecai as he reached over with a napkin to attempt to blot off some of the coffee. "Forgive me please. I'll pay for your lunch. Here, here let me dry you off."

"Get out of here stupid fool!" Viktor shouted towards the rapidly approaching waiter, "Here, fool spilled coffee on me. I leave. Give him bill!

As Viktor turned to walk away, he looked back at Mordecai. "You stupid, clumsy Jew!"

Apologizing to the waiter and handing him enough money to cover the bills, Mordecai knew his prey, the Russian, was just that—a Russian. Mocking Mordecai as being a Jew was what a non-Jew might say, especially a foreigner. It was the mocking by a man who thought everyone else here was different from him and so they all must be Jews. He knew he was different and so did Mordecai know that Viktor was different and decidedly dangerous.

With all the fuss around Mordecai, Eric, Sonja and Elana discovered him and rushed over to his previously hidden position. "Are you OK?" asked Elana.

"I'm fine," an energized, but brusque Mordecai answered, "but you just missed a little lesson in counter-intelligence."

"What happened?" asked Eric now genuinely grasping the gravity of the situation.

Momentarily surveying the people around them, Mordecai continued. "The guy that just left, the one I intentionally spilled my coffee on, was taking photos of your table."

A startled Sonja stared at Elana, then back to Mordecai, "Why was he shooting us?"

Mordecai couldn't resist giving Eric a disparaging look that said 'I told you so' about sitting out in the open. "Speaking in Russian code and taking photos of the three of you, who knows why?"

Looking confused, Eric couldn't grasp what really happened. "What're you talking about?"

Constantly eyeing the crowd to see if anyone was listening, Mordecai continued. "I'm not sure, but I think this guy is involved with someone who killed the relic dealers. None of the three of you could have made any enemies, especially Eric with his recent arrival. And it's not a coincidence this guy was talking in code and taking your picture. Coincidences just don't happen!"

"Who would the someone else be that he was speaking to?" asked Elana whose nose now was uncontrollably twitching.

Eric did the answering this time. "Who knows who or where he is?" Turning to Mordecai he added, "What do we do to keep the women safe?"

Mordecai couldn't stop looking around at who might be watching them, but answered without looking at Eric. "I'm not sure what to do, but let's get out of here. You never know who might be watching our reactions? Let's get the women home and I'll have security at their apartment. Tomorrow we fly to Khor Virap, and then you can tell us about your Vatican trip. Let's leave now, morning comes too early and we'll need to be the airport by 6:45 AM."

Chapter 19

Doubts had dropped in from everywhere, but driving along in his undercover police car, Mordecai's optimism overrode the eroding thoughts that crept into his mind. This Armenian excursion might be a good starting point to make something positive happen. He picked up his three partners with more than adequate time to check in at the Austrian Airline boarding area. He had already contacted his friend, Aghim Chobanian, in Yerevan, Armenia and arranged for a Security Forces van to be awaiting their arrival. An Armenian intelligence officer who previously worked with the Mossad, Aghim remained undercover for Israel.

With the smooth, sedating silence of the plane ride to Yerevan, Mordecai watched his partners drift off into their own private worlds of deep sleep. Whether due to the early morning departure or the stress of the previous day, Mordecai expected they would be tired and talk later, but the only sound he heard was a muffled 'no' from Eric. Mordecai couldn't deny the burden Eric carried, nor his responsibility for it. That long ago misguided mission against al-Azziz deeply wounded Eric's psyche and Mordecai's career. Now he understood that magma of despair erupting from within Eric—a molten uttering from somewhere deeply embedded in a tortured soul.

As the plane circled the Yerevan airport, Mordecai awakened his partners for a glimpse of the mountains, especially Mt. Ararat. Attempting to clear the residue of sleep from their drowsy eyes, they could hear Mordecai's hurried words, "Take a look and see beautiful Mt. Ararat."

The slumbering squad had a good view of Ararat before the plane banked away and prepared for its final approach to the runway—an approach to an Armenian adventure about to begin once they set foot on the tarmac.

Mordecai led his support team into the Yerevan terminal to be immediately greeted by a somber, yet hospitable face. "Mordecai," said the stranger in fractured English as he wiped his sweaty brow with a magically-appearing handkerchief, "so good to see you here in Armenia."

Spitting out that ever present toothpick, Mordecai opened his arms and embraced Aghim Chobanian. "Aghim...what a pleasure to see you!" He then pointed to his partners. "Let me introduce my team: Elana Dutros, Sonja Martin and Eric Stanfels."

Extending his hand to each of these sleep-walkers, Aghim shook their hands and warmly greeted them. "Welcome to my lovely Armenia. I trust your flight was uneventful and your trip will be worthwhile because our beautiful mountains and our friendly people are here to embrace you. But now, forgive me while I take your Mordecai away to speak in private."

Leading Mordecai to the other side of the reception area, Aghim engaged in what appeared to be an animated and very serious discussion. After several minutes, they returned as a frown found its way onto Mordecai's face. "Aghim told me there were some problems at Khor Virap. There was a murder a few days ago."

Aghim interjected, "Sometimes it takes several days for reports to travel from deep in the countryside. If I had known sooner, I would have told you so."

Mordecai continued, "Aghim told me the head monk at Khor Virap was murdered, so gaining access to the monastery might be difficult. He'll go with us to help where he can."

Seeing the apprehensive looks on the faces of Mordecai's team, Aghim put them at ease. "Not to worry, I have the security clearance to enter the monastery and talk to the local police."

Perceiving somewhat of a slight towards the women, Mordecai tried to draw Aghim's attention to Sonja and Elana as he spoke and pointed in their direction. "I've told Aghim we've come this far and need to see what's at Khor Virap, but I'm suspicious about someone being killed at a place we've come to see. A coincidence? Not likely!"

Elana spoke to Aghim. "Will any monks be there?"

Aghim focused on her while wiping away that ever present sweat from his brow. "I suspect so, but we must go see what happened."

As the five of them in the van rode south towards Mt. Ararat, Mordecai updated Aghim about what had already occurred in this relic search.

With the face of a doubting Thomas, Aghim inquired, "You think something might be here in my Armenia, at Khor Virap? It's only a small monastery with no wealth, art or antiques."

Knowing his friend had no time for foolishness, Mordecai got right to the point. "Something could be there. This type of place gets overlooked."

Sonja's searching eyes finally caught Aghim's attention. "We were told there were some relics of the crucifixion either here or at St. Catherine's monastery on Mt. Sinai. We came here first, but obviously someone got here before us—just like they did when my antique dealers were murdered before I had a chance to speak with them."

Elana spoke-up. "Do you think there's any chance the monk's murder could be a coincidence, maybe connected to some local problems?"

Nodding towards Mordecai, Aghim replied. "No, I agree with Mordecai. Not a coincidence! For those of us in intelligence, there are no coincidences. The real question is who is out there shadowing you, and then why?"

Looking confused, partly by sleepiness and partly by innocence, Elana inquired, "What do you mean 'shadowing'?"

This got Aghim's attention as he turned to her. "Someone is aware of your moves and your thoughts, and you must ask yourself how are they doing it." He turned back to Mordecai. "What's your read on this?"

Mordecai looked stumped, but pointed towards Aghim. "I agree with you, but I'm dumbfounded how it's happening. With the relics dealers, one or more of the three might have talked to the wrong person, but here at Khor Virap, it makes no sense. When I'm back to Jerusalem, I'll get an electronic sweep of everybody's apartments and offices."

Eric interrupted, "Is there anything to be had here?"

Aghim responded first, "You're already here, so why not go to Khor Virap and see what's there."

Looking over at Eric, Mordecai added. "Yea, let's go. It'll give you a chance to tell us about the Vatican."

The thought of the Vatican experience brought a smile to Eric's face. "The trip was good. President Smathers clearly had the contact we needed in this Monsignor Bertani, and he's willing to open doors for us, if they can be opened at all. I know he's already talking to Archbishop Bournias, the head of St. Catherine's."

"Can this Monsignor get the job done for us?" asked Elana.

Eric's gaze now met her tension-free eyes, eyes that had previously been prickly enough to invade and almost destroy their previous relationship. "There could be a problem because the monks at St. Catherine's are still skittish about dealing with Protestants, but I think this Monsignor Bertani can overcome that. With its physical isolation and its fortress-like impenetrability, nobody uninvited gets into St. Catherine's."

The van continued southward and snaked along the Arak River until finally making a left turn up the hill away from the river in the direction of the monastery. Ascending the hill with their backs toward Mt. Ararat, Aghim reassured his four passengers, "It won't be too far. I have been here often since each year we Armenians worship our patron saint, St. Gregory, the Illuminator. His remains lie in a crypt in the floor at Khor Virap."

Sonja looked surprised. "Even in the Soviet time with their anti-religion policies?"

A suddenly pious Aghim smiled. "Religion is no different from the search you are on. The more obstacles that are put in the way, the more the true believers seek it. Our Armenian Church grew during all of those years of Soviet religious repression."

"Why?" chimed in Mordecai.

Beaming with pride, Aghim's words were sprinkled with a sense of spirituality. "Seeing how uninspiring were the godless, occupying Soviets, the Armenian people were stimulated that much more to believe in the value of faith and the existence of their God. They understood how religion gave meaning and purpose to their lives."

After driving the rough road up the mountain, Aghim finally pulled into Khor Virap and shouted to awaken the sleepy searchers and get them out of the van. "We're here! Follow me!"

Walking to the monk's residence, they could see the separate monastery was roped-off with a sign that Aghim interpreted as: 'Crime Scene'. Reaching the rectory, Aghim spoke to a policeman who then led them inside. Turning to his trailing team, while toweling from his forehead those ever-present beads of moisture, Aghim's voice was hushed, "The inspector is inside. I will see what he knows and who might be here to talk about any relics."

Just as Aghim finished speaking, a heavily-bearded, swarthy man came into the room and greeted him. They spoke for a few minutes before the man exited out a doorway. "He is the inspector and will get the monk in-charge to take us to the monastery."

Trailed by a monk, the inspector returned and spoke to Aghim. With an open-handed gesture, the inspector pointed the way to the monastery as the monk led the way out.

The walk to the monastery was short and silent. Upon their arrival, the inspector and the monk removed a barrier and all seven entered through an elaborately carved stone archway. The monk took them to a hole in the floor and described in Armenian how below lay the bones of St. Gregory—bones which were disturbed by the horrible people who killed the senior monk. Aghim translated this to his fellow travelers who had already sensed the intense emotion of this mortified monk.

Eric reached over to touch Aghim on the arm. "Ask him if the killers took anything."

Aghim spoke briefly to the monk who then shook his head. "He said nothing was taken. They had the senior monk over here looking for something, and when they didn't get what they wanted, they killed him."

Now looking at the monk, Eric inquired, "Sure nothing was taken from St. Gregory's resting place?"

Aghim turned back to the monk and they spoke for only a minute, followed by the monk again shaking his head. "The monk said no. He said the lid of St. Gregory's ossuary was removed while the ossuary itself was overturned. Some of the bones were on the stone floor of the crypt, but he is not aware of anything missing."

Sonja's eyes met Eric's. "An ossuary? We're here looking at another ossuary?"

Eric continued with Aghim. "Has the ossuary scene been undisturbed or were the bones placed back into the box?"

Turning to the inspector, Aghim mumbled something and more head shaking followed. "The inspector said despite the attempts of the monks to get in here and restore the ossuary, the crime scene, including the ossuary, remains undisturbed."

Elana caught Aghim's eye, a difficult thing to do since he seemed to avoid the women. "Can you ask him if we can go down into the hole?"

Aghim again spoke to the inspector and a smile came upon the faces of Mordecai's team as finally they saw a nod. Aghim turned back to Elana. "It will not violate the holiness of this place if one person, a male, goes down into their very sacred crypt. St. Gregory was held captive down there for many days and they believe it is only a man's place."

Sonja just smiled as she thought about the presence of sexual bias—universally present and universally accepted!

Noticing both women rolling their eyes in bewilderment, Eric tried to placate them. "I'm sure it smells musty and you'd be happier anyway if Mordecai or I went down. Mordecai, any preferences?"

"Yes, I prefer you go down. You're much younger, and I'm a Jew. They probably don't want our kind down there either."

This brought a bigger smile to the women, and even to Aghim. The monk and the inspector looked befuddled about what was said.

Taking his cue from Mordecai, Aghim spoke to the monk who again shook his head.

Mordecai wagged a finger at Eric. "I don't even have to wait for Aghim's answer, because there's got to be an invisible sign: 'No women or Jews!' "

They all laughed, except the monk who had a bewildered look on his face until Aghim translated the discussion.

Ready to descend into the hole, Eric looked around. "Does anyone have a light?"

Aghim was ready to translate, but before he could say anything, the inspector provided a flashlight from behind a post. Aghim handed it to Eric who then descended down into this solemn subterranean site.

Sonja caught Aghim's attention. "Is it OK if we crouch down and look into the crypt?"

Aghim spoke to the monk who nodded his approval to the women.

Sonja and Elana stuck their heads down into the hole and could see what Eric was seeing as his light panned around this cave-like tomb. A stone-lined concavity comprised the perimeter of the pit but the floor was inlaid with semi-precious stones which reflected different colors as the light shined upon them.

219

They could see the overturned ossuary, with its lid as well as the bones lying askew.

Elana turned to Sonja. "Looks like the same-sized ossuary you bought from Moshe Levin."

Sonja nodded in agreement. "Who knows, maybe they made them all the same size."

Eric pushed aside the ossuary lid as he rummaged through the bones and searched the inside of the ossuary for any hint of something left or hidden inside. He turned to look up at those attentive pairs of eyes surveying his every move. "Nothing here in the box."

Pointing down at something, Sonja shouted, "Eric, the lid! Hand it up."

Picking up the lid, Eric hoisted it up to Mordecai who laid it flat with the underside showing. All could see what Sonja's persistence provided as Mordecai commented on the obvious, "Looks like a carved animal!"

Gloating wasn't her style, but Sonja quickly added, "Just like the one on my ossuary. Unbelievable! There's more wear on the one I bought from Moshe Levin, but they look the same." She got Aghim's eye. "Could you ask the monk if he was aware of this carving before today, or if it has any symbolic meaning to the monastery?"

Turning back to the monk, Aghim spoke briefly with him, but this time there were no head movements of any kind before Aghim answered. "He said the monks were aware of the carving, and from the monastery's oral history it appears this is the original ossuary from about 1,700 years ago. The carving has always been acknowledged in their oral history as being on the lid, but he doesn't know why."

Now out of the hole, Eric caught Sonja's attention, "Use your camera to get some photos. This might show up better than the one on your lid. There's less wear on whatever you think this animal is."

Climbing back into the hole, Eric shined the light around to see if he was missing anything; then picked up the ossuary and examined it again. He looked back out at a peering Mordecai, "Nothing else on the ossuary. Gimme the lid and I'll replace it."

After replacing the lid, Eric pulled himself out of the hole and turned to Aghim. "Can you ask the inspector if they have any information about the killers?"

From watching Aghim talking to the inspector and then to the monk, it was obvious they knew nothing. The head shaking returned, and Aghim turned to Eric. "The monks know nothing more, and there was no one at the rectory when the murderers came."

"Murderers? How many were there?" asked Eric.

"The inspector said there were three men. On the day of the murder, three men in a van stopped a farmer down the hill and asked for directions to Khor Virap. The farmer came to us when he heard the monk was killed. He also saw the same three men driving unnaturally fast down the hill about 1 ½ hours after they originally got their directions. We assumed those three were the murderers."

Mordecai persisted. "Did he remember anything else?"

Aghim spoke again with the inspector. "He told us the three men were in the robes of priests, but didn't look like priests. And one man spoke in Russian."

"Anything else?" Eric asked impatiently.

Aghim again turned to the inspector and got what appeared to be a short verbal answer while the inspector pointed to the back of his right hand.

Turning to Eric, Aghim pointed to the back of his own right hand. "The farmer remembered something else. On the back of the Russian's right hand were tattoos of three stars in a slanted line. He saw them clearly because the Russian pointed at something on a map when he was getting directions to Khor Virap."

Sonja, Elana and Eric all looked at each other with their heads nodding in unison. Eric then looked at Aghim. "Like Mordecai said, not usually a coincidence."

Aghim looked puzzled.

Eric saw it and responded accordingly. "The men who killed the two antiquities dealers back in Jerusalem—one of them had three stars on his hand."

As he looked at Aghim, a serious pall was cast over Mordecai's face. "We know someone out there thinks we're on to something, and they're willing to kill as many people as they need to beat us to it. But for what? Something important or just a wild goose chase for some relics that don't even exist?" Now looking at Eric, Sonja then Elana, Mordecai took the lead. "Let's get back to Jerusalem." His eyes met Eric's. "What's your next step with the Vatican?"

"I'm going back there once we return to Jerusalem. Saw an e-mail at the Institute saying the Monsignor arranged a meeting for me with the Archbishop of St. Catherine's in two days. I'll leave tomorrow evening."

Mordecai continued, "Well, let's get you back." He turned back to Aghim. "Thanks for your help, but I need two more favors from you. First, get us back to the airport as soon as possible so we don't miss our flight."

"No worry," Aghim said as he patted Mordecai's shoulder and then wiped his brow again. "If there are problems, the plane waits. The Security Force still has some clout."

Mordecai smiled. "Good, but could you also contact the Interpol Evidence Data Bank and start a computer search on unsolved crimes where somebody had tattoos of stars on his hand? It'll take a few days to get this done and if you can start it for me today, that'll save me a day." Handing a card to Aghim, he continued, "Here's a special e-mail address. Have the results sent there."

Aghim looked at the card, then back at Mordecai as a smile emerged. "Ahhh, you have a Mossad address. I worried they dumped you completely."

Without noticing the quizzical looks on the faces of Eric, Sonja and Elana, Mordecai responded. "Just a place to get special info."

Turning to his three companions, Mordecai nodded towards the van, "C'mon, let's get Aghim moving back to the airport. We've got a lot to think about once we get back to Jerusalem."

Chapter 20

His concrete confidence crumbled after the frustrating conclusion at Khor Virap—only a box of dust and bones from a Saint Somebody who didn't matter. Pacing the floor at 8:00 AM at the King David Hotel, Rigel was confused over his next moves, and the beautiful view from his posh suite wasn't enough to settle his creeping anxiety. Khor Virap was an ego buster with too much time and energy spent with nothing to show, and now thoughts wandered and confidence was frayed. *What will they think if there's nothing at St. Catherine's?* But suddenly Rigel's arrogance kicked-in and rejuvenated his belief in planning and executing another mission. Maybe Khor Virap didn't hurt Orion's morale too much after all. He taught his men to be positively confrontational—identify problems early, confront them with a positive attitude and then give quick solutions a chance to emerge. While Khor Virap created enough fertilizer for doubt to sprout, Rigel concluded that bold planning for the St. Catherine's mission would bridge any holes in Orion's confidence.

Liam walked in on this solitary, pacing Rigel. "Your e-mail ta the lovely Miss Dutros has no reply."

With the remnants of his childhood search for comfort-in-the-sky locked away deep within his subconscious, Rigel looked out the window, yearning for peace from the heavens. "Doesn't surprise me, give it a few hours, then recheck it. If they got back from Armenia late like we did, she won't get ta her office for several hours."

Smelling the pungent coffee wafting through the air, Conor and Viktor came from their rooms and sat in the big, comfortable wing-back chairs to be entertained by Rigel's pacing. Conor reached over to the cluttered table and poured some coffee while nudging a sweet roll onto a napkin. "What's next? What makes sense ta ya?"

Turning back to this caffeine-energized band, Rigel stopped his pacing and focused on Conor. "It's best ta let the women take the lead because it won't be easy for us ta get in St. Catherine's. Use the Church model—let the women do the work, then screw them out a the riches. This guy, the professor, let's see what he finds at the Vatican. We've got a front row seat and a front row ear, but I'm still frustrated we wasted our God-damned time at Khor Virap. Now let the other team do the finding and we'll do the taking."

Heaping his spoonfuls of sugar into his coffee, Viktor added, "Just sit and wait?"

Rigel looked to Viktor, Conor and then Liam before slyly crowing, "No. I sent an e-mail ta my friend Elana ta meet for lunch where Conor can download her burst transmitter."

A short silence was broken with a computer message. "You've got mail!"

Hustling over to see what Elana said, Liam was surprised at what he saw. "Rigel, it says here your Salvador Dali has sent ya a message."

Impatient, Rigel barked, "Damn it Liam, open it and read it ta us!"

"Here's what he said. 'Rigel, I await your direction here in Glasgow. My research convinces me we can expect a brilliant resurrection from the DNA. Tell me when to come'."

Not particularly directed to anyone, Rigel's smile lit up the room as its power projected the confidence he had in his 'Salvador Dali'. "My Dali's waiting in the wings for us ta find the relics."

Still not totally sure of the role of this Dali, Viktor looked lost in this confusion. "Rigel, what is he for us?"

"For me ta have my Church a the Internet, don't forget I need some genetic engineering. I need a genetic genius ta be a part a our team, and that's Salvador Dali. As I told ya before, once we find Jesus' DNA, we'll sell a little ta every pregnant Christian woman in the world. A little bit a Jesus for all God's children! E-mail Dali that I'll be in touch within the week."

In an uncommon display of dismay, Liam shook his head, still not totally sure where this would lead. "With what ya plan with your Church a the Internet, ya better hope God is dead because if he isn't, you a all people will most assuredly burn in hell—and probably us with ya!"

Hurt by Liam's sharp words, Rigel eyed him with a sinister look on his face. "God's not dead, just so sick a what He's created He's got His head in the shitter. Driving the porcelain bus and puking his guts out! He, or She, isn't dead, just disgusted and disowned everyone a us poor bastards. And ya think He sent his only son ta save our miserable souls? If that was the case, God should've been given a bloody prize for blind and foolish optimism."

Walking over to the computer, Liam saw Rigel had a message from Elana. "Rigel, your Elana says she's fine for lunch at 12:00 noon, but where?"

With a casual wave of his hand towards the computer, Rigel crowed with the pride of a man who had just envisioned his victory. "Tell her it'll be at the Crown Plaza Hotel on Hayourkon Street—at the Bellissima restaurant. Maybe tomorrow I can mine her brain for a few gold nuggets. And hopefully they'll not be fool's gold. I know she doesn't trust that professor, so who knows what she'll tell us? We'll all go ta Tel Aviv, but you guys can sit in the van and monitor the information from her transmitter. While you're doing that, ya can also be hearing what she and I are saying."

Doubt dominated Viktor as he looked up from his coffee. "What if she doesn't bring her purse to lunch?"

Rigel sipped away at his coffee, and without looking, responded. "She will. All women carry a purse when they go ta a restaurant, and she told me at the Ossuary a James symposium she had only one purse. That's why I planted the bug in it. Tomorrow, we'll find out what they're up ta, but until then, we'll just keep hacking away into their computer."

Chapter 21

Early mornings are ugly mornings for late night travelers. With Eric leaving later that afternoon for Rome, Mordecai's opinion was they needed to organize their options now. Arriving before everyone else, and bored at the computer, Eric thought this meeting wasn't necessary since everything was totally dependent on what Monsignor Bertani could do, and he wouldn't know that until tomorrow. Despite his tiredness, Eric's thoughts of seeing Sonja brought pulsars of pleasure to his emotionally-depleted brain. Ever since the Golden Ram, he saw her, or more importantly, sensed her much differently. She was bound within his very existence in a way he had not experienced before, with a binding fusion that no atomic force could dislodge. Overwhelmingly indebted since she broke him out of his stupor, Eric also knew, as the clouds of his confusion parted, how close he came to kissing her lips instead of her hands. He couldn't, and hoped he wouldn't shake the memory of those luscious, quivering lips acting like brilliantly beaming beacons bringing a lost soul through such emotionally unchartered waters.

To Monsignor Bertani went a simple e-mail: 'Will be arriving at your office at 10:00 AM. Hope Archbishop Bournias will be as interested in meeting me as I am in meeting him.' Eric's message was well-received by a whole cast of characters, one good and the rest not so good.

Leading Elana and the newly-arrived Sonja into the room as Eric was finishing Bertani's e-mail, Mordecai was surprised to see him. "What're you doing here even before the women?"

Not looking up from the computer, Eric waved him off: "Confirming my plans for tomorrow in Rome."

Walking over to the computer table, Mordecai set down his cup of coffee. "Good, but now let's look at what we need to do today. You're leaving later today, and Elana and Sonja need to get out of here for the rest of the day so my men can electronically sweep their office cubicles and apartments. So ladies, get out of here! Take your hat, purse and shoes and leave everything else behind. Give me the keys to your apartments and go spend the day shopping or sightseeing, but one of my men will be with you at all times."

Sonja looked at him. "Are you part of the sweep?"

Mordecai shook his head 'no'. "I'm not qualified for that. I'll go back to my office and do some work, but I'm not exactly sure what since I don't expect any information until later tonight or tomorrow. We'll meet for lunch tomorrow at 11:45 and I'll tell you what we find."

"What are you expecting?" asked a confused-looking Eric.

Rolling his eyes, Mordecai sarcastically replied, "Hopefully something from you in Rome as soon as you know anything, and then maybe something from Aghim's Interpol search. You'll be in Rome, so I won't try to tell you what we get from Interpol, but as soon as possible I expect to hear what happens with the Archbishop."

Elana hesitated as that little twitch invaded her nose. "I... I can't make it tomorrow. I've a very important meeting at Tel Aviv at eleven. Why don't you plan on me being back here about 4:00, and maybe by then, we might have heard from Eric."

Nodding his approval, a disappointed Mordecai continued, "Fine, I guess, but let's get out of here now. Have a good trip Eric, and girls, have a great day off. I'll wait around to see what the sweep turns up here or at your apartments, then off to my office to wait for the Interpol report."

Leaving the office, Sonja noticed a dreamy look on Elana's face. Now she was curious about the vague reason she wouldn't be around tomorrow. "Business or pleasure in Tel Aviv?" Sonja asked without trying to be too nosey.

With eyes brightening like a multitude of stars taking up residence in her brain, Elana whispered, "Pleasure, of the Irish kind, but just for lunch. Rigel has some business up there and can't spare too much time. But since Eric is busy the rest of today, why don't you and I have lunch."

Sonja had already turned and was looking longingly at Eric as if some gravitational force seemed to be drawing her to him. Resisting this tensional tug, she turned to Elana. "Sounds good, but where and when?"

Noticing Sonja's diverted attention, Elana added, "Why not 12:30 at Eucris, that cute little restaurant not too far from your apartment."

Suddenly turning away to walk over to Eric as he was putting some papers in his briefcase, Sonja knew she was distracted and had turned her back on Elana just as the lunch meeting place was confirmed. She now twisted her head back to face her. "A great choice! I've gone by Eucris several times and it looked marvelous."

Drawn to Eric, and unwittingly, in an almost unconscious stupor, Sonja reached over and touched his right forearm. "Be safe, and I'll look forward to hearing from you when you get back."

As light as the touch was, Eric was momentarily mesmerized by its warmth, and her proximity to him sent a stream of her pheromone molecules up his nose. Like a primordial caveman, he could smell her, sense her and, surprisingly to him, want her even though the meaning of all this was still foreign. He never had this feeling about any woman, and it made him uncomfortable. Now he was out from under his cloak of control and discipline and exposed to the vagaries of the cascading emotional forces he feared he couldn't harness. He instinctively grabbed her and looked at her hazel eyes framed by that long dark hair, and it seemed strange to him how he never noticed the rich color of those eyes unblinkingly locked onto his. "You'll be the first person I talk to when I return."

Uneasy about making a public display of her affection, Sonja timidly gave a kiss to the index and middle fingers of her right hand and planted it on his cheek. "Do well and be safe."

Chapter 22

Strange feelings fueled Elana's emotions as she exited the taxi in front of the large wood and highly-polished silver door at Eucris. Not often did she go to a restaurant, and this brought back some of the mixed feelings she had when she met Rigel. Now she was walking on what she hoped would be a comfortable emotional landscape at a stunning restaurant with its huge windows allowing passersby to look in at the patrons who were looking out at them. Walking by the windows, seeing the tables set with pristine white tablecloths and crowned with sparkling crystal begging to be filled with ruby red wine, she tried to not look too inquisitive. She knew it would soon be her turn to be one of the 'anointed' ones, privileged enough to be seated inside, and hopefully at a window table.

Entering the restaurant, Elana was greeted by the host, who, with a friendly nod, inquisitively addressed her in Israeli-accented English. "Welcome. How may I and my staff here at Eucris be of service today to such a lovely young lady?"

Nodding her approval, an embarrassed Elana, a virgin to such flattery, smiled at him while hoping her blushing wasn't as red as the wine in the glasses. "Thank you. I'm pleased to be here, waiting for a friend of mine. We would love to sit at a window table if one is available."

"Yes. Yes," so excited was his answer. "I have a lovely window table that will give you a wonderful view of the outside. Please," he said as he pointed the way with his stack of menus, "if you would like to be seated before your friend arrives, follow me this way."

Elana followed and then sat down on the chair he had so properly pulled away from the table. As he slid her chair in, she looked up and saw Sonja about to enter. She turned to the host, and as she laid open the palm of her right hand and pointed it in the direction of the front door, she exclaimed, "There she is now!"

"Ahhh...your friend? Yes, your friend. Please, allow me to go and bring her to your table. But, if I look surprised, I was expecting a male friend. Forgive me, but someone as lovely as you, I... I thought some lucky man was to be enjoying the presence of your company as your beauty graces my Eucris."

Appreciatively, Elana smiled while feeling the heat rising in her face from his continuous flurry of flattery. "Thank you, but today I'm with my best friend. Tomorrow I'll be with that 'lucky man'. Or maybe it's me that's lucky tomorrow."

"I can assure you it will be him that is so lucky!" he said as he then excused himself to go over to direct Sonja to her table.

Watching him approach Sonja, Elana did some quick introspection about what impacted their relationship since Eric arrived. Certainly grateful for his mission-saving money and expertise, she couldn't deny it came with a price. She lamented the change in her relationship with Sonja, and wasn't sure why and to what extent. Surely she could see the seedlings of romance, probably sown sometime years ago at Strayton University, were fertilized here in Jerusalem and were now coming into full bloom. Yet she wasn't totally sure what she felt about this Eric. Or for that matter, what she felt about Rigel and what he felt for her. She wasn't sure whether she was jealous of Sonja's blossoming bounty or simply distrustful of Eric. And she hoped the attitude she projected when they were walking to the Golden Ram wasn't seen too negatively in Sonja's eyes.

With the gracious host leading her towards Elana, Sonja could see the lost-in-space look on Elana's face. "Elana! It's me. Remember me? I'm the person you're going to have lunch with, or at least I hope so."

Rising from her chair, Elana reached over to give her a hug. "I'm sorry, kind of got lost in my train-of-thought and must have gotten on the wrong tracks from the time I saw you enter the door. Have a seat." Elana said as their host quickly pulled a chair away for Sonja.

After adjusting her chair opposite Elana at this table-for-two, Sonja gazed out the window and then back to Elana. The radiance of a woman-in-love was all over her face, and the energy it brought to Sonja was unmistakably present when she spoke. "Tell me dear, why did you want to meet me here today? Something mysterious about your lunch with Rigel tomorrow, or is there something else I should know that you've been holding back?"

Pursing her lips, Elana raised her eyebrows and then gave an indifferent response. "No. Not really. Is there something you haven't told me about your relationship with Eric? Looks like you're the love struck undergraduate back at Strayton."

Sonja laughed as she spoke but sensed some underlying current of friction. "C'mon, not really love struck—after all, I'm not a 20 year old schoolgirl anymore."

Surveying Sonja's defensive pose, Elana couldn't help but comment, "You may not be 20 or a schoolgirl anymore, but love struck? You look like a poster child for being a woman-in-love. Look it up in the dictionary and there's your picture."

Easing back in her chair, Sonja was flushed with a sense of self-righteous propriety. "I didn't think it was that evident, and I'm really trying to keep my focus on the job. I don't think my feelings, whatever they may be, are getting in the way of doing my job. Or are they?"

"Relax dear," a smiling Elana added. "Don't get uptight. I agree with you. Your personal life and your professional life haven't had any earthly collisions."

"But how do you feel about Eric? How does he come across to you?" asked a little too needy Sonja as she leaned towards Elana.

Lifting up her water glass, as if to examine its contents, Elana replied, "Do you mean how do I see his performance in our search for the relics of the crucifixion?"

"Yes," nodded Sonja, "that and maybe how do you see him as a person? Do you see what I see? Or maybe it's what I've always seen in him since Strayton,

232

and now this whole venture is unmasking my psychohistory of what I repressed from my past."

Elana put down the glass and looked directly at Sonja. "I do see what you see in him. He's tall, dark and handsome, and yes, there is something mysterious about him. You were right about that, but... "

"But what?" said a surprised and a little defensive Sonja.

Hesitating, Elana then overcame her reticence to say what was on her mind. "Well, I'm not completely sure what I really think. I'm not sure what it is about Eric that still leaves me suspicious about what he's doing here now or what he's done before with or without Mordecai."

Sonja could feel the heat radiating through her body and the emotion rising in her voice as she couldn't help but assume the mantle of a woman needing to protect her unjustly-accused man.

"Do you think Eric's doing something illegal or something dishonest with us? Certainly you don't think that, or do you?"

"No, I don't think that. But sometimes I'm concerned. There's something still unsettling."

Staring into Elana's eyes with an electrified intensity that could scorch metal, Sonja tried to constrain her voice, while knowing it was tweaking a few decibels too high. "What aren't you sure of? I'm not sure of you right now—not sure of where you're going with this. What's really bugging you about Eric, or is it Eric and me? Is there some jealousy rearing up its ugly head and getting in the way of what's always been a wonderful, trusting relationship between you and me?"

Embarrassed and confused, Elana avoided eye contact, then turned away as she sensed that noxious nose twitching. "I don't know what it is, just a feeling. Maybe I'm being more emotional than rational, but I've had this unsettling feeling ever since Eric joined us. Don't get me wrong, I know we couldn't do what we're doing without him, but it's just not the same since he came—and bad things have happened since then!"

Leaning towards Elana, Sonja whispered, or what she thought was a whisper. "Are you saying you think Eric's responsible for the deaths of the antique dealers? What're you thinking about? He's been nothing short of great for this venture."

An anguished look replaced what had been Elana's friendly smile. "I'm not sure what I think or what's behind it. Maybe I just feel now that he's here, we're not the same. You and I were such a great team and now it's not that way anymore."

A piercing pain penetrated through Sonja's eyes, all the way from her heart, as she spoke softly in a voice that assumed an estranged distance from Elana. "Are you sure that's what it is or is it something with Rigel? Is it that I'm building a relationship with Eric and you haven't had enough time with Rigel, or enough history with him, to allow something to gel? Is my hope of something with Eric the cold water that's chilling yours and my relationship?"

"I just don't know what's right. Maybe you're right. Maybe my failure to build some type of relationship with Rigel is the problem, and my subconscious could be working on me when I see you and Eric together and me on the outside."

Reaching over to clasp Elana's hands, Sonja tried to reconcile Elana's remarks with her own need to rebuild their relationship. "But don't you and Rigel have some chemistry? When you're with him, doesn't something happen? Lights go on? Temperature gets hotter? Doesn't something different happen?"

As she caught her image in the mirror on the wall, Elana could see her eyes looking glazed, a nose twitching and a face void of its vigor. "No, I can't really say that's happening, or at least I can't say it's happening on his part. On my side of the emotional equation, yes, I feel those things, but I haven't had much experience with boys, or for that matter, men. Or really all of them—boys and men! I've never had any real romantic relationships in my life. Sure, dating and simple platonic pals, but nothing that ever made the whistles blow and bells go off. And certainly nothing ever with some steamy, sensual involvement"

Still holding Elana's hands, Sonja looked up to meet her eyes, and stayed locked on them. "What's he like when he's with you? Does he hold your hand? What does he do, or doesn't do?"

234

Momentarily looking away, Elana then turned back to Sonja. "Well, yes, he's held my hand, but I can't say it's been with a clutching that says 'I never want to let you go'. And maybe it's that kiss, the one kiss that we shared."

"He kissed you?" exclaimed Sonja excitedly. "So early in the relationship? That means something, doesn't it?"

Staying focused on Sonja, Elana tried to generate the courage to expose her emotionally exasperating moment. "It might have if it had been a kiss that knocked me off my feet, but it wasn't. It's that kiss that's haunting me the most!"

"Haunting you? Maybe a kiss can leave you cold and emotionless, but haunting?"

"Oh, I just don't know if I'm being cruel, insensitive, naïve or all of the above. It was a kiss that wasn't a kiss. Yea, his lips met mine, but it was like kissing a stone—like kissing a corpse! That kiss was like getting that limp handshake from a wimpy male when you know he wants you to shake the tips of his fingernails. Those lips could've been artificial, rubber or silicone, because there didn't seem to be any emotion attached to them. Am I the problem? I just don't know, but if you based anything on that one kiss, as far as romance is related, I could be a disappearing act. What do you think? You know more than I do about men."

Lost in her own cauldron of confusion, Sonja shook her head. "I wouldn't call me experienced, but I am puzzled with his lack of emotion if he at least had the gumption to give you a kiss. To have the courage to kiss carries a charge to the actual contact that brings some type of electric jolt. I'd think that anyway, unless… "

Elana interrupted before the sentence could be finished, "Unless what?"

"Unless he's gay. Who knows? If he's gay, maybe he needs to put on some sad show but doesn't have the emotional reservoir, at least for women, to at least do a good job of faking it."

235

Now Elana was the one leaning down and forward as she sensed the tone of her voice was rising as she wanted to only whisper. "Gay? How would I know that? And if he's gay, why would he want anything to do with me?"

"I'm not sure what he wants or why he acts the way he does, and I don't know how you can tell if you're the cause of his detached emotions or distant sexuality. We don't even know if his sexuality is detached, damaged, diverted, perverted or simply non-existent. I'm lost on this and don't want to give you advice for something I don't understand. But don't blame yourself! You're seeing him tomorrow, aren't you?"

"Yea, off to Tel Aviv for lunch. He's tied up with business there and I'm more than willing to drive up in the good, old Biblical Institute van."

Trying to console Elana, Sonja's sense of guilt grabbed at her since she had none of these problems. "See how it goes tomorrow. You can tell me all about your luncheon when you get back. I'll be like a doting mother waiting for the report from her daughter after her first date."

Picking up her menu, Elana cast a chilled look into Sonja's eyes, "My report? My God, you make that sound so clinical. Let's order and get this lunch over. This discussion killed my appetite, but I'll make sure I save some of it for an enjoyable lunch tomorrow. But 'Mom', don't worry, I'll give you a full report when I return from Tel Aviv—just like a little girl should! Who knows, maybe tomorrow will be the start of something big, even for a loser like me."

Crushed by the cutting edge of Elana's words, Sonja tried to heal this rancorous rift. "Please, I'm sorry I've offended you. I was just trying to help, and obviously failed. Let's try a new start. Please, let's enjoy this lunch as a form of 'breaking bread' by two friends whose love for each other will always transcend any misunderstandings."

Nodding her approval, a conciliatory Elana conceded, "You're right. I know you're only looking out for me."

Reaching over to clasp Elana's hands, Sonja proceeded to say a simple grace which blessed this lunch, their inseparable friendship and a wonderful future.

Both women continued on with their lunch with a better sense of understanding than one would have expected considering the emotional territory they'd covered. They hadn't necessarily resolved many issues, but at least they understood there was an emotional bond between them that could never be broken.

Chapter 23

Nagging doubts devoured a dour Mordecai who considered the investigation's objectivity compromised by his investment in it—his affection for the women and the guilt for failing Eric. Sensing some tick of fear had burrowed into his usually well-fortified confidence and left a gapping sore that wouldn't heal, he looked for help wherever he could find it. *Need Aghim's help to jump-start this thing,* he whimsically thought while looking at the frayed toothpick remnant he had nervously chewed to shreds.

And Aghim did his job well! At 9:00 AM the report finally arrived and Mordecai, speeding in his police cruiser, couldn't suppress his schoolboy eagerness to share this privileged information with Sonja. Now he possessed the key to understand the evil force shadowing their efforts, and even though it didn't solve the murders, at least they could figure out how to protect themselves. They didn't and couldn't know who their adversaries were, but the blanks were now being filled in by faceless foes whose aggression could now turn their way.

Barging into Sonja's cubicle with the Interpol report in his hand, Mordecai sat down with a very startled Sonja. "Well Super-Sleuth, what did you find out?" she asked before he could open his mouth.

Pitched from his hand, Aghim's report fluttered onto her desk. "Interpol confirmed it. Someone's out there, one or more people, and they committed crimes where witnesses remembered seeing three diagonal stars on someone's hands."

With eyebrows raised and a hand momentarily over her mouth, and almost too stunned to speak, Sonja cross-examined Mordecai. "Same man or men? Same hand or hands?"

"Who knows," he answered. "Eye witness accounts are rarely completely accurate. Could have been multiple men and some with tattoos on the right hand and others on the left hand. We'll probably never know everything."

Projecting an odd sense of satisfaction, she continued, "But at least we know our imaginations aren't running amuck—something's really out there. What's in the report?"

Pointing to the report, he moved a chair close to hers. "Evidence from three unrelated and unsolved crimes. In two of the crimes the evidence is pretty direct, but in the third it's circumstantial."

"How so?" she asked.

Cradling a cup of coffee in his left hand, he leaned back in his chair. "Let me tell you what's known on the two cases, and then you'll figure out the third. First, in Belarus, a group of thieves stole two highly explosive bombs from a former Soviet nuclear weapons depot. Interpol isn't sure whether the Russians even knew these bombs were there; probably unaccounted for like so much of the ex-Soviet arsenal. Anyway, Interpol questions why the Russians would divulge this heist unless they're desperate for help to get them back. In the process of stealing the bombs, a Russian-speaking man removed his gloves to put duct tape over the mouths of the security guards. That's when the guards saw a tattoo on this guy's right hand that matched our interest: three diagonal stars."

"OK," she nodded while focusing more intently on his papers, "makes sense. What's next?"

"Off ta Ireland, County Kerry ta be specific," Mordecai said with a decidedly poor Irish accent.

"Irish Republican Army bombs?" Sonja asked.

"No, that only occurs in Northern Ireland. This is about two priests murdered in separate incidents within a month. Both bodies mutilated the same way."

Uncrossing her legs, Sonja leaned toward Mordecai as he had her attention. "Murdered the same way?"

239

"No, murdered differently, but abused in the same way. And these mutilations are no coincidence, not with two highly-beloved priests in the same county and both within a month."

Now she sat back in her chair. "How are they connected to Belarus and our problems?"

Mordecai got up off of his chair and started to pace the floor, incisors whittling away at that wooden object of his affection. "The only evidence of the murders comes from a bed-and-breakfast proprietor in Waterville, Ireland who remembered a strange foreigner staying with him, supposedly to golf. But the foreigner, who sounded like a Russian, didn't know anything about golf, not even what's a hole-in-one."

Sonja smirked, but Mordecai didn't see it since he was looking past her. "I've never golfed, but I know what a hole-in-one is."

"Anyway, you have this phony golfer hanging around during the time the one priest is killed in Waterville, and the B&B proprietor remembers one other thing—a tattoo of three diagonal stars on his right hand. Saw it when the foreigner signed the guest register."

Her head nodded its assent. "Sounds like a match for our man, but what about the other priest?"

"That, my dear, is where we look at the circumstantial evidence, and you'll see, it's pretty compelling. The second priest was mutilated in exactly the same way as the first one; both with their penises cut off and stuffed in their mouths."

Sonja turned her head away to gag, then turned back to hesitatingly reply, "As you've always said, no coincidence!"

His turn to nod, he then spoke, "Now you understand, it's no coincidence at all! Two priests, same county in Ireland, same mutilation. You can assume the crimes were perpetrated by the same person or persons."

Getting up from her desk, Sonja went over to her coffee pot and poured a cup for herself and another for Mordecai. "Where do we go from here?"

Turning away from her, Mordecai delayed his response for all of 20 seconds before turning back to face her. "It's hard to say, but we need to be careful and keep out a sharp eye for the guy or guys with the tattoos."

"Anything show from your electronic sweep of my apartment?"

"Nothing," he said as he picked up his Interpol report. "It doesn't add-up because someone, somehow is getting information and watching what we're doing. Speaking of keeping out a sharp eye, where did Elana go today? She left without my security guy. Was it really just pleasure up there at Tel Aviv?"

"There might have been some business involved, but probably monkey business. We lunched together yesterday at the Eucris and she told me she was having lunch at noon with a guy she met at that Ossuary of James symposium."

"Some guy she just met?" Mordecai said alarmingly as he jerked his head back in Sonja's direction. "Who?"

"An Irishman. His company is involved in the restoration of ancient manuscripts. He seemed like a nice guy when Elana and I first met him."

"I don't care about all of that stuff. What's his name?"

"Rigel. That's how he introduced himself to us the first time we met."

An incredulous looking Mordecai persisted. "Rigel? What in the hell kind of name is that? First or last?"

Sonja gave a blank look. "He told us it's his only name. He goes by Rigel."

"Odd name," replied Mordecai. "Doesn't sound Irish!"

"I thought it was Irish, something Gaelic, like R-a-i-'-j-e-l. Let's look on the computer and see if his name is on any of her e-mails." Looking over, she saw 'Rigel' written on a pad on Elana's desk. "This looks like this must be the name, R-i-g-e-l, let's Google it. Sonja started to type the name and was stunned as her superior memory kicked-in. She shrieked, "My God, how did I miss this? Rigel's the name of the brightest star in the constellation Orion!"

Startled, he knocked over his coffee. "What are you talking about?"

Shaking in shock, and frozen in a fear that momentarily was a mask that covered her face and seized her heart, Sonja desperately exclaimed, "The constellation Orion. That's it—the sheath for the knife! Don't you know anything about the constellations?" she said as she slammed her fist down on the desk.

"No!" he replied, looking both dumbfounded and at the same time insulted by her question.

"The Constellation Orion depicts Orion as a Hunter," Sonja proclaimed with a tremble in her voice she couldn't suppress.

"A hunter of what? What are you talking about?"

"Mordecai, the stars in the tattoos on the hands come from Orion. Google a search for Orion and you'll see."

The monitor quickly produced the constellation Orion and Sonja showed Mordecai a schematic drawing with three diagonal stars jumping out at them. There they were, the three stars representing the sheath for the knife of the hunter—unmistakable, unforgettable and unfortunate. Barely holding back a scream, her panicked eyes radiated sheer terror as they caught Mordecai's. "The stars… the stars on the tattoo are from Orion and so is Rigel. He's the one who's tracking us and murdering everybody!" She could feel the panic welling up inside and she was ready to burst with fear, "And Elana's with him right now!"

Mordecai rubbed his chin as his thoughts bounced between Elana and this Rigel. "It's Rigel or someone else working with him. Did he have any stars on his hands?"

"No. I remember when Elana and I first met him his hands looked so manicured and smooth, they almost looked effeminate."

Mordecai sprang to action. "Get her on the phone. If she's having lunch with him right now, we need to get her out of there!"

Reaching into her purse, Sonja was autodialing before she had it up to her face. Redialing, then redialing again. "I'm getting a recording to leave a message, and I don't know if she's talking or shut it off."

"Do you know where they're meeting?" asked Mordecai with a look of fear washing over his face.

"She told me she got an e-mail where to meet him." Sonja said as she reached over to the computer and brought up Elana's e-mails. "Here's the last one from Rigel@hotmail.com. Says to meet him at 11:00 in the Bellissima restaurant at the Crowne Plaza hotel."

Mordecai bolted to the door. "Grab your stuff and let's go! I can get there quick with my siren. But once we get in my car, I'll call the police to get her out of there."

Chapter 24

This time was different. Now she was comfortable with herself and very much in command of her emotions. Maybe it was the discussion with Sonja or maybe her time had finally come to successfully arrive at that intersection of hope and reality. But whatever it was, Elana knew she was more self-assured and even bold enough to grab that brass ring of life. One thought dominated her—*Just empower his emotional side*!

Floating into the Crowne Plaza on clouds of optimism, Elana alighted from this euphoric state to face the reality of Rigel standing alone and waiting for her. The 40 minute drive in the Institute's van seemed like it took forever, but now she was finally there, ready to reach out and touch him. But the lightness of her step might make her appear to be bouncing along, too eager to jump into his arms, and much as she might want this to happen, she sensed some type of emotional void between them. She knew the one kiss, the virginal kiss, was not a kiss of emotion, and feared worse—only a kiss of convenience. With his emotions cold and distant, and like getting a kiss from an amorously absent e-mail, she hoped she could now stoke some fires of emotion within this mysterious man.

Walking briskly towards Elana, Rigel's blue eyes projected warmth, but he only delivered a marginal kiss that slid off his lips with nary a hint of heat and hardly a portion of passion. With a mood fractured and now brought back to a harsh reality, she couldn't divest her mind of the thoughts gaining credence: *His romantic core must be a black hole whose gravity won't let his emotions escape.*

His eyes contacted hers, but with the electrified impulse of energy now gone from those blue orbs, they had the same stale stagnation as his kiss. "Elana, my

244

dear! How wonderful ta see ya. I apologize for having ya drive up here, but I've a meeting with a very serious client after lunch."

"No problem," responded Elana as the sensitive inflection in her voice tried to mask the disappointment over his vacuous kiss, "it's not really that far and I loved the thought of seeing the hotel right on the beach—something you don't see when you're headquartered in Jerusalem."

"Allow me," Rigel said as he grabbed her arm to lead her. "You'll love the Bellissmi. It's just perfect for you."

Shoulder-to-shoulder, riding the escalator to the third floor, they were duly deposited directly in front of the Bellissmi's reservation desk. Rigel addressed the very proper host, "Da ya have the reservations for Rigel?"

"Yes Mr. Rigel," he said with a flair while holding their menus and ready to open a pathway to their destination, "for you a table for two. Our best, overlooking the Mediterranean, and without the sun in your eyes so you'll enjoy seeing the whitecap waves of the sea. Please follow me."

After allowing the host to first seat Elana and then himself, and after the menus were placed on the table, Rigel reached over with both hands, and in an affectionate way, grasped Elana's. "Ya simply look so radiant, just so lovely. How foolish a me, a crazy man I must be not ta have driven ta see ya sooner!"

The blushing was boundless, and the smile on her face and the light in her dark brown eyes were undeniable signs of her renewed optimism in Rigel's presence, and hopefully in his intentions. A chuckling "Thank you," flitted from her luscious lips, "you may flatter me all you wish and I'll soak it up like a sponge."

He sensuously rubbed his fingers over her hands and as she spread open her fingers to let his between hers, his dreamy look locked onto her eyes. "Your fingers are so delicately beautiful, like they were chosen ta be the model for those ya see on so many wonderful sculptures."

"That might be a bit too much flattery, but I'm glad you noticed." Elana said as she looked at his hands and noticed a gold ring. An immediate shock reverberated in her mind as her judgment was weakened by a dose of doubt. *A wedding ring?* Her confusion dissipated as she realized it was the wrong hand, since in her panic, she got flustered because he was facing towards her. Trying to hide her embarrassment, she admiringly stroked his slender fingers, but the ring caught her attention again. Even though it was slightly rotated she could see enough of the flat surface to make out what was engraved on it. *Oh my God,* she thought, *three stars!* Now she needed a critical diversion, but wondered if her voice would be quivering like her hands as they transmitted the percussive pounding of her heart. And her nose, the barometer of her state of mind—there it was just twitching away. Elana took her hands away from his and clasped them over her nose. With the shaking visible, she then put them on her lap as she tried to divert the attention away from herself. "A beautiful ring, is that an old family crest on it?"

"Not really," Rigel said innocently enough. "The stars are ta represent the constellation Orion. My employees gave me the ring in appreciation for something I did for them."

Struggling to regain her composure, and trying too hard to look interested in what he might say, she forced some conversation. "Is Orion a favorite of yours?"

His retort seemed proud, yet distant, almost like he was responding to someone other than her. "Ya might say it's always been special. They guessed right when they chose this gift."

"How fortunate," Elana said as she started to cough, and then continued more frequently and violently. She could think of no other way to leave the table and knew it better be quick. The coughing covered-up the spastic shaking spreading through her extremities. "Forgive me," she choked out in the midst of pushing from the table, "but I need to go to the restroom—quickly!"

Watching her leave in this very distressed circumstance, and with a rare flirting relationship with empathy, he tenderly asked, "Are ya OK? Shall I call the waiter?"

As she walked away, she gave him a hand sign she was OK. "No, just wait there for me. I'll be right back."

Like crows abandoning road kill, Rigel's elusive empathy quickly took flight. Out came his cell phone to call Liam sitting outside in his van. Empathy gone, and with opportunities needed, Rigel questioned Liam, "Have ya been able ta listen in?"

"Loud and clear," Liam proudly spoke. "We're fine. Been listening ta ya at the table and got the bug working perfectly." No sound on the line for a moment before Liam added, "Rigel! She's talking on her cell phone in the bathroom. Pleading for the phone ta ring!"

Sunk in a tub of turmoil, Elana implored the phone to come alive. "Ring! Ring! For God's sake, please ring!" Suddenly she had contact with Sonja. "I'm in trouble here at the restaurant with Rigel. He's wearing a ring with three stars on it, three diagonal stars just like the stars on the killer's hand! I don't know if he's the killer or if the killer works for him, because he doesn't have any tattoos on his hands."

"Don't worry, I'm here with Mordecai and we're on our way to get you. He thinks Rigel's behind the killings of the dealers and also some priests in Ireland."

Mordecai took the phone from Sonja. "Get out of there as soon as you can!"

Not being able to hear clearly in the bathroom, Elana needed to repeat what she thought was said, and though Mordecai could hear what she said, so could the bug in her purse. "Mordecai, I can't hear you that well, but you want me to get out of here right away? Rigel is part of the killing? Murders in Ireland? OK, I'll tell him I need to leave. I'll drive the Institute van out of here as soon as possible."

Mordecai's voice now came through clearly to Elana. "Good, but leave now! We're on our way up there and I've called the police, but get out of there as soon as you can. They'll get Rigel, but you leave and drive down the highway to Jerusalem. We're coming up, and we'll meet you along the way."

247

Alerted to what Elana just said, Liam dialed Rigel on his cell phone. "She's on ta what you're doing, and her people in Jerusalem have linked ya ta the killings."

Speaking slowly, Rigel eliminated any emotion from the decision. "There's no way we can't let her get away back ta Jerusalem. Gimme Viktor!"

"Rigel, what you want?"

"Moy chornee Ruski brat. We can't let her get back ta Jerusalem."

After waiting a few minutes, seeming like an eternity, a wobbly Elana walked out of the washroom back to Rigel's table. Weaving from side to side and creating the impression of not being stable on her feet, she waved Rigel off as he stood up to help her with her chair. "I'm sorry, but I feel so horrible. First it was a cough and now my stomach is tied in knots—and it's not a good time of the month. I'm so sorry, but I need to leave right away! Can you walk me to my van?"

"That I can do my dear. I can see you're not feeling well. And your nose is twitching—maybe the allergies got ya." He got up and grabbed her arm and spoke the words that might be his last noble gesture. "If I may, allow me ta help ya down ta your van."

"Waiter!" Rigel called as he waved to the man in black-and-white. Handing him something, he spoke quickly, "Take this money and keep the change. It'll cover our bill, but my friend and I must leave now."

As they left the restaurant, descending down the escalator and walking out the revolving door, Rigel held Elana's arm and put his other arm around her shoulder. He spoke as he gave her a reassuring hug, "Are ya sure ya can drive safely?"

Turning her head towards him, and with the look on her face projecting nothing short of dire sickness, she pointed to her van, "Yes, I'll be OK. My van's over there to the left."

Helping her to the van enabled Rigel to look across the street where Viktor, Liam and Conor sat in their surveillance sleuth-machine. Once Elana got in the van, Rigel kissed her hand and closed the door. "Be careful driving home, you're very precious ta me."

As she drove away and waved good-bye, Elana gave a quick turn of her head as she proceeded to exit the driveway and off into traffic. With only seconds elapsing, Viktor scooped-up Rigel and this band of decadent desperados quickly followed.

The main road from Tel Aviv to Jerusalem was four lanes of undivided highway, with no barriers between the two northbound and two southbound lanes. Mordecai thought this convenient as a way to meet up with Elana, but Rigel and his crew, now following closely behind her, knew this to be perfect for their purposes.

Too busy to look in her mirror, Elana hadn't noticed who was behind her. She autodialed Sonja and made an instant connection. "I'm out of there! Tell Mordecai I'm OK. I don't know where Rigel will be when the police get there. He paid his bill and left with me, but who knows where he is now. Just don't worry, I'm safe." Steering confidently at the wheel of her van, she had no doubt things were going to be OK—the twitching of her nose had stopped.

Mordecai interrupted. "I heard what you said, so don't worry about Rigel, just drive safely."

Seated in the front passenger seat, Rigel had the perspective he wanted for watching and planning while Viktor paid attention to the traffic and Elana. Rigel gave Viktor his directions. "She's aggressively passing cars like she doesn't want anyone ta hold her back. When she's back in the slow lane, pass her. Me and the guys in the back seat, we'll duck down so she can't see us. Once we get in front a her, I'll tell ya when ta slow down ta force her ta pass us. Understand moy chornee Ruski brat?"

Viktor's repulsive response was a nod and an evil sneer. "I know what you want."

With a smile erupting like some sinister, satanic force, Rigel then patted Viktor's arm, "Ya got it right! Just wait till I give ya the signal."

Driving aggressively, Elana quickly passed a trailer truck in front of her and then pulled back into the slow lane.

Rigel gave Viktor the direction to pass the truck and then Elana, after which he pulled into the slow lane four car lengths ahead of her. Rigel then pointed, "Viktor, look down the road, there's a truck coming. Slow down and make her pass ya. When she gets right next ta ya, speed up and don't let her pass ya. Then I'll tell ya what's next."

Oblivious to what was in front or went past her, Elana reached over to turn on the van's radio. Knowing she was out of that mess back at the hotel, she felt her heart's pounding gone, replaced by an overall sense of tranquility.

A short play was about to unfold before a very limited audience—Elana, Rigel, Viktor, Liam, Conor and one unsuspecting truck driver. Waiting in the wings were two supporting characters, Mordecai and Sonja, desperately trying to be included.

Just as Rigel planned; Viktor slowed, she sped and upon Rigel's orders, Viktor turned hard to his left and pushed her in front of the oncoming truck. All so quick with horrible smashing sounds of the van being crushed by the truck and the explosion that reverberated all the way back to Ireland.

Rigel's van sped down the highway, rapidly separated from the accident scene and the human pathos of his creation. Inside, a satisfied, smiling Rigel gazed back at the smoke and the sudden traffic jam. Just as he thought, no worries about being followed—everyone stopped at the accident scene. *Good Samaritans? They would've been better Samaritans if they'd tried to catch us!* thought Rigel as his van passed an oncoming police car with its lights flashing and siren blaring.

Speeding northward, unknowingly past Rigel's southward traveling van, Mordecai looked ahead at the traffic jam. Above it, he saw the spiraling, dark

250

smoke rising up to smudge a serene sky. With no traffic on the opposing lane, he pulled onto it while fear, a stranger to his mind, now found a home in his thoughts. "Tell her we're stuck in traffic."

Sonja hit the autodial and waited. Nothing! She tried again. Again…and again. "I can't get anything. Please hurry!" she said with a sense of desperation dominating her voice.

Arriving at the head of the northbound traffic, a fear that had been building in Mordecai's stomach belched out its ugly head destroying the hopes of this small rescue squad. Out of the car he got, but Sonja was quicker. Her premonition of disaster was stronger than Mordecai's worst fears, and the devastation of the horrible wreck and fire was clearly visible and palpable in her hyper-stressed heart. Sonja clutched at Mordecai's arm as she caught a glimpse of the only thing legible that could identify the smaller vehicle. There on the back of the burning van was the name, 'New Testament Biblical Institute'. Just as her brain processed those letters, it shut down and she instantly collapsed.

Mordecai grabbed her, and clutching her to his chest, knew her young life would be permanently scarred by this demonic beam of blackness that snuffed out the dazzling brilliance of Elana's life. Throwing that damned, frayed toothpick into the fire, Mordecai knew this horrible loss was no coincidence.

Chapter 25

With a pleased look plastered all over his face, Eric presented himself at the Monsignor's office where the security guard looked up from his desk. "Ahhh…Professor Stanfels. So good to see you again. I know the Monsignor is eagerly awaiting your arrival."

After shaking the guard's hand, Eric was overflowing with joy and optimism. "Thank you. I'm so happy to be back to meet with the Monsignor and his friend."

"Yes, the Archbishop," replied the nodding guard.

An inquisitive look wiped away Eric's enthusiasm. "How do you know that's who it is?"

"Monsignor arrived earlier with an Archbishop, a Greek Orthodox Archbishop, but I don't know who he was. But, from his dress and Greek cross, obviously he was a Greek Orthodox archbishop." The guard reached over to open the entry door. "Please, you may enter and go directly to the Monsignor's office."

Eric gave a courteous nod, and like a hunting dog sniffing a trail, he sensed his direction and was off to find the Monsignor.

Tracing his steps along the corridor, Eric thought of how this time his shoulders were square and his head held high as the imposing power of the hallway wasn't intimidating at all. Continuing to the office and opening the door, Eric was greeted with the very accommodating smile of the reception desk priest.

"Professor Stanfels, so pleased to have you return to us. The Monsignor and his guest are expecting you. Please follow me," the priest said as he rose from the desk, walked over and opened the door leading into the Monsignor's private office.

Entering through the door, Eric could see Bertani and a man in a dark cleric's cloak he assumed was the Archbishop. "Eric, it is so wonderful to see you again," said the Monsignor, in his courtly style, as he walked over to shake Eric's hand. He turned towards the Archbishop with an open hand pointing towards him and continued. "And I would like you to meet my friend, Archbishop Bournias, who has heard so much about you."

Tall and powerfully-built was the Archbishop, who, apparently in his late 60's, hid half of his face behind a long, gray, bushy beard. But his dark brown eyes had a piercingly strong quality that penetrated above that gray, swirly mass. His large right hand dwarfed Eric's as he extended it towards him. He spoke perfect, if deliberate English and Eric could sense the influence of his native Greek language on the enunciation of some English words. "Professor Stanfels, it pleases me to make your acquaintance. Monsignor Bertani has been very generous with his praise of you, and I am most assuredly confident you are worthy of his trust and support."

Momentarily assessing his appraisal of the Archbishop, Eric then followed with a courtly ceremonious bow. "Thank you Archbishop. It is my distinct pleasure to meet you, and if I may say so, to impose upon your good graces just as I already have with Monsignor Bertani."

The smile on Bournias' face somehow found its way through his beard like a laser cutting its way through dense underbrush. "I'm sure you will not be imposing whatsoever. Monsignor Bertani has already told me some of what interests you, and obviously, since I am here, I must have some interest as well."

Bertani took both men by the arm and led them to one side of the room. "Please, let us to have a seat on the sofas, for our conversation may be much too long and involved for an old man like me to stand. Please, have a seat," he finished as he pointed towards the sofas.

While Eric and the Archbishop sat facing each other at different ends of a large sofa; the Monsignor sat on a smaller one facing them. "Professor Stanfels, the Monsignor told me about your Strayton University and its close relationship with the Vatican. It pleases me to know of such an ecumenical relationship between Catholics and Protestants; something not always in existence over the years."

Humility was the behavior for the day and Eric made certain no hint of hubris would show its ugly face to the Archbishop. "Thank you Archbishop. We at Strayton have had a long and very trusting relationship with the Vatican for many years, and we hope the relationship has been as good for the Vatican as it has been for us."

The Archbishop made strong eye contact with Eric. "Monsignor Bertani has convinced me your interest in St. Catherine's is valid and that I should give you an opportunity to present your case. Fortunately, I had previously planned to be here in Rome since I hardly would have traveled here for such a speculative cause."

With eyes now humbly looking down to the floor, Eric paused then raised them to meet the Archbishop's unwavering gaze. "I'm pleased we could meet since I understand your reluctance to travel far just to talk to a stranger. If you believe in such a thing, maybe destiny brought us together." A chilling dagger of fear struck at Eric's heart as he wondered if he said the wrong thing—all that stuff about destiny to a member of the Orthodox clergy.

Bournias chuckled and leaned over to Bertani to touch his arm as he spoke. "While I think destiny might have had a hand in this, most of the credit belongs to the Monsignor."

Worried he might look silly, Eric sheepishly nodded his approval first to the Archbishop and then to the Monsignor before continuing. "Thankfully, Monsignor Bertani believed in my vision and gave it a breath-of-life with his intercession. Needless to say, for that, my associates and I are very grateful."

"Understandably so," said Bournias as he got up from the sofa to stand behind it. "I hope we both will be thankful for the Monsignor's intercession, but for now, tell me of your interest in St. Catherine's."

Still seated on the sofa, Eric found himself intimidated by this large, imposing man, and needed a few seconds to gain his composure to quiet the quivering in his voice. "My interest, and that of my colleagues at the New Testament Biblical Institute in Jerusalem, is based on rumors of relics at St. Catherine's. Our archeological and genetic research capabilities initially were focused on the discovery of the Ossuary of James, the alleged brother of Jesus." It crossed Eric's mind, *Better say alleged or a theological dispute could derail this whole thing.* "Had you followed that discovery?"

Coming from behind the sofa, and brushing the hem of his cloak out of the way, Bournias sat back down on the sofa. He leaned in close to Eric. "We did follow it and, if the truth be told, found it very intriguing. While being somewhat isolated, geographically and scientifically, the research that was to be used was of interest to us. We were aware of it, but did not anticipate genetic research would have any merit in our religious world. Frankly, I was disappointed the ossuary was not legitimate. But now, please tell me, what does all that have to do with us at St. Catherine's?"

Eric's flitting eye contact bounced from Bertani, then to Bournias. "In the course of my colleagues' research on the James' ossuary, opinions were given that relics of the crucifixion might actually exist. We were told any relics might be at a Russian monastery, and that Khor Virap and St. Catherine's were the best bets. We were confused since St. Catherine's is now Greek Orthodox, but a little research told us of its Russian Orthodox connections."

The Archbishop looked first at the Monsignor and then to Eric. "Yes, the Emperor Constantine was driven by his mother, the Empress Helena to construct the monastery in the 300's A.D., and it is easy to be confused since it had been Russian Orthodox from the time of its completion in 563 A.D. until 150 years ago. Forgive me professor for using A.D. since I'm too old to change to B.C.E."

After searching the faces of both men for some small sign of approval, Eric continued. "Anyway, we went to Khor Virap first and found nothing of interest. Obviously, we realized St. Catherine's was the place to look. Now we find ourselves here to determine if you actually might have something of such great antiquity that it could be from the crucifixion of Christ."

"Was there nothing at Khor Virap?" asked the Monsignor.

"Yes, a murder. My partners and I found the monastery's senior monk had been killed. But we did come across something of collateral interest." He then reached over to his briefcase, and after fumbling through it, produced a photo of the chiseled animal. "This photo is what was chiseled into the lid of St. Gregory's ossuary at Khor Virap. We also saw this carving on the lid of another ossuary, the fraudulent Ossuary of James."

The Archbishop took the photo and viewed it with an increasingly inquisitive look taking over his face, then turned back to Eric. "You must understand your inquiry does intrigue me or I would not have met with you. And, to persist on a point, the science of today is equally intriguing and perplexing. You must also understand that St. Catherine's has many rare and valuable objects, but we choose to be isolated from the world community for the sake of their protection. What is it specifically that you seek?"

"Our assumptions are based on the projection that if some relics from the crucifixion of Jesus do actually exist, there's a strong probability they would be metal. If they're metal, they, or it, would be the spikes which nailed Jesus to the cross. If one or more of the spikes exist, then certainly we have the potential for two things. One would be that with the use of carbon dating, we could verify that the spikes were approximately 2,000 years old if there is some organic residue on them. Actually, we'd be determining if the organic residue was 2,000 years old since the spikes could be even older, but you can't carbon date the metal of the spikes. Then, if organic residue exists on the spikes, we could determine if it's blood residue."

"You could find blood on something that old?" inquired a surprised Archbishop who looked at an even-more-surprised Monsignor.

"Yes," replied an increasingly confident Eric, with his focus still on the Archbishop. "Traces of blood and its DNA were extracted from stone cutting tools that butchered wooly mammoths twenty thousand years ago. Those were stone, and metal also could have lasted 2,000 years in this part of the world, especially if it was in dry caves."

The Archbishop smacked Eric on the knee as a gesture of some growing trust. "Professor Stanfels, you do intrigue me! I will admit to you that we do have three items we believe to be relics from the time of the crucifixion. And I must tell you these relics have been stored in a stone box which is two feet square, and on the inside of the box's lid is a carving of an animal exactly the same as the one in your photo. Bear in mind, these relics were not in our possession for 2,000 years since we are only 1,500 years old. But we do know our relics were stored in very dry caves for hundreds of years, which, I assume, is why they are still in existence. We at St. Catherine's would be interested to determine if you might find something worthwhile about those relics."

Monsignor Bertani straightened up in his chair and as usual spoke to Bournias in his very proper style. "Does not the thought of analyzing what might be the blood of our Savior cause some concern for you?"

The Archbishop now aimed his attention solely at the Monsignor. "No, not really. I hadn't thought of this as an option, but a DNA analysis would be something noteworthy only if it showed something positive. What does the professor think?"

Nodding approvingly, Eric chimed in. "I agree. A common result of a DNA analysis is meaningless, and if there's blood to be found, it's only significant if it's something dramatic. But I'm very curious why you're so interested in pursuing this discovery with us?"

"My dear Professor," said the Archbishop as his right hand tugged on his beard, "the real motivating factor is simple, unadulterated curiosity."

Shocked by such an answer, Eric's mouth hung open for seconds before responding, "Curiosity?"

The Archbishop nodded. "We have been curious for many years whether we had something of legitimate value. More recently, we thought we could consider carbon dating, but figuring out the issue of carbon dating only organic residue was outside the scope of our imagination. We knew about DNA testing, but it was also unimaginable that this testing had any relevance to our needs."

Not to be entirely excluded, the Monsignor leaned in and added, "What changed your minds?"

"At St. Catherine's we were aware of the search for the legitimacy of that Ossuary of James. It provided great stimulation for many debates regarding what we should do with what we had. In that setting, you can see how the scientific discussion of DNA testing was brought into the religious sanctum. I had seen a reference by some investigator that if there was any residue within that ossuary, they would do a DNA test on it seeking a DNA link back to Jesus' brother. Now, as an Orthodox, I certainly don't believe some of that, but I know you Protestants believe differently. But that really isn't the issue here. You could say the potential for DNA testing simply got me thinking about what we might have in our limestone box."

Turning away from the window, Eric stared at the Archbishop. "May I ask why you've chosen to help us? Was it because of Monsignor Bertani or something he said about us?"

"Professor Stanfels," the Archbishop laughed as he swept his hand in Eric's direction, "the Monsignor certainly said good things about you, but it wasn't about that. You simply came along at the right time—you were the first one to ask us!"

Eric persisted. "Why do you believe these relics, from so long ago, are from the crucifixion? If your monastery has only been in existence for 1,400 years, these relics would've been sitting around for 500 years before they ever got to St. Catherine's. How could they have existed so long before St. Catherine's was built?"

The Archbishop sat back in his seat. He paused, then took to stroking some of that huge beard. "I can answer that for you and the Monsignor if he is equally curious. It is all about Canis lupus, the wolf. And, your photo adds a dimension of confirmation to my answer, since that chiseled animal is a wolf."

Monsignor Bertani stood up. "Forgive me for interrupting, but I ordered lunch to be served at this time, not thinking we would move so quickly into such depth in our conversation. Let us sit at my luncheon table by the window and continue our discussion there."

As all three men moved over to the table, the staff brought in plates piled with broiled fish on beds of vegetables. While wine was being poured, Eric motioned to the staff to be bypassed. "Professor," asked the Archbishop with a devilish look on his face, "passing on the wine? You should not let that opportunity go by. Here we have a holy meal with fish, a symbol of Jesus, and wine which speaks to His sacrifice of blood." he said while finishing with a big, belly laugh.

A huge smile furrowed his face as Eric lightened up. After seeing the Archbishop make light over the wine issue, he understood the Archbishop and the Monsignor were actually enjoying the dialogue more than he. "I agree with you, wonderful symbolism but there's too much for me to learn from the two of you to risk having a brain confused by the grandeur of the grapes. And speaking of symbols, you mentioned the symbol you called Canis lupus, the wolf. How did my photo of that carving bring that up?"

Not letting Eric's disinterest in the wine limit his love of it, the Archbishop continued drinking and talking. "The wolf? The wolf was a symbol of a group of very secretive men who were very important after the crucifixion. Since you have something with this wolf chiseled into its surface, this implies your object came from the time of the crucifixion or within 300 years after it. We at St. Catherine's believe these objects, which have this likeness of the wolf, were special holy containers holding precious treasures from the time of Jesus' life. Bear in mind that I just told you the wolf was carved into the lid of the stone box holding the three relics at St. Catherine's. Where did you say you saw this animal?"

Without realizing how much he was leaning in towards the table, Eric replied, "I first saw it on the lid of James' ossuary, then, the second time, it was at Khor Virap on the ossuary that held the bones of St. Gregory. If you think the carving

259

means the box contained something very special, why do you think the James' ossuary was a fraud?"

Shrugging his shoulders, the Archbishop raised both hands with their palms upward as if to say 'who knows' and continued in his very formal style of speech, yet slightly affected by the wine. "It is hard to say what was fraudulent, but some of the chiseled letters were a fraud. Science showed that to be true, and in this instance, I believe science to be true—something I don't always do. But just because the lettering was a fraud, doesn't mean the box itself was not from the time of James. Who can say?" Bournias looked over at Bertani. "Can you?"

Bertani just gave a negative head shake.

Bournias looked at Bertani, then Eric. "It may have actually contained the bones of James and the chiseled wolf may be its best clue. That chiseled animal tells me James' ossuary and the one at Khor Virap are probably of the same origin as ours at St. Catherine's. We actually suspect our relics came to us from Khor Virap. In ancient times, we had a special relationship with them, and since our monastery is an impenetrable fortress, the monks of Khor Virap may have sent their treasures to us for safe keeping. There is no question that during the early times of Christianity, around 560 – 1,400 A.D., St. Catherine's was the safest place in the world for items of great religious value."

Eric's impatience was imploding. "What about the wolf? What's that all about?"

The giddy effect of the wine worked on the Archbishop as he chuckled while responding. "We did get away from that didn't we? This is a part of our oral history, and since I am the one responsible for the oral secrets of the monastery, I can tell you some things we've never shared with anyone." After another long drink of wine, Bournias continued. "There was a society of men from the time of the crucifixion that took upon itself the task of perpetuating the works and love of this man Jesus."

"Forerunners of the early Christian Church?" asked Eric.

The Archbishop vigorously shook his head. "No, they do not show up anywhere within the written histories of the early Church because these men were of the Roman army. Not combat soldiers, apparently their job was to clean up the crucifixion site. Obviously something not assigned to the magnificent men of the mighty Roman fighting machine."

Interrupting when he could, the Monsignor got Bournias' attention, "Are you saying there were other believers at the crucifixion, other than those we know from the Bible?"

"Yes. Our oral history says so and it would have been naïve to think such a spiritual event as the crucifixion impacted only a few people at the foot of the cross."

Eric's curiosity continued, "Are you telling us Christian history didn't accurately record the total impact of the crucifixion?"

Looking at his half-empty glass of wine, the Archbishop paused, then looked up at Eric. "The crucifixion had a very powerful impact on many who were there, but not necessarily the Roman soldiers who were an unthinking fighting machine. But the support members of the force at Golgotha had a number of men who apparently understood the Son of God died there. Bear in mind, the Roman Army was a very repressive society, and these men of the Army would need to be even more secretive than the early Christians."

"Are you implying these are the men who took the relics?" queried the ever-impatient Eric.

Bournias kept his focus on Eric, while the Monsignor, wanting to be even more included, found himself moving his seat in closer. "Professor," Bournias half-shouted as the tint of the wine had influenced the tone of his speech, "our oral history tells us these were the men who removed the spikes from the hands and feet of Jesus. Rather than laying the cross and its remnants aside so that the people who took Jesus' garments could also take what they wanted, these men probably hid the materials from the cross once everyone took Jesus' body to what they thought would be its final resting place."

Never having heard even an inkling of such a history, Bertani was transfixed by it. "And you and preceding generations of the keepers at St. Catherine's believe somehow these men were inspired to preserve these relics? How? Why? Was there anything else?"

Turning to the Monsignor, the serious look on Bournias' face was accompanied with an equally serious tone in his speech. "You must understand what we are discussing has been only for those ears at St. Catherine's. I will tell you now only because I sense something very special can be done with the relics of these early men who stored them in jars in dry caves. As their written histories deteriorated, these men, these Lupus men, resorted to relying on oral accounts, but the relics themselves didn't deteriorate in the caves."

"Like the Dead Sea Scrolls caves?" asked Eric.

"Yes, something like that," replied the Archbishop with a dismissive wave of his hand.

An incredulous Eric asked disparagingly, "And they just lay in some cave for 500 years?"

"No. Don't forget, you asked me 'how' and 'why'. I am still telling you 'how. Now, these men, we assume 10 to 20, believed in Jesus and wanted to perpetuate him, his mission and his beliefs. We don't know why they didn't join mainstream developing Christianity, but we do know they called themselves Lupus, the wolf. And their symbol was just that, the wolf—hence the carving."

Eric interjected even before the last sound left the lips of the Archbishop. "But why a wolf? A ravenous beast inspiring love and sacrifice?"

"Professor, you must remember two things as I try to answer the 'why'. First these men were committed to nurturing the work of Jesus, and secondly, they were Romans. Have you forgotten the mythology of Rome's founding?"

His hands signaled to 'go on', but lost the race as Eric's tongue moved even faster. "Yes, Romulus and Remus, two little babies abandoned on a hill to die."

"Correct, Professor! But they didn't die because they were nurtured by a she-wolf. This wolf, Canis lupus, was the savior of Rome, the nurturer of Rome."

With his elbows resting on the table, like a little child attentively listening to his mother's story, Eric was enthralled. "You're telling me these men took the name Lupus because they wanted to nurture the work of Jesus just like Canis lupus, the wolf, nurtured Romulus and Remus?"

The Archbishop lifted his wine glass in Eric's direction. "A toast to you. Correct again! But you must understand these men, this Lupus secret order, did not last much longer than 300 years."

Entranced with what he was hearing for the first time, the Monsignor couldn't resist asking, "If the Lupus didn't last much longer than 300 years, how did the relics, and whatever else, get to St. Catherine's since it was built so much later?"

An ebullient Bournias continued. "While Lupus eventually did die out, their parchment writings lasted at least long enough to be recorded into our oral histories. As I said, once these items left the possession of the Lupus, they were at Khor Virap. Trace the trade routes! You will see Armenia is not that far from Jerusalem and abundant trade existed between them. St. Catherine's ultimately took possession of items from our brother monks at Khor Virap because we were always a safer and drier place."

"And you believe what you've told me and the Monsignor—the writings and relics were the real items?"

Bournias nodded as he replied. "Yes, we all believed that over the years, but now, we have no papyrus and only the relics. And, my dear Professor Stanfels, since I believe they are from the crucifixion, I am intrigued with what you might be able to do with them."

"What are you suggesting?" asked Eric.

Reaching under his cloak, the Archbishop took out a brown envelope. "I brought with me these fragments from the relics just in case I would feel favorably inclined towards you. Which I do! I would like you to obtain the carbon dating of these fragments since we need to know if the relics are actually from 2,000 years ago, or if this is a wild goose chase."

263

An elated Eric tried to temper his enthusiasm. "Carbon dating may not be able to give us an exact year, maybe pretty close, but not exact. And the dating can only be done if there's some organic material on these metal fragments."

Maybe too lubricated by the wine, the Archbishop nodded in approval as he reached for his wine glass. "I know it can't be exact, but we need to be in the correct range, give or take 50 years. And what I am giving you is not metal, it's wood! We don't need to find organic material on these fragments, we need to carbon date the wood itself. If the age of the wood is appropriate, we can then worry about finding the blood residue.

Staring with a startled look cast first at Bournias, then Bertani, Eric queried. "Why are you so fixated on the wood, but not any spikes?"

The Archbishop paused for a sip of wine, then turned back to Eric as he clumsily set his glass on the table. "Don't worry Professor. Only concern yourself with these wood fragments, and if they are 2,000 years old, we can then concern ourselves with finding any blood residue – trust me! And if you find any blood residue, you may analyze it for its DNA content at St. Catherine's. You must transport your laboratory equipment there. After Tischendorf—von Tischendorf that arrogant fool called himself—stole our Codex Sinaiticus, we won't let anything out of the monastery. What I do with the DNA analysis depends on what it shows. It may be of no value to us, and to Christianity, or it may be very valuable. We can cross that bridge when we get there. But you must understand, and provide to me in writing, that St. Catherine's has complete ownership and control over what is done with any results of the testing."

Reaching over, Eric took the envelope from the Archbishop. "I'll get the carbon dating on these wood fragments, just as you wish, and we will comply with your demands just as you have stipulated them. And you can't imagine how grateful I am for trusting me with such an opportunity."

Sitting back in his chair, under that bushy beard the Archbishop was smiling at an obviously elated Eric. "You have the Monsignor to thank for that. Bear in mind, I don't have to answer to anyone regarding what I do with the relics, but

Monsignor Bertani may have to answer to someone higher in the Vatican if they don't like what we find. He is the 'risk taker' here."

Eric's look towards the Monsignor was one of absolute appreciation. "Thanks for creating enough trust with Archbishop Bournias that he would even consider bringing these wood fragments."

Bowing his head as a sign of his appreciation, Bertani replied, "I believe there are occasions where science and religion can work together, and if we have the opportunity to show something great, it will be great for all Christians. But, if you find blood and analyze its DNA, I want to be there when it's done. I will come to St. Catherine's as soon as you have some scientific evidence."

The archbishop raucously roared with a voice lubricated by wine. "That is some statement coming from the center of Christianity that at one time repressed scientific thought."

The Monsignor rolled his eyes upward in a sign of disdain. "Yes, my Church has been on the wrong side of some past issues. From my personal perspective, one which doesn't represent anyone else's thinking here, I have been stimulated by genetics ever since I read there may even be a genetic predisposition towards religion."

Startled, the Monsignor's words caught Bournias' attention. "That concept, a genetic predisposition, wouldn't be acceptable in my Orthodox faith. I am surprised you would have been exposed to that kind of thought here. What did you read?"

Bertani continued since it was obvious his opinion was now the center of controversy. "What I read was there appear to be certain DNA nucleotide sequences that are associated with spirituality—people who weren't inclined towards being spiritual didn't have this sequencing. How true it is, I don't know, but I do think there is more to be discovered through science that is not exclusionary to Christianity."

"I am too isolated at the monastery to have exposure to such thoughts," said the Archbishop with a dismissive wave of his right hand. "What direction would your theology take if you believed we were genetically predisposed towards religion?"

The monsignor hesitated, "I don't know. I had not thought about that."

An enthusiastic Eric interrupted. "May I join in on this? It's like... WOW! I can't believe I'm hearing this from a Roman Catholic priest. But you might consider God created us not only in His physical image, but also in a genetically-predisposed image, and here I mean a DNA sequencing towards a religious devotion to Him. The concept of original sin may mean that humanity, with its ability to make choices like Adam and Eve did, could unfortunately override that genetic predisposition. Now, bear in mind, I'm not saying I believe this to be totally correct, but it's something to consider."

Stifling a big belly laugh, Bertani replied, "You might have a good theory, but please don't attach my name to it. I still need to keep this day job. I don't think the Vatican is ready for me to be speaking on this subject. But now let us finish our lunch, since I know you both must leave and I must attend to other issues not as controversial as genetics and religion."

Eric leaned over towards the Monsignor. "Before I leave, may I impose upon you again to send an e-mail back to my colleagues at the Biblical Institute?"

"Certainly!" nodded Bertani. "You may do that while I will take the Archbishop with me as we bid you good-day."

Getting up to leave, the Monsignor and the Archbishop stood up and shook hands with each other and then with Eric. But Eric's thoughts drifted as he thought of the excitement he would soon share with Sonja and Elana. As they left the room, Eric sat at the computer and sent his e-mail: 'Great day here at Vatican! Archbishop Bournias of St. Catherine's brought fragments from relics for carbon dating. Will test them at Tel Aviv University once I return. May have found the relics of the crucifixion!'

Sure his good news would unleash a stream of elation flowing to his friends in Jerusalem, Eric got up from Bertani's computer. He was correct about the elation, but it was only Rigel and his men enjoying the euphoria from reading the message. The gloom and despair at the Biblical Institute dominated the

266

atmosphere so that no one had any interest in anything, let alone the internet. Repeated phone calls to Eric had not been answered when he was at the Vatican and he had no idea of what lay ahead when he returned. It wasn't until Eric listened to his messages at the airport in Rome that he stumbled into a senseless sinkhole of devastation.

Chapter 26

E-mail euphoria was the elixir of optimism oozing through Orion's psyches as they read the recent report of Stanfels' relics recovery. Rigel was back on top of his game—prancing on tiptoe with an uncommonly huge smile dominating a face framed by tousled red hair and lit-up by the light in those intense blue eyes. He proved again, that despite conventional wisdom, his planning was far more reaching; deeper in its probing and broader in its vision than that of most mere mortals. As always, Rigel had simply been correct! And now Liam's hacking produced the fertile seed from which their bountiful harvest would sprout. From Stanfels' e-mail, it was clear that Orion, by proxy, had struck gold, or in this case gold in the form of some old iron spikes. And Rigel's plan was perfect; let Sonja and the professor establish the basic discovery and analysis process. His men might not understand why his smile was getting broader with each bigger thought. *When they need to transport a laboratory to St. Catherine's, that'll be when I insert Orion into the monastery. And thank heaven for you Monsignor, you'll be our vehicle to get in the door.* Couldn't ask for more for the cause of Orion—the Monsignor requesting to be personally present when they analyzed any blood from the spikes!

A tad apprehensive as he addressed the boss, Conor didn't avoid what was working on him. "What da ya have in that cold, cold heart a yours? Didn't ya love her just a bit? Aren't ya in just a bit a mourning?"

Taking in the panoramic view from the hotel window, and always fixated on the heavens, Rigel paused, then answered without looking Conor's way, "What are ya thinking?"

A confused Conor persisted. "About that woman Elana, didn't ya have even a wee bit a Irish love for her?"

With a head shaking and a heart not breaking, Rigel now turned to Conor. "No, I didn't love her, and I don't miss her. A nice girl, but knew too much. A casualty a my war against the Church. In times a war, the death a innocents is unfortunate collateral damage, but it still happens."

Looking up from his computer, Liam queried, "Ya killed one a the two people who could identify ya. What'll ya do now? Kill this Sonja?"

Returning his gaze out the window, Rigel was searching for something looming in the far off Heavens—a habit imprinted in his own DNA that he couldn't discard from his childhood. "You're thinking the right way! At some time I'll need ta kill her and the professor, but for now, keep her alive ta do the genetic research. She'll still be our handmaiden a the Church; doing our handiwork with the DNA and then getting screwed out a the glory. It always happens that way ta women, and it doesn't matter if it's the Catholics or the Protestants, and who knows what the other religions do? Why should our Church a the Internet be any different?"

Stifling a snicker, Liam couldn't help adding, "Ya never quit hating the damned Church, da ya?"

With a face screwed-up with an intensity of searing bitterness, Rigel turned back to Liam. "Nah, I'm what the Church isn't. I'm consistently consistent, and ya can count on that! I'm an equal opportunity hater because I hate the Father, Son and the Holy Ghost all ta the same degree. I hate all the churches, but especially the Catholic Church. Abandoned my mum and my Michael, didn't it! But don't ya worry, I'll get my revenge and you'll get rich along the way. Then we can be done with computer theft and certainly nothing again like that craziness in Belarus. We could've gotten killed or, at the least, put in jail. With our own church, we'll be professional thieves above the law, just like all those Protestant televangelists. "

Speaking his piece, Conor added, "But Rigel, the Castle Gondolfo caper netted us $15 million dollars by the time we were done with the Vatican. That's enough ta be free! What more da we need?"

Understanding Conor's point, Rigel started walking his way. "I agree we have enough ta live on, so there'll be no more foolish risks once we get the relics and the royal blood a Jesus."

Up from his chair, Viktor paced the floor. "Rigel, what we do next? What is plan?"

Turning to meet Viktor's questioning eyes, Rigel raised his index finger. "First, we'll wait until the carbon dating is done ta see if we go on ta the next step. Then let this Sonja set-up a lab ta see if there's blood on the spikes. If she finds blood, the Monsignor will be coming ta St. Catherine's, and that's when we make our move—he'll be our passkey into the monastery. Just read their e-mails, and when it all comes together I'll activate my genetic wonderboy, the good Dr. Geoffrey Salvatore."

Wanting to show he understood, Viktor piped in. "You mean Salvador Dali!"

"Yes, my Salvador Dali," replied Rigel with a smile now smoothing over his deeply creased concerns. "I'll let him know when we need him. Anybody else need anything?"

With no one responding, Rigel gave a hand motion to Liam. "Out a that seat! I need ta send an e-mail ta my Dali."

Liam hopped out so Rigel could sit, but he looked over Rigel's shoulder as the letters 'Dear Dolly' fell into place on the screen.

Interrupting Rigel, Liam quickly added his discovery, "Ya got it wrong! It's D-a-l-i, not D-o-l-l-y."

Not looking up from the keyboard, Rigel cast Liam's confusion aside. "The good Dr. Geoffrey Salvatore knows who I'm talking about."

Chapter 27

Sitting solemnly on the flight back to Tel Aviv, the news of Elana's death draped an exhausted Eric with a dark cloak of depression that snuffed out his discovery's radiant beams of exhilaration. The text message strangled, then suffocated the exhilaration he hoped would empower their mission. Now this noxious news threatened to provoke a spiritual and emotional collapse. Simple words on a hand-held device, but with such a destructive impact: 'Rigel murdered Elana! Horrible car crash!' As some cold, dark subterranean force snatched this victory from their hands, Eric was thrust into the harsh reality of 'had—had not' conflicts.

His team now had entrée to St. Catherine's and the Archbishop. Whoever were their antagonists had not these advantages. He, Sonja and Mordecai had a sense of impending success in their mission, but they had not the companionship of Elana. Eric's team had every reason to expect their investigations would bear them the succulent fruit of a momentous discovery, but they had not any inkling of why Rigel would try to destroy part or all of their team.

As his plane made its final descent into Ben Gurion Airport, Eric's doubts surfaced about the relics. Not whether they were legitimate, but who else could find out about them? How did they know about them, and what would they do to get them. When the plane's tires smacked the tarmac, Eric was jolted back into the reality of being in Jerusalem; into a quagmire of ill-tempered, misdirected people who would do anything to get their goals and his relics. But he was struck with a bolt of doubt as he wondered whether these killers were any different than he was when guiding that killing bomb in Gaza seemed justifiable. He couldn't shake the harsh conclusion that killing was practiced by anyone whose hubris made them think their cause was more worthy than someone else's life.

Departing the plane, Eric was surprised to see Sonja and Mordecai standing there, waiting for him before he even got to the reception area. Looking at Sonja, Eric could see she was simply struggling to keep it together. Then she lost it, and like being projected through a time-warp, she leaped towards him, thrust her arms around his neck and grabbed for dear life. Between sobs, he could barely understand: "Elana's dead! Why would anyone kill her when it was my project? Why didn't they kill me instead?"

Tasting the salt from her tears, Eric saw those pregnant puddles of despair, the precipitate of her pain, as he whispered, "If I could take away your grief, it'd be gone in a heartbeat—but I know I can't."

Grabbing his neck even tighter, her tears continued flowing almost as fast as the sobs sped up. "It should've been me, not her. It's all my fault!"

Clutching her tightly, Eric kissed her cheek as he tried to wipe away her torrent of tears. He knew the depressive devastation of 'survivor's guilt', and now it owned her as she thought she should have died instead of Elana. "It's not your fault, it's not about you. When bad things happen, it's the ugly destructive forces of evil colliding with good people's lives…and the evil usually wins out. This isn't about you! It's the nasty negative forces in the universe and for us, it's this fear-mongering force, this Rigel—whoever or whatever he is."

Appearing a tad guilty, Mordecai looked at Eric and caught his attention. "She left for that lunch without her security team."

Shooting a stern, sterile look towards Mordecai, Eric knew they both understood that his men had failed Eric before, and now they did it again. "Make sure you have 24-hour security on Sonja, and this time, no excuses!"

Mordecai nodded, but then looked away without making eye contact. "My men'll be there."

A frustrated Eric fired back, "Yea… Yea… Yea. Don't give me that crap! Your men failed me before so don't let it happen again!" Holding onto Sonja and still aware of the tension in her embrace, he gazed back at her. "We gotta go. C'mon, let's get back to your apartment."

Looking up at him with those pools of pathos filling her eyes and distorting their shape, color and hope, she choked on her words. "I spent all last night suffocated by the stifling shadows and shrill sounds spouting out that Elana is dead. And it's all my fault! The walls, the floors, everything is coated with that rotten, repulsive residue of her death. I can't go back there. Take me with you— I won't go back there!"

Mordecai nodded his approval.

Holding her at arm's length, Eric suddenly stammered, "I... I can't take you to my apartment. It's only an efficiency with not even a sofa I could sleep on."

Grabbing his arms with a vise of desperate determination, her face was filled with a resolve borne of fear. "Eric, what can't you understand? I won't be alone and I don't want to be in that apartment. I'll stay with you and we'll sleep in our clothes." She clutched his arm even tighter as she sensed he wasn't getting it. "For God's sake, Eric, what's wrong with you? I'm worried about losing my mind, not my virginity!"

Finally forcing himself into this spat, Mordecai added, "What are you thinking about? You're not living in sin. For God's sake, you're living in life—give it a life! Get out of here and take Sonja with you. My driver'll take you to your apartment."

Momentarily dropping his head in shame, Eric then looked up and placed his finger and thumb on Sonja's chin to gaze into her eyes. As he did, they both instinctively initiated a kiss. Simple in its innocence and powerful in its meaning! As he pulled away, his eyes were now transfixed on the radiance of her's, although they were framed by a red sea of emotion. They both sensed some faint element of a smile, either on their faces or in their eyes which transcended the veil of tragedy that had smothered their relationship. As he led her by her arm, Sonja reached over and grabbed his. She was not about to let him go!

273

A security car deposited Eric and Sonja outside of his apartment where Mordecai was already talking to a man at the apartment building door. He now came over to their car. "Everything's OK. My men searched your apartment, the windows, the door, closets. You name it, they looked at it and it's all safe."

Sonja gave Mordecai an incredulous look. "Your men searched his apartment without getting his key?"

Mordecai smiled. "I could've waited until we all got here, but what if someone was inside? Do I want to find that out when you and Eric are here, actually going into the apartment?"

She persisted. "How'd you get in?"

Eric intervened, "Where Mordecai wants to go, there are no doors or locks left unopened."

Putting his arms around both of them, Mordecai pushed them towards the apartment. "And no two people who I'm going to talk to anymore out here on the street. Now get in there! My men will be here all night."

Entering the apartment and closing the door behind them, they were now face-to-face with the awareness of being alone for the first time since they met back at Strayton. As he took her coat, she spun around and now found the two of them staring intently into each other's eyes. Two sets of quivering lips were overwhelmed by their magnetic attraction, then gratified by the tenderness of their kiss. The intensity from releasing such repressed emotions was amplified by the innocence surrounding their actions. That shield of purity separating Sonja from Eric became an all-embracing envelope of simplicity and undiscovered sensuality as their bodies fused together in a way that forged them as one single entity. As they took off their shoes and turned off the light, their world was now spinning on an axis, the center of which was them.

Sonja realized how her great loss was blunted, if only slightly, by what she had found in Eric.

His feelings were like those that penetrated his on-board emotional defense mechanism amidst the explosion at the Golden Ram. He sensed then some power projected by Sonja had kept him from falling deeper into that chasm of despair. Now he understood the magnitude of her emotional force-field that re-aligned those misguided neurons which mired him in his Problem. Love, or whatever it was, had saturated deeply into his wounded psyche, empowered some healing and stabilized a sense of security. It now dawned on him that when he heard of the explosion and the flames surrounding Elana's death, his revulsion wasn't revisited by another psychological rebound back into his Problem.

"Good night Sonja," Eric said as he laid his head down and wrapped his arms around her. "With so much to do tomorrow, we need to get some sleep."

She reached over and gave him a simple kiss on his cheek, then turned away. "I'll have a good night, and hope you do also. See you in the morning."

Sleep came quickly to Sonja but she wasn't sure if she was dreaming or if she actually felt Eric's finger tracing the outline of something on her back.

For Eric, that heart he traced was an acknowledgement that she owned his.

The 'morning after' meant different things for many people, but for Eric and Sonja, this morning's purity was greeted by the tainted reality of what had to be faced at the Biblical Institute. Elana's death, with its percussive power on the collective psyche of the staff, was still reverberating through the empty canyons of each co-workers' seared consciousness. No one could hold a head high enough or look with a clearly focused eye. They were all partially destroyed and totally distraught by the intrusion of her death into their lives.

Arriving at the Institute, Sonja and Eric were greeted by Mordecai as they walked into the lobby. "Don't worry! No one knows about last night. But we need to tell the employees what happened with this investigation. They're understandably concerned, if not downright frightened."

Entering the conference room, Mordecai stood front-and-center and took over. He introduced himself as the detective-in-charge of the investigation of Elana's death, and his body language asserted that authority. "You need to know we don't believe Elana's death was accidental. A witness, driving behind her, told us a vehicle forced her over into the path of the oncoming truck. Eric and Sonja know they're at risk, but it's not likely the rest of you are. Still, my security men will be watching you and checking your homes with you each night."

After a quick and empowering squeeze to Eric's hand, Sonja stood up. "When will Elana's body be released?"

Looking over at Sonja, and then to the staff, Mordecai added, "Later today. I know her parents are flying in today from Athens, but I can't get her body until after 5:00 PM."

Repressing a torrent of tears, Sonja chokingly replied. "I'll get her parents at the airport and bring them here tonight so they can be alone with her. Their devastation has to be beyond any realm of comprehension."

Mordecai spoke, but Sonja noticed the crack in his demeanor and his voice. "When's the service?" He paused to regain his composure. "I'll arrange for a plane to take her and her parents back to Athens."

Sonja scanned the still-stunned faces of the staff, drifting in the dark over any plans. "We'll be having a small service tomorrow at 10:00 AM at her favorite place out in the courtyard. After that, I'm sure her parents will want to take her back to Athens as soon as possible."

A sullen Eric was the focus of Mordecai's attention. "Are you going with her to the airport?"

Shaking his head while still gazing longingly at Sonja, Eric's answer was somewhat detached, "No, I've got to take the relic fragments to Tel Aviv University."

Sensing Eric was caught in some emotional quandary, Mordecai lowered his voice. "How long will it take? Do you need my men? I'll send one to the airport with Sonja."

Hesitatingly Eric added, "No, I'm OK by myself. But I'd appreciate you getting me a .38 revolver."

Noticing how quickly Sonja's head turned towards Eric with the mention of the gun, Mordecai minimized the impact of his answer, "I'll get it." He didn't know there was a part of Eric hidden deeply away from Sonja that she still couldn't grasp, and probably didn't want to know. Trying to deflect Sonja away from staring at Eric, Mordecai tried to change her focus. "How long for the carbon dating?"

Now in her element, she understood the process. "A couple days depending on the method they use. They'll need to prepare a test sample and that could take one to two days. The actual testing might take a few hours."

Turning from Sonja, Mordecai spoke in hushed tones to Eric. "Why don't you get going? I won't have the .38 for you right away, but we'll deal with that later." Mordecai caught the glance Eric and Sonja gave each other as it was clear their separation would be difficult. "Eric, why don't you get going so we can get some results, and so Sonja can go meet her security detail."

"Wait!" Eric replied, "I need to send an e-mail to Strayton." Going over to the computer, Eric fired off a quick e-mail to President Smathers. "Have samples of relics possibly from the crucifixion. Carbon dating to start today. If relic fragment is 2,000 years old, we'll take lab to St. Catherine's to find blood from our Savior. Monsignor Bertani insists on traveling to St. Catherine's if we find it. Keep you in touch."

Leaving the Institute together, Eric was off to Tel Aviv while Sonja left for the Ben Gurion Airport. Like two lovers who think their smallest actions are invisible, the sensitive touching of their hands was something broadcast to virtually everyone. Upon parting, Eric whispered, "Meet you here at 6:30. If you're with Elana's parents, they'll want to be alone, and I'm sure you won't. I'll be there."

Time jumped quickly by and the shadows of dusk strangled the life out of the streets and alleys of Jerusalem. Eric finished his task at Tel Aviv University while Sonja was trying to fulfill her obligation to Elana's parents. She spent most of the day trying to bring some comfort and conciliation to cavernous eyes that spoke of those empty shells of humanity—lives that had been totally eviscerated by the tragedy snatching this life blood from their hearts and minds. No one can realistically console a family that lost what defined its existence.

When the negative forces of life conspire to destroy the hopes and aspirations of parents, outside of their faith in God, there is no other mental, physical or emotional resource capable of soothing such searing wounds that scorched their dreams. Sonja knew she couldn't really comfort Elana's parents, but was committed to bringing some sense of light to them in this time of absolute darkness.

As the day passed towards the evening hours, Sonja received the call from Mordecai she was awaiting. Looking over at Elana's parents, she struggled with the words, "It's time. They've released her body and soon she'll be at the Biblical Institute."

Grief saturated every fabric of these two people as they quietly rose with eyes afraid to raise and face a reality they could no longer deny. The blackness of their clothes radiated like bright sunshine compared to the darkness in their hearts and souls. Not a word was spoken, and Sonja understood that nobody could provide any sense of meaning or comfort for this immeasurable grief. She knew her role was just to be there as a gentle touch and an occasional warm word in this vacuum of emotions that defied any outsider's intrusion.

Arriving at the Institute, Sonja realized Mordecai had done all he had promised. The simple oak casket was placed outside in the courtyard with effusive arrangements of lilies caressing the coffin and somehow hoping to bring the epitome of God's love into a hollow hole of hope and repulsive repository of despair. When Sonja brought Elana's parents through the Institute to the courtyard, she saw Mordecai in the shadows. Acknowledging him with a nod, she witnessed a rare exhibition of sensitivity as Mordecai nodded back with a look of grief frozen on his face. *Strange,* she thought, *a man who'd been on the killing side of life still had some capacity to grieve!*

Approaching the courtyard, Sonja backed away from Elana's parents, allowing them to proceed in total privacy. While a genuine gesture of respect for their privacy, Sonja also knew she couldn't bear what was about to ensue. She felt horrible, but knew her feelings could never begin to touch what Elana's parents were experiencing as they were alone with their daughter. The penetratingly painful, deep howling of the two abandoned parents was more than she could bear. As she turned and walked outside, she was confronted with a blurred image of Eric coming through the distorting drops of her tears.

Sensing her emotional fragility from her body language, Eric moved quickly, grabbed both of her hands and pulled her towards him in an all-consuming hug. He felt the desperation of her arms grasping him and he responded in-kind as he heard the muffled sobs coming from her face buried in his chest. He whispered to an ear he had been gently kissing, "Are they inside?"

Sobbing spasmodically, she shifted her head to speak, "Yes, but how can killers be so unaware of the consequences? That mass of cells and organs representing a human being isn't just a thing—it's the culmination of a lifetime of love, sharing, hope and optimism. We only exist with and through those we love! How can someone so callously take that away?"

Eric wasn't going to get a pass on this one, nor did he deserve to. Those words momentarily shot him back to Gaza, but he recovered quickly enough as he looked at Sonja's eyes brimming with loss and overflowing with pain. "There's no answer to it. If we're spiritually alive, we struggle to honestly resolve the continuing conflict of the good and evil forces that dominate our lives." Looking away from Sonja to where Elana's parents were stuck trying to force-feed some meaning into their existence, he asked, "How are they holding up?"

Silently shaking her head, she could barely reply. "Badly! What do you expect in a time empty of emotions where all the love and meaning of their lives has been sucked out by some uncontrollable, destructive force?"

Gazing over at Elana's temporary resting place, Eric disdainfully closed his eyes as he shook his head. "We can't do much more here, but at least we do know Elana still exists. And she knows of us, our love, our grief and our pain. Her parents will come to understand she's still there with them in more than just a memory. She'll be a spiritual presence residing alive, deep within them, everywhere around them, and then finally guiding them during the last minutes of their lives—comforting and leading them to the next phase in the hereafter."

Uncontrollably sobbing, Sonja reached to Eric, kissed his cheek and let her head rest on his chest. The intensity of her sobs competed with the pounding of his heart; both sounds of the pain and love that hammered then bound them.

Pulling away to make eye contact Eric added, "I know how bad it is, but we need to go inside. They don't need to wonder who's with them here in this strange place."

Consumed in the pain of despair, she shook her head. "I know we need to go back, but stay here for just a second. Being surrounded by the pain and gloom of death isn't the best time to say I love you, but I know it can't wait. Maybe I sound like a simple little schoolgirl from Vermont, but seeing how quickly life changes, I need to tell you now how much I love you and probably have ever since Strayton."

With thoughts running rampantly through his mind, a captivated Eric looked at her in silence. From the time he saw her in Jerusalem, he knew he couldn't escape the emotional gravity that sucked him into her magnetic field, only drawing them closer. Still not sure how to respond, a tentative Eric could only say, "I... I'm not sure how it happened or when it even started, but President Smathers wondered all along if I had some emotional residue of you from our time at Strayton. What I thought I knew was what I remembered about you as a student. Who knows, with my frame-of- mind at that time, maybe I did have some chink in my emotional armor. Maybe I don't understand the past, but I'm pretty sure of the present and hope the future happens as I'm planning it."

Emboldened by an awareness of their mutual attachment, Sonja's inquisitiveness replaced her sadness. "What really happened before Strayton? I know Mordecai talked about it and he failed you and you then failed in your mission. Can you tell me about it? I got you involved in this situation, but I get the feeling you've been here before."

The sympathetic smile on Eric's face was suddenly replaced by a distant look of dismay as he looked away for a few precious seconds, then turned back to meet her penetrating eyes. "Some things I can't tell you, but you already know I was in the CIA and Mordecai was with the Mossad. He probably still is. We worked together on only one mission over a period of two months, and we got to know each other fairly well."

"At times, you had worked well with me and Elana, but at other times I can see the heat of some underlying combustion that sizzles between you and Mordecai."

Eyes rolling, and with a mouth twisted, Eric chose to look away again from those probing hazel beacons. "You're close. He's been great for this search, and I'm comfortable with his handling of the security. Just don't forget, he's the one influencing factor behind me coming back to Strayton."

Sonja reached over to touch his cheek, and he responded by meeting her penetrating gaze. "Was he a good influence or a bad influence?"

Shaking his head, Eric looked away again, fleeing some confrontation with the innocence of her eyes and questions. "A horrible influence! He was the reason a mission to eliminate a terrorist turned into an intelligence fiasco. Instead of killing two terrorists, I also killed the wife and two children of one of them. And Mordecai? He insisted no women and children were in that house. Instead of an intelligence coup, I smeared the image of my country, destroyed my own humanity and instantly severed my commitment to the CIA. It was time to get out, and I did—off to Strayton where President Smathers greeted me with open arms. There I took a soul lost in some cataclysmic inversion into the depths of despair and found hope, peace and a love I couldn't identify and didn't understand."

Stepping away as she sensed her questions might have been too threatening, Sonja was greeted with a return of his eyes to hers. "I remember you saying something like that on the day I saw you jogging back at Strayton. You told me you weren't there to rehab your body, but to rehab your soul. Powerful stuff for a young woman to hear from the first guy that stirred some infatuation in her; whether she recognized it or not."

Eric smiled, but abandoned her eyes again as he sought something off in the distance. "I remember that day," he said while turning back to face her, "but this day is what needs some tending to. Let's go see what we can do for Elana's parents."

She took his arm, leading him in the direction of Elana's casket. As they walked, Eric stopped her and asked. "After we're done, what'll you do tonight? Back to your apartment?"

She shook her head with a firm finality. "I'll never go back there! You stay at my place and I'll stay at yours."

"OK," he sheepishly said, "I understand. I'll tell Mordecai so his security knows what's happening."

Smiling for the first time in a long while, she reached over to give him a kiss on the cheek. "Not that I didn't enjoy your company last night, but it wasn't the best night's sleep."

The next day's morning sun brought a new set of hopes and expectations. The magnificent radiance of the Jerusalem sun completely carpeted the courtyard of the Biblical Institute. But the warmth of the sun was impotent to dispel the emotional chill collecting over this small group of Elana's parents, friends and co-workers. While the service was simple, yet touching with numerous remembrances about her, Sonja had the distinct sense that Elana's parents longed to quickly close this chapter of their lives. They just wanted to take her home to Athens.

After the service, Mordecai and his security detail took the casket and her parents to the airport while Eric and Sonja followed in their security car. But before they left, Mordecai took Eric and Sonja aside. "Let's meet here at the Institute when we return. We need to talk about where we go from here."

After an Israeli plane with no visible markings departed from a special military airport with what remained of the Dutros family, Eric and Sonja drove back to Jerusalem. The dynamics between them were what might be expected. A man not showing emotion spent his time staring out the window, and with the muscles of his firmly clenched jaw rippling with tension. A still devastated Sonja lapsed into bouts of subdued sobbing. Eric's mood focused firmly on the murderers, while Sonja's mind was fixated on loss—ugly, hateful loss.

Arriving back at the Institute, Mordecai wanted to meet in the conference area, away from Elana's desk and the impact it might have on them. Languishing around the conference table, Mordecai assumed the role as team leader. "We need to find out where we go from here. Eric, what's going on with that carbon dating?"

Turning away from his perpetual peering out the window, a noticeably distracted Eric replied. "I expect to hear by tonight or early tomorrow if we're lucky. They were already calibrating for some other carbon sample, so our test shouldn't take long."

With that toothpick perched passively on his lower lip, Mordecai now turned his attention to Sonja. "What if they say the relics are 2,000 years old? How reliable is that?"

Looking up but not saying anything to Mordecai, she turned to let her gaze fall onto Eric. "They'll give us a range of years, something like 1,965 to 2,020 years old, but not a specific year. They can get close, but can't give an exact age."

"Is that a problem?" asked Mordecai.

"Not really," she responded while still looking at nothing but Eric. "That's the standard for carbon dating."

"But then what do we do?" he continued. "Eric said any further testing of the samples must be done at St. Catherine's. Can that be done?"

She was already one step ahead of him. "I'd already made plans to lease lab equipment from Tel Aviv University for that Ossuary of James scam. They had a lab packed and ready to go when I had the money to lease it. With Eric controlling the Strayton purse strings, that's not an issue anymore."

Now Mordecai was looking at Eric, who added, "Money isn't the issue. This is exactly what President Smathers wants us to do."

Tilting his chair back from the table, Mordecai looked at Sonja. "Check back with that lab, and tell them we'll need to move quickly whenever we contact them. Once we hear about the carbon dating, getting to Mt. Sinai won't be difficult since the roads are good, but we'll need to pass through Egyptian customs."

Eric slyly smirked, "And I assume you can take care of that like you're taking care of everything else."

A rare smile slid smoothly over his lips as Mordecai eyed Eric. "You know once you leave intelligence, you still keep some contacts. Customs won't be a problem. The only problem I'm concerned with is who's watching us? How did they get to people before we did? Are they out there somewhere watching what we're doing? I even put a 24-hour security detail at the lab at Tel Aviv University since it could've been a point of vulnerability for us. But from here on, if the relics are old enough, we need to wonder where they'll be coming at us next?"

Sonja spoke with a rare optimism flowing. "Who knows? After this Rigel found out we know about him, maybe he and his men disappeared."

Putting his hands in his trouser pockets while dismissively shaking his head, Mordecai brought a different perspective. "Maybe, but probably not, because what we're after is also very important to them. I had my security people cross-check hotel occupants in Tel Aviv, looking for an Irishman registered alone or with someone else. Nothing! But we've got to assume they'll be around. Look, it's been an emotionally trying day, so let's wrap it up. Just confirm with the lab you'll need the equipment again. Let them know it'll be short notice we give them, and if they have any questions, call me. Now, let's get going! Your security will take you home."

The first smile of the day found its way to her face as she spoke to Mordecai while being stuck in the warmth of Eric's gaze. "We're switching apartments. Eric's staying at mine, and I'm at his."

Understanding his present insignificance, Mordecai smirked, "Good! I'll tell my men. And double-good, you'll be well-rested tomorrow. I'll go tell them and give you thirty minutes together. Make the most of it!"

Before Mordecai had even left the room, Eric's hand reflexively reached over to Sonja's. In a moment's notice, they were in each other's embrace. Kisses of passion, coupled with a clinging desperation, created a union of unique synergy. The intensity of their passion empowered the depth of their commitment to this emerging love. But an invading intuition still reminded them there was more out there to fear—more elements of doom and despair, personified in this Rigel. But they still used their thirty minutes wisely. Silent gazes were punctuated by the high voltage intensity of the emotion passing between their eyes. Kisses met by mutually-inclusive lips of lusciousness defied any scientific description of what they should have felt like. Love blossomed, only to be constrained by the call of the security driver. This day was done and tomorrow would come quickly.

At 8:00 AM, Mordecai arrived at the Institute and wasn't surprised to be there first, even though his security detail was told to get Eric and Sonja to the office early. As he sat at the computer, he saw an e-mail came from the Tel Aviv University. While reading the incoming message, he failed to notice Eric and Sonja entering behind him.

Interrupting with a loud clearing of her throat, Sonja asked, "Find anything?"

Mordecai's eye never left the screen. "Eric's got something from the Tel Aviv University. I was just ready to open it."

Eric teased, "Go ahead. It might not be your desk or computer, but you're welcome to snoop into my private e-mail."

Disregarding both of them, Mordecai opened the e-mail and read. "Professor Stanfels: Your wood samples were able to be carbon dated. Our results show they are between 1,970 and 2,030 years old. What is next?"

"Great!" said Eric moving over to nudge Mordecai aside. "Let me in there. I'll tell them I'll pick-up the samples when we get the lab equipment."

"Awesome!" exclaimed Sonja, whose momentarily radiant face now had a sudden curtain of gloom descend over it and into the tone of her voice. "But it's not. Elana can't be here with us."

Moving over to her, Eric took her in his arms. In their embrace, Mordecai could see Eric was whispering something in her ear, waited a few seconds, then interrupted, "Are you two OK? Can we go on?"

Sonja turned away first from the embrace. "We're OK, so go on."

Mordecai only smiled at the young lovers. "I understand you two need to work this through together, but all of us need to move on from here."

Looking at Mordecai without flinching, and from some place she couldn't control, Sonja asked critically. "And you? What does her death do to you? Nothing at all?"

"No," answered Mordecai. "I know that deep pain inside you is something I can't perceive because I didn't have the relationship you had with Elana. Even though you think I can't feel badly, there's a pain I bear in her loss. But my pain is different than yours. You have youth, with purer emotions and simpler optimism. I mean optimism not tarnished by the harshness of life, although, I suspect Eric, due to me, is also tainted in these areas. And for me, it is different. I've been in this life too long, seen and killed too many people, and lost the ability to love honestly and grieve completely. I may have screwed Eric on that Gaza mission, but he should be thankful for what I did, or didn't do. He got out while I didn't. Love escaped me and knows to never let it's shadow grace the portals of my emotions." Mordecai paused and reflected on what he had just said, and then looked back at this youthful pair. "OK, enough. Sonja, why don't you take a break from this and call the University about that lab equipment?"

As she sat at her desk to call the Tel Aviv University, Eric went to the computer.

Mordecai's frustrations got the better of him as he looked over at Eric. "Who are you e-mailing now?"

"President Smathers and Monsignor Bertani. I'll share the good news about the carbon dating, then ask the Monsignor to call the Archbishop. Once we have an idea of a departure date, I'll let them know." Eric turned to Sonja. "Once we get set up at St. Catherine's, how long will it take to find any blood residue? And if you find any, how long to analyze it for DNA?"

She looked up from her desk just as she was to telephone the University. "Using spectroscopy, a day for the presence of blood or any other organic residue. If we find any, it'll take two more days to check for the DNA."

Hands eagerly knocking at the keyboard, an enthused Eric couldn't contain himself, "Good, that'll work. I'll tell the Monsignor so he can make his plans to come over to Tel Aviv and then have the Vatican counsel in Jerusalem drive the Vatican Range Rover to St. Catherine's." Eric turned to Mordecai. "I assume you can take care of his directions and customs considerations."

Mordecai rolled his eyes while shaking his head. "I don't have to take care of everything. He'll have no problems with customs with or without me. In that Range Rover with its Vatican diplomatic flag, even the Egyptians will let him through with no trouble. But, I'll still make a call, and send the Vatican counsel a set of directions on how to get there."

Sonja hung up the phone. "It's all done. The university still had everything in the crates and we can pick them up today if we like."

Mordecai nodded as he turned towards Eric. "Good, let's go, but don't you want to let President Smathers, the Monsignor and the Archbishop know we'll be on the road tomorrow? Tell the Monsignor if we hit pay dirt, to plan on arriving in Tel Aviv in about three days."

Eric laughed and reached over to squeeze Sonja's hand. "I will, and I'm sure these e-mails will bring great joy to a special few people."

They would be the cause of very great joy to more than a few!

Chapter 28

Hastily exiting the elevator on the 5th floor, Dr. Geoffrey Salvatore briskly walked along the luxuriously expansive hallway of the King David Hotel. This pathway through opulence allowed him to reflect on how he should have stepped out of scientific obscurity and into a realm of adoration and greatness among his peers—those molecular geneticists. But that was not to be! He was denied his scientific legitimacy because he had been too good, too aggressive and not pliant enough to satisfy the Honors Committee of the Royal Academy of Biologic Scholars; and yes, too Catholic!

When Dolly, the first cloned sheep, was introduced to the world, there was Dr. Salvatore, the Catholic Scotsman of a very distant Italian heritage, relegated to a position of insignificance with no awards, acknowledgements, kudos, laurels or any type of praise for the man whose ideas on rejuvenating partially-deteriorated DNA had placed him light years ahead of his fellow scientists. And he also knew how threatened were his former genetics colleagues by his visionary intelligence, keen insights and dogged persistence. Geoffrey was the face of innovation in molecular genetics and they would try to do whatever they could to deny him his just place in history. Smarter and better wasn't enough reason to hate him, but they needed to do it anyway because he was a Catholic working in a Protestant-dominated Scotland. And a socialist Catholic at that! It was easy to see how he and Rigel became soul mates from the time they first met at Trinity. Rigel being screwed by the Church even though he was a Catholic, and Geoffrey being screwed by the Protestants because he was a Catholic!

Following Rigel's directions, Geoffrey went directly to room #507. Knocking on the door; three knocks, then two and then three again, he waited, then saw someone looking through the security peephole. The door burst open and there he was, in all his magnificence: his great friend and chief collaborator —Rigel!

Opening the door and struck by that flaming red hair and beard of his friend Geoffrey, Rigel blurted an old greeting. "My dago red! How wonderful ya could come ta see us. Come in." Extending his right hand to shake Geoffrey's, Rigel followed with a big bear hug that bound them together once again. "It does me good ya could visit us here in our little part a Israel. I hope everything went OK for ya."

With the ear-to-ear smile wider than the opulent hallway behind him, Geoffrey knew the sincere greeting and the emotion behind it. Thoughts instantly tracked through his mind of how good a friend Rigel had been ever since those university years when a non-judgmental sense of brotherhood united them. And the name 'dago red' provided fertilizer for a mind full of memories of his youth. One of his Scottish playmates had a father who regularly went to the United States and drank the homemade wine that old Italian grandfathers called 'dago red'. But the son, as young schoolmates can do, used the name to innocently, yet cruelly, tease his red-haired friend Geoffrey with the Italian name Salvatore.

When the words 'dago red' rolled off Rigel's tongue, it reminded Geoffrey that he would never be accepted by the Scots, but of how with Rigel, it was always a sign of endearment. Geoffrey answered in his rich Scottish baritone. "No problem at all laddie. My only worry was security might ask me who I was going to visit, and I didn't remember your Russian's name."

"Then come in and let me introduce ya ta him and the others," Rigel said as he led Geoffrey into the conference area where Liam, Conor and Viktor were standing. After introducing the good Dr. Geoffrey Salvatore to each man, they vigorously shook his hand and gave their own greetings.

A smiling Liam finally got to meet this secretive Salvador Dali, with his head full of red hair not like the artist's black, slick, sinister strands. "It's good ta finally meet this mysterious friend a Rigel's. He told us all about ya and your role in building his Church a the Internet."

289

"Church of the Internet he said?" responded Dali with his Scottish speaking style more formal than that of the Irishmen. "What else has my good friend Rigel told you about me?"

Sitting back down in his wingback chair, Conor added. "He said you're the man for us, the one person we need ta do our genetic engineering so we can scam the Christians who join Rigel's church. Says ya got a mist inhaler that'll deliver wee bits a Jesus' DNA ta the internet nerds a the world."

"Nerds of the internet you say?" asked Geoffrey with a devilish look that would have made the real Salvador Dali proud.

"Yea," Liam said as he sat down. "That's our market. All the computer nerds who don't go ta church but worship their computers more than their God. We'll merge their techno-love ta the love a Jesus with a little a your genetic manipulation. Rigel says we'll make more money than those phony Protestant preachers. Didn't he tell ya about this?"

Watching from the sidelines, Rigel now stepped into the discussion. "No, not really lads! Didn't tell him everything. Just the big picture. And there are some things Geoffrey and I planned that I haven't shared with ya either."

Having wandered over to the bar, a surprised Viktor turned around to face Dali. "Like what?"

Geoffrey reached into his pocket and pulled out a business card. Handing it to Liam, he gave him a few seconds to digest it. "Liam, what do you see on the card, under my name?"

Liam read the card, and turning with utter confusion on his face, made eye-to-eye contact with Geoffrey. "Under your name is 'Dolly' and you're spelling it D-o-l-l-y. Why didn't ya use your code name Dali, D-a-l-i?"

Smiling at Liam with his bright green eyes a perfect contrast for his red locks, Geoffrey added, "Dolly, D-o-l-l-y, is my code name, the name I want all the world to know me by. That's where I built my lovely reputation and had it stolen from me when they screwed me out of the Dolly Project credits. All because I was a Catholic, and just maybe too smart for them! Now with Rigel, I'll get the resurrection of my career and the acclimation that's owed me. That resurrection might just be a new religious resurrection with a reputation that was dead now coming alive!"

A deeply puzzled Viktor left the bar to stand next to Dali. "But what means this to us? What's this Dolly thing?"

Looking at Viktor, then hesitating since he hoped he remembered his name, he addressed him. "Viktor, now I know Rigel didn't tell any of you what I'm here for. I'm the one who created the critical elements for the cloning of Dolly, the sheep. And got screwed out of the credit because I had some clones that weren't perfect! I'm not D-a-l-i. That was a ruse by Rigel to keep my identity hidden so nobody got loose lips and sunk this project."

Slapping him on the back in a sign of newfound camaraderie, Liam reached over to shake his hand again. "I'll call ya Geoffrey instead a Dali or Dolly. But since you're saying Rigel didn't tell us everything, what's next?"

Rigel sensed it was time to let the cat out of the bag. Now was the time to tell all they needed to know as he moved into the midst of his men. "You're right Liam, I didn't tell ya everything, and it won't be the Church a the Internet. Once we find these spikes with Jesus' blood on them, then my church will be the Church a the Living Jesus!"

With the smile never leaving his face, Geoffrey nodded towards Conor. "We'll need to create that inhaler system, but we're going to do one better, we're going to clone Jesus. Naturally, you don't just clone Jesus, but you need to use His DNA to create the human Jesus. Then you can clone from this one human all the Jesuses that you need. And your church, it'll be the Church of the Living Jesus, with Jesus himself as our spokesman. Or maybe a whole bunch of Jesuses—more than you could think of."

Seeing the shocked look on their faces, Rigel let a huge smile dominate his. "Yes, lads, we're going ta clone Jesus, and what a wonderful Church a the Living Jesus it'll be."

Shaking his head in disbelief, Liam could only smile as he looked at Geoffrey. "Then why da we need the inhaler?"

The Scotsman chuckled, "You'll not be able to instantly create and clone Jesus as an adult; he'll only be a baby. And it'll take twenty years or more to mature. How do you think we'll keep the attention of our flock if we make them wait so long for Jesus? Some will die off waiting for their newly-cloned messiah. Die before they had a chance to see him! The inhaler system will deliver altered genes to be part of the gene pool of who breathes it. We'll use the inhaler to give the flock a little taste of Jesus' genetically-manipulated DNA. Why not let them have a wee bit of their Savior while they wait for him to grow up?"

Rigel added. "We'll tell our unsuspecting flock that having a bit a Jesus' DNA in your genes will guarantee a first-class trip ta heaven, just in case they depart this earth before our mature Jesus or Jesuses arrive on the scene. Which loving parent wouldn't try it? Who wouldn't give their kids a free pass ta Heaven whenever they depart this earth?"

Like an obedient schoolboy, Conor raised his hand to get Dolly's attention. "Da ya believe it'll work? Can ya really clone Jesus if we even find His DNA?"

Rigel started to answer, but Geoffrey waved him off. "Conor, don't worry about what I can do once you deliver me His blood. Creating a person or animal and cloning is much farther along than people know. And, damn it, they would have known more if those Scots hadn't destroyed my work. But, the Japanese, not even knowing what I'd done, are projecting to create a wooly mammoth within twenty years."

Still having a hard time believing what he was hearing, Conor asked, "But didn't ya say ya had problems with your cloning a the sheep. Some weren't perfect?"

An indignant Geoffrey fired right back. "Yes, I said that, and it's true. Not every clone did come out looking like a perfect sheep. Some had deformed heads or bodies and we destroyed them in the early phases of their lives, still in the womb. That's what the hypocritical Scots didn't like about my work, but still they used most of it and then let someone else take all the credit."

"Why no credit?" a constantly confused Viktor asked.

Geoffrey understood the dilemma. "It was because my work showed you could partially deteriorate and then reconstitute DNA. My co-workers on that project predicted this could never be done, but I made them look bad by succeeding. When they said I would fail, I didn't and they hated me. But partially deteriorated DNA is what I would expect to find on the blood of those spikes. With my unique techniques, I can reconstitute it and make a living Jesus from it. Then several clones! Or hundreds, if we need them! We'll have many Jesuses for our Church. For God's sake man, we could even franchise Jesus and create thousands of Him! We could have a Rent-a-Jesus.com. There's no end to it!"

Relaxing, as he could feel Orion's tension diminishing, Rigel pursued the issues. "Geoffrey's correct. We'll need a lot a Jesus clones. If some come out of an experiment with too many heads or whatever, we'll need ta have some waiting in reserve. We wouldn't want ta need ta start all over again, would we? Some could die at any phase a the development."

Geoffrey added more, "There's another consideration. From the Dolly experiment, we know the clones age quickly, and we can't simply re-tread Jesus if he ages quickly. We'll always need a few spares hanging around if we want our Church to be a vital force."

Surveying the faces of his men, Rigel could only laugh to himself as he read their surprise. "Maybe now ya understand why I wanted ta stay with this project and not live off our earnings from those other ventures. I needed some a that money for Geoffrey ta build his lab in Scotland. We still have tons a money, but it'll be seed money for our Church. Ahhhhh…what a noble experiment!"

Turning to Geoffrey, Rigel continued the discussion, "Are ya OK with this woman, this Sonja, setting up the lab at St. Catherine's? Does that work for ya?"

Dolly scratched his chin, looked at Rigel, then to the other men, before replying. "Yes. If she has access to it, and obviously she must, that equipment to analyze the blood and its DNA isn't too complex. From the e-mail you sent me, it makes sense to wait till she tells that Vatican priest they've found the blood. From there on, your plan is fine. Just get me the blood if it's on those spikes!"

With his focus now on Geoffrey, Liam asked him. "And the stuff she'll be analyzing, da we want ta get her samples or her data?"

Moving over to an arm chair, Geoffrey plopped himself into it. "That would be nice to get and see what she's discovered. But I expect there's more blood on the spikes, since she wouldn't want to use all of it for her analysis."

Now turning away from Geoffrey, Rigel directed his words to Liam. "All a us will be going ta St. Catherine's except ya and Dolly. Ya two stay here in Jerusalem, and when we come back from St. Catherine's, we'll need ta get some sleep and then fly out a here the next day. We'll call ya when we leave the monastery and then ya can make our airplane reservations. OK with that?"

"Yea," replied Liam with disappointment dawning over his sad face.

An empathetic Rigel tried to salve his pain, "Good. I'm sure ya would like ta come with us, but I need ya here. And you've had no problem hacking into the Monsignor's Jerusalem counsel, have ya?"

Liam's facial and body language perked up as he was being called on to verify his special computer skills. "None at all! I've got the directions that were sent ta him by the professor. Don't worry, when messages for the Monsignor are now sent ta the counsel, I'll have them before the Monsignor gets them."

Turning back to Geoffrey, Rigel gave him a 'thumbs-up' signal. "My Dolly, all systems say GO! Once that woman says there's blood on the spikes, the good Monsignor Bertani leaves the Vatican and flies ta Tel Aviv. From there, we'll follow him ta St. Catherine's and he'll be our doorway ta riches."

Still unsure of the plan, a dubious Viktor asked, "How will Monsignor help us at St. Catherine's?"

Going over to Viktor, Rigel put his arm around his shoulders. "Viktor, my boy, don't worry about a thing. Once they leave Israel and go into Egypt, we'll just trade vehicles with him."

Confusion still shrouded Viktor's face. "Why would he trade?"

Taking his arm off Viktor's shoulder, Rigel stepped away while still facing him. "He'll have no choice! You'll see what happens at the trade. And we'll look much better riding into that monastery in a Vatican Range Rover with its diplomatic flag flying in the wind. Once we're inside, ya never know what we'll run into, so bring some a that plastique explosive."

Chapter 29

Meticulously packed in ten medium-sized boxes, the lab fit easily in a van not designed for comfort, but that wasn't Sonja's primary concern. She was fearful the suspension of the van might create too rough a ride for the glassware she hoped was safely packed. And on top of that, she had to deal with the testosterone-fueled driver competition.

Barely able to tolerate Eric's and Mordecai's jockeying over who would be the driver, Sonja finally imposed her will as she pointed to Mordecai. He consistently fit the role of 'team leader', but Sonja thought there was something else brewing in this team chemistry. He seemed to be overdoing something with Eric, like trying to not only impress her, as older men had a tendency to do, but also to impress him. *He failed Eric once*, she thought to herself, *so is he now overcompensating?* The chemistry between Eric and Mordecai had been better since they apparently resolved whatever deep-seated hostility previously divided them. But despite the good-natured bantering between them, Sonja couldn't stamp-out the premonition of trouble if they couldn't permanently conclude their conflict—the threat of Rigel was ever present. She leaned forward to interject her presence into those alpha males in the front seat. "Are you sure of the route, or do we need a map?"

Without taking his hands off the steering wheel, Mordecai looked back. "Not to worry. I haven't been to Mt. Sinai before, but I know how to get there. Probably don't even need a map, but I did bring one. The main highway from Jerusalem takes us to Hebron, then on to Be'er Sheva. From there we go south and then west through the Negev desert to the Nitzana border crossing into Egypt. And from Nitzana there's only one road to Mt. Sinai. Once we get close I'm sure there'll be signs, since the mountain is still a major tourist attraction for

Christians and Jews. Finding the monastery on the mountain won't be the thing to worry about."

Fiddling with the air conditioning, Eric turned and gave Mordecai a look of surprise. "What're you worried about?"

Mordecai's eyes stayed on the road, but his mind was elsewhere. "The other people. This Rigel, then some guy with three stars on his hand and who knows what else. There might be even more than one guy with stars on his hand."

With words overflowing with tension, Sonja butted in. "You think they're still out there somewhere?"

Keeping his eyes on the road and both hands on the wheel, Mordecai spoke without looking at her. "They haven't gone away. They're out there or in the desert, or back in Jerusalem, but they're out there somewhere. Don't even begin to think they've gone away." Now he turned to her, with both hands still clutching the wheel. "Reach under Eric's seat, there's a box. Pass it up to him."

"What's in it?" she asked while passing it to Eric.

Mordecai took his eyes off the road for an instant as he looked over to Eric. "Open it. There's something you asked for."

Tearing open the box, Eric found a .38 revolver with ammunition. Half-smiling, he looked up at Mordecai. "I thought you forgot."

After a quick glance, Mordecai added a few sharp words, "If you were concerned enough to ask for it, I wasn't going to let you down again. Who knows what we'll run into? Keep it with you at all times, even at St. Catherine's."

The pitch of Sonja's voice rose with an arousing sense of alarm. "You think Rigel would even come to St. Catherine's?"

In the rearview mirror Mordecai could see Sonja's questioning look and a hint of fear in her eyes. "Can't take anything for granted! This Rigel and whoever else is with him, if they know about the relics, expect them to try to get them. Whether it's here or somewhere else, we need to be alert and prepared."

The ride through the rest of Israel to the Nitzana border crossing assumed a strange silence where nobody wanted to expose their thoughts or doubts.

Not able to keep Elana out of her mind, Sonja's reflections on the proximity of the prize and what they lost to get there left her trapped in an unresolved web of worries. *Would it be worth it? Could it justify the price we had to pay?*

Realizing he viewed this quest as a policeman, Mordecai understood if they found blood, it would be interesting, and maybe even a little threatening to his Jewish faith. But his thought process was still dominated by the police work mutated into his genes. What's out there? When will they try to do something? How much of a threat was Sonja to them, especially to this Rigel who knew she was the only person alive who had a good look at him. Mordecai couldn't shed his anxieties over Sonja's risks. *How safe is she? Am I using her for bait?*

An equally anxious Eric questioned what he'd gotten Sonja into, and whether her enthusiasm for finding the relics may have clouded his judgment. There was a huge element of risk out there as long as Rigel existed, and now he understood how his fears of loss were being driven by his other emotions fertilized by his emergent attachment to Sonja. He was in love for the first time in his life, and with that unsettling emotion came a new one—fear, fear of loss. And the haunting seeds of his past failure with Mordecai were still sown deeply within his psyche. *I'll be damned if anything will happen to her*, he thought. *With or without Mordecai, this time I'll get the job done.*

Time passed quickly as the meandering miles along the road to Nitzana disappeared as the surrounding desert embraced the asphalt sliver of civilization dissecting it. The Nitzana border crossing finally loomed ahead. Mordecai drove up to it and stopped as the Egyptian border guard emerged from his booth and swaggered towards the driver's window.

The guard looked at Mordecai with a sneer before asking, "What can I do for you who leave this land stolen from the Palestinians?"

Playing it very casual, Mordecai acted not the least bit offended at the remark and certainly not intimidated. "We're leaving Israel to search for the fifteen tribes of Moses."

The sneer disappeared, replaced by a sudden smile and enthusiastic word. "You are confused! There were more than fifteen."

An indifferent Mordecai looked away before re-establishing eye contact. "Sorry. I'm old, sometimes I get my numbers confused."

With his hand pushing open the gate, the guard smiled again as he waved Mordecai through. "Good luck on your visit to St. Catherine's."

As the van pulled away, Sonja leaned forward, loaded with rapid-fire questions. "What's this about fifteen tribes of Moses? And how did he know we're going to St. Catherine's? You didn't say anything about it. He didn't even check to see what's in the van? We could've been drug smugglers."

Mordecai gave a smile with those ever-arching eyebrows climbing upwards to evade the pupils of his eyes chasing them. "Who knows, maybe everyone coming through here goes to St. Catherine's. What are you asking me for? You should've asked him."

Shaking his head in dismay at such a humorous farce, Eric looked longingly back at Sonja. "There's no limit to the strings he pulls." Turning to Mordecai, he added on an upbeat note, "Keep it up. This time you're doing a great job!"

The ride through the Egyptian desert to Mt. Sinai was uneventful, as one would expect when driving through a land of deserted nothingness. The long stretches of road slowly rose to a crest then gradually flattened out only to have the desert floor distorted by the heat rising from the sand. But the duration of this phase of the trip allowed for some deep introspection on the part of these three voyagers who were approaching an objective seeded with opportunity and doubt.

Even though finding the relics was valuable in its own right, Mordecai suspected they might be the bait to lure this Rigel and friends into a trap. Hidden deep within his subconscious, but sometimes creeping into his repressed conscious state, was the doubt that maybe he was trying so hard to compensate for his past failure with Eric that he was putting him and Sonja at risk. Was he going to fail Eric again just to achieve his own selfish goal?

Finding the relics and DNA would culminate a mission Sonja created with Elana, but the excitement of the impending success was still clouded by the constantly hovering gloom of her loss. Now on top of the world, Sonja found herself unable to dispel the guilt not only about the relics, but also about her newfound love with Eric. Had she betrayed her sense of loyalty to Elana by being so in love at such a time of soul-penetrating despair?

Eric's joy at bringing Sonja and Elana's vision to fruition, fueled his optimism, but his past failure in this part of the world was a constant reminder that an apparently successful mission could quickly deteriorate into a calamitous failure. With tendrils of tension tugging at him, he clearly understood Rigel's threat was ominous and probably out there lurking, ready to strike from somewhere in the desert or back at Jerusalem.

Mt. Sinai was obvious and imposing from a distance of many miles, and as the road cut a straight path through the desert, it was clearly evident to anyone going to Mt. Sinai or further west to the Red Sea. To get to the actual base of Mt. Sinai, a smaller two-lane road turned southward, and when Mordecai made the turn they found themselves facing directly at the mountain; another mountain of religiously historic significance even greater than Mt. Ararat. After driving for what seemed to be thirty minutes, they reached the base of Mt. Sinai where Mordecai could see a small parking area with a security booth from which a small road wound up the east side of the mountain. He assumed the road led up to what appeared to be a small plateau carved into the mountain, but to get there, they had to approach the security gate where a frowning guard emerged from a booth.

When Mordecai lowered his window, the guard immediately asserted his control with a firm, confrontational style. "What is your business here?"

Not to be intimidated, Mordecai boldly replied, "We're here to see Archbishop Bournias. He's expecting us."

"What are your names?" inquired the guard without a change in facial expression or a trace of emotion in his speech.

Knowing the unwritten rules of security forces, Mordecai stared forcefully into his eyes, "I'm Mordecai Rubin and with me is Professor Eric Stanfels and Miss Sonja Martin."

Stepping back, the guard pointed while he spoke. "Good! You are expected. Follow this road up to the monastery. When you get there, a guard will meet you."

A narrow, twisting asphalt road led up the mountain, though barely wide enough for two vehicles. At the top, the road ended at a plateau where the monastery was seated in all of its statuesque majesty.

"Magnificent!" a breathless Sonja said while looking out the window. "But how do we get in?"

Craning his neck to get a better view, Eric couldn't help adding, "That's what friends and foes alike have asked for centuries. Look over to the right," he pointed for Mordecai. "There's the security guard."

Mordecai drove over to the guard and while the three got out of the van, Sonja asked, "Why are there so many guards?"

Reaching over to take her hand, Eric replied, "They've got a treasure in art, old biblical manuscripts, gold and jewelry. You name it, they've got it. This place may look desolate, but it's the greatest collection of ancient biblical history outside the Vatican."

Nodding his approval to Eric, Mordecai allowed a smile to penetrate through his austere, tight-lipped countenance. "Since you know that Mr. Biblical Genius, go over to the security guard and see how we get in."

A very deliberate and confident Eric approached the guard with his wallet and passport in hand. They talked briefly and then Eric, with the guard trailing, walked back to the van where the guard spoke in his highly disciplined fashion. "The archbishop is awaiting your arrival. You are to leave your equipment here and follow me. We will transport your equipment separately."

"How will you get our laboratory equipment into the monastery?" asked Eric. "The back of this van is loaded with very fragile glassware."

In a terse style, without an expression change on his face, the impatient guard responded, "It is only important to know that you will be getting into the monastery. We take full responsibility for transporting your equipment into St. Catherine's. Please follow me and give me the keys to the van."

The guard led them over to an opening in the base of the perimeter wall, opened a control box, and after pressing a button, a door opened to expose a hidden stairway. "Follow me," he said as he went up the stairs into a lit, but damp, stone passage.

As the steps got steeper, Mordecai looked down at Sonja and Eric, and with a shortness of breath wheezed-out a joke, "Do you think they had this same electronic control box for all the centuries they kept people out of here?"

The voice reverberating through the narrow passageway belonged to Eric. "Who knows what they had, but whatever it was, must've been a combination of unique camouflage and superior deception."

In a moment of levity, Sonja laughed at what he just said. "Aren't they the same?"

With hurt feelings, and unable to hide the emotion in his voice, Eric replied, "What? Camouflage and deception? Oh, I don't know, I think they could be different. What about you, Mordecai?"

Mordecai looked back again at the both of them. "I don't think, and you two sound like you're squabbling. Drop it! Just pay attention to getting up this passageway."

Without a word, Sonja looked away from Mordecai and gave a big smile to Eric before placing her finger over her lips.

From the top of the stairs the guests were led to a large hallway into which opened numerous massive wooden doors. To the eye, the enormous impact of architectural power was in competition with the saturating sensation of the musty, stagnant smell emanating from this dark, old corridor. The 2 ft-by-4 ft chiseled limestones lining the great hallway had so exact a fit they sandwiched no mortar between them. As the guard led them along this long and imposing corridor of such structural magnificence, the size and apparent sturdiness of its huge wooden doors created the impression that doors of such magnitude must restrict entry into rooms of equally great importance.

At the end of the hallway, the visitors spilled out into a large, high-ceilinged room where they could see Archbishop Bournias awaiting them. With arms spread wide, the welcoming Archbishop approached his new visitors. "Professor Stanfels, it pleases me you were able to safely make the trip here to our venerable St. Catherine's. Might I impose upon you to introduce your companions?"

After a ceremonial hug, Eric pulled back as he pointed to Sonja. "Thank you Archbishop Bournias, we are so pleased to be here at St. Catherine's. This is my associate from the New Testament Biblical Institute, Miss Sonja Martin, our resident genetics expert. And this worthy gentleman to her right is my Israeli friend Mordecai Rubin, a colleague of mine from past explorations."

Extending his hand first to Sonja and then to Mordecai, the Archbishop then clasped his hands together and gave a ceremonial bow to all three of his guests. "It pleases me to welcome you to St. Catherine's. But now, come and allow my aide to take you to your rooms. You must be tired after your long drive and need to be refreshed. After you have a chance to bathe, we can meet for dinner in approximately 90 minutes. Brother Demetrius will lead you to your rooms."

Following Brother Demetrius, Eric, Sonja and Mordecai could see why St. Catherine's was so impregnable. The floors, walls, ceilings and doors—everything here was immense and powerful in proportion and substance. Upon arriving at their rooms, the wide-open doors invited them into an ancient world of monastic lifestyle. The rooms were sparse with stone floors, a small rug on the floor and a simple, narrow wooden bed. Despite the absence of bathrooms, a bath could be taken in each room in what appeared to be a portable galvanized tub, already filled to the brim with steaming water. Spartan accommodations, yet thoroughly appreciated by the three travelers who were eager to leave the dust of the desert behind. They would freshen-up quickly in order not to keep the Archbishop waiting.

While waiting for the arrival of his guests in the dining hall, the Archbishop took advantage of the time to reflect on what was about to transpire. His exposure to genetics was limited and he had concerns about what could actually be found. But he knew in this world of diminishing Christian values, if he could discover something profound, it would be a tremendous boost for the faithful and even the not-so-faithful. He was struck by the contrast of how he was now looking to science, historically the great destroyer of faith, to be the generator of even greater faith. The old church and even some of today's leaders would never comprehend the diverse mission upon which he had so entrepreneurially embarked.

Brother Demetrius led Sonja, Eric and Mordecai into the dining hall as the Archbishop rose to greet them. "You all look wonderful!" he said while spreading his hands pointing to both sides of the long table where he was seated at the head. "Come and sit, as I am sure you may have some questions for me."

Taking their seats, Sonja initiated the conversation. "Where will my lab equipment be sent?"

A courteous nod of his head in Sonja's direction preceded the Archbishop's reply as his deep voice bounced off the stone walls of this cavernous space. "As we speak, my men are putting it in a special room where we have enough electrical outlets for your needs. We generate our own electricity and most of our rooms," he pointed to the walls, "are serviced only with candles."

304

While keeping her focus on the Archbishop, Sonja continued. "How do you get the internet out here in the desert?"

"We don't have the internet here. I use it for references, but to do so, I must telephone my requests to friends in Jerusalem or Cairo and they send me what I want. But we do have telephone and fax here."

Realizing the dilemma, and as if his mind had strayed elsewhere, Eric perked-up, "But if we find blood, I'll need to contact Monsignor Bertani."

Turning his attention to Eric, the Archbishop raised a bushy eyebrow as he spoke. "It may be desirable to call your office at the Biblical Institute in Jerusalem and have them e-mail what you need. This avenue may be best since I suspect you would also want to e-mail your President Smathers. And since he is such a good friend of the Monsignor's, he might want to hear of your discoveries even before the Monsignor." Now turning to Sonja, he continued. "Tell me Miss Martin, what do you expect to discover if you find any DNA from the relics? What did you expect to find in that Ossuary of James?"

"My genetic work based on the Ossuary of James was to find some DNA from bone or residue and compare it with a known DNA marker that could be traced back to Aaron. And since this DNA marker, really a sequence of DNA building blocks, could be linked through Elizabeth and her cousin, the Virgin Mary, I had a very good chance to show it was what I might call a holy DNA sequence, and that James was a blood relative of Mary, not born of another woman."

Cringing at what Sonja just said, Eric could feel himself slouching in his seat, wondering what Bournias must be thinking about these Protestants.

"Quite a leap in scientific thought," said the Archbishop while scratching his chin. "And certainly a problem for us of the Orthodox faith! Believe me, if this is what I heard first from Monsignor Bertani, I would not have had any interest in your work. But fortunately for you, and even for me, that ossuary was a fraud, or we would not be here today."

A meek smile covered over her anxiety as Sonja continued, "It was fortunate for us, because otherwise we would never have discovered the existence of these spikes. And since it was a fraud, I bought that ossuary for a lot less money.

When I saw that animal carving on the underside of the lid, it got my attention, but if it hadn't been for Abraham Weissberg," she started choking up as she thought of him, "this search wouldn't have happened."

With a wave of his hand, the Archbishop pointed to Eric. "Yes, Eric told me all about the carving and how you also saw it at Khor Virap. A carving, I might also proudly mention, we have here in the box which holds our relics. One never knows whether your box, at one time, might even have been here at St. Catherine's. Over the years, so much has been lost from here that we even think the Gnostic Gospels of Thomas, which were discovered in 1945 at Nag Hammadi, could have been here at St. Catherine's. One can only guess what your ossuary held at some ancient time, but ours probably never held spikes."

A shocked Sonja twisted her head in a panic after processing the meaning of his words. "You mean you don't have any spikes here? I know we carbon dated wood fragments, but we all thought you had spikes here somewhere."

Vigorously shaking his head in disapproval, Bournias' reply "No, no, no!" bounced off the walls like bats following their on-board radars as they traversed through the stone columns. "We have no spikes here. I know that is what you were looking for, but we have none. Who knows who might have them? At the Duomo in Milan, they think they have one intact. Two others supposedly were melted by the Roman Emperor Constantine's mother, Empress Helena, to make him a crown and a fitting for his horse's saddle."

Almost falling off his chair, Eric could sense Sonja's and Mordecai's eyes now beaming streams of shock at him, and knew he better resolve this crisis of confusion. "But what were the wood fragments all about?"

Through that bushy beard seeped a sly smile as he first looked at Eric and then Sonja. The Archbishop then held-up both hands, palms facing them, before answering, "I know you have been fixated on the metal spikes, thinking only metal could last 2,000 years. But that is not so! The wood fragments you carbon dated are from the relics that were stored in our limestone box. The one with a wolf carved on it!"

Stunned, Eric slowly stammered, "You mean you only have some wood fragments?"

With eyes sparkling brightly before he erupted into a volcanic laugh, the Archbishop was simply uncontainable. "My dear Professor Stansfels! I would not have brought you here for a foolish reason. I know the wood I have is from the real Cross of the Crucifixion. But in the treasuries of the large cathedrals from the Middle Ages are found many crosses they thought were the original Cross. There were so many phony crosses from those times that there is enough wood to build another cathedral. And Empress Helena? She was after more than building a monastery. Such a prolific buyer, she bought any relic of Jesus' crucifixion she could find, including those spikes she melted down. She even purchased the marble steps from Pontius Pilate's palace, the ones Jesus would have walked on. Those steps, the Scala Santa, still exist today in Rome at San Giovanni in Laterano where the pious climb them on their knees. That Helena was such a buyer," he chuckled again, "that as you Americans say, you could have sold her the Brooklyn Bridge! But let us get back to what brought you here. Have you told Miss Martin and your Mr. Mordecai the story of the Lupus group?"

Simmering with doubt and more than a little frustrated, Eric nodded. "Yes. I told them all about Lupus and how they would've kept the spikes from the crucifixion and stored them safely enough that you and your predecessors could secure them.

Now Bournias' face, what you could see of it, turned stern with his dark eyes piercing the aura of confusion surrounding Eric. "A good story based on your assumption we had spikes, but I never spoke of spikes, only relics. For you see my young friend Eric Stanfels, the wood you carbon dated is of infinitely more value to you and me than the spikes—spikes which we don't have! The wood is what Lupus rescued from the crucifixion site at Golgotha. But not just any wood. These men, responsible for destroying the crucifixion site, kept the wood, at least a part of it, from Jesus' Cross. And because of our Lupus relationship, we know what we have is the real thing!"

Interrupting what was evolving into a two-way dialogue, an emboldened Sonja spoke, "If this wood is from the cross of Jesus, what does that have to do with His blood? Without some residue of His blood, we have nothing. At least with the spikes, they would have had contact with Jesus' hands and feet. The wood? What chance is there the precious drops of Jesus' blood just happened to fall on some little sliver of wood that also just happened to be stored at St. Catherine's?"

With Bournias' dark eyes once again bursting with beams of radiant energy, one could only assume a smile was seeking to escape from under his dense forest of a bushy beard. His words came faster and more emphatically. "So correct Miss Martin, but this wood is special— very special because the Lupus men understood how important was our Jesus and His holy blood. When they had the Cross, they removed the small end sections of the wood which held the spikes. In our limestone box are those three sections of wood which soaked up the precious blood of Jesus!"

Eric seemed to sense the validity of Bournias' argument but still asked, "You don't think the pitted spikes would be valuable?"

Bournias shook his head dismissively. "No, probably not, but the wood of the Cross had spike holes in it, tunnels that couldn't be cleaned no matter how hard you tried. And with its fibrous structure, that wood was saturated with the blood that could never be removed."

Changing the tone and direction of his interest, the Archbishop turned to Sonja. "Tell me Miss Martin, since you will be working only with wood, how do you see your work evolving? Do you not think there is a better chance of finding just a trace of His blood from the wood than from some oxidized metal spike?"

Leaning forward with her elbows on the table, Sonja clasped her hands together. "I'm a little shocked, but frankly, optimistically so. I agree there's probably a better chance to find blood in this wood than on the spikes. The three of us should be able to set-up the laboratory tomorrow, and I'll have the spectrometer operational after only a few hours. Then I can determine if there's any blood on the spikes... er..., wood. If there is, I'll need the rest of the day and part of the next day to complete my testing."

The Archbishop's satisfying smile spewed forth its approval, but lost in his forest of fur, it couldn't be seen. "I agree there is no reason to set-up the whole laboratory if you can't find any blood residue. But please, enough of this. You are tired, so let us enjoy our dinner and then you can go to your rooms to sleep. Tomorrow will be a big day for all of us."

Before he could close the discussion, Sonja blurted out, "Excuse me Archbishop, but may I ask one more question?"

Looking curiously in her direction, he was receptive to whatever she might ask. "Certainly Miss Martin! What would you like to know?"

Sonja sat back in her chair, away from the table. "Since we are on Mt. Sinai, why is this monastery called St. Catherine's?"

With a hand tugging on the tufts of his beard, the Archbishop tilted his head towards Sonja. "Yes, I can understand why you ask that question. To be on the mountain where Moses received the Ten Commandments, would it not be more appropriate to call this monastery something other than what we do?"

Her enthusiasm empowered her as he legitimized her question. "Yes, that's what's been on my mind, and I just had to ask it before you left."

Folding his hands as he brought them up to his face, a pensive Archbishop paused as he reflected on her persistence. "St. Catherine of Alexandria was murdered because so great was her love for God, she would rather die than forsake the purity of her virginity. Her body was taken by the angels and carried on their wings here to Mt. Sinai where her bones were ultimately found on the top of the mountain. She was a miracle sent from God, and a saint like that deserves to have a monastery named in her honor. Would you not agree?"

As a look of approval washed over her face, Sonja dripped with exuberance from being bathed in the wonder of St. Catherine's story. "Yes, I do. A wonderful name for a wonderful monastery."

Bringing an air of finality to the table, the Archbishop terminated the session. "Now let us finish our dinner and retire for the day. You have had a long trip and there is much to do tomorrow."

Chapter 30

Excitement ruled the day—one that finally came, despite the long, arduous process to find His blood. A day permeated with anxiety, yet glowingly tinted with a healthy dose of optimism. It was easy for this group to reflect back on when they first lost their enthusiasm for James' ossuary, only to be rejuvenated by renewed rumors of relics of the crucifixion. The disjointed path to discovery was made more complex with the lack of definitive information from the antique dealers. These diligent seekers had done their duty and now sat around anxiously waiting to hear if blood, maybe His blood, was to be found on the relics. Yes, Orion was ready, and tired of waiting.

Rigel came bursting into their new suite at the Crowne Plaza and confronted the inquisitive faces of his band of hunters. "What are ya doing sittin' around? What are ya thinking of? Anxious are ya?" "Ya've been sitting here way too long wondering what's going on. Let's go for a walk, but only as individuals, not as a group. Who knows, when ya return, maybe we'll find if our girl down at Mt. Sinai has a little Irish luck for us today."

Moving towards the door, Viktor stopped and turned to Rigel. "I'm not happy about cloning Jesus with many heads or whatever Salvador Dali will do."

Conor couldn't resist adding his two cents. "I agree! Ya know I'm not a Jesus freak, but I'm not interested in creating a bunch a freaky Jesuses. Dali, how often did ya create those freaky sheep?"

Geoffrey looked at Rigel before answering. "Not very often! We were able to monitor them in the belly of their mothers. We can do the same here. Trust me! No multi-headed Jesus babies will be born."

Sensing the discord, now Liam turned towards Rigel. "I'm guessing ya'll pay women ta carry these babies, but don't ya think they'll resist if you're going ta kill their babies?"

Knowing this was an issue that needed quickly defused, Rigel was emphatic. "Liam, the Catholic in ya is coming out! Don't worry lads, we'll get Asian women ta carry the babies. When ya look how those poor, unfortunate creatures get sold into sexual slavery by their own parents, they'll do anything we want and we'll give them a better life than what they had. If one child is aborted, we'll get them another. They'll all see how everybody has babies, and only healthy ones at that. I can assure ya there won't be any Jesus freaks, only healthy ones. Ta franchise them, we'll need good looking ones, perfect ones. Ya know, if each congregation wants ta buy its own Jesus, we've got ta provide something a great pride. Don't let it bother ya, there'll be no freaks! We'll destroy them just like nature uses miscarriages ta destroy its own freaks. Now, get along with ya while I stay here with Liam ta see if he can hack into anything we can use."

While Orion was enduring its impatience, that same experience was being imposed upon Eric and Mordecai as they sat around in the expansive living area deep within the bowels of the monastery. They helped Sonja set-up her lab and now were consigned to wait while she tried to detect some blood. They were eager but edgy with no place to walk and nothing to watch or hear. Just like the monks, they were isolated in thought, word and deed. They wondered what was taking so long, or whether she was stuck in her lab, unable to pull open that huge wooden door. But now they heard footsteps in the hall, reverberating between those sacred stone surfaces, and with them came Sonja.

The look of elation on her face still couldn't cover the residue of pain persisting in her heart; the pain of knowing how much Elana would have enjoyed this moment. "There's blood on the wood! Let's ratchet this thing up to the next level. I'll extract the blood and get the process going."

Goofy grins, from ear-to-ear, covered Eric's and Mordecai's faces before Mordecai gained his composure and spoke, "I'll call the Biblical Institute on my satellite phone and tell them to e-mail the good news to President Smathers and to Monsignor Bertani."

Not able to take his eyes off of Sonja's radiant beauty and exuberant enthusiasm, Eric couldn't deny some sense of mutual ownership of her emotions. "My guess is the Monsignor can't wait to get here and see what you've actually done. It'll be a great message for some very important people who've closely followed our work."

And without fail, great excitement erupted in the U.S., Rome and at the Crowne Plaza in Jerusalem.

Chapter 31

The flight from Rome was quick, especially on the wings of good hope and high expectations. Now on the ground, elation dominated the good Monsignor as he rode in his chauffeur-driven Range Rover with its Vatican diplomatic flag waving vigorously on the right front fender. The road from the Ben Gurion Airport to Mt. Sinai might be long, but the Monsignor was on cloud nine thinking of nothing other than what could be a miraculous discovery for his Church. Despite a history of theological and cultural conflict between the Roman Catholic and the Orthodox Church, the Monsignor was pleased that he and Archbishop Bournias had collaborated in a most ecumenically-driven and genuinely generous gesture to support this Protestant-led search.

A smile rippled across the weather-bitten creases of the Monsignor's face as he thought of how much his good friend President Smathers would enjoy being here. The Big-Three, Smathers, Bournias and Bertani, were pursuing a scientific venture of which some superiors may not approve. He understood maybe Smathers didn't need to report to anyone at all, but he and Bournias lived and worked in the shadows of superiors. What would they think? *Science? Genetics? What good could come from this?* Now he understood why, for some uncertain reason, he believed in the intentions and vision of this young woman and Smathers' Professor Stanfels. The third man, the Jew, he wasn't so sure what he brought, but he trusted the other two enough to overlook the inclusion of this Mordecai character.

Liam and Salvador Dali, the Sheep as Liam was calling him, had been following the raven black Vatican Range Rover from the time it picked up the Monsignor at the Ben Gurion Airport. Their responsibility was to discretely follow him all the way to Be 'er Sheva. Finally arriving at their check-point, Liam called Rigel, notifying him they reached their destination and would return to the King David and wait.

Listening to that predetermined message from Liam, an eagerly awaiting Rigel was ready to pounce as he heard the message, 'The blackbird arrived at Be 'er Sheva. Good hunting!' He closed his phone and prepared to implement his 'Iced Blackbird' plan even though he was still in Israel, 20 minutes ahead of Bertani, as he approached the Nitzana border crossing station. Arriving at the checkpoint, he made one last attempt at levity with Conor and Viktor as he viewed them in their priestly garb. "Well lads, da ya think we look enough like priests ta bless these un-anointed guards?"

Looking proudly at his very proper appearance, Viktor commented, "I look Russian Orthodox, and you two look like Catholics."

Father Rigel laughed. "Your Holiness Viktor, what's the difference? Ya look the same as Father Conor and me. Let's see what the guard thinks."

The border guard motioned for Rigel to lower his window, while giving his toughest, territorially-protectionist look as he surveyed these clergy. "Where do you go? Show me your passports. Why do you leave this country and come to Egypt? Why leave such a wonderful country that steals our land and kills your Jesus?"

Never taking his eyes off those of the guard, Rigel showed no hint of nervousness. "We're on a pilgrimage ta Mt. Sinai ta do the good work of our parish back in Ireland. And I agree with ya, its lovely ta be coming away from Israel ta your wonderful Egypt."

After returning the passports, the guard opened the gates and waved them through. "Enjoy your stay in Egypt, and stay long."

Driving along the hot, black asphalt road, Rigel then stopped at an elevation where he could observe the border through his binoculars. "We'll stay here til the Monsignor comes through."

Twenty minutes passed quickly as Rigel saw the Range Rover bringing the 'blackbird' through the Nitzana checkpoint with virtually no hesitation from the guard. Like a predatory falcon, Rigel honed in on his unsuspecting target traversing the blacktopped road toward an ultimate conflict with a harsh reality. Positioning his car with part of it blocking the road, Rigel hopped out and raised the hood.

Seated in the front passenger's seat, Monsignor Bertani first saw the disabled vehicle with its priest standing on the side waving for them to stop. With the priest virtually blocking the road, the Monsignor's driver had no option but to stop. As the Range Rover came to a halt, a second priest came out from under the hood of the disabled car. The Monsignor and his driver got out but Rigel seized the initiative. "I'm sorry your Excellency, sorry ta stop ya but our car broke down."

"I am Monsignor Bertani. My driver is very handy. Let him see if he can be of assistance."

As Bertani's driver approached the stalled car, out jumped Viktor from his hiding place in the front of the car. With one swift karate blow to the driver's neck, Viktor dispatched him to a meeting with his Lord. Rigel instinctively turned to the Monsignor and attempted to wrestle him to the ground, but he resisted with a surprising strength for a clergyman. Bertani was almost getting the best of Rigel when another swift chop from Viktor rendered the Monsignor immobile and dying. A grateful, but embarrassed Rigel looked at Viktor. "Thanks moy chornee Ruski brat. Let's throw these in the car trunk and find a place along the way ta dump them. You drive the car and Conor will ride with me in the Range Rover."

The two-vehicle caravan snaked its way through the Egyptian desert until Rigel finally stopped at some mounds of sand and rocks. After Viktor hid the bodies there, the only possible hint of their existence might be the vultures swooping in for a sumptuous feast.

Rigel waved Viktor over to the Range Rover. "Once we get ta St. Catherine's, we'll park that car somewhere near the mountain. We'll need it ta get back ta Jerusalem because we won't want ta be seen driving this Vatican vehicle."

Arriving finally at the base of Mt. Sinai, they parked the car out of sight and then Rigel drove them in the Range Rover to the security post. As the guard approached, Rigel confidently confronted him first. "We're expected by Archbishop Bournias. I'm Monsignor Bertani from the Vatican."

Recognizing the Vatican Range Rover he had been told to expect, the guard opened the gates. "Please proceed up the road. The Archbishop is expecting you. When you see a security guard at the base of the monastery, park there."

The Range Rover proceeded past the guard and up the hill, clinging precariously to the winding, narrow two-lane road with no guardrail while Rigel's thoughts skipped back to Ireland. "Reminds me a the road from the Ring a Kerry down ta Bantry. No safety railing there either. Only a single strand a barbed wire ta keep ya from falling off the road into the sheep pastures. Those damned sheep! Once I had ta stop my car because they were all over the road and one was sucking on the tit of another—wouldn't move no matter what I did."

Arriving at the base of St. Catherine's, the second security guard approached their vehicle. "What is your business?"

Knowing never to show any hesitation or doubt, Rigel caught the attention of the guard and spoke in a very proper English style, with none of that Irishness. "We told the guard below that Archbishop Bournias is expecting us. As you can see from my diplomatic flag, I'm Monsignor Bertani from the Vatican. And we were told you would guide us to our meeting with his grace, Archbishop Bournias."

"I will lead you. Leave your vehicle here and the three of you will follow me."

317

Already planning his exit strategy, Rigel had the presence of mind to ask, "Will our Range Rover be here at this spot when we want to leave, or do you park it somewhere else?"

The perplexed guard paused, then responded while pointing. "We can park it for you, or if you like, you can park your vehicle right over there".

Realizing their exit from St. Catherine's may not be as orderly as he might prefer, Rigel planned for quick access to his vehicle. "We'll park it over there, and if you don't mind, we'll keep our special Vatican keys. We never let them out of sight."

The guard nodded his approval and Conor proceeded to park the Range Rover.

"And Father Conor," Rigel said to him, "why don't you be the keeper of the keys?"

After Conor parked the Range Rover, the guard led the three men into and then up the hidden stairway. The dank, moist smell of the old massive stones and the poorly-lit corridor reminded Rigel of a time long ago when he was led by the priests into the old hidden recesses of the churches of his youth. He had been young and naïve and believed their lying stories of how they could show him some very special secrets only they knew about. Special secrets they would show and share with him—do with him, if he promised to never tell anyone. They told him it was OK to do those repulsive things because they were their very special gifts from God that they were supposed to share. Even though the passageway was filled with hot stagnant air, Rigel could still feel the chill go down his spine at the thought of his destitute desperation before the constellation Orion rescued him.

Reaching the top of the stairway and turning into a well-lit corridor, Rigel was struck with the size and complexity of the inner bowels of St. Catherine's. He asked the guard, "Sir, it's so big and with so many huge doors, will you be taking us to meet the Archbishop?"

"Yes," replied the guard. "I will take you to his study where you can meet with your friends."

"Ahhh…yes, our friends," Rigel continued. "And I know Sonja has her laboratory already functioning. Can you show us where it is?"

"Yes," said the guard as they turned the corner which then exposed a row of heavy wooden doors going around a circular corridor that went to the right and to the left of where they stood. In the center of this circular corridor was a massive stone wall. "The woman's laboratory is the last room we passed," he said as he pointed back to its door. "Now to the Archbishop's study which is the first door here on our left. If you must use the restroom facilities, they are further ahead to the left."

A never-wavering focus is what Rigel cast on the guard. "No, we're fine. I can't wait to see the Archbishop."

As the guard knocked on the study door, Viktor quietly removed three revolvers from his backpack, kept one and handed the others to Rigel and Conor. When the Archbishop opened the door, Viktor shot the guard and Rigel pushed the door wide open as he alone burst into the study and closed the door behind him.

But Viktor's shot resonated down the hallway and even into Sonja's laboratory. Unknown to those in the study, Sonja opened her door to see what caused such a commotion. Viktor and Conor turned as the door opened and rushed it. Frozen in her gaze, but with an evolutionary instinct for preservation whose origins she could never comprehend, Sonja made the mighty push to close the cumbersome door and latch it just before the two strangers hit it with all of their weight. She then heard two more gunshots and though they hit her door latch, it didn't give.

Having just left the bathroom, Mordecai heard the first shot as he came around the corridor. Gun-in-hand, he bolted around that circular stone wall only to see the guard on the floor and two strangers with guns in their hands. But the one wasn't a stranger at all—he was the foreigner from the Golden Ram. While 'Moy chornee Ruski brat' exploded out from somewhere in Mordecai's memory bank, they saw him first and fired. He returned two volleys while disappearing backward in the corridor as the two strangers jumped down the hallway towards Sonja's laboratory.

Mordecai couldn't hear Viktor as he told Conor, "Take Semtex and mold it against her door. Blow that bastard down!"

The push into the Archbishop Bournias' study knocked Rigel off-balance, and falling to the floor, he pulled the Archbishop with him. But in the fall he lost his gun-in-hand advantage, and Eric had time to take his .38 revolver from under his jacket. Now both men had their guns drawn, but Rigel still had the Archbishop. With their eye contact beaming messages of surprise, fear and hatred, these two adversaries were fixated in a face-to-face confrontation. While each could hear the shots ringing outside the door, neither took their eyes off the other.

Rigel wasn't sure what was happening outside the room but he trusted the abilities of his men.

Knowing Mordecai had gone to the bathroom, Eric hoped he confronted those other men he saw at the door when it was pushed open.

Intensely focused on each other, Eric and Rigel were keenly aware of the smallest movement of the other man's eyes. But Rigel still had the edge—he had the Archbishop as his shield!

Never batting an eye, Eric still couldn't ignore Rigel's revolver pointing at him. "And who are you? Rigel?"

"Ya might call me that."

Eric gave a rapid retort. "What about the Monsignor? Where is he? Or have you killed him like you killed the antique dealers?"

A sinister smile slowly spread over Rigel's face. "What does it matter where he is? He can't help ya now. He couldn't even help himself, but at least he's helping ta feed the vultures."

Struggling, the Archbishop tried to turn around but Rigel warned, "We'll have none a that old man. Struggle again and I'll kill ya! And why would ya even worry about your friend the Monsignor? He's happily on his way ta Heaven, or just maybe on that ecclesiastical erotic express ta Hell where so many a the God-damned priests belong."

Looking up at Eric as they faced-off with their guns pointed at each other, Rigel slowly put his gun in the Archbishops ear. "Is this what ya want? Ya try ta shoot me but I kill the Archbishop and then you?"

An unwavering reply escaped Eric's tightly pursed lips. "Somebody might be killed, but it'll be your people not mine."

Rigel gave Eric a dismissive look for only a second, then pointed his gun in the direction of Sonja's lab. "And what about your woman? Killed or worse?"

Staying focused on Rigel, Eric repressed the shiver of fear that hit him as thoughts of Sonja jolted him. "Why harm her? We know you want what we have, but why?"

Rigel mocked Eric by pointing his gun back-and-forth between him and the Archbishop. "Who gets shot first? You or him? Nah, tell me something else dear professor. We're both after the spikes a the crucifixion, but why da ya want them? We know your Sonja found blood, but is it that a Jesus?"

Not to be intimidated, Eric rigidly responded, "We think it'll be His, and His DNA will be different, uniquely holy."

A laughing Rigel tossed back his head, "Uniquely holy ya don't say? How arrogant can ya be? Why da ya think it would be different, let alone holy?"

Eric shot back, "We think the DNA will be partially human and partially divine since God was the Father!"

Rigel laughed again, but with a steady head and an even steadier hand on his gun. "A fool ya are about the divine nature a Jesus, the Christ. And da ya think He'll save ya now? Save ya from Hell or purgatory or any a those places the faithful need a travel agency like the Church ta get ta or from?"

Eric's unwavering focus stayed fixated on Rigel's eyes. "Why do you want the blood? Is your religion stale, needing a transfusion?"

Bursting with pent-up bitterness, Rigel spewed out his intense hatred for the Church. "Transfusion, my ass! The only transfusion I ever got was the priests' sperm, all in the name a your loving God. No, my religion isn't stale, it's post-menopausal—there's no more a my blood ta be had!"

Archbishop Bournias crossed himself as his shaking head dropped onto his chest. "My God! My God!"

Looking at the Archbishop, Rigel then turned his attention back on Eric. "And you? Are we that much different? Ya loved your God since being a little lad and he brought ya peace, love, optimism and might I even speculate, a dose a tranquility. Ya don't even seem ta be shaking with that gun in your hand."

Knowing he had to quickly defuse this desperately deteriorating drama, Eric took a chance. "Rigel, there's peace when you're with God. Give God a chance!"

"With God? My, aren't ya the team player! I was with God and loved Him but He was no better than the Romans. No, He didn't throw me ta the lions, He threw me ta my priests. With the lions, my pain would have been short. With the priests, it wasn't just their abuse, but as just a wee lad I lost my faith and innocence. Abandoned by a God I loved as much as I did my mum!"

Twisting again, the Archbishop made eye contact with Rigel. "Your God has never stopped loving you!"

Erupting from deep within some reservoir of pain, Rigel's shouts unleashed decades of repressed hostility. "Shut up you old fool! It wasn't my God never stopped loving me, but the damned priests never stopped loving me! I couldn't get the priests ta stop fucking me and telling me this was their special gift from my God. Our special sickly, seminarianly-sweet secret only between them, God and me! An unholy Trinity it was, with me, a sacred vessel for their holy sperm. And my poor brother Michael," Rigel choked-up as he slowly spoke, "may there be a real God ta rest his soul. Killed himself jumping off the church because he couldn't stand being the priests' whore any longer! Did your God bring peace ta his tortured 15 year-old soul?"

He turned to Eric with nothing but hatred coating the raw edges of his words. "And you Professor, tell me why our God took care a your family and not mine?

322

Da ya think our faith, the faith a my dear mum and the other poor people was less worthy in God's eyes than yours?"

Trying to stifle the seeds of compassion that were starting to sprout, Eric couldn't deny the devastation of Rigel's family, and now it's creeping impact on him. "I… I can't explain why bad things happened to your family. But pray to God, He'll make it right for you!"

With a stupefying shock dominating his face, Rigel incredulously inquired with a tongue inflamed with some molten psychic pain, "Make it right for me? Are ya fucking nuts? How can He make right what He allowed ta be so wrong? Only I can make it right—and I did! Just ask those deviants in County Kerry who died with their damned dicks stuffed in their mouths."

Eric needed to look unfazed, but with this outpouring of pain, chronicling a youth of abuse, he couldn't deny Rigel's reality, nor that of his despair. "We knew you, or someone with you, killed them. But not why."

Torrents of tormented tears bathed his eyes, then flowed down his face only to be halted by a quivering upper lip somehow connected to a ferociously fluttering heart. Rigel's voice quivered, "My only regret was I couldn't kill them again and then again another time. They were the worst, especially ta my Michael. They were the only ones buggering the beautiful boys, and nothing was as rotten as them." He started to sob with a mouth starting to spurt the terrible turmoil he always repressed. "I wish I could've killed them a hundred times, and that still wouldn't be enough suffering and pain for what they did. Did ta my poor Michael!"

Understanding how the depth of Rigel's pain had destroyed his humanity, Eric's resolve was now under attack. But he knew he couldn't weaken because Sonja's life was hanging in the balance. "The Church failed you, but what does that have to do with Jesus' blood?"

Baring his teeth with the viciousness of an ugly sneer, Rigel contemptuously spat at Eric. "With the DNA a Jesus, I can create the ultimate scam on Christianity—my Church a the Living Jesus. We'll re-create Jesus then clone Him. Maybe hundreds a Jesuses, and then franchise Jesus ta all my churches!

And best a all, the DNA research from your New Testament Biblical Institute will legitimize my work!"

Tugging at Rigel's arms to free himself enough to look back at him, Bournias pleaded, "My son, hating the Church is no reason to destroy something that has done so much good for so many."

Overwhelmed by his burgeoning hostility, Rigel mocked the Archbishop. "Your holiness, I hate it for all the helpless children screwed by the good shepherds—left unprotected by a God who let those wolves ravish them at night, during the day, on the altar or in the confessionals. I just want ta repay the hypocrisy a the Church; a payment long overdue and still earning interest!"

With his eyes averting the intensity of Rigel's, the Archbishop turned away in shame.

Eric looked at Rigel with the sadness in his eyes a reflection of the pain filling his heart. "Will that bring you peace?"

Rigel's tear-filled eyes pierced right through Eric, and then his nostrils flared as his aggressiveness overruled any sense of appeasement. "Peace ya ask me about? Da the sexually-abused ever find peace? Nah, none for Rigel, the brightest a boys named after the brightest star in the Orion. But my hatred a the Church burns even hotter than the star—a searing pain that can't be drenched with the fucking holy water a forgiveness! Let those priests drown in their own cesspool of god-damned holy water!"

Too much for the Archbishop's heart, the stress shattered his system. His face turned white and his eyes rolled up into their sockets as he wretched, heaved and collapsed to the floor. Letting the Archbishop fall to the floor, Rigel could feel the life go out of him, but now realized he was naked in his confrontation with Eric. He lost his protective shield and, even worse, he unwittingly lowered his gun.

Eric's CIA training didn't fail him. His gun never moved off Rigel even though the death of the Archbishop stunned him. Without a flinch or the bat-of-an-eye, Eric stayed focused and commanded, "Don't raise your gun! Check him! See if he has a pulse."

Applying his index finger on the side of the Archbishop's neck, Rigel then looked up. "None, but what does it matter?" he said mockingly. "He's probably found more peace than I ever could."

Eric couldn't take his eyes off of Rigel's. His sense of pity was now in conflict with his sense of duty, but duty ruled as he spoke in a tone indifferent to the pity. "Don't raise your gun or I'll put a bullet in your head!"

"A bullet ya say? Might be better than what I got from the god-damned priests. A bullet in the head is better than a dick in your mouth! Why did our God bless ya so much while I got a bad screwing in the deal?"

Like a searing stream of supercharged electrons escaping from his damaged emotional core, Rigel's palpable pain penetrated every level of Eric's perception. But Eric's resolve didn't waiver as he ordered, "Drop your gun now!"

With a face twisted by his grimacing agony, Rigel's tears continued cascading downward. "Professor, it looks like ya win and I lose... again!"

Unable to deny the pathos in Rigel's tear-filled eyes, nor the empathy trying to gain a foothold in his own heart, Eric's CIA experience kept his voice from breaking and his heart from overriding his brain, "What did I win?"

Shaking his head in bereaved bewilderment, Rigel blasted out, "Professor, ya haven't really figured it out, have ya? This isn't about Jesus' DNA, it's about D&A, Divinity & Abuse! That's the D&A that binds us, yet divides us. Ya got the Divinity and I got nothing but the Abuse! Ya stand there the winner, and I, abandoned by the loving God a my mum, the loser." After a sad, calculated confrontation with Eric's sympathetic eyes fixated on his own, drowning in their tears, Rigel glanced at his revolver, then bent his head down to meet it. In this last instance of phallic abuse upon little Donovan O'Rafferty, he thrust the revolver into his mouth and pulled the trigger. A hollow-point bullet finally brought the peace to Rigel that his loving God never did.

The sound of the gunshot in the study was followed by the opening of the door and there stood Viktor, revolver in-hand and aiming it at Eric. In his Russian-accented English he ordered, "Drop your gun or I kill you like I kill woman with this," as he displayed his detonator. "Don't know why Rigel bring us here. Had enough money and power. Didn't need Church of Living Jesus! But you killed my leader, and I kill you!"

Standing in the doorway, Viktor didn't see Mordecai inching his way along the inside of the circular wall. Without a clear kill shot, Mordecai needed to get Viktor's attention without exposing himself to the other gunman. He called out the only thing that came to mind, "Moy chornee Ruski brat!"

Acting instinctively to a familiar sound, Viktor turned outside of the door frame to see if Conor had called him. Seeing Mordecai with his pistol aimed at him, Viktor realized for a second he wasn't the only professional killer in the corridor, and for only a fraction of that second he was aware of being the second-best.

In a flash, Mordecai fired three rapid shots, all of which hit their target. With the sound still roundly reverberating in the stone, circular corridor, no one could hear Mordecai's last words to Viktor. "Moy mertviy chornee Ruski brat! My dead, black Russian brother!" But to Mordecai's dismay, as Viktor fell heavily, he seemed to be tossing the detonator away from the doorway. Mordecai's Mossad training triumphed and he instinctively knew to keep going since there was another man somewhere in the hallway and he now knew where Mordecai was.

Down the hallway, across from Sonja's laboratory where he had planted the plastique explosive, Conor came around the corner to see a startled Mordecai coming at him. At his feet was the detonator which he grabbed and then ducked behind the corner. He then jumped back into the hallway and fired first. Mordecai fired back. Being a professional killer, Mordecai's highly trained hands didn't shake under fire and he was the only one to hit his target. Conor fell to the floor, clutching something in his hand. As Mordecai fired another shot into his head, it struck just a millisecond after Conor's corpse had instinctively pressed the detonator. The explosion ripped through the hallway coming out onto the circular corridor. The percussion knocked down Mordecai and threw Eric, who had just exited the study, against the door frame. They weren't knocked unconscious and both instantly sensed their worst fears came to life. Flames were still shooting out the door from Sonja's lab, but Eric didn't have time for old flashbacks. Now his time had come to salvage their future.

Despite the stunning effects of the explosion, Eric and Mordecai moved swiftly to the shattered door into Sonja's suffocating space. Smoke filled the corridor and her lab was enveloped in a ferocious fire. Hurtling himself through the remnants of the massive door into that intense inferno, Eric was directionally driven by Sonja's screams and found her back in a corner, away from the flames. Covered in blood, with the worst flow coming from her arms and legs, she was lapsing in and out of consciousness. Using his belt as a tourniquet to stop the worst site of bleeding, Eric finally freed her from under a tumbled table. The force of the explosion had broken her body, but Eric could still carry her out of the room after Mordecai cleared away a broader path through the doorway.

Outside the room, in corridors clogged with smoke, but with stilettos of light cutting through this smog, Mordecai led Eric and Sonja to the steps leading to the outside courtyard where curious monks surprisingly stared in fear and panic. For these men, so isolated from anything, it would have been hard for them to act—except one did. He grabbed a first aid kit and brought it to Eric, hoping he knew how to stop the bleeding.

In and out of consciousness, everything for a physically-fractured Sonja was now a blur, obscured in some fog of fear and haze of hopelessness. Engulfed in this desperate dusk of despair, as darkness seemed to lead her to some terminal transition, a brilliant light shined through, just like she read about in those near-death experiences. Finally, an emotionally-depleted Sonja knew this was her time to ride that silvery shaft to salvation.

But Eric, empowered by some energy form surpassing any realm of reason, somehow brightly beamed a healing power like plasma photons that pierced through the darkness, past the doubts and pulverized the despair. His faith and actions had snatched her away from a dismal death, directly to a world of hope and healing. Yet, despite this resounding rescue from the hands of a fickle fate, he sensed Mordecai on a satellite phone, and now confusion clouded his mind.

Shouting at Eric in a firm, yet confident voice, Mordecai took charge. "Keep her under control, she'll be OK! We'll have a chopper here in a few minutes!"

Eric's look at Mordecai defied any level of credibility as fear fueled his breakdown. "Chopper, my ass! Don't bullshit me now! How in the hell are you getting a chopper out here in the middle of nowhere?"

At that moment, Sonja returned back to the realm of the conscious. "What's happened? I can't see and can't feel anything!"

Finding morphine in the first aid kit, Eric injected it into her thigh. "You'll be OK! Lie back! This'll take away the pain. Don't worry. Mordecai said a helicopter will be here soon."

Accurate to the second was Mordecai! Much to the amazement of the monks who had never seen one before, a helicopter hovered overhead. One of the monks, astounded by the presence of this spiritual semblance of a Sikorsky, spoke in a hallowed, reverent tone while watching the chopper descend. "My God! My God in Heaven! The wings of angels! On the wings of angels! It's a miracle! Like St. Catherine's body being brought here to Mt. Sinai on the wings of angels!" He turned to bend closer to Sonja. "You will be saved my child on the wings of angels sent by our God! You will be saved by a miracle—by St. Catherine!"

With blood dripping down her left arm and pooling under a shattered elbow, Sonja looked to Eric as thoughts of what she first told Elana coursed through her shock-challenged brain. Between her sobs, she was barely able to say, "I told Elana you were a man a woman would just die for, but I didn't think I'd have to."

Eric bent down to her blood-splattered forehead, and kissed it while caressing it in his hands. "You won't have to! The morphine'll kick in soon and you'll make it—don't worry, we'll make it."

Tears cascaded down her blood-caked cheeks, leaving paths of pain on those patches of parched blood. "But I don't know what's even left of me, I'm so badly torn to pieces."

He tried wiping her face but her tears kept coming as he whispered in her ear, "Don't worry, you'll be fine. I love you! You'll be fine!"

Looking away, and then with what little strength she had, Sonja turned back and through her streams of tears, gazed into his eyes. With words barely energized enough to escape her lips; words covered with fear and layered with despair, she poured out what might be the last of her emotions, and her life. "I'm hurting so bad, how can I be fine? And how can you love me? I'm so badly blown away I'm not even a whole woman anymore. How can you ever love me?"

Eric knew Sonja had been the force that snuffed out those explosive, burning horrors of his past Problem and he was not about to let her become terminally seared and scorched by this man-made inferno. He brought his face down as close to hers as he could. "Sonja, listen to me!" His voice now became even more forceful as he tried to keep it from breaking-up. "Listen to me! You're not going to die, you'll live! Damn it, I'll make you live!" He took a piece of white first-aid tape and after cleaning her bloody left hand, placed the tape, like a wedding band, on her left ring finger. He then did the same thing on his left ring finger and held up their hands so she could see both of them intertwined. "You're all that I have to love, and I'll always love all of you. Trust me! You'll live. We'll live and dance at the weddings of our children."

Trying to raise herself up from her stretcher, she was constrained by Eric trying to preserve her energy, all of which she would need if she was to make it. She turned her head to him with a look of deathly desperation in her eyes and mouthed the words that Eric thought were 'I love you'. And as he prepared to load her onto the helicopter, he took her head and gently placed it onto a makeshift pillow made from a monk's robe. "Lie back! We're going to put you on this chopper and get you out of here."

Eric and Mordecai loaded Sonja on the helicopter, and before he and Mordecai jumped in, Eric took one last and puzzled look at the markings on the aircraft. Then the chopper lifted off from St. Catherine's, and despite the howl of wind and dust, Eric looked out the porthole at the monks with hands uplifted to Heaven and lips proclaiming:

"A miracle! A miracle from St. Catherine!"

Chapter 32

Four weeks in an Israeli military hospital gave Sonja and Eric sufficient time to deal with their questions about the events of the past month. They had all the time they needed to resolve those reoccurring doubts which crept into their compartmentalized consciousness of the St. Catherine's affair. Really a miracle? Did the angels who carried the virginally-pure body of St. Catherine up to the highest point of Mt. Sinai somehow intervene to save Sonja's equally pure life?

With her pain finally fleeting and now under control, Sonja was able to slowly start her physical therapy. Still haunted by the reality of what happened to her and how much she lost, Sonja knew she might never have a total grasp on what actually occurred on Mt. Sinai: Rigel and his two men killed and Archbishop Bournias dead of a heart attack. She had no idea of what happened to her blood sample, but she knew Eric had saved her. And while she couldn't remember everything they said to each other that horrendously horrible day, she knew of his love and trusted in the simple symbolism of their tape rings.

Having the opportunity to be an observer for the duration of Sonja's commitment and pain, Eric knew she'd never be the same after such an experience. His love had not wavered, but only intensified. With the closure of the Rigel escapade, he knew no threat existed for Sonja. If anyone had escaped the carnage at St. Catherine's or hadn't even been present, Eric correctly assumed Orion would be a headless monster that would disappear and only exist somewhere up in the heavens. With the threat of Orion gone, he now realized he hadn't been able to talk to Mordecai about the markings on the helicopter, nor resolve how they ended at an Israeli military hospital.

Mordecai had only spent a little time with Eric and Sonja since her recovery had been slow, and her memory only haltingly coming back on line. From where he stood on the issues surrounding the relics search and the death and destruction, he was satisfied with the resolution. He only had one item that needed to be taken care of, and this meant he needed to be more candid than usual with Eric. Shuffling down the hallway to Sonja's private room, he knew Eric would be there—a permanent fixture he rightly assumed! Poking his head around the door into her room, Mordecai interrupted what appeared to be a simple, yet meaningful kiss. "Um... excuse me. Sorry if I'm interrupting something, but may I come in?"

Wiping Eric's post-puckered saliva from her lips, a laughing Sonja answered, "Of course! Eric was just whispering in my ear what a wonderful person you are. Can you believe that?"

"Absolutely not!" laughed Mordecai. "He's not capable of that, but I did want to come over and see how you two were doing. Everything OK? Physical therapy coming along alright?"

"Yea, the last three or four days have made a big difference, and I don't need to be sedated as much now that the pain has pretty much disappeared. A little pain is still there, but from places I know don't even exist. Hey, I'm fine! I'm going to make it." A tear welled-up in her eyes. "So much of me is gone that I'm only part of what I was, but if Eric can accept me, or as much of me that's left, then I'll make it."

Reaching over to caress her brow, Eric's eyes locked onto hers. "There's more there than I could ever want," he laughed, "and probably more than I can handle. We'll face together whatever life has in store, and when a big ball of trouble comes rolling our way, we'll just give it a swift kick right out of our lives." The tears streaming down her face only served to lubricate the kiss Eric placed ever so gently on such quivering lips. "We'll be fine," he said.

"Now let me be nosey," Mordecai added with those eyebrows arching high as his eyes were chasing them. "With all this behind us, what did you really find? Anything in the DNA make any sense?"

Staring at Eric, Sonja couldn't look away as she spoke to Mordecai. "We really hadn't talked about this since I was so out of it from the morphine. But now's the time! I did get the basic analysis done before the explosion, and I was just ready to come out of the lab when all the commotion started. The analysis was like nothing I'd ever seen or imagined. It was human DNA, but different. It had that same DNA microsatellite sequencing from the Jewish Priest Study, but its sequence was so unique it appeared there was even an additional nucleotide, or something like a nucleotide. Not just adenine, guanine, thymine and cytosine, but something else, something special, something uniquely different. It's not hard to conclude it was probably something divine."

She paused as if now struck with the significance of her discovery. "That's it, that's what the sequencing was; Divine! I was looking at the Divine Sequence of God's DNA! That trace of blood was really THE Trace! The Holy Trace! A Trace of Jesus' DNA that came from God!" Momentarily she looked away from Eric, then back to the warmth of his eyes. "Can you believe it? I found the Holy Trace of God's DNA!"

A stunned Mordecai was drawn closer to Sonja. "Wow! Even being Jewish, I can guess that's what you might have expected from the Son of God—DNA that had to be different."

Nodding in agreement, Eric added, "You got it! What we were looking for, some scientific evidence of God. You actually found the Divine Sequence!"

Focusing now on Mordecai, Sonja continued. "For once, we had science supporting religion, not subverting it. Even to the skeptics, we could say we proved Jesus was the Son of God." Then she hesitated and turned to Eric. "But the relics, where are they? What's happened to them?"

Mordecai chose to respond since he thought the question was directed to him. "When I knew you two were OK, I went back to the monastery but couldn't find any trace of them. Whether they burned somehow or were taken, they weren't there."

Rubbing her hand in a tender, yet consoling way, Eric tried to assure her, "Your work was conclusive—you found what we were after."

Starting to get a little wound-up, her frustration was distorting the look on her face. "But who'll ever believe us? Believe me? We're back to believing in faith, when for once we had science confirming God's existence!"

Sensing she was becoming too frustrated, Eric put his hand on her shoulder and with a warm, yet conciliatory look, spoke as comforting as he could. "Honey, we'll have a lifetime together to figure this out and discuss it. But for now, why don't you get some rest? Mordecai and I will go for a little walk."

As they turned to go, Sonja's voice halted them. "Wait! There's one more thing I didn't tell you. When you're doing any research testing, you need to standardize your testing and reagents. You basically do a 'dry run' on something else so that you don't take a chance of wasting your real test item on a procedure that fails or blows-up. I did that type of standardized testing on some of the bone from that Moshe Levin's Ossuary of James. Well I'm not so sure it was a total fraud after all! My DNA testing showed what I extracted had the same genetic sequencing microsatellites found in the Jewish Priest Study. My guess is there was a good chance the bone residue could have been that of James. And here we are again, we've got science supporting our concepts, but not being able to definitively prove our position."

Eric was stunned. "No end to the surprises you're dropping on me. But what'll you do with that ossuary when you're able to do more research?"

The strength of her resolve emerged, "I don't know what I'll do. I bought the ossuary with my own money and I'm certainly not going to give it to that fool, Reverend Lewis. He didn't pay for it and doesn't deserve it. I'll probably give it to Dr. Smathers. He'll know what to do. But you're right, why don't you two be on your way. I'm tiring and need some time alone."

Waving goodbye, Eric and Mordecai left to walk down the hospital corridor. Once far enough from Sonja's room that they couldn't be heard, Eric took the initiative. "What can I say to you? Worked on two projects with you and lots of people got killed. Only this time, you saved me and Sonja, and I owe you a lot for her life. If that chopper wasn't there, we would've lost her."

Mordecai reached over to Eric and put his arm around him just like a father. "Eric, my boy, you and I did it together. For once, we were working together as a great team, and our God, the God of Jehovah, blessed us. But I could never forget I'd failed you once before. I owed you one after I failed you at Beit Hanoun when you eliminated one of the most hated enemies of Israel. You took care of us, but I let you down. I couldn't fail you again."

Eric laughed. "Look, I know you're still with the Mossad, regardless of what you say, but what I can't understand is why the markings on that helicopter were those of the Egyptian Intelligence Service. What were they doing hanging around what was supposed to be a biblical relics search? They couldn't have been there by coincidence since you and I both know coincidence doesn't happen."

Mordecai looked at him, then stroked his chin before speaking. "There's something else I need to tell you. The Egyptians, the Israelis, the Americans and even the Russians were involved in some way. Remember that Interpol evidence search I did to find out about the stars on the hand? There was a little more to the story than I told you. Didn't tell you everything I told the Mossad, but this Orion group committed a crime in Belarus. They stole some bombs from an old Soviet weapons depot. Not just any bombs, but two suitcase bombs. Two small nuclear weapons! One they used against the Vatican at the Castle Gondolfo where they blackmailed the Vatican into giving up a lot of money. Can't be certain how much because the Vatican is close-lipped on this issue. They'd like those of us in intelligence to not know they paid for some extortion scheme, but they had to use Italian intelligence, and those guys rarely keep a secret. The thing that concerned everyone else was one suitcase bomb is still out there somewhere and no one knows where."

Eric was shocked and more than a little hostile. "You used Sonja and me as bait to lure Orion out where you could catch them?"

Shaking his head and waving his hands in such a way as to connote the negative answer that would follow, Mordecai protested, "No, not at all! I was with you on this project with my primary mission to support the two of you and protect you. Regardless of where you went, Orion was going to be following, and they were the most dangerous if we didn't know where they were. We kind of flushed them out into the open where we could get them."

"And the remaining suitcase bomb?" Eric probed. "Any ideas on it?"

Another shake of the head from Mordecai. "No. We're all stymied on that. No idea where to look. But fortunately for us, this Rigel lost his direction, and his hatred for the Church may have been a blessing for mankind. It took him off his focus with that remaining bomb. And look at you, you found your relics and know what you discovered appeared to be the DNA of Jesus."

Eric looked down while disdainfully shaking his head. "And now it's been lost in the heat and destruction of that explosion."

Mordecai gave him a consoling look. "But at least you know Sonja's work supported your faith and didn't undermine it. Who would've believed you were on the right trail?"

"I guess you're right," Eric acknowledged as he looked away from him, out somewhere in space for some meaning. After a pause he asked, "What'll you do now? Go back to being a simple detective in Jerusalem—if you ever were one?"

Again, Mordecai's raised eyebrows made the scene. "Don't know. Mossad wants me back, and I'll probably do that. More importantly, what'll you do?"

A huge, warm smile crossed Eric's face like the sunrise at dawn bringing warmth and succor to the waiting lands. "I have a woman who I love and I promised her we would dance together at our children's weddings, so I better get started with our own wedding first. I've got a lifetime to give back to the woman who gave me more than I can repay. With her and through her I've been able to cast off those demons of Beit Hanoun. It's ironic, when I first ran into her, when she was a student at Strayton, I made the remark to her that I'd returned to Strayton not to rehabilitate my body but my soul. I could've never imagined that first conversation, unknown to both of us, was the first step in a healing process, and a bonding process. I just needed to come back to the Middle East and complete the task. Surprisingly, I did it with your help, and then found a life, or regained a life that I'll spend with Sonja wherever she takes me."

Mordecai took Eric's hand and shook it. "That's what you've gotta do, and whatever you do, don't turn back! Love and be loved as intensely as you can for as much of your life as you can. For tragic reasons, part my own fault, you left the CIA at the right time—a time when you could still find a life and a love. Nurture it! Worship it! Put it on a pedestal for all the world to see. I wish I could do it, but I stayed in intelligence too long— too many years within that shroud of hatred and killing leaves a veil of suspicion and cynicism. What's left for me is to keep the world safe for lovers like you."

Muted for a moment, Eric looked back towards Sonja's room and then to Mordecai for what seemed like ten seconds before he spoke. "For lovers like us? Yea, the world should be safe for people to feel each other's love and the love of God. But why isn't that love of God spread evenly over His flock? Why does a Rigel end up on the losing side of God's love? Rigel? Hell, I don't even know who or what he was. Just some guy who hated the Church for what it did to him and his family."

Hands in his pockets, Mordecai shrugged his shoulders, hesitated, then persisted. "I wasn't sure if you even wanted to know, but we were able to trace who he was. Donovan O'Rafferty was his real name and originally from Tralee, County Kerry, Ireland, where the two priests were murdered."

Eric's piercing, squinting eyes never left Mordecai's. "And his family? Who were they?"

Reaching into his pocket, Mordecai took out a piece of paper and proceeded to read. "Mother Margaret and a father, Ryan, who abandoned the family early. Probably drink got the best of him, like it so often does with men."

Eric reached over to point to the paper. "What else?"

Mordecai nodded his approval. "A brother and two sisters—sisters named Molly and Shannon and a… "

Eric interrupted. "A brother named Michael."

"You're a genealogical genius! How'd you know that?" Mordecai asked incredulously.

"Hardly that," replied Eric. "I just knew Michael was his brother who'd been sexually abused so bad that he killed himself. Rigel shouted that out during those final minutes of his life in all that pent-up rage and hostility he felt towards the Church. Michael committed suicide when he was fifteen years old and jumped from the church tower to his death".

Disapprovingly, Mordecai now shook his head. "My boy, you're not really such a genius after all. You're wrong on this one. Rigel's, Donovan O'Rafferty's, little brother was Michael, but he was just that—little. Died of leukemia when he was barely three years old! Not very likely to be targeted by the priests for sexual abuse at that young age, and couldn't have climbed high enough at any church to have jumped off."

It was an incredulous look that Eric shot at Mordecai. "You can't be right! I heard Rigel with my own ears and I know he told Elana about his brother Michael's abuse at the hands of the Church. She told it to Sonja. Rigel definitely shouted out that his brother Michael was the 'whore of the priests'!"

Mordecai reached to grasp Eric's shoulder. "I'm not doubting that you and Elana heard that story, but it couldn't have been his brother Michael he was talking about."

Turning away from Mordecai for a few moments, Eric whirled back with a look of confusion all over his face. "Then who could it have been? Who was the Michael he spoke of?"

Mordecai unflinchingly looked Eric in-the-eye. "Maybe it wasn't 'who' but 'what' that Rigel spoke of. What really was Michael to Rigel? Remember, Rigel had already changed his name to create a new persona. Maybe this

Michael was a figment of Rigel's imagination, only a protective mechanism for Rigel to escape the horrific psychic pain of his own abuse?"

With his head shaking in bewilderment, Eric pushed away from Mordecai, as he muttered half to himself, and the other half to anyone out there . "I don't know. I just don't know! Was Michael really Rigel? Or just another layer of Rigel's pain?"

Mordecai reached over to give Eric a pinch on his right cheek. "You're young, my boy. You'll have a lifetime to sort this out. Then call me when you've figured out the whole caper, including whether or not this Rigel's genetic engineer really could have used the DNA to create and clone Jesus." Mordecai then gave Eric a pat on the shoulder and turned to walk down the corridor.

As Eric watched Mordecai trudge along the corridor, he called out to him. "Where will you be when I need you?"

Mordecai turned with a smile that had been a long-lost stranger to his face. "Be there in Jerusalem! You found me before, you'll find me again."

Eric's smile was uncontainable and bursting with pride. "I'll need a best man at my wedding. Will you be able to make it?"

Walking away, and right before he took that toothpick from behind his ear and put it in his mouth, Mordecai shouted back, "I'll be there with bells on my toes and a ring in my nose. Mazel tov!"

Watching Mordecai walking the length of the corridor, Eric felt the tear that trickled down his cheek. A tear of joy and one of sadness, for he knew he was looking at a man with a heart of gold, yet a heart partially torn asunder by the sacrifices he had made to fulfill his obligations to keep his people safe.

Chapter 33

Three months later.

Sheer exhilaration permeated every nook and cranny of the Smathers Chapel at Strayton University—the perfect place for a wedding for Strayton's most perfect couple. The chapel had been designed for President Smathers by a Strayton graduate, and its lofty design was based on an inspiring work President Smathers had seen in California by the renowned architect of spectacular buildings, Gin Wong. With the marriage of marble and highly finished steel, the Smathers Chapel's vertical lines provided an upward, awe-struck view of how the steeple actually appeared to reach to the heavens and be touched by the grace of God. It was an architectural testimonial to the God of all people.

Embracing the chapel, the dogwoods were in full bloom and the blossoms reminiscent of the love of Christ as made manifest through his crucifixion. Today was a day for love, a perfect love being consummated on the part of Sonja Martin and Eric Stanfels. President Smathers proudly officiated at the service which united two of his most illustrious alumni. Not marrying two strangers to the campus at Strayton, but uniting his Professor of Middle Eastern Studies and his Chair of Biological Studies in Religion. And the good Dr. Smathers was overwhelming in his praise of these two. They not only represented Strayton in the best of ways, but more importantly, they had represented God and love in the eyes of all who knew them.

The wedding service was perfectly performed in the packed chapel where folding chairs were needed for the overflow of guests. The Stanfels family was exceedingly pleased to see their son back in the service of their God, and doing so here at Strayton with his lovely Sonja. The Martin family, and all of its extended members, had come south from Vermont and were overjoyed with the union of two such fine people. The extent of their daughter's injuries had been devastating to them, but they were so thankful for the purity of Eric's love. There was no confusion that with a lesser man the results of the St. Catherine's fiasco could have doomed their Sonja to a life constrained by the shallowness of human superficiality. Sonja's and Eric's love had been tested by fire and, like metal being tempered by the heat of the flame, had only grown stronger.

The wedding party was unique, possibly one of the most extraordinary in the memory of virtually anyone in attendance. There was only one member other than the bride and groom, and he was resplendent in his morning coat, with his gold Star of David on his lapel and a quite noticeable toothpick wedged behind his right ear. The maid-of-honor position was vacant as Elana, *in absentia*, served Sonja through her presence within the hearts and minds of all who knew and loved her. Her parents, sitting at peace with Sonja's, and comforted by their faith-based tranquility, had come to realize that Elana's spirit was there with them now and would be for every remaining minute of their lives. They knew their God had not abandoned them and would unite them together again at their Day of Judgment.

During the wedding service, President Smathers' voice boomed throughout the chapel filling it with a resonance that penetrated every bone in the pews. But at the time for the exchange of the wedding rings, very few in attendance could have understood the significance of the act which took place when Sonja and Eric removed the old, frayed, first-aid tape from their ring fingers and replaced it with their simple gold bands. No finer moment had ever existed in that chapel as when an exultant President Smathers, with a tear of joy running down his cheek, turned this young couple towards the attendant congregation. "I and Strayton University are so proud to present to you Mr. and Mrs. Eric Stanfels!"

Consistent with the tradition at the Smathers' Chapel, the congregation would empty first in order that the bride and groom could come down the outside steps to this waiting assemblage and be showered with rice and good wishes. With her brown hair flowing out from under her elegant tiara, and with those radiant hazel eyes making contact with everyone, Sonja tentatively walked down the final steps with her husband proudly keeping a firm grip on her arm. Once she reached the flat landing area at the bottom, in a surprising, yet lighthearted moment before the rice started flying, a large, green fluorescent child's ball came rolling out of the crowd toward her feet. The child's mother was aghast! Eric started to bend over to pick it up but Sonja held onto his arm to stop him. "Don't forget what you told me! When a big ball of trouble gets in our way— just kick it out of our lives!"

With a smile on her face not dimmed by her doubts or disability, she knew now was the time to deal with her last issue. She lifted up her wedding dress so she could kick that ball away. It was then all could see her beautiful, elegant and very athletic left leg planted as she still had enough strength to swing her right metal-frame prosthetic leg and deliver a striking blow that sent the ball up in the air like a Super Bowl kick. The cheers of the crowd were exultant and their shower of rice was explosive!

That leg may have been cold and artificial but the emotion between Sonja and Eric was pure, intense and a healing force that would bind them forever. Sonja had helped Eric eliminate the Problem in his life and his love had done the same for her. His love made sure the effects of that horrible explosion at St. Catherine's would never be a Problem in her life! Mrs. Eric Stanfels knew she was now whole in the eyes of her husband and of everyone else who mattered.

The monks at St. Catherine's were right—it was a miracle!

Epilogue

Sonja and Eric would live together in a state of love and respect permeating every aspect of their very existence. The pain they experienced together, especially at St. Catherine's, had been a molten, welding force unifying two strong people with backbones of steel and an integrity of even greater strength and duration. Their love had an atomic bond of such strength that nothing could break it apart. It was truly theirs with never a trace of doubt of their commitment to each other. While they were still too young and unable to see far into the future, it would be a lifetime of love for them and their four children. And Eric's pledge to Sonja would come true far into that distant future. There were to be no physical limitations in her life and they would one day dance at the weddings of their children—and even at the baptisms of their grandchildren! Eric made a vow to love and cherish Sonja, and there would be no limit to the devotion he had for her. She was truly perfect and whole in his eyes, and would be until the last ray of sunshine in his existence on this earth would no longer be able to create a sparkle in his eyes; eyes that only existed to behold her. That inner and outer beauty of Sonja had eliminated the Problem forever in Eric's life as she had been the ultimate Solution for him!

Liam avoided the carnage at St. Catherine's being safely ensconced in Rigel's suite at the King David. When Rigel didn't return one day after schedule, consistent with his directions, Liam knew to leave Israel as quickly as possible and return to Ireland. He did so via a circuitous route that ultimately took him to Slovakia, Latvia and then finally on a freighter to Larne, Northern Ireland. Upon disembarking at the Larne pier, his small amount of luggage was of no significance. The two larger boxes listed as 'library books' were never searched and passed customs readily. Always unhappy with the British domination of the

Irish, Liam could think of no better place for the one remaining suitcase bomb than Northern Ireland.

While Rigel may not have been able to get what he was after, Liam was sure the Catholics of Northern Ireland would be able to someday settle the score with the repressive British Protestants. And maybe he would be the savior the Catholic faithful had needed. He might just be the coming of the next Michael Collins, yet different—an Irish hero who would not tolerate any treaty with the British. Having been raised on the pabulum of true Irish independence, and even though he had been a follower with Rigel, Liam knew now was his time to lead. Why not lead the battle for total Irish independence. With his suitcase bomb, Liam would settle the bloody score for a battle that reverberated deep within the devastated psyches of his fellow Irishmen, emasculated by the evil British who would enslave anybody they could in their quest for Empire!

Dr. Geoffrey Salvatore escaped from Israel with the same degree of stealth as did Liam. Fortunately for him, he planned for Rigel to deliver the spikes to him back at the King David. And like Liam, he followed Rigel's directions to depart Jerusalem if Rigel fell even one day behind his return schedule. After the debacle at St. Catherine's, he had chosen to march onward with his quest to use his cloning skills wherever he could find his fortune and fame as well as perpetuate his political vision. While he was suspected of being a part of Rigel's operation, nothing was ever definitively proven. His whereabouts were of concern to the intelligence communities of many nations as well as some of the scientific authorities. It seemed he had disappeared from public view after having made several trips to Moscow, where, with the huge fortunes that accrued to the Russian mega-industrialists, there was an opportunity to be had. Salvador Dali had at last found his niche, and his association with the faction of neo-Stalinist Russian multi-millionaires was just what Dr. Dolly needed. Open the encased tomb of Josef Stalin and enough DNA could be taken for all the cloning they would need—the neo-Communists would re-gain power, and Joseph Stalin, and a bunch of little Joseph Stalin's, would be resurrected!

Geoffrey smiled as he thought back to his schoolboy teasing, *You were so right to call me the 'dago red'—the Italian red! That is what I'll be. The Italian Red— THE Italian Communist!*

Dr. Harland Smathers was extremely pleased with his investment in Sonja and Eric, and he had been rejuvenated with the energy and commitment of these two young people. And, as a bonus, Sonja gave him the disputed ossuary she had bought from Moshe Levin with her own meager savings. Even though he didn't get the DNA from the crucifixion relics, he trusted Sonja's conclusion that the DNA from that wood was like no other in genetic research. Now that he had the discredited ossuary in his possession, with all of its bone residue intact, he would figure out some way to utilize the DNA 'marker' of the Jewish Priest Study with the DNA from the bone residue of the ossuary.

Dr. Smathers had also benefitted in another way. He had gained an energized affection for the realm of New Testament studies in Jerusalem. With Strayton's vast endowment at his personal disposal, he readily concluded that the Jerusalem New Testament Biblical Institute needed a patron. Yes, a patron with deep pockets who could finance further innovative research and explorations. Naturally, his $1,000,000 donation to the Institute did come with some strings attached. Dr. Smathers became the dominant force at the Institute with the power to hire and fire, and his first order-of-the-day was to replace the misogynist Reverend Simon Lewis with a new Chairman of the Board of Governors. The plump, pompous and scheming simple-minded Reverend Lewis was stupifyingly stunned when he was handed his immediate termination papers by his successor, the Reverend Doctor Angela R. Whitmore.

Mordecai was wrong—life and love had not passed him by! Whether it was the joy he sensed through the commitment Eric and Sonja had for each other or simply the fact he was growing older, he finally did find his love. Smitten like a young schoolboy, he had fallen head-over-heels for Esther, a Mossad operative. It was only now that Mordecai could truly understand what had taken place as he had watched Eric's and Sonja's love blossom. And he was struck! He became so intoxicated with the nectar of love that nothing other than Esther seemed to matter. He couldn't wait to see her in the morning, afternoon and evening. Got to work later, his lunch hours became much longer and he left work earlier. And he loved nothing better than meeting her for a hand-holding lunch or a glass of wine to toast their love. Even though Mordecai had been hardened by the life he previously led, his love for Esther took him on a path, the likes of which he could never imagine. From a simple wedding at the spot of Elana's memorial ceremony to the birth ten months later of the first of their two children, Mordecai knew he had been blessed by being bathed in the glow of Eric and Sonja's love!

Book Club Study Guide

Was the use of colloquial Irish spelling more phonetically realistic? Did it make the characters more realistic?

Can a genetic study like the Jewish Priest Study have a real impact in religion?

Have you experienced a man like Rigel who could love a mother so much yet devastate other women?

Did the male author depict the female characters adequately? Was Sonja strong enough? How was Elana projected? Was Eric too alpha male?

How did the ending of the book match any preconceived notions that evolved during your reading?

Do you understand the Irish nationalism of Dan Keating—a poor man hating an "illegal" Ireland so much he did forsake his pension at age 65 and a $3,500.00 bonus when he turned 100?

What made Khor Virap and St. Catherine's valuable as protective repositories of faith for early Christianity?

Was Rigel correct that women really are the "rock" upon which the Christian church is built?

Did the ending change your feelings about Rigel?

How was Mordecai's emerging character?

As you were confronted with Sonja's loss of physical wholeness at the wedding scene, was the sense of loss felt or anticipated by the reader?

Was the romance in *Trace* intriguing enough without strong sexual content?

Did the author's use of x-rated language appropriately portray the depth of Rigel's pain? Could it have been done differently?

What do you feel is the role of multi-media sexual saturation upon sexual abuse by the clergy?

Does the concept of cloning wooly mammoths within the time frame of contemporary genetics seem realistic?

347